THE BLOOD CONNECTION

THE FADED PHOTOGRAPH SERIES

Book One

By

CHARLIE B. HOPKINSON

ISBN-13: 978-1-9162648-0-9

DEDICATION

To Marijo Spehar (Dreadcop) — the first novel is for you.
Thank you for being a werewolf.

CONTENTS

ACKNOWLEDGMENTS

To Kriss Dudek – for your enormous support with editing and pointing mistakes. You are the star that navigated me through my darkest hours, when it was so hard to keep writing.

To Piotr Czajka – for being my first reader, who is the one witnessing how the novel had changed and how my storytelling skills have grown.

To Kamil Jurczyk – for sharing knowledge about filming and for friendship that last for decades despite all hardships.

To Anna Zaras – for listening my monologues about stories, characters, creating scenes over so many coffees in town.

And finally to myself for believing that I can do it.

CHAPTER 1

16th June - In the Forest

'Jessica, wait! I can't run that fast,' shouted Gary, barely breathing. He was standing on the path that was located in a thick and vast forest in the middle of England. He stooped down, corrected his rifle, put his hands on his knees and wheezed. He was panting loudly, trying to catch his breath after chasing his female companion. They were both running for some time now, but it was Gary who was trying not to get left behind alone in the frightening woods. After sunset, the woodland was looking less friendly. Long shadows, moving shapes and dark bushes cast uneasiness and a cold thrill into the souls of those who dared walk at night amongst the old trees. The night sky was coated with clouds, covering the moon and stars, making the surroundings look creepier than they did during the day.

'You shouted that some lunatic was chasing us,' replied Jessica angrily.

'I don't want to get shot. Besides, it was a long time ago,' snorted Gary.

They were both standing on a narrow track of trampled grass, made mostly by locals living in the villages surrounding these vast forests. Alongside the track there were old-fashioned Victorian street lamps standing on one side, with an electric cable hanging from one to the other. The lamps were about two metres high but emitting only a weak, dim light. This made some places look even scarier than the rest of the woods. The electric cable had many small bulbs with blue lights attached to it. There were also shinning red arrows pointing in one direction. It looked more like Christmas decoration in a park than a footpath's lightning.

'With your fish memory it was a long time ago, but down here on Planet Earth it's only five minutes, Gary,' said Jessica, kneeling on the ground. She was his companion, wearing a similar black, military uniform to his. Their helmets had cameras attached to one side and quite bright but relatively small LED lights on the opposite side. Her backpack was stuffed to the brim, whereas Gary's looked pretty flat. She struggled for a while, muttering in anger, and trying to untangle an oblong-shaped item from the bushes. There was a breaking sound as she pulled it out of the shrubbery using all her strength.

Gary was still wheezing, but he stood up straight, smoothed his uniform and corrected his helmet. He took off his backpack, pulled out a big bottle of water and drank greedily. He was a tall, twenty-two-year-old, with average looks and a few curves on his body. He had a smooth-shaven face and a few drops of sweat running down his cheeks. He had long brunette hair, pulled tight in a ponytail, now matted and tangled with leaves.

'Jessica! Haven't you just destroyed a new drone?' asked Gary. Although he didn't smile, his question sounded like he was amused rather than annoyed by her action.

'It seems I did. I need to practice flying this bloody thing a bit more,' she answered, clearly irritated. She rolled her eyes huffing, sighed, and took off her helmet.

She got up and dusted down her trousers. She was slim, much shorter than Gary, with long, now tousled, curly red hair. She took off her hairband, smoothed her hair then turned around as though she was looking for something that might still be behind them. She had pale skin, face covered with freckles, her eyebrows and eyelashes were the light colour of a natural red-head.

The drone she had pulled from the bushes had four propellers, but one of them was broken. Jessica picked it up, checked the battery level and detached the small camera from the bottom of it. She held the power button and watched as the red light blinked and went out.

'And we lost it. No more filming from above,' she said, showing the camera to Gary and shrugging.

'Never mind. Let me see what we've got from it,' said Gary, taking the camera from her. He removed a micro card from inside the device and gave it back. He took a large tablet from his backpack and put the card inside. The light from switching on a screen illuminated their faces with a bluish hue. Gary searched the memory card, found the last recorded ten minutes and started it. They both watched a green night-vision movie on fast-forward.

'I bet there was nobody there. You watch way too many horror movies, and please don't start with vampires and werewolves,' said Jessica, smiling.

Gary muttered in reply. In his mind, he was counting all those cameras still attached to trees in so many locations around the contest zone. He wanted to record the Airsoft event from as many angles as he could. He aimed to make a good impression by making a video with eye-catching fast-paced movements and action scenes. He hoped this event would help with his freelance film career. Although Gary was sure the cameras were still recording around the forest this late evening, the fact he had lost the flying night-vision view was kind of heartbreaking for him.

'Who is this then?' asked Gary boldly, staring straight into Jessica's eyes. He pointed to the human-like silhouette that appeared suddenly on the screen jumping out from a large bush. The cold shiver of fear ran through Gary's body, giving him goosebumps and putting his senses on the maximum alert, but he smiled gently, covering his fear with a straight face and a slight arrogant smirk.

'A vampire?' asked Jessica sarcastically.

'Stop mocking me. They don't exist,' answered Gary, smiling broadly.

'He looks odd. He doesn't belong to any of the teams. And he isn't a crew member either,' said Jessica, staring at a paused video.

'What's he doing alone so late at night and how did he see to walk in total darkness?' she asked perplexed.

There was a pinch of fear in her voice. The video was stopped at a precise moment when the silhouette was seen fully. It was a man, but the picture wasn't sharp enough to expose his face. He was moving fast as though walking on the well-lit pavement. She reversed the tape, going back a couple of seconds on the recording and played it again. They glanced at each other in silence and then, like a well-synchronised watch, they looked around surveying their surroundings, searching for signs of anything that might indicate they were still being followed.

'I heard something,' she whispered. She frowned and put the finger on her lips, indicating that Gary should stay silent. They both stood motionless. Gary looked at her with concern.

'Okay, stop it, or we'll conjure up some monsters in our heads like-' Gary didn't finish.

'You definitely will, but not me,' she snorted.

'Or maybe you are both overly dramatic?' a mysterious voice asked.

'Mark! Stop creeping up on us,' yelled Gary, nervously turning in the newcomer's direction, who was standing just right behind them with his hand on Jessica's shoulder.

'God, help me! Mark, you scared me to death! You always creep around soundlessly like a cat. Stop sneaking up on me! I've told you this so many times,' shouted Jessica as Mark squeezed her shoulder. She turned and smacked his arm.

'As intended,' replied Mark, grabbing her hand and pulling her closer to him so fast that she lost her balance, landing on his chest. She blushed, pushed him away and turned her head to avoid catching a glimpse of his amused expression. He archly looked at Gary and switched on the LED light he had attached on the side of his helmet.

'Oh yeah. He is very good at disappearing and reappearing like a genie out of thin air. Where have you been?' asked Gary, raising his voice a little bit too high. He realised now that Mark surprised them walking straight from the darkness without any light on.

'Wow, did someone piss in your Cheerios?' asked Mark cheerfully. He came closer to Gary and tried to put his arm around him, but Gary turned, took a step and stood aside.

'Dude! We should've met an hour ago!' said Gary, staring at Mark angrily. His anger didn't last long, because, after a few seconds, Gary was busy brushing off dry grass from his clothes. This was his usual way of behaving to avoid going too deep into an argument with his older brother Mark. He peered at him one more time, and then the green-eyed monster of envy started poking Gary's ego.

Mark was tall and very handsome. His dark, longish hair was always flawless. He usually had a three-day beard perfectly trimmed and shaped. He was wearing black military trousers and a tight-fitting T-shirt, highlighted shapes of his muscles. Mark was very fit, and he loved emphasising it by wearing enhancing clothes. Gary saw many times how women were attracted to him and how quickly Mark abused it.

'Enough, guys! We should go. Sean is waiting for us,' said Jessica firmly.

'Well, something is lurking in these woods, that's why I'm late. I was checking on-' Mark didn't finish. He saw their faces and decided not to continue the story.

'Oh, please. Stop with these lame excuses,' replied Gary sharply.

'Yep, let's move,' said Jessica, interrupting the possibility of an argument.

Gary turned off the tablet and put it into his backpack. *I'd love not to be around here knowing an unknown figure might be following us,* thought Gary. A cold shiver ran down his spine. As he walked away quickly, he turned on the GPS on his mobile, searching for their position inside the forest game zone.

*

They were walking in silence for a while, but Jessica looked over her shoulder more often than her companions. In this quiet and dark place, only the sound of their footsteps could be heard on the path.

Gary was walking behind everyone, feeling uneasy. He felt fear scratching his back with cold and paralysing fingers. He tried to focus on something less terrifying than the threat of a mysterious figure wandering around.

His mind went back to Nottingham, the town where he grew up. Gary was an orphan who was brought up by his grandparents after his parents were killed in a car accident. He was only a twelve-year-old boy back then, and he remembered his parents quite well. But he suppressed the memories of their life together so severely that now he barely thought about his past. His grandmother gave him his first camera and had sown the seeds of his love for fantasy stories and movies. Although it was mainly to keep Gary's mind occupied and far away from the tragedy of his parents, it created a deep passion in him.

Two years ago, he completed a media course at college and moved to London, hoping to be accepted at the University to study film and media. He wanted to be a movie director, but he wasn't accepted on the course, as he had planned. That fact didn't kill his ambition. He promised himself that he would never give up chasing his dream and that one day he was going to make films like a professional director. In the meantime, he was filming weddings, hen and stag parties and crazy birthdays, as well as students' stunts, just to earn some money. He was putting some of his movies online, not only to get peoples' attention but for his portfolio as well. Sometimes he made video clips for young bands at gigs but didn't get much from it.

That was why he was very excited when this event knocked on his door. The Airsoft competition was significant to him, not only for the money's sake, but also because he hoped to use the material for his university admission next year.

Gary's half-brother, Mark, was included in the event alongside uncle Sean, Jessica and Simon, his friends and housemates. They were taking part in the contest as crew members. Mark didn't work directly for the company organising the tournament, but he had loads of connections in London and that gave him the opportunity to get, from time to time, well-paid casual work for an extra cash boost.

In that way, Jessica and Gary were members of staff operating one of the biggest Airsoft competitions in England. Three clubs were fighting for a high prize. It wasn't only about the money but also about the opportunity for the winning team to participate in an international competition for a much larger reward. Tonight, the final fight was taking place, and the next hour would be the last time where three groups could earn bonus points to win. Two days of massive struggles placed the groups at almost the same level. And now the last task to be completed had made them all very irritable. Even those who were only working as personnel could feel the vibe of rushing and the 'want to win' excitement emanating around, like a subtle aroma of a delicious dish that everyone couldn't wait to taste.

The first day's matches were straightforward. Every team attacked the enemy base and got points for the seizure of it or for eliminating the opposing team. The stations looked like large wooden castles with four towers, wide main gates and two small side entrances on the opposite walls. There was a wooden construction inside each of the castles that looked like a big shed in the middle of the courtyard that was shaped like a citadel. It was all well-lit inside with spotlights on the battlements which illuminated the neighbouring area in places.

*

But this evening, the last activity was more complicated than during the regular contest. It wasn't just an Airsoft brawl anymore, but a live-action role-playing game full of quests and tasks that tested their creativity and ability to work as a team. The teams had to complete several missions around the woods, such as sneaking up to the opponents' bases and capture the flags that were kept inside the shed. But the most challenging project, and therefore the one that could earn them the highest number of points, was to find and catch the rogue's crew hidden among the event personnel. The rogues looked exactly like the rest of the staff. The clues about them were hidden inside quests that if completely finished, revealed their names one by one. This was a test of the contestants' social skills, intelligence and creativity. The way to discover who was playing the rogue role and where to find one was designed around asking right questions, and for some people, it was the toughest of all. Gary, Jessica and Mark belonged to rogue's team, now hiding in woods, mainly because they had a tricky mission to do.

*

Gary scratched his cheek. He was so deep in thought that he bumped into Jessica who had stopped suddenly. He rebounded and pushed her into Mark. Mark smiled broadly, catching her in his arms. Mark peeped at his brother, but seeing irritation on his face, moved slightly away from her.

'Guys, half an hour left to the end. I want to win so badly. I wish to wipe the smile from Waller's fat face. I hate that guy…' said Mark with notable competitiveness in his voice.

'What do you mean by winning?' asked Jessica intrigued.

'We can win as rouges this game?' asked Gary. His anger disappeared under the vision of the opportunity to earn more money than he first expected.

'Yep. It's in the terms and conditions section right at the bottom.

I've made sure, it's written there. Nobody ever bothers to read it anyway,' replied Mark, looking pleased with himself.

'Are you cheating, Mark?' asked Jessica.

'No, I don't. The trick is, nobody would ever think it's possible,' said Mark without any remorse, shrugging his shoulders.

'How?' asked Gary. He remembered that this fact was mentioned at the beginning of the competition, but no one paid any attention.

'We need to capture all their flags before they find out that Sean's chaos, it's a decoy,' said Mark, walking behind Gary.

'Whoa, hold on for a second. Who's doing what?' asked Jessica.

'Sean? No way. He's a curator at The British Museum for goodness sake. Putting books in the wrong places is the most evil thing he could ever do-' Gary didn't finish.

'What's he doing, classifying their flags based on carbon from all fags they have smoked so far?' asked Jessica sarcastically.

'You'd be surprised at him if you spent more time with us, Gary. So, if Sean invites you for dinner, move your arse and pretend you are as happy as Larry in our small family gathering, however boring it might be for you,' snarled Mark. This time he seemed annoyed not only at Gary, but now at both of them.

'Enough!' shouted Jessica, 'Get off Gary's back Mark, or I will tell him-'

'Whoa, Jess, stop right now!' shouted Mark.

'What?' asked Gary, sensing some shady story about his half-brother that she might know.

'I'll start with how Mark got that job,' said Jessica, grinning and raising her eyebrows.

'Okay, you win, you red-headed devil. Besides, we don't have time for the sweet family reunion. Let's go folks,' said Mark and nobody opposed.

'What we should do then?' asked Jessica.

'Before I explain my plan, you should know about these additional rules. If the rogue's team has all flags, the price is tripled. I've got one already,' stated Mark, cutting off any further quarrel. He smiled broadly with a mysterious glint in his eyes. He pulled the Green team's flag from one of many pockets in his trousers and waved it vigorously. It was a small table flag, that could fit in the palm of a hand, attached to a stainless-steel pole with the end shaped into a loop that allowed to stand on its own.

'That's why you were late?' asked Jessica.

'Pretty much,' answered Mark, grinning.

'But why did you go there without us?' Gary sounded a bit resentful.

'I'm faster alone,' replied Mark, walking in the Blue's camp direction.

'By the way, Mark, have you seen Simon anywhere?' asked Jessica. She was walking behind Mark who was now holding a very modern GPS system showing their position in the woods and remaining distance to the base.

'I have and he'll be here after midnight with some food. We need to hurry. It's already late,' said Mark, choosing a dark path between pine trees.

*

'How are we going to do it?' asked Jessica. She was looking at Gary expecting answers, but he just shrugged and shook his head indicating that he had no ideas.

They were laying on the ground among spruces only a few metres from Blue team's fortified base. It was built like a fortress with four towers, high wooden walls and quite a large shed inside that looked like a castle. The whole construction was extensive, with battlements on the top and two hanging bridges, that were connecting the roof of the shed with surrounding fortified walls. There were many arrow slits that gave the opportunity to shoot attacking opponents. The gate was two metres tall and wide enough for an off-road car to get through. It was now wide open, showing everything that was going on inside, including two quite large minibuses standing near one of the wall.

'We have to hurry before they close it. Some of the crew are coming back, so Sean's distraction tactics won't last much longer. Any idea how we can get in and grab two flags?' asked Gary. He was peering through night vision goggles into the base, skimming the woody foliage growing in places near the walls, searching for human activity.

'Damn it! We're too late. We need to get there now before the rest of their team appears. We could try just running inside and taking it by force,' said Mark with a bit of panic in his voice, pointing at a few groups of people walking on a path. Although the bulk of the Blue team had a bit of way still to get to the base, they were noisy and could easily be seen with all those torches and lights they were carrying.

'It won't work. There are two guards above the gate. They'll shoot us before we reach the entrance,' said Jessica, pointing out silhouetted figures barely visible on the top of the rampart. Mark took the goggles from Gary's hand without asking.

'We can't wait any longer. If only we could impersonate members of the Blue team, we might blend in. It's dark so we could be inside before they find out who we really are. Shame we don't have their unit armbands,' said Gary, clearly irritated, and trying to take back the goggle but without success.

'I think we can,' Jessica shouted excitedly, a bit too loud. She covered her mouth with her hand and looked around in panic, ducking deeper under hanging branches. The trio lay motionless and silent for a couple of minutes, observing the activity around the gate. Three of the Blue team members, passing only two feet from the hiding rogues, stopped and used their flashlights to investigate nearby bushes.

'Ben, there is nothing there, are you high? Oh, man! You should get over it. That shit is messing you up. Do you see evil yellow eyes again?' one of them asked mockingly laughing.

'No! I'm not stoned. I've only smoked one joint this morning. I know what I saw. Some big animal is sneaking around, and it'll strike tonight, you mark my words. Didn't you hear those horrible stories in the pub yesterday? Of course not, you were too drunk to stand,' the second man muttered, cursing under his breath. He shone his torch only a few centimetres from the place where Jessica was laying.

'Oi, you! What are you going to do if it jumps out from bushes? We don't even have so much as a butter knife with us. I'm going back. I'm hungry,' said a third one turning around and walking back fast towards the base. The rest of them followed, leaving the place where the rogues were hiding, unchecked.

'Guys! Hurry up! We're going to close the gate now. It shouldn't have been open so long,' shouted one of the guards from the nearest tower. Three of the Blue team murmured something incomprehensible as they walked towards the gate. They closed the doorway leaving the dark forest behind and nothing but silence all around.

'Damn! We've lost our chance. Thank you, Jess,' Mark whispered sarcastically. He switched on a small torch but kept it partly hidden behind his backpack.

'I'm sorry guys, but we can still get in. Listen, do you remember in the first hour of the event where nobody knew what to do, and it was just a chaos?' asked Jessica, raising her voice again with excitement.

'That was hilarious. We were assigned to three different support groups, and you were in the place you hate the most: the kitchen,' said Gary, trying not to laugh.

'You know very well that my cooking skills are based on survival instinct. Besides, Mark is champion of the frying pan in our house, and I'm not going to compete,' replied Jessica, pulling a funny face and sticking out her tongue.

'Okay, okay, what's your plan? Just please don't tell me we should start digging a tunnel with our bare hands,' said Gary, smiling broadly.

'With these,' replied Jessica as she pulled out four white armbands, with a thick red cross in the middle from her pocket.

'How did you get them? You're not supposed to have any equipment from the medical team. They're not part of the competition, but only for the emergency services to use,' said Mark.

Jessica looked at him with such a fierce expression on her face that made Mark feel uneasy. He put his head down and loudly cleared his throat.

'So, any other ideas and smart solutions, Mark?' asked Gary, interrupting the awkward silence. He was staring from one to the other expectantly. Jessica made a gesture with her hands to Mark, meaning of hurrying up with a solution, but he only shook his head without answering.

'I totally forgot to give them back, seriously. I found them when I was looking for spare batteries. We'll pretend that we're on the medical team and we need to get inside the base for the medical kit,' replied Jessica smiling.

'It's a very lame excuse, and nobody will ever buy it. Therefore, we need to stage serious performance with lots of bruises and blood. Maybe we could spin a tale about being bitten by a rabid animal,' said Gary enthusiastically.

'Blood! No chance. I'll faint or puke if I see blood. How about somebody's faking an injured ankle. You don't need blood for that, and they have to open the gate. There are the only minibuses available within a few miles' radius from here, and they're standing just inside the castle. They'll have to give the injured person a lift to the main camp,' said Jessica smiling with a spark of excitement.

'That's brilliant. Let's move. Only twenty minutes left until the end of the game. Jess, when we get up, you should start to moan. Don't forget to cry and occasionally swear. The closer we're the gate, the more you should cry and grumble,' said Mark, checking his big and very masculine watch.

'Why me?' she asked surprised.

'Because you're a pretty lady and they're mostly men, so they'll feel sorrier for you than they would for me even though I'm lovely, and Gary is not good at pretending anything,' replied Mark, silently laughing. Jessica looked at Gary and rolled her eyes.

They put on the armbands, emerged from out of the bushes they were hiding in and started walking towards the fortification. Gary tried to drape Jessica's arm over his shoulders, but Mark outmanoeuvring him, pulled at her other arm so fast that she lost her balance and tripped over her own feet landing fully on Mark's chest. She groaned when one of her shoes caught in protruding tree roots. Mark grinned even more widely. He caught her around her waist with one hand and pressed closer to his body, smiling like someone who'd just received an unexpected gift. Gary peered at them and frowned, clearly irritated.

'Gary, you will sneak around and take the flags. They should be inside the castle on the table. Me and Jess will keep them busy and keep their attention on us. I'll ask where their first-aid kit-' Mark didn't finish, interrupted by Gary who was now visibly annoyed.

'Why me? Why I can't distract them?' asked Gary jealously.

'Because you can't lie and you're not good at improvising. They won't take you seriously. No arguments. Hurry up, guys,' said Mark, turning around and heading towards the main gate of the Blue team's camp.

Mark dragged Jessica through dense bushes making as much noise as he could. He was a bit too rough with her, so the complaints sounded very realistic. Gary thought about what his brother had said as he could not argue with him, so he didn't answer. Inside, Gary knew he was so bad at lying that his voice automatically changed to a higher pitch. Deceit was written all over his face and body language showed that something was very fishy when he was being dishonest. Therefore, on many occasions, Gary had kept quiet rather than make something up that might put him in a very uncomfortable position.

'Ouch, that hurts, Mark,' she shouted angrily.

'It supposed to. You are playing an injured damsel in distress so wail and weep louder, sweetheart,' said Mark without sympathy. He changed his pace, speeding up now. Jessica started grumbling loudly about the pain from her imaginary accident, but Gary wasn't sure if it was only acting or she really was uncomfortable. She used such colourful language declaring Mark a real Prince Charming that some of the phrases could make vicious pirates blush from embarrassment.

'Open the gate! Open the gate! Someone is seriously injured and needs medical help,' shouted Mark to the guards who were looking down at them from the tower.

'Hey down there! The new car is coming! You don't have to come inside. Just wait a few minutes,' shouted one voice from above. Mark, Jessica and Gary gazed at each other in amazement. They were stumped and didn't know what to say to force the guards to open the gate. The rogues turned and saw car's headlights still far away in the distant but definitely approaching here.

'Hey, moron, do you know how many points your team will lose for not helping the medical team? She is hurt and we need bandages from your first-aid kit. Have you read the terms and conditions of this event thoroughly?' shouted Gary loudly.

Mark and Jessica stared at him in astonishment. Mark frowned, gave the thumbs up and then nodded approvingly at Gary. The guards were talking between themselves but too quietly for Mark, Gary and Jessica to hear them.

'I can be very spontaneous when I want to be,' muttered Gary, not looking at his companions but observing the oncoming Blue team and the car still way behind them in woods.

'When did you read the rules?' asked Mark quietly.

'I didn't, I just made that up. I bet no one else here read them either, only you and only to cheat,' Gary replied, avoiding eye contact with his brother.

There it was, his first serious lie and he made it out of desperation. Gary felt himself blush and the bizarre sensation inside his body that made his stomach somersault. He was really very grateful that he was standing in a spot not lit by the floodlights installed on the top of the gate so at least nobody could see his discomfort. The darkness worked to his advantage of hiding his embarrassed. Gary felt weird lying because he wasn't accustomed to such behaviour. But maybe sometimes the end justifies the means, he thought trying to comfort himself.

'That was a good one, bro. I would have never expected that you are capable of such things. I'm truly impressed,' answered Mark with undisguised admiration.

Somehow Gary didn't feel proud of Mark's approval, although he wanted to win the competition as much as his half-brother. *At the end of the day, somebody would be walking away with this cash prize so it might as well be me as anyone,* Gary thought, excusing his action to himself.

They were standing in silence when the gate slowly opened. Although, the approaching car was still quite far, its strong headlights lit up the path well and they could hear the drumming bass beat of loud metal music. Some of the returning Blue team members stopped and looked at the coming car.

'Damn! Simon's too fast, our brilliant plan just failed,' whispered Mark more to himself than his companions. He pushed the wooden doorway so forcibly that a man standing behind it was knocked flat on his back. The rogues hurried inside. They passed a few surprised men and headed into the centre of the base. There was a timbered shed with a castle-like layout with gaps shaped like windows big enough for an adult to walk through. There was no glass in them, but only shutters which were now wide open. Screens were installed inside the shed.

In the construction, on two oblong benches, two men in military uniform were sitting, drinking beer and eating doughnuts. There were empty cake wrappers, scattered chips and half-empty juice bottles laying on the square table. The men were laughing at a dirty joke one of them had just told. They all jumped at once, surprised to see the advancing rogues. When they saw the medics armbands, they nodded and made space for Jessica to sit down. Mark hauled her onto the nearest bench. She hung her head, trying to hide her face with sported a broad grin under her hood and long curly hair. She was still whimpering but had to choke back laughter.

'Your mates are calling you; they need help getting something from the car,' said Gary to the Blue team members still sitting on the benches. *And I was lying again,* thought Gary, feeling more confident this time than before. Gary pointed out the chaos in the square, but it was Mark who shooed them away using a strong, assertive voice. The men moved out reluctantly, seemingly unsuspicious of the medical team imposters. The heavy metal music from the arriving car was turned down. More of Blue team members emerged from the gate. It was the returning group that had left their base to check Sean's decoy. The cacophony of laughter and voices was increasing outside. People were shouting excitedly and triumphantly screaming that they had won the contest.

'You are a lame actress, Jessica. You almost ratted us out,' said Gary, but couldn't help laughing with her.

'I didn't. Sorry, I just couldn't…' she said, still with a big grin on her face as Mark interrupted her talk.

'Stop talking, the dickheads have hidden the flags! Guys, start searching for them. They should be somewhere here. We only have eight minutes left,' shouted Mark, closing and bolting the door. He started to rummage and search in the room for flags. Gary and Jessica rushed to joined him. They looked in all the obvious places with no success.

'They are not here. Maybe the leader has taken them with him?' asked Gary panicking.

'It's not possible. Flags have to be kept inside the castle at the end of the game, or you lose points. They couldn't take them out. They have a GPS tracker inside, that's why Simon is here. He has to check them before the game is over,' said Mark kneeling down and looking under the table.

The main gate was open, and the rest of Blue team members were walking back to base chatting elatedly about their upcoming victory. They were all congratulating a tall, beefy man who was their team leader, praising his strategy and reminiscing about the best actions they had made as a team.

'Hey, guys. I can see that you've caught the last three rogues. That'll add up nicely to your score,' cried Simon, surrounded by Blue's and shaking hands with random team members.

'What rogues? Who did it? Where are they?' and more similar questions could be heard all around.

'I've just seen them. They are inside your base, folks,' said Simon, waving to Jessica whose head was easily seen in one of the shed windows.

The crowd cheered even more and burst into a victory song, well known among football fans. Some of them were walking to the shed-castle.

'It's over. Not only we've failed, but we're raising their score. They didn't even have to catch us. Damn, stupid idea,' snorted Jessica as she sat resigned on the bench and helped herself to biscuits.

'No, it's not over yet, five minutes left until midnight. We still have a chance if only we can find those bloody flags. Help me, guys, we have to lock ourselves inside,' said Mark, hurriedly closing one window shutter.

Jessica unwillingly got up and, taking one more biscuit, headed to the window next to her. Gary jumped to the nearest flap, tripping over a rotting floorboard. The tip of his shoe caught in a hole as he felt, slamming the hatch quite loudly and attracting the attention of a few game participants standing near the castle.

The moving plank on the floor revealed a hiding place beneath.

Mark, Gary and Jessica looked at each other with surprise. Mark closed the last window's flap and hurried to Gary, arriving at the same time as Jessica. But it was Gary who put his hand into the black hole beneath and drew out two flags, one belonging to the Red team and one to the Blue's. Mark took out the Green team's flag he had in his trousers pocket and yelled so loudly it shocked the people standing outside into silence. Mark tore off his medic's armband and hid it inside his clothing. Gary and Jessica followed suit, also taking off their armbands and hiding them. They were shouting with joy, babbling nonsense about mischievous pirates and winning the jackpot. Gary's foot was still stuck in the hole, but he didn't care. In his mind, he was counting all the prized money that he would have got after this event and the fact that he now could afford to buy his new professional computer. That would definitely change a lot in his life, he thought, smiling and feeling proud that his career prospects had finally started to look up.

Moreover, he had recorded a lot from this event, including their final moment of nervously searching for the flags. The cameras on his and Jessica's helmets were still recording. Mark unbolted the door, opened it and energetically waved all three flags, laughing loudly. The rogues were cheering as Simon and a few Blue's members entered to the shed after banging on the door for some time.

'We won. It's five past midnight. The flags were under the floor. But we searched the whole place, and we found them. We outsmarted you, guys,' he cried, pointing into the Blue team leader's face as he entered the castle walking behind Simon.

'No! What? How? You can't win!' shouted the leader, grimacing with astonishment and anger. He clenched his fists, looking like he was ready to fight someone. He was the kind of man who loved to give orders as much as he loved his beefy, muscular appearance. Although his posture and voice intimidated most of his team standing around him, Simon remained calm and unflappable.

'Let me check the rules,' said Simon calmly in the tone like a government official. He pulled out a tablet from one of the pockets in his green, woodland jacket and started searching some files on it. For a few minutes, everyone was silent, staring at him attentively. Simon was tall, quite muscular and bold. His chocolate-colour skin contrasted with his white T-shirt. He wore rimless glasses and had a thick gold chain around his neck.

'Well, it's written here that rogues are a team, paragraph 24 terms and conditions. They don't have to have a base or a leader, and as far as I remember, all that was said at the beginning of the game. But you, sir, were not interested in participating in the first organisational meeting. You all knew about the contract before you signed it. Moreover, it says here that you can't hide the flags, so I have to disqualify your team entirely for not following the rules, and I can do it according to paragraph 55. Here's the note about how rogues can win, and it seems it's not as easy for them as it is for you guys. So be polite and give them credit for creativity and for tricking you all. If anyone disagrees with this verdict, there'll be a discussion panel tomorrow after breakfast summarising all the groups' teamwork. Everyone will have an opportunity to speak their mind. I'll personally check the cameras from this base for the last half an hour, and see what's recorded on them, alongside with the GPS data. So, thank you all very much for the lovely time we've had together, and I hope that you all learnt something valuable for future reference,' declared Simon, loud enough so that everyone could hear him well. He was eyeing all those around him, searching for signs of troublemakers. Meanwhile, the Blue team leader moved beside him and took the tablet from Simon's hands and began to silently read the contract. Everyone was agog, waiting for the verdict.

Gary admitted to himself that Simon didn't have any problems with confidence when public speaking.

'Wait a minute. They were pretending to be a medical team. Is it even legal to fake who you are?' asked one of the Blues who was sitting inside the shed before the rogues arrived. He was now standing next to his boss, trying to read from behind him.

'Of course. That's why we call them The Rogues. Guys, stop arguing, it's all in the contract and you, sir, signed it yourself,' said Simon in a condescending manner, staring at the leader. The game participants were calmly observing the situation.

'This is bullshit, I'm going to the pub. Who's with me?' the leader interrupted the uncomfortable silence, looking around at his teammates to see who was up for a boozy session in the pub. Some of them cheered, but many were still muttering about unfairness and the cunning ending to the competition. They all left the shed, boarded minibuses and drove away, leaving some of the equipment and a lot of rubbish behind. Only the rogues and Simon were left at the base.

'Who had the evil plan? I bet Mark had a hand in it. All our staff will congratulate you for winning over those bullies. That was awesome guys,' cried Simon excitedly. They were standing outside, watching the Blue team departing and praising themselves for their bravery.

'Oh, God, let's clean some of this mess because if I sit for one minute, I won't get up at all,' said Jessica, picking up empty wrappings and packages. Simon brought black rubbish bags and handed them out. They cleaned the area and put the filled bags in the boot of Simon's SUV. After finishing, they went back to the shed carrying food and drinks brought by Simon.

'I hope all the cameras are working properly in every base,' said Gary, looking at Simon who was the one responsible for the equipment.

'No worries. Thank goodness the bases are all wired with each other, otherwise the radio connection wouldn't work so well. Someone did an excellent job building and adapting this place as a permanent event area and they predicted there would be filming,' said Simon, sipping a can of beer.

They were sitting inside the castle recounting their victory, laughing, drinking and eating burgers brought by Simon when suddenly, the soft thump of feet landing on the wooden roof interrupted their conversation. They were staring at each other in silence, listening to footsteps walking above their heads. The first few steps sounded very soft, like someone was uncertain where to go, moving back and forth in different directions. But after a while, the steps walked fast towards the edge of the roof of the shed directly above the door. The friends looked at each other and with a tacit agreement they silently got to their feet. Mark and Simon jumped up and hid behind the open door and stood quietly in the corner. They chose a place which was perfect for setting a trap or at least surprising someone.

Jessica and Gary hurriedly hid under the table. They put their bags on the bench in such a way that it was quite hard to notice them hiding there. A few seconds later someone jumped from the roof and entered the shed castle.

*

The man rushed inside. His clothes were torn in a few places and covered with dried blood stains. He looked ordinary, not too tall, not too short, with a non-distinguishable shaped face and blond hair. But one thing made him different to the average person, his golden eyes which attracted immediate attention.

He had taken only one step inside the shed with one hand holding the doorknob as another figure appeared just behind him and pushed him in with such force that he plunged into the room like a rag doll. Losing his balance, he landed flat on the table knocking off some empty bottles. The door slammed towards the wall, hitting Mark and Simon who were standing behind it. They both groaned silently in pain but didn't make any sudden movement. Mark was standing in the corner. He cushioned the impact of the door using his hands, but it was Simon who caught the door-knob to prevent it from bouncing off them. Mark put his finger on his lips and nodded at Simon, indicating to stay silently hidden for the unknown newcomers. Simon smiled like a boy who was playing hide-and-seek with his mates, but Mark remained calm as he leaned over Simon, trying to take a glimpse of the scene, but the gap behind the door was too narrow for both of them. He took a long, deep breath and raised his nose like a dog trying to catch scent.

Meanwhile, Jessica and Gary were observing the scene with their mouths wide open. They were both sitting deep under the table, sheltered behind bags laying on the bench. They shivered lightly when glasses smashed to the floor leaving broken pieces all around. Gary put his finger to his lips indicating that Jessica should stay silent as they watched the second figure enter the place. But it wasn't necessary as she seemed so deep in thought, staring at the creature that she didn't notice Gary's gesture.

The second individual who came in wasn't like any living being Gary had ever seen. The creature was more than two metres tall, a humanoid shape with a massive torso and a posture that overshadowed everything around him. He was bulky and barely fit beneath the ceiling. His head was wolfish, the snout was much shorter with more human facial features including slightly larger than average canine-like ears. He had long, white, sharp fangs which made him look dangerously savage and emphasised his partial animal nature. He was standing on two legs in an upright posture, growling fearsomely. He had five-fingered hands, but they ended with massive, sharp, black claws. He had muscular legs, but his feet were shaped precisely like wolf's paws. His body was made of perfectly formed muscles covered with short hair on his stomach but long grey animal fur on his back. He had a long, hairy tail that was now hanging alongside his legs. In the middle of the room stood a werewolf, in its fully shape-shifting battle-form.

The werewolf jumped up and grabbed the man lying on the table, tearing at his clothing, narrowly avoiding piercing his skin and placing his muzzle so close to him that his long fangs touched the skin on the man's cheek. With his other hand, the wolf clutched the man's neck and pressed slightly, just enough that his claws pierced his skin and drops of blood oozed down his neck. A slow growl reverberated inside the shed, freezing everyone with fear. The beast growled louder. His whining prey tried to say something, but he stuttered and couldn't articulate a coherent sentence. His face was so pale, and he was so still he could have been mistaken for a shop dummy.

The werewolf squeezed his claws on the man's neck, opened his mouth as if he was smiling, baring his teeth. He then froze as he heard a deafening shout from outside.

'Robert, stop!'

A third man appeared in the doorway just behind the beast. The half-wolf, half-human creature turned his head and said something, but it sounded more like a bark than any language known to Gary. The werewolf gazed at the intruder and the tension visibly left his body as he relaxed. Robert, the beast, took a slow and deep breath and said with a more human voice,

'I'm not going to kill him yet. But I've chased him for more than two hours-' Robert didn't finish.

'How so?' asked the new man, sounding more interested than frightened.

'I shot him with a Daurel's bullet, the best hunter's drug,' replied Robert with a strange laugh.

'But of course, you did,' replied the newcomer, as though stating the obvious.

Robert turned his head and sniffed the air and took away his sharp claws from around the captured man's neck but still held onto his prey with his other hand. The man tried to see who had entered the shed. He stretched himself in a way so that the werewolf's massive bulk wouldn't block his view.

'I know the Prince of Vampires wants him very badly, and there is a price for his head, but …' said the newcomer, coming closer to the werewolf.

He was brisk despite his chubbiness. On his round smiling face he had a few scratches with tiny lines of fresh blood, made by the brambles he had been running through. His mid-length hair, pulled in a short ponytail, was matted with bits of dried leaves. His long beard had greying patches and two long braids braided in it. He had several piercings and visible tattoos which started on his neck just below his ears. He was wearing a similar military uniform, two rifles and a gun as all the game participants, but he had a yellow armband with the word 'Organiser' on it. He was quite short, reaching only half of beast's chest, but he looked straight in his eyes without fear.

'Don't call this schmuck the Prince. There is no such thing like a Vampire Prince in London. Just because he calls himself that, doesn't mean he is one,' said Robert, spitting his every word angrily and clearly showing his disagreement.

'Okay. Stop now. Please, don't hurt him, I need him alive and in one piece so calm down and let's talk like gentlemen. I don't assume you have high-class manners but at least let's pretend you do possess some *Savoir-Vivre*,' said the new man sarcastically, grabbing the werewolf's hand and pulling the beast towards him. The werewolf growled a warning, showing large fangs, but the man didn't show any sign of being afraid.

'Sean! Is that you? Help me for goodness sake. I just came back to England, and I couldn't find you,' cried the captured man. The werewolf looked puzzled, watching the ongoing conversation with rising curiosity.

'Yes, it's me. I twice picked up your scent in the forest but you're fast, even if you're drugged, Draco. I tried to leave some markers to let you know that I'm here, but you just passed through them like a wind. Man, I thought that you were dead. Where have you been all this time? Robert, let him go for goodness sake. I seriously need him,' said the new man named Sean, addressing the werewolf. He put his hand on the beast's massive claws trying to unclench them and prevent Draco, the captured man, from being torn apart.

'Since when do you hang out with vamps, Sean? That's so not you,' said the werewolf, still holding Draco close.

'I'm working for the Guild. It's my job to keep in contact with many supernatural beings,' answered Sean calmly.

'Bullshit! Are you drinking his blood or is there something more exciting about this scumbag that turns you on?' replied Robert, raising his voice.

The werewolf turned his head towards Sean. Sean didn't react but stayed calm and confident, staring straight into wolf's eyes, even when the drops of the beast saliva dripped onto his face. He didn't move his head or the rest of his body back, but the colour of his eyes changed. Sean looked like he was focused and alert, ready to take more aggressive action. They were sizing one another up in silence.

'There is no need for that language, Robert. Just please, let him go. I need Draco. He is more important than you think,' said Sean, placing his hand on the hairy wolf's arms and squeezing gently. There was visible tension between them, and both were observing each other intensely without blinking. After a few seconds, the wolf's grip on Draco loosened but the beast didn't set him free.

'You are lucky, blood-sucking maggot,' growled the werewolf to Draco, 'I don't care about your weird, so-called friendship with Sean, next time you'll be mine, mark my words you hideous, slimy bastard,' said Robert. He pulled Draco's face so close that his fangs slightly pierced his cheek, leaving a small wound which started oozing black fluid instead of blood. Suddenly, the werewolf pushed the vampire so quickly that he fell down on the floor. Robert spat on him with disgust.

'Thank you, Robert. I do appreciate your kindness,' said Sean, sighing with relief and smiling softly.

'Don't flatter yourself, Sean. I'm doing this only because you're an adviser in The Guild. Besides, you're protected by the law, otherwise you'd have to fight me and that is the last thing you want to do. I'd snap your head off before you could say "sorry". So, I guess it's this motherfucker's lucky day. There is nothing illegal in chasing off vamps, is there?' ask Robert, pointing out at Draco.

'Technically speaking, you have to have a reason to exterminate him and The Guild's permission, I believe. As long as he doesn't kill anyone by his rage, you-' but he didn't finish because Robert roared.

'I don't care about your bureaucratic bullshit. I work for Scotland Yard, and my department is not a part of The Guild and I know our laws better than you think. I found him at the crime scene. You've heard about Boyle's Farm, haven't you, Sean? I knew as soon as I got there they didn't get what they came for, so sooner or later somebody would be back. This little shit was there. I saw him searching the storage units in the yard. Did you miss something when you tortured the little girl?' asked Robert angrily. His sneered, exposing his sharp fangs. He took one step towards Draco, but Sean held up his hand.

'I swear I had nothing to do with it. I wasn't even in England when the murder happened. I can show you my plane tickets. I have all of them in my flat,' replied terrified Draco. He was shaking and his voice indicated that he was very stressed indeed. He got up slowly and stood behind Sean who made a protective gesture trying to create distance between them and Robert.

'See, he can prove it, I'll bring it to your office. If he doesn't have them, I'll personally hand him over to you, you know I can. So, how's it gonna be?' asked Sean, offering his hand as a sign of agreement. Robert hesitated for a while, still staring at the vamp intensively, but then he reluctantly grabbed Sean's outstretched hand.

'Just scan and email them to me,' said Robert to Sean much calmer now. There was a silence between them for a while, only interrupted by the rain tapping on the roof. It had started to rain just before they entered the shed but now the downpour was heavier.

'Someone is here,' said Robert, suddenly freezing in one position. He started sniffing more thoroughly around the table and the doorway. Sean and Draco looked at each other in surprise.

In the meantime, in the hiding place behind the door, Simon was trying not to laugh. He couldn't see what was happening, but he could hear everything. His face contorted in disgust. He pinched his nostrils with his fingers and put a hand over his mouth. He couldn't bear the emitting smell of wet fur, but he didn't know it belonged to the werewolf. The scent was slightly different to an animal's, but still quite strong in this relatively small place. Mark was squeezed in the corner and couldn't see anything either, but his face was frozen in terror. It seemed that he knew what the newcomers were talking about.

Meanwhile, Gary was dumbstruck, staring at the scene through the gap between bags on the bench. Deep down he couldn't believe what he was witnessing. The whole scene looked like it was taken straight from a horror movie. Somehow, he didn't feel frightened mainly because he couldn't see the beast clearly and, in his mind, this all looked like play acting with excellent costumes and facial prosthetics. Maybe that was the last surprise, the last quest to finish to get extra points in the competition, or perhaps that was Sean's grand master plan which the rogues didn't see coming because it was very secret, thought Gary, flabbergasted. He knew that the cameras were still recording, not only in this base but at other points in the forest, so he convinced himself the scene was made up to end the Airsoft competition in a very theatrical way. Gary thought that maybe this had all been created as a surprise for the participants and similar scenes were being enacted at other game locations. He realised that he missed the part explaining how the competition ended at the first organisational meeting. Now he recalled that at the time he was busy with Simon setting up cameras around the camps and in the forest. He hoped that Simon didn't turn the cameras off after midnight so Gary would have beautiful, dramatic pictures he could include. He was admiring the details of the theatrical work and the werewolf's costume and mask. He wondered how it was possible to make the beast so big and realistic at the same time. He thought about all the tricks of disguise he knew but couldn't think of anything as professional as what he was currently seeing. But on the other hand, Gary admitted, he was only an amateur and had never been inside a professional film studio. Therefore, what he saw now was something new for him, and he was more fascinated by it rather than scared.

He couldn't believe Sean was such a brilliant actor, as good as any Hollywood star. He looked so different from the usual calm and reasonable uncle, thought Gary watching Sean. But on the other hand, Gary never had been too close to this side of his family. Sean was the brother of his mother's first husband, John Miller, who was murdered, and his killer was never found. From that relationship,

Gary had twin half-brothers eight years older than him and Mark was one of them.

Gary's mother, Helen Rogers, had died ten years ago in a car accident, alongside her second husband, George Rogers. Gary was twelve years old back then and was spending the summer at his grandmother's house in Nottingham.

After his parent's death, Gary stayed with his grandparents and Sean cared for the twins. Gary quite often visited his relatives in London, but he didn't know them well. Even after he moved to London, he lived separately in a rented room and he stayed quite distant with Sean's side of the family. He probably wouldn't have too much in common with them if it weren't for Mark. His half-brother was ubiquitous and annoying in forcing his presence into Gary's life. Sometimes, Gary had an impression that Mark possessed some mind-reading ability with his tendency to appear and disappear in the weirdest situations. It took Gary a while to get used to Mark unexpectedly showing up out of nowhere.

And now, Gary was stunned watching his uncle as though observing a total stranger. This puzzled him even more. What else didn't he know about his family, Gary brooded deep in his mind. Maybe his family was more interesting than he'd suspected and perhaps they weren't as dull as he'd judged them to be. And perhaps he could ask them for help with his film making career. If only he had a good story and some talented actor friends, he pondered, it might work pretty well. His mind was running wild as he daydreamed of his future on a red carpet illuminated by thousands of flashes from paparazzi taking his pictures.

At first, Gary didn't see Jessica's body curved up behind him. She had covered her head with both arms and murmured something unintelligible. Her body swayed gently and softly touching his back. Gary turned to her, put his hand on her arm and shook her softly. She reacted to his touch by curling her body even more into a foetal position and hiding her head deeper in her arms.

When Gary saw her, he felt fear freeze his blood when he realised there was something seriously wrong with her. He leaned over and whispered her name a few times and shaking her arm intensely. She stopped muttering and it seemed as though she relaxed a bit upon hearing his quiet voice. She grabbed his hand tightly and pulled it towards her chest. Her arms were no longer clenched around her head and she started to breathe more evenly. Gary let her hold his hand, but he turned his head to nervously observe the scene. But this time, something deep inside him was shouting, as he realised this wasn't characters play acting. He watched what was going on around him speechless and with his mouth slightly open.

*

The werewolf was sniffing around the door more thoroughly. He grabbed the door handle and pulled it quickly, exposing Mark and Simon hiding. Simon froze at first sight of the large beast face. But then, in a split of a second, Simon punched Robert hard straight on the nose. The wolf's fangs sank into Simon's fist, instinctive in self-defence. At first, Simon didn't feel a thing but only stared at the large wolf's jaw clenched around his hand. Blood flowed from his shattered, clenched fist, but he was so surprised that he didn't feel pain. There was a pause when they looked shocked at each other, trying to process what just had happened. After a few seconds, when the pain woke up all the nerves in his body, Simon started screaming at the top of his lungs.

Gary, watching the whole situation, felt a wave of anger and fury overflowing him and raising adrenaline in his blood to uncontrolled levels. He wasn't aware of what he was doing but acting on impulse when he grabbed a large torch, the first thing near him that was reliable and sturdy enough to use as a weapon, as he leaped out from under the table. He beat the werewolf around the head without any fear or hesitation. Unfortunately, he jabbed the beast in the temple with such force, that it resulted in even more fierceness from Gary's opponent.

Robert released Simon's hand, turned rapidly and thumped Gary so hard that he flew across the table like a rag doll, landing on the opposite side of the room, banging his head and losing consciousness. A slow stream of blood flowed from Gary's ears.

Jessica began to howl like a banshee when the table was knocked over by Gary's flying body. She was sitting on the floor, covering her ears and staring at the scene with horror. She was rolling her eyes and rocking back and forth. But suddenly she felt silent as she passed out cold at the moment when she looked directly into the werewolf's eyes. Her scream had stopped Robert in his tracks and made him realise what he had just done. He looked around with hesitation.

'No, no, no!' shouted Sean as he tried to push the massive werewolf's body away but without any success. Simon passed out. Mark, who was standing speechless right behind him, caught Simon's collapsing body and gently laid him on the floor. He then bounced up from his crouching position so high and so fast that he surprised not only Robert but the two other men as well. He landed on the werewolf, punching him in the head with his fists and knocking him down onto the floor. Robert yelped like terrified dog. He covered his head and curled his body, shielding his stomach. Mark's face changed drastically. Upon his usual cheerful, smiling face appeared a grimace of anger mixed with revenge. His pupils turned thin and vertical. His body was changing radically. He was much taller than a few moments before, his face transformed with delicate feline features. His hands grew, sprouted short ginger-ish fur and long sharp claws. He looked like a man with perfect control over his transformation, changing only the parts of his body he wanted to.

'What have you done stupid dog?!' shouted Mark while pulling out a Samurai sword. The blade was purple, transparent, and about one metre long which looked as if it was made from pure light. With incredible speed and without any hesitation, he placed the blade against the wolf's neck.

*

Mark leaned forward and gazed at Robert in a very intimidating way. He smiled softly, showing his long, upper fangs. He whispered something that sounded like a soft growl. The blade in his hand elongated slightly, puncturing the werewolf's skin to the point of drawing blood. Draco clenched his fists, staring at a trickle of blood on Robert's neck. He closed his eyes and took a few deep breaths. Sean looked scared.

'Mark, calm down. Gary needs you now. We don't want any more problems than we already have, right?' asked Sean calmly as he moved slowly towards Mark. He put his hand on Mark's arm, gently pushing it down. He seemed more frightened by Mark's actions than when he spoke with Robert for the first time. Sean knew that stopping his nephew would be more difficult than the werewolf.

Although the blood from the incision on Robert's skin started streaming faster, staining his fur, the cut began to regenerate itself, and soon the wound was fully closed. Draco's eyes had red marks with dark lines inside when he saw the fresh blood. He turned over, walked to a window and opened the shutter a bit wider. He clenched his fists and jaws even harder, breathing deeply in a controlled way. He looked like he was fighting a battle in his mind and could barely restrain himself. But his sudden movement broke the uncomfortable silence that was hanging around like a bad stench in the air.

'And now what?' asked Sean, angrily staring at the werewolf.

Robert got up but hung his head low in silence. His body started to shrink rapidly to the size of an average human. In one blink of an eye, where the big beast once stood, there was now an ordinary, fully dressed middle-aged man. He was quite tall and thin with a long face. He had a week-old beard and spiky, dishevelled black hair with white strands making it appearance more grey than black. He was wearing black jeans and a reddish t-shirt, both worn out in a few places with small holes giving the impression that the best time of their existence was behind. He was holding a black thick cane which, on the contrary of his clothes, looked like it was bought yesterday. It seemed expensive and had a lot of thin silver symbols engraved on the surface and a silver handle shaped like wolf's head.

The marks on the cane slowly disappeared, leaving the cane completely black. Robert's arms were covered in tattoos of glyphs, reminiscent more as if they were scratched by animal claw, rather than as human writing. His tattoos shone softly with red light, but then faded away and vanished in a few seconds, leaving his skin thoroughly clean. Robert took a few steps, visibly limping on his left leg, and leaned over to Simon. He seemed not to care about Mark's blade still close to his body.

Draco, now calm and without showing any emotions, made himself busy trying not to react to the smell of blood that was all over the shed. He crouched near Gary, checking his pulse, lifting an eyelid and testing the pupil's reaction. He nodded to Sean a gesture suggesting that Gary was still in this world. Meanwhile, Sean was checking on Jessica. Mark was observing every move Robert made, but this time he included Draco in his mission for keeping an eye on potential danger. He hid the blade with such speed and grace that nobody knew when and where he put it.

'Thank Goodness, she is still alive. In a deep coma but still with us,' said Sean checking the pulse on Jessica's neck and her eye response using the light from his phone. His statement softened the tension that had grown between them to the point of violent outburst. Sean knew that Mark was able to kill Robert if something drastic happened to Gary or his friends. Sean sighed, relived when he saw Mark's face relaxing when he heard that Jessica was alive.

Jessica had a soft smile on her face, but her skin was still white like paper. Even her freckles were barely visible. Sean patted her face gently, but she didn't show any sign of waking up. He sighed once again, put his hoodie under her head and went over to Gary. Mark was already there checking Gary's head, chest and spine as much as he could without moving him.

'He needs to go to a hospital. He might be seriously injured,' said Mark in a trembling voice, wiping a single small tear away before anybody could see it.

'Shall I call an ambulance, or will you do it? They will need names and details, so maybe you Sean?' asked Robert, taking out a mobile phone from a pocket of his jeans. His voice was calm and soft. He looked at Sean with expectation, wiping the blood from his neck using his worn T-shirt. Sean shook his head incredulously and yelled at him.

'But of course, you have no idea what to do. Your work usually begins after mayhem leaves blood and smashed bodies all over the place. Your department is not interested when there are no casualties and nothing to collect as evidence in plastic bags. I need to talk to your brother-' but he couldn't finish.

'Don't you dare involve James in it!' Robert's truculent response rapidly interrupted Sean's accusatory tone.

'If things turn very badly, I'll have no choice,' said Sean calmly.

'I know, but we don't know yet how it'll all end up,' replied Robert in a friendlier tone. A light smile appeared on his stern face, but nobody was smiling. Sean caught sight of Mark's face and saw that his anger was brewing once again. The threat of a fight was looming, and Sean didn't want to let that happen.

'Don't panic, Mark. They are still alive, and we'll do everything to help them, right Robert? I'm talking about you as well. I hope you don't think you can escape the consequences of this event,' said Sean, staring straight into Robert's eyes. Sean put his hand on Mark's arm and squeezed it quite hard.

'No, I don't, but it wasn't all my fault-'

'Oh, please. Don't start with some crappy victim speech. The Guild will investigate anyway, and you know very well, we can't lie, and neither can you. They'll find out what just happened, and they won't necessarily need to ask questions. Simon and Gary didn't have delirium so for shamans it'll be easy to check their body's memory. Anyway, I'll deal with it later on. Now we need to come up with a convincing explanation for this mess to the company we're still working for. And don't forget the cameras. There is one here. Thank goodness they don't have our marks, otherwise, everyone could see you in the ferox form. I told you, Robert, many years ago, one day you'd cross the line way too far, and your temper would get you into big trouble. I think there is a Viviter doctor in the local hospital, I'll call him,' said Sean firmly to everyone, but he held his gaze on the werewolf's eyes without looking away. Robert seemed ashamed.

'Maybe I should-' started Robert but he was interrupted by Mark who had jumped fast towards him, catching his throat and said through teeth clenched with anger.

'You've caused enough chaos for today. I don't want to see your dirty fur here anymore, or I swear to God I'll tear you to shreds when I fully change. You may terrorise Sean, but I'm not a lazy fluffy kitten, so try again with someone who can match you, and we'll see how good you are,' hissed Mark, straight at Robert. Only Sean's hand still holding Mark's arm, like an anchor holding a ship on a rough sea, prevented the conflict from escalating to the point of no return.

There was silence for a minute, as everyone waited for the course of events to unfold. Robert turned his head and closed his eyes. He couldn't look into Mark's light green eyes; whose vertical pupils gave him the appearance of a focused cat.

'That's enough. Let him go. You have work to do,' said Sean, firmly turning Mark's head in his direction. Mark took a deep breath, pushed Robert aside and walked away. Robert staggered but kept his balance thanks to his walking stick.

*

They all worked in silence. Sean and Mark checked everyone over.

When Sean was making the call to the nearest hospital, Robert took the first-aid kit and took out all the bandages.

Simon's hand looked terrible. The werewolf's fangs had pierced through his skin, crushing the bones which could be easily seen. It seemed like the bite had left a few fingers paralysed. There was a fast-growing pool of blood beneath his wounded hand. Draco's eyes widened, and his golden pupils glowed lightly at this view. He swallowed, clenched his teeth and covered his eyes with his arm. He turned, looked at Sean, shook his head with disapproval, picked Jessica's body up and left the room. He didn't see the watchful gaze not only from Robert but Mark as well. Robert hobbled after Draco, stood in the doorway, lighted a cigarette and watched his every move. Draco didn't have any difficulty carrying her body. He opened the backseat door and placed her inside the SUV.

In the meantime, Sean and Mark bandaged Simon's hand as much as they could to stop the bleeding. Sean twisted his face with disgust and retched. He covered his mouth and turned his head away but was still holding Simon's arm to make the whole dressing process easier. Mark finished it with a deadpan face, concerned about leaking blood through the layers of dressing. He called the manager of the event company and explained the situation very briefly in a few sentences. He knew that the director, whom he knew well, would demand more specific descriptions as to what had just happened and that there would be a price to pay for asking her to help cover up the accident. Mark smiled thinking about all the negotiation tactics ahead of him. The small details that they always dispute over and over again made him realise how exciting the whole process was for him. He had to admit she was the best in keeping contract terms to the bitter end.

*

They were waiting for some time for the doctor to arrive. They didn't talk much but were sitting in the shed drinking juice and finishing the food. Even Robert sat with them and drank a beer. The atmosphere was still hostile, but the tension loosened up a little bit.

The doctor was a middle-aged lady who looked quite terrified about Jessica and Simon's condition, but Gary's state petrified her. She didn't say much but she made a phone call, standing in a voice distance. Sean told her everything that had happened in the last half an hour as she had to fill out a report for The Guild. It appeared the accident was way too dangerous to ignore its nasty outcome that would definitely come to light sooner or later.

There was only one place in the ambulance for Gary, so Simon and Jessica were driven to the hospital by Mark. He got into the SUV, drove off and was swearing to himself that he would do everything possible to save his younger brother. He also knew that he had to take care of his friends too, and that life would never be the same again for any of them. They were not only Gary's friends but his as well. Although they were just regular human beings and not connected to anything behind the supernatural veil, but that was what he liked about them the most. He was thinking about all the usual, typical stuff he had with Gary, and the fact that he didn't want to lose it motivated him even more. He knew that Gary would never forgive him if something terrible happened to his friends.

*

Sean watched the departing vehicle and felt the dangerous calmness soaking his mind. He knew now was the moment when the silence was a harbinger of oncoming events which would turn their world upside down. His inborn, intuitive spider-sense could feel the upcoming tremendous changes, that kind of inversion which always cost sweat, blood and possibly someone's life.

Last time he felt precisely the same as he did now, was ten years ago on a day Gary and the twin's mother, Helen, died alongside her husband and his other friends. He had the same feelings of stillness like he had before the event of closing Erick, one of the most influential vampires, inside a powerful artefact. Back then they had a perfect plan, but it all went very, very wrong. And now, the story was repeating itself like an old, broken and long-forgotten engine, which all of a sudden started working, pushing events into motion with double the speed. He could feel the intimidating rush, the rain of unwanted questions and wrong attention he had to face. Even worse, the unknown outcome of today's event started to harass him like a cold thin finger of death, scratching the bottom of his skull. How did this evening turn so bad, he wondered? He had done everything to protect Gary from the world behind the veil, the world of Viviters, and sending him to live with his grandparents in Nottingham was part of it. Sean wanted Gary to stay on the safe, lull-ish like a dream side of the world, but this was only his wishful thinking. He should have known that in this family, a normal and quiet life would never be possible.

'Are you okay?' Draco's voice rapidly burst into Sean's thoughts.

'No, I'm not okay and I'm more than sure nothing will be okay, like ever, from today onwards. I wish this evening had never happened,' said Sean, sighing deeply.

'You just overdramatise-' started Robert but was interrupted by Sean.

'Do I? The worst scenario is that Gary is dead because of internal bleeding. Jessica has to be locked up in an asylum suffering severe paranoia and Simon will become a bloody rogue werewolf, or did I miss something?' replied Sean angrily, emphasising every name he just said.

'What? A werewolf? There's little chance for it,' said Robert surprised.

'You forgot it's a full moon today,' said Draco calmly, as though very tired.

'Holy fuck!' cursed Robert, without hiding his utter surprise.

'You're not allowed to be in your ferox form during the full moon. You do know The Guild's law about it, don't you?' asked Sean sarcastically. Robert looked stunned.

'The moon isn't only full, but it's The Red Moon, one of the rarest in the sky. He might not survive the change,' added Sean with a slight tone of resignation.

'The last case I know of when someone was bitten under a red moon was a woman, more than a hundred years ago. It was in Paris, and I saw the whole process. The transformation was excruciating, like being tortured for days without a break. Not everyone could survive that, but she got through. She was never the same again. I don't know what happened after I left the city, but she mutilated more than one hundred humans in furies she got during the next full moon. It's not about becoming a werewolf; it's about living with it. Totally different than being born as one. The turned humans are more vicious and bloodthirsty than others in a ferox-battle form. You're perfectly capable of controlling yourself during a full moon, but they might have a huge problem with it. They're exactly like in all those bad stories about werewolves written throughout the centuries. You'll have to face the consequences of creating him,' said Draco coldly.

'But I didn't mean it. It all was an accident. He didn't have delirium like she had. Humans always black out when they see our shape-shift form. Gary and Simon didn't react like that. It'd never happened to me before. I know, there is a tiny percentage of human population who are immune, but two of them in one place? That is weird,' said Robert. The tone of his voice indicated that he desperately wanted to give a good excuse for his action to escape the dreadful unknown lurking in his future.

'Shit happens every day. When you're ferox there is always a possibility someone can see you. Do you think the law was created to make our life miserable?' asked Sean. He sat on a bench, dropped his head on his hand, and sighed. Draco was sitting next to him.

'Every day the Guild has to deal with similar cases. It's not only me who's made a mistake, so it's no biggie. I didn't change in their presence. They just happened to be in the wrong place at the wrong time. But the question, what he was doing on the farm, remains unanswered,' said Robert pointing at Draco. There was a silence among them.

'And why did you search for him in the place where the vicious murder took place? I saw you once near the storage. Nobody sane would go there without a good reason, not after what happened a few days ago,' said Robert, more confident than moments before.

Sean and Draco looked at each other first and then at him. Robert smiled and took out a new cigarette. He lit up and took a deep breath. The silence was long and built up more tension than the whole situation with Gary and his friends. Robert gazed attentively at them as he pulled on his cigarette, filling the shed with a cloud of smoke.

'Well, I was curious about all those rumours from the pub, so I took a stroll to the scene in my free time. Maybe I could sense something important. I have friends who might be interested in my opinion. There is nothing special or mysterious in it. And it just so happened that Draco was there. What a funny coincidence?' said Sean calmly. He tried to smile, but it looked a bit too artificial.

'And you were there because-' Robert held the rest of the question, staring at Draco with expectation. Draco hesitated for a long time. Robert could not see any emotional reaction from him.

'I rented one of the storage containers. Before I left London, I put my belongings in it. I paid for keeping them safe. I came back for them, only to find out what happened on a farm. Unfortunately, not only my box was robbed,' said Draco, still not showing any human emotions.

'So maybe you should go and report your stolen property to the police and give a statement. I can help you with that. I'd love to know what you were hiding in there. It's a bit far from London to bring some of your handy stuff for a fresh start when you come back, isn't it?' asked Robert sarcastically, staring at both of them. Sean and Draco again exchanged glances in muteness.

'Maybe I will. I don't need your help to report stolen, vintage items with no value other than sentimental attachment. Why are you so interested in what I had there? You're supposed to check facts first before you jump to conclusions,' said Draco with a weak voice.

'I don't believe in coincidences. There has to be a deeper reason for you two to be in the same place at the same time,' said Robert firmly.

'It doesn't matter what you believe or not. Two people immune to delirium shouldn't have been in the same place at the same time in your opinion, but it happened. You can't deny the facts. So maybe this evening is just one long chain of coincidences, like winning a hellish lottery being cheated by the devil himself. It just fucking happened,' said Sean, raising his voice, visible annoyed with Robert. Robert was smoking and looked deep in his thoughts.

'Besides, stop asking stupid questions in an attempt to misdirect me from your case. Fact is you had bitten Simon, and that's what's important now, not Draco's heirlooms. Besides, it's not your department who will deal with it,' said Sean angrily, accenting some parts of his speech.

'Wait a minute. Now you avoid my questions. You said I had to spare this shitty vamp because you need him. Why? For what?' asked Robert, raising his voice.

'Look, you know who his father is. As The Guild's adviser, I need him for a legal matter regarding the contract with the vampires. The time is running out and I can't tell you everything. If you want answers, you need to request them in writing from your department. It's standard procedure-' Sean couldn't finish.

'Bullshit bureaucracy. I'm not going to do it. You'll respond with some nonsense with no meaning at all. I'll find out anyway,' replied Robert confidently.

'I'm sure you will. The contract with vamps will end in three months. If Draco can't manage to extend it, we might have a new war. Had you forgotten about it?' asked Sean angrily.

'So, that's why you came back to London?' Robert stared at Draco.

'Yes and no. Yes, I can extend it only once, but I can't take Eric's place as the vamps' representative. Nobody can, not without his written authority,' said Draco not looking at either of them. For quite a long time Robert looked deep in thought. He finished his cigarette, drank his beer, glared at them and in a much calmer voice said;

'I'll keep an eye on both of you, mark my word. Sean, call me when you know what's going on with Simon's wound. I want to see him when he's conscious,' said Robert as he dropped the cigarette end on the floor, stepped on it, then turned slowly and limped out the shed without saying anything for a goodbye.

Sean watched him walk through the gate and disappear in to the dark.

He and Draco left the castle construction together, walking along the still dimly lit path towards the event's main camp.

After a while, when they were standing in the middle of the fortress in the most illuminated place, Sean frowned, looking at Draco's ashen face. Suddenly, Draco dropped to his knees and slowly lay himself on the ground. Sean knelt next to him checking for a pulse in his neck.

'You're very weak. You need blood, Draco. What's happening? I've never seen you in such a bad condition. Hey, can you hear me? Talk to me!' yelled Sean with a demanding voice, tagging Draco's arm. For the second time this evening, Sean felt fear scratching his skull making a cold shiver through his whole body. Draco opened his eyes and took a rumpled, half-empty bag of blood from one of the pockets inside his jacket.

'No! You shouldn't,' shouted Sean holding his hand.

'I know, but I don't have a choice. It'll be worse if I don't drink now. I was so worried after Adam's texts that I haven't drank for days and that's weakened me too much. I tried to sip blood from a lady in the village, but Robert found me. He shot me and made me really sluggish and sleepy. I'm quite old, so it didn't work on me in the way he expected. I ran again, but he almost caught me. I was near the small local hospital, so I sneaked in there and took two bags of blood. I'm so hungry I could drink the whole village in one gulp without controlling myself,' said Draco, slurping blood through a small tube. His skin became more human-like in colour, and his eyes lost their red marks.

'Can you manage to walk to the village now?' asked Sean after Draco had hidden the empty plastic bag inside his coat.

'Yes, I can,' answered Draco, getting up from the ground. He sighed deeply with relief.

'I hope you won't have the rage after not drinking directly from humans,' said Sean.

'I won't. You're the only one close to me now, but if I attack you, your instinct will take over, and I'll be dead in seconds,' replied Draco in a livelier voice.

They were walking in silence through the dark forest. Sean shone a bright torch on the well-trodden path. They heard howling coming from behind, but it sounded more like a large dog than a wolf. Sean looked back but kept walking. The forest was becoming less dense. The weather had changed. The wind increased, clearing the clouds out to expose the night sky illuminated with stars and a big, red, shiny moon. Sean stopped and looked up stunned by the unrealistic picture. The red moon beams shone throughout branches of trees creating rays that reached the ground. They both stood precisely in the middle of one of them. Sean's eyes brightened in the delicate red light.

'The Bloody Moon. I have an awful feeling that Simon is going to die. He has maybe two days left to live,' Sean murmured more to himself than to his companion.

'Did you take the coffin from the farm before the Prince attacked?' Draco's quiet question broke the long silence.

'Shush. Not here. Someone might still be lurking. But yes, and that's the second big problem we have.'

CHAPTER 2

12th June - The Vampire's Prince

Patric drove into his garage and closed the gate remotely. He switched the engine off and unfastened his seatbelt but stayed inside his luxurious new car for a while. He closed his eyes and recalled his last hunt. The memory made him shiver with excitement. Patric loved challenges and hunting vampires was one of his favourite sports. Even though he had caught the old vampire with such ease, he was pleased with the luck he had had this early morning. He got out of the car and walked towards the trunk, opened it and looked at a curled up, unconscious figure of a small, thin man lying inside. With the body size of a teenager, the captured man didn't look like someone who could live for more than three hundred years, Patric thought as he stared at him. Patric lifted him easily, and then unlocked the door to the next room just behind the garage.

The lights switched on immediately, reacting to the installed motion sensor, illuminating a large storage room. There were metal shelves full of plastic boxes alongside the walls and one large window-wall with a door leading to a garden which was now covered with a shutter from the outside. Patric placed the man gently on the floor and then used an app on his phone to lock the gate. There was a small control panel near the entrance with a green light continually blinking.

Patric never thought he would ever bring anyone to his secret house. The house was a hiding refuge for him, the one and only place where he finally could stop pretending to be someone else. It was a small, semi-detached house on the outskirts of London, with a garage, a storage room behind it and three upstairs bedrooms. The house was the first property he bought a long time ago when he finally had enough money. Back then he was still a young Upir, a type of vampire without any family of his kind. He smiled to himself thinking about all those years of hard work, killing his opponents and political effort that finally paid off, making him the of The Prince of Vampires in London.

He had a strong sentimental attachment to these walls as they had witnessed most of his deeds leading to his current wealth and position in London's Vivider's society. He smiled, thinking about how much it had cost him and how willingly he had paid for it. He started walking around the person on the floor, pondering what to do next. Although he had a few places for various occasions in town, today everything was different. He knew he had to kill this man and that made him feel happy, but there was a strong possibility that Roseanne would find out about his death. Patric wanted to keep this to himself for as long as it was possible.

Roseanne was the head of the Acherons, the vampire dynasty of Erick, one of the oldest and therefore most influential in the whole world. She was the oldest of his vampire's daughters. Even though Patric wasn't the formal leader of the dynasty, he was master of all the achievements they had made throughout the last ten years and every vamp in London knew him. Patric's romantic relationship with Roseanne gave him the unwavering position of the boss. She started calling him the Prince and that was something he wanted most, finally being recognised as a member of the higher society.

Moreover, this little man was one of her so-called vampire sons. She had an addiction to partying with alcohol and drugs on the main menu. That was her aristocratic lifestyle she had learnt throughout her more than five-hundred-years vampire's life. During these times she created new vamps, just for her amusement, to see if they would survive the excruciating pain caused during the transition. She still had the urge for producing more children of the night, but after signing a contract with The Guild, it was no longer legal for her to do so.

*

Quiet moaning from behind pulled Patric out of his reverie. He turned and watched the figure moving slowly on the floor. The man looked shabby in his dun-coloured, plain clothes. He sat up and looked around with dazed expression.

'Where am I? Who are you? Do I know you?' he asked, touching his head and hissing in pain.

'Who am I? Oh, I think you know me well, it's who you are that matters to me. So, tell me where Draco has been hiding for so many years?' Patric smiled gently as he paced around the captured man.

'Who is Draco?' he answered, avoiding Patric's arrogant gaze.

'Your name is Adam. You're more or less a three-hundred-year-old vampire, and you're one of the jokes spawned by Roseanne during one of her drunken nights. Erick spared you only because Draco interceded for you. You're Draco's bitch. I can't say friend, more like a skinny cunt who hangs around like a fucking leech. Draco doesn't have friends or even his own bloodline…' Patric didn't finish all what we could say about the history of the captured man. He could go on and on, a tirade of facts about past events and dirty businesses he knew about Erick's close family members. He just watched for Adam's reactions in silence. Adam froze and for a long time stared at Patric visibly weighing up in his mind what to do and what to say.

'I don't know where he is. He never contacted me after he left England on the day of Eric's disappearance. Last time I saw him was when the utter carnage shook London,' answered Adam slowly and evidently considering every word.

Patric came closer, grabbed Adam's long hair and in one swift movement, pulled him up off the floor. He was holding Adam's head with one hand and slowly lengthened his nails on the second one. The nails turned black and were about thirty centimetres long with edges sharp as razors blades. Patric stabbed Adam's chin with three long nails. They pierced his tongue, like soft butter, and exited near his nose, very close to Adam's eyes. Adam squealed like a little puppy in pain. Patric was holding his head still but the rest of Adam's body was jerking uncontrollably. Adam's blood flowed down Patric's hand, dripping on the floor. Patric's eyes darkened so completely that even the skin around them showed black marks resembling small veins. He smiled with unfeigned pleasure and then started licking the blood from his hand. Patric grinned widely, baring long white fangs with tiny black drops of venom at the end of them. Adam's eyes grew wider with undisguised horror like he couldn't believe what he was witnessing. Adam tried to push him away, but Patric's grip was too strong. This lasted only about a minute but it made Adam faint. Patric slowly withdrew his sharp claws, letting more blood trickle down his hand. He threw Adam's body like a discarded rag doll so fiercely that he slammed against the metal shelves and fell to the floor. Patric was licking the blood off his hand, savouring every drop like a connoisseur of vintage wine.

Patric was pacing back and forth in the room. He shortened his long nails to a regular length and glanced at Adam from time to time. He knew Adam's wounds needed time to heal before he could speak again. Patric was patient, engaging himself in meaningless activities such as checking emails and messages on his phone, waiting until Adam woke up.

'I believe this might refresh your memory regarding Draco's whereabouts,' said Patric after a while. He came close to Adam and grabbed his arm.

Adam reacted with panic at Patric's touch, pulling himself away as far as he could. His wounds were perfectly healed and had left no scarring, but he still had dried blood on his face and clothing. Adam looked like someone facing the devil himself. The only sound that came from his throat was a quiet moan like a terrified cornered animal. He covered his head with his hands but kept one eye on every one of Patric's movement.

'Are you going to talk, or shall I continue with the torture?' asked Patric softly with a big grin on his face. He came closer to Adam, extended his claws just a few centimetres, laid the tips of them gently on Adam's hand and made a long cut with one fast scratch. Adam screamed in terror and leaned back, hiding his hand. Patric squatted next to him and repeated the trick with nails, but this time he cut Adam's cheek leaving long bloody furrows. Adam had nowhere to retreat. He froze with dread, breathing very fast and squeaking. Drops of tears ran down his cheeks. Patric smiled broadly, more to himself than to the man he was observing. He admitted in his mind that he liked watching the fear in his victims' eyes and hearing the begging at the moment they realised their life would last only minutes.

'You're an Upir,' stammered Adam. His whole body was shaking.

Patric said nothing but nodded in agreement, a little surprised by the question. Patric was an Upir, the kind of vamp-predator that mainly drank blood from other vampires. He showed his long, white fangs with small drops of toxin gathering on their tips.

'You can't be. They're a myth. They're extinct. Erick killed them all,' shouted Adam in desperation and hope that his wishes could change the terrifying reality. He started to cry loudly, rocking like a small child.

Patric couldn't wait any longer. It was fascinating for him, seeing how much fear was overflowing Adam's body. It was so intense that he could almost sense it in the air, like a scent of flowers luring bees with their nectar. With one swift move, Patric grabbed Adam's chin, lifted it up to expose his neck, and then bit deeply into it. The flavour of warm blood, filling Patric's mouth in a rhythm of Adam's heartbeat, tasted like a delight dish reserved only for the Gods. Although Patric wasn't hungry, he couldn't refuse old, mature vampire's blood. Adam wouldn't pass out because of the toxins from Patric fangs which kept him in a half-sleepy, dreamlike state, but at least he wasn't afraid any more. Instead of feeling abject horror, he became very relaxed, blissfully happy and a sensation of erotic ecstasy slowly flowing through his body.

Patric needed all his willpower to stop drinking Adam's blood, as that would surely kill him. He couldn't remember the last time he had drank such exquisite blood, full of adrenaline, fear and despair, he loved so much. The taste of terrified prey was the most desirable for him. He always felt the kick of ethereal energy at the moment his fangs pierced the live being. He felt the spirit and the power of all the years of Adam's life when it mixed with his own blood inside. He thought that he had drunk way too much, but he couldn't restrain the desire. When he had finished, Adam was unconscious but still alive. Patric left him lying on the floor. He tied Adam's ankles and hands behind his back and put a gag in his mouth. Patric knew Adam would wake in few hours. His body needed to regenerate the blood loss. The thought about sipping Adam's blood again the next day put Patric in an excellent mood. He retracted his nails and checked every pocket of Adam's clothing, taking everything that he found. Patric unlocked Adam's phone using his fingerprint, reviewed his last calls and Internet search history. He smiled, pleased with himself and the fact that he found emails sent to Draco during the course of the previous year. He was thinking about how lucky he had been this night as he opened the inner door and walked into the living space of his house.

*

It was early afternoon. The garage was lit by sunlight coming through the fully exposed window-wall and framing an idyllic picture of a summer garden filled with flowers and green trees. A few hours later, Patric went back to the storage room. He looked very refreshed and pleased with himself. Even his skin had a more natural colour with visible, slightly blue, blood veins just under the surface. Adam was awake, trying to cut the plastic cord binding his hands together behind his back. He was rubbing the cord on the post of the metal shelf he was leaning on. He flinched at the view of Patric approaching and pulled his knees up to the chest. Patric brought two massive wooden chairs and put them down in the middle of the room. One of them he placed directly in a sunny patch near the window. The second was situated opposite the first one but in a safe distance from the intense light. Patric lifted Adam and put him on the chair near the window, and then, took the gag from his mouth. He sat opposite him silently watching his prey. Adam looked normal; the sun didn't seem to affect him.

'It won't hurt me. I'm too old,' stuttered Adam quietly, without looking at his torturer.

'Oh yes, it will. The weaker you get, the more damage the sun will do. It might take hours to burn your skin, but I can wait. You'll boil slowly inside, and I'll be delighted to sip your pain again. Your blood tastes delicious when you're terrified,' said Patric with a wild grin. He came closer and with only one long, black, sharp nail, he ripped Adam's shirt tearing it apart and exposing his bare chest.

'You'll be alive for a few days. I feel like I've won in a lottery,' continued Patric, observing Adam's reactions through half-closed eyelids.

'What do you want?' asked Adam panicking.

Patric showed Adam's phone and the emails he had found earlier.

'You have contact with Draco. Where is he?'

'Okay, I'll tell you everything I know, but first, you have to take

The Derelict Oath…' said Adam, without finishing the sentence but a tone of hope was audible in his voice.

'What?' asked Patric surprised, losing his arrogant confidence.

'The Derelict Oath. You should've heard of it,' said Adam with a more calm and confident voice.

'It's a myth,' replied Patric, snorting.

'Like you?' asked Adam with a gentle smile.

Patric stood up and walked around the room, lost in his thoughts, but said nothing.

'You can torture me as much as you like, day after day. I'll die telling you lie after lie laughing maniacally at your stupidity. You'll lose a century trying to find out what was real and what was made up based on all soap operas I've watched since television was created,' said Adam, confidently spitting out words in a wave of anger. Something changed in him. Desperation and vision of his death triggered energy hidden deep inside his soul.

Patric looked confused. He had never come across such an oath. He had heard rumours about old dynasties' customs and rituals from the past, believed to be magic by many, but nobody took these tales seriously.

'What is it?' he asked, trying to cover his curiosity with toneless voice.

He admitted that it was pretty clever how Adam tried to escape death. Patric smiled, thinking that his prey always tried something, but today, it was something new.

'You'll have to swear, on the blood of your father, you won't hurt me, and you'll let me go free right after I tell you the story. In return, I'll swear to tell you everything I know about Erick and Draco and what had happened ten years ago between them. It'll be sealed with our souls' energy and blood,' replied Adam, now staring at Patric confidently as equals.

'What if you lie? What if I kill you anyway?'

'The oath will be broken, and we both will die an extremely painful death,' replied Adam gravely.

Patric was thinking intensely. After ten years of searching for

Erick, so many tortures and killings to find the answers, he could now solve the puzzle, but the price was very high. If Adam were to walk freely away, Patric's identity might be exposed. He would be hunted by every normal vampire living in the whole of Britain or even in the whole Europe. Patric was an Upir, the last apex predator who fed on the blood and spiritual energy of mundane vampires. He was a vampire that relished on the blood of other vampires more than on humans. Upirs were almost extinct due to years of a merciless chasing. He had heard stories about his kind caught by dynasties and tortured for a several decades. Everything he had achieved, every penny made by his political manipulations, even the love of Roseanne he had to fight so hard to win, all might be destroyed by this scumbag, thought Patric, struggling in his mind.

He tied Adam to the chair and left him alone. Patric went back into the house to think. He poured himself a strong whiskey from the bottle he kept in the living room, filling his glass to the rim and then drank it down one gulp. After the third full glass he smiled when he realised there was something he could do to keep the oath and kill Adam, but it was hazardous. He didn't like deal with those outlaws, but he didn't have any other option.

Well, my entire life is based on taking risk after risk. It's worked so far, so what the hell, he thought, walking back to the storage room. He came to the chair that Adam was sitting on and cut the cord tethering him, but this time using a knife from the kitchen.

'Begin the oath, or I'll keep you here for a year as my dessert,' said Patric, reaching out to touch Adam's hand.

Adam smiled, looking somewhat unsurprised. He seemed confident, like someone who knew he had just won the battle. Adam grabbed Patric's hand and used the knife to make a deep, bloody cut on both of their hands. They entwined fingers and clasped their palms together, mixing the blood. Adam swore the oath, ending the sentence with an ancient Latin word and then he recited the formula ordering Patric to repeat it. They could both see the subtle light of energy binding their hands and spreading over their bodies. Patric felt fear and panicked but he didn't show it as the ritual began. He learnt he couldn't pull his hand from Adam's grip and that made him feel even more terrified. He felt the warmth overflowing him from the top of his head to toes. Somehow, on the subconscious level, he could feel some spirits watching the ritual. For the first time of his entire existence, he felt sure that he would never raise his hand to harm Adam.

*

'So, start at the beginning,' said Patric after the ritual ended. He sat on the chair opposite Adam feeling pleased with his decision.

'Well, this is what I know. It started years before I woke as a vampire and I know only a small part of the story. Some bits I heard and saw by being around them. They always treated me like a piece of garbage. I was nobody to Erick so automatically nobody to anyone but Draco. Erick ordered to kill me, but Draco took me under his wings. It wasn't friendship, more like feeling pity for me-'

'Stop whining and get to the point. I don't care about your sob story,' Patric warned him while making himself comfortable in his chair. He didn't look at Adam but closed his eyes and smiled gently.

'Right, to the point,' murmured a crestfallen Adam. He cleared his throat a few times, stroking his chin in places where Patric had punctured his skin with his long, sharp nails as if he was still feeling the pain. Adam was always afraid of suffering and would do everything to avoid it at all costs.

'Anyway, soon I found out about some kind of war, that is still lying in depth and beneath the lovely family facade they try to sell to others. Especially Erick, who was attached to Draco and loved keeping him close like no other from his dynasty. But Draco, for reasons known only to him and Erick, never wanted to be one of us and hates Erick for changing him. Nobody knows what kind of motive Erick had when he made Draco his first son - the Chosen One. Erick created many other night children before and after, but only he was the one who got all just like that ...' Adam stopped telling the story, snapping his fingers a few times. He looked at Patric trying to gauge his reaction but found none. Patric was staring at Adam, still sitting almost motionlessly looking lost in thoughts.

'So, you can imagine how the others felt about that. That made Roseanne truly jealous and apparently, from what I heard, she started acting the way she does now because of this. She's inherited nothing and had to learn everything herself. And as you know, she's from an old aristocratic family, so she used to get a lot for free. Regardless of being vile to Draco, she stuck around Erick for centuries,' Adam interrupted his monologue and looked at his abductor. Patric didn't move but reminded him more of a plastic figure than someone alive. Adam waited for a few minutes, but Patric stayed mute and rigid. Adam didn't know what to do so he continued the tale.

'The story I know began when Draco met Helen and her husband George Rogers, the most gifted witch hunter in England. George had all of his ancestor's skills and abilities and I heard his presence could bend a witch's spells. I can picture their disappointment when they realised their magic wasn't working,' Adam made a sound that was mixture of laughing and grunting but his voice was rising to the high pitch and the end. Patric frowned at him in astonishment and disbelief.

'Do it again,' ordered Patric and standing up rapidly.

Adam was surprised and had no clue what it was all about. He straightened up in his chair when Patric came closer, looking vicious and extending his nails to the maximum length.

'You were spying on me, you stupid cunt. I recognise your laugh. You were following me a few times. I'm sure,' he yelled, outraged.

'No, I did not. I saw you maybe twice near a metro station, but that's my usual spot. I'm a drifter. I play the guitar on the streets for money. Oh, that hurts! What's going on with me-' he didn't finish the sentence but jumped suddenly to his feet and tried to push Patric away, but he couldn't do it. The nails on Patric's right hand touched Adam's chest but didn't pierce it but made only small cavities without breaking the surface.

Suddenly, black lines appeared on Adam's hands spreading over his whole body. They were glowing from the inside, like burning coals and the terrible smell of burnt meat was emitting around. Adam screamed, patting his hands, trying to extinguish the fire lines emerging over on his skin.

Patric bounced back realising that he had a bigger problem. Patric's long nails from his right hand, the one that touched Adam's skin, suddenly became incandescent to the point where they looked like they were made from molten iron. Their colour started to change from black to orange-yellow and looked precisely like a heated iron rod in a blacksmith's forge. Small pieces began to drip leaving black, scorched spots on the floor, and the hideous smell of burning flesh filled the whole room. Patric began to howl like an animal. He grabbed his burning nails with his other hand and pulled them fiercely, ripping them from fingers. It came off with a creepy popping sound leaving his fingertips with black marks of deeply burned tissue. Patric was moaning through clenched teeth with pain and rage on his face. He walked around, roaring and shaking his wounded hands. The last time he felt so much pain was the hours of his birth as an Upir. The transformation into that type of vampire took him a few days. He shivered, picturing the endless hours of agonising torture imprinting new life not only in his body but in his entire soul. He stood for a while with closed eyes, gasping for air and holding his hand on his aching heart.

The silence brought Patric back to reality as he realised that the panic and the pain was only a memory of events from more than century ago. Patric glanced towards Adam and saw him lying on the floor swearing to the Gods that he would never lie under oath again. Adam's skin was clean without any dark marks, but the scent of seared flesh was awfully intense in the room. Patric opened a window, put both chairs furthest away from the sunny places and helped Adam sit on one of them.

'Apparently, your spell works,' said Patric in a low voice. He watched how the black lines on his palm made by burning nails were healing but it was a slow process. However, his blackened fingers didn't show any signs of regeneration at all. This puzzled Patric because he was used to fast healing, especially after drinking old vampire blood. Patric brought bandages and poked Adam indicating that he needed help. They both glanced silently at each other from time to time. Adam dressed his wounds, and it looked like he really knew what he was doing.

'I didn't know it'd work that way,' said Adam softly in an apologetic tone.

'What did you know then?' asked sarcastically Patric.

'I didn't know it'd work at all,' said Adam not looking at Patric.

'What?' asked Patric without hiding how shocked he was.

'Well, I learnt the oath, but it's the first time I've ever used it.'

'You were bluffing?'

'No. I knew there might be consequences of breaking the oath but this?' Adam made a hand gesture that included both of them.

'So, what was the lie?' asked Patric, accenting the last word.

'I have spied on you since Draco left. But only because you were my number one suspect,' said Adam trying to avoid Patric's gaze.

'Suspect?'

'Well … yes. When some prominent members of vampire dynasties started disappearing, I knew someone was hunting them. I read about Upirs, and I thought that it might be their work. But, you know, I'm a pushover. Nobody would ever believe me.'

'Did you tell anyone about me?'

'No, I swear I said nothing,' said Adam putting his hand on his heart and patting his chest gently. Patric knew he wouldn't lie this time. The vision of burning internally was too terrifying for him to want to go through it again.

'What about Erick, where is he? Hurry up. I don't have much time to listen to your lecture on long-forgotten vamp abilities. So?' asked Patrick yawning constrainedly.

'I don't know details, but Draco promised to help catch Erick before the agreement with The Guild was signed. But they were too late. What I know is that Draco dragged Erick and put him in the Tritus' End. Do you know what that is?' asked Adam, but one look at Patric's face made him realise how deep the ancient knowledge of skills and artefacts was wiped out, not only form the world but from customs and traditions of the children of the night.

'Tritus' End is a special coffin made centuries ago for all those creatures too powerful who witch hunters couldn't kill straight away. Roger had this artefact and used it on Erick. It won't kill him, but it'll strip his strength and make him weak and vulnerable after a long time being trapped inside. Draco can't kill his own blood father just like that because he'll die as well, but the coffin will help. After a few years of being there, Erick can be killed without annihilating the whole dynasty-' Adam didn't finish. His story was interrupted by Patric's exiting shout.

'Wait a minute. Do you mean that Erick, the oldest known vampire in the whole world, was captured by witch hunters and now he's trapped somewhere, weak like a baby?' asked Patric in disbelief.

'Well, Draco helped. They wouldn't do it without him. But, yes. In a nutshell, that's the story behind the riot ten years ago and the beginning of you as the Prince,' said Adam wearily.

'Draco would never let you know about this if he didn't have a reason. What's your part in it?' asked Patric slowly, looking at him intensely. Adam hesitated a long time before answering and it seemed he considered carefully what to say.

'I don't know where the coffin is hidden, he'd never tell me. But I'm kind of guardian of the artefact. I have a lot of contacts on the streets. If someone were to search for Erick, I might be the first to hear about it,' declared Adam.

'And?' asked Patric smiling broadly. He realised now Adam was the key to finding Erick.

'Well-' Adam hesitated for seconds. Patric stood up, came close to his chair, leaned over him and grinned broadly, showed his long fangs. Adam didn't move but after seeing the result of the oath, he felt more confident. Patric kept quiet, staring at him.

'I should text one guy what I know of,' continued Adam calmly. Patric took Adam's mobile from his own pocket, passed to him and commanded.

'Text him and Draco now. I believe you have their numbers just in case, right?' Patric didn't look at Adam. He knew his assumption was true. All that he could think about now was the fact that for the first time in his life he had the opportunity to not only to kill his opponent but also to take control over his dynasty and therefore have power and influence over the whole world. The excitement started to grow in him very fast. He could picture himself on the top of the vampire community and the dream of drinking from the oldest blood made Patric excitingly nervous. He knew he had to calm down otherwise he might start making stupid mistakes. But the vision of power he could possess, and killing those he hated the most at the same time, was too much for him to bear and remain calm. His hands started shaking, and he was walking around in circles waving his arms like he was talking to himself.

'Give me the phone!' he yelled angrily and pulled the device from Adam's hands. Patric made a new message window and gave him back the phone to put the correct contact names as a receiver. Although, Adam used some nicknames as contacts, but he couldn't lie about the identity of recipients because has still obliged to tell the truth under The Derelict Oath. When he finished, Patric snatched the phone again and started to type the message, 'Erick is in danger. Patric knows everything. Change location now. I need help.'

He sent it and was waiting impatiently for a response. Unfortunately for Patric, he got nothing back within ten minutes and the waiting made him agitated. Patric knew he needed to busy himself doing less important things just to keep his mind off the issue.

He tied up Adam again and left him lying on the floor in lethargy. Patric entered the house, read messages on his phone related to his business, he called his office, nagging subordinates to do their jobs, and scheduled a few meetings. He spent more than an hour chatting with Roseanne about new rumours she had heard although he couldn't care less.

Most of his mind was occupied by making plans involving Erick, The Guild and Draco. Nothing was easy and all of the problems he was facing now demanded drastic and fast decisions. Patric didn't like the fact that he couldn't see any clear solutions. Moreover, he had a faint, deep feeling that the situation could go wrong on so many levels. On top of it all, like the cherry on the cake, was what to do with the tiny man lying on the floor in the garage.

Patric had to find the way of getting rid of him completely but the impossibility of killing him was very irritating. Patric imagined many possible scenarios in his mind, but only one was good enough to sound credible to Rosa. Although he felt happy finding the way out from this impasse, Adam's knowledge made him shiver.

What if Adam's skills were far beyond the one oath? What if he learnt something more powerful than any other vampire, including Erick, and could easily use it everywhere he went. Adam said that he dedicated his long life to collecting knowledge and skills of long-forgotten vampires' powers and rituals. What if he was like a ticking timebomb that could easily explode at any time? All the 'what if's' swirling around Patric's head made him feel uneasy and yet at the same time gave him a thrill. This wasn't excitement though but a fear in its purest form, the feeling Patric hadn't experience since he was re-born as a vampire. That made him want to kill Adam even more.

The sound of incoming messages reminded him that Adam's case was only the beginning and the most significant battle was still yet to come.

The first text was from a number named Sdr2, 'Will remove it from the current location in next 24h. Do not contact me again.'

Patric had to wait for the other message from Dr1, about fifteen minutes after the first one came in. It was even shorter than he had presumed. It said only 'OMW'. Patric knew this meant 'on my way', but it didn't specify where. There were no dates, times or addresses included regarding neither the location of the coffin nor the name of receivers of the texts. He expected a bit more, and a lack of the information made him nervous again. What if he should have used a specific code when he was sending messages to them? He didn't ask Adam about that.

Moreover, Patric texted them not Adam. He noticed this was the mistake he had been trying to avoid. He was too agitated about the fact he could find Erick and kill him to think clearly. Moreover, Patric was waiting way too long for answers. He now realised that while he was busy with meaningless conversations, the first one who got this message was already running to the place where the coffin was hidden to move it. Patric screamed furiously and threw the half-full whiskey glass at the wall. It smashed into pieces leaving a wet mark with a dent on the surface.

Patric was mad at himself but didn't dwell on it. He knew that he had to make a swift decision and try to trace their movement.

There was only one way to do it. He knew exactly where to go, and who would help to find the exact location of the phones. Patric called and gave instructions knowing that at this moment, Adam had become an unnecessary burden. Even the fear of his unknown skills wasn't important to Patric anymore. He made a decision of letting Adam go, and he meant it. He made a call feeling happy that there were underground outlaws willing to take care of Adam. Moreover, Patrick might get quite good money selling him to the arena's fights and keeping his oath in the same time. After all, he was only giving information where the toughs could catch Adam.

Patric came back to the garage feeling hungry. All of these exciting news and overwhelming plans made him desire more blood than he usually needed. He wondered what would happen if he tried sipping from Adam's veins but one look at the bandages on his right hand stopped him from doing anything irrational.

Adam was awake. He looked even thinner that before, with greyish skin and deeply sunken eyes surrounded by dark shadows. Patric cut the cord on Adam's ankles and wrists and helped him to stand up. Patric supported him all the way to the car and helped him to sit into the back seat, even fastening his seatbelt.

Patric locked his house and sat behind the wheel. He set off and appeared to be driving aimlessly, but he was looking for the perfect spot to let Adam go without catching anyone's attention. He knew Adam was starving so his first reaction would be to jump someone for fresh blood. Patric pulled over on one of many small side streets near Regent Park. He realised that he had spent the last four hours with Adam and that it had been one of the most intense times he had had since Erick disappeared. Patric got out of the car, opened the door for him, and with a hand gesture showed Adam that he was free to go.

Adam was too hungry to show any emotions. He unfastened his seatbelt, vigorously jumped out from the car and run. He didn't look back at Patric but was only interested in finding the nearest human and how to get their blood without drawing attention.

Patric sat back in his car, but he continued to observe the whole scene. Although Adam still controlled his blood desire, he was too focused on the hunt to realise that he was slowly surrounded by three tall and menacing-looking men. He couldn't see Patric's car parked at the end of the street nor Patric watching the event from a distance with a charming smile. Adam was trapped. He saw the moment when one of the men took a gun from the pocket and shot him with a dart full of tranquilising liquid. He passed out before his body reached the ground.

One man turned around and gave the thumbs up, indicating success in Adam's capture. One of toughs picked up Adam's body and put him inside the trunk of their car. Patric sighed and thought that now it was time for him to eat something delicious.

CHAPTER 3

17th June - The Hospital

Gary was terrified. He couldn't move at all. Even the smallest fingers in his hands were stiff. He couldn't open his eyes or even breathe. He felt trapped in his own body, and those feelings caused a nervous breakdown in him. He wanted to scream and cry, but his body was perfectly immobilised. He panicked and shouted for help to God he had never believed but he felt too desperate to not do it. In this black and cold place, Gary felt someone's presence, but it was so delicate that this person could be standing miles away. Gary had a severe headache and couldn't bare this anymore. The pain was spreading all over his body. He had impression that his whole existence was shaking regardless being paralysed. He wanted to get out and stop the torture using his willpower, but nothing had changed. And in this moment, when he thought that he couldn't fight for even slight movement anymore, something broke inside him like a soap bubble. He was still in a pitch black, but he could see a tiny patch of light ahead of him. That gave him a hope of ending suffering he was feeling now. The light drew closer and closer to Gary making the nearby surroundings greyish. Gary's fear and pain disappeared and was replaced by relief and something warm inside him, but he couldn't name this feeling.

On the edge of the dark, Gary could catch the sight of moving human-like shapes. The forms had a lighter colour, but they were still in dark-grey shades like most of this place. He heard some voices, but it sounded more like a quiet underwater murmur than any recognisable language.

All of a sudden, he saw himself lying on the hospital bed,

attached to medical devices and surrounded by nurses and two doctors. Gary was flying above his body connected only by blue cord coming out from his navel. He felt so light like the gravity had never existed.

One of the nurses injected him with three different syringes and somehow Gary felt not only the sting but the bitter taste of the medical liquid as well. He felt uneasy with it because he didn't want to go back to be trapped in his own body. He tried to stop her, but he just went throughout her like a wind. Although he didn't physically touch her, she looked into his direction like she could sense his presence. She shivered and goosebumps appeared on her skin. When she finished the third injection Gary felt a sharp stabbing pain in his heart and blacked out.

*

Mark was walking fast in a long corridor in one of London's hospital. It was getting late, ending the visiting time, but there were still people standing in groups and whispering. He got to Gary's room on the intensive care unit, following a doctor who wanted to privately discuss the medical condition and treatment for his brother. Mark tried to ask a few questions on the way, but the lack of response by the doctor and his impassive face only worsened the terrible scenario that stuck in Mark's mind. Mark knew his brother's accident was serious, but he had hope that Gary would get back on his feet very soon.

The room was small with only one hospital bed standing in the middle of it. Gary was lying unconscious with a medical equipment attached to him. He had a pipe put inside his throat showing that he wasn't able to breathe without help. He had a drip in hand, cervical collar around his neck and bandages on his head partially covering black bruises on his face. Mark looked at Gary and felt cold when fear froze his body to the point when he felt so weak that he had to sit on a chair.

'Sir, are you okay?' asked the doctor, staring at Mark.

Mark sighed deeply but said nothing. The doctor checked Gary's medical forms, turned a page on a clipboard and ticked in some places. The doctor explained Gary's health using professional terminology but it didn't make any sense to Mark.

'What's the diagnosis?' Mark interrupted him, cutting the monologue.

'Please understand, we are doing what we can for your brother, but with that serious spine damage and a fractured skull, the treatment will be long. We need to run some more tests, but it doesn't look promising. He might never fully recover, and there is a chance he might be paralysed from the neck down,' said the doctor calmly. There was a thick silence hanging in the room interrupted by Mark's deep breathing.

'I'm so sorry, sir. I'll leave you to it now. You know where to find me if you want to talk,' said the doctor, walking out from the room. He closed the door behind and left Mark alone.

Mark covered his face with his hands and remained motionless for a long time. He clenched and unclenched his fists automatically, but after a while he got up suddenly and started to walk to and fro inside this small room. Time passed and changed Mark's anger into deep sadness.

The hospital was quiet and almost empty this late evening. Mark turned off the main lights in the room leaving only a small lamp on that was standing on a small cabinet near Gary's bed. He sat down on the chair, wrapped his hands on his head and cried silently.

*

Gary regained consciousness in the same place and the same state he had had before he fainted. His ethereal being was sitting near, watching himself lying down on a bed and barely recognising who he was. He definitely was in hospital, and the number of machines, pipes and things attached to his face and body frightened him more than ever. That was the moment when Gary realised that he was dying. The last thing he saw in his mind before he fainted again was the picture of electronic timer counting down how many earthly hours he had left.

The next time when he felt awake, he saw himself standing not far from the bed where his battered body was in a deep coma. But this time, he saw one more person present in the room. His eight years older half-brother Mark was sitting on a chair just near Gary's head. Half of Mark's torso was lying on Gary's arm and shaking from the silent cry.

Gary noticed that he didn't feel fear any more, like everything he had cared in life didn't matter. The memories of his family, friends and daily issues started fading like emotions and knowledge of a story in a movie that he had watched a day before. Gary felt light-hearted. He had the urge to get out of this place and jump to a new adventure that he knew it was waiting for him just behind this door. He felt very cheerful and somehow he knew that soon or later he would find out something exciting.

He heard some noise behind the door that attracted his attention. Some people were talking and even laughing after one of them said a joke. Gary headed to that direction but could still feel the blue line attached to his navel, keeping him on a leash near his broken body. He had to use willpower to stretch the cord to the point that he could get out of the room. Behind the door, there were five ghostly human silhouettes standing, talking and laughing. They looked like a bunch of friends getting on well and having a perfect time at a party. Gary could see and hear them correctly. He hemmed and hawed, first time shy and quiet but when he couldn't attract their attention, he repeated it pretty loud. The fact that he could make any noise gave him a lot of hope for finding help with understanding where he was and what he could do about it. All of them turned silent and stared at him with wonderment.

'Go back! Go back! It's not your time yet. You're still attached. Your life isn't finished,' shouted one of them. The ghost came closer and pushed Gary back to his room. Gary couldn't resist nor stop him. He felt so weak compared to the ethereal being who shoved him back with such force that Gary flew a few metres and landed on his still living body. Gary's body had one spasm of convolution, but his spirit stayed outside of it. Mark raised his head and looked around like he felt something. His eyes and Gary's met and they both had impression that they were staring at each other like two living beings.

'It's you, Gary?' asked Mark who looked like he was waiting for an answer. Gary tried to touch him but without any effect. He gave up after dozens of unsuccessful attempts. He sat disappointed near his half-brother Mark, feeling hopelessly trapped in a place and in a situation where he had no influence and could only wait for some miracle but at least he didn't feel pain anymore. Gary wished to pass out again, but it didn't happen. All that he could do was observing the whole scene, feeling utterly useless.

*

Mark was staring at Gary's broken body and still couldn't believe what had happened. Everything was going way too fast in to the extremely wrong direction and he felt terribly helpless. About this time yesterday, they were standing in the middle of forest making some stupid plans to earn extra cash. Today, those issues were so irrelevant, like dinner problems in a soap-opera set somewhere in a faraway tropical country.

Mark was sitting in the dark hospital room wiping his tears. He felt the vibrations of his mobile a few times, but he didn't bother to look at who was calling. He knew it might be Sean, but Mark didn't know what to tell him about Gary's state. Mark was sure that Sean would start organising all those supernatural treatments he knew of and started to test one by one on Gary. But Mark was very sceptical about their possible effects on his brother. Gary was just an ordinary boy who was born into a family he would never fit in. Mark smiled involuntarily, thinking that being normal wasn't typical for all Gary's kin. That was the reason Gary was living with his grandparents in Nottingham, to separate him from rest of his relatives.

Mark kept contact with Gary, as much as they both could, but keeping secrets about the Viviter's society, made a lot of boundaries and prevented from having a deeper relationship between them. Gary's mind couldn't accept all of those differences and his brain might turn into mashed pulp, giving him severe mental health issues if he would ever see the creatures existing behind the secret veil. The threat of Gary's madness was still hanging like a sword of Damocles above, not only Gary's head but to all with whom he was related to. Mark had a nap, still half-lying half-sitting near Gary's bed, so tired of his tears he couldn't stop for so long and constantly thinking to find the best solution.

*

After a while, the door opened, and a nurse entered. She looked at the sleeping Mark but said nothing. She was smiling broadly, and her face expressed internal bliss and happiness. She stepped vigorously towards Gary holding a small, metal medical tray with three large syringes filled with dark liquid. She took one of them and injected it into the cannula that Gary had attached to his hand and humming some old love song. Mark, now completely awake and alert, frowned and looked at her with concern.

And then he saw the colour inside the second syringe she was pumping into Gary's veins. He jumped, being fully alert and feeling the rapidly growing rage. He caught her arm and pulled so strong she turned and fell on the floor. The tray flew out of her hand spreading the syringes around the room. She looked surprised and seemed to not recognise the place she was in. She reminded him more of someone who was dipped into a happy dream that even falling on the floor didn't change her mind-state. Mark knelt near her, lifted her chin and checked her neck. His sight adjusted and now were like cat's eyes glowing in the dark. The room was quite dim, so he ran his fingers on her skin along the jugular, searching for freshly closed punctured wounds that might leave small protruding scars. He found them. They were barely visible. They were matching perfectly the size of vampire fangs, leaving only a reddish mark on her neck. Mark's senses sharpened putting him into fighting mode. His pupils changed, resembling hunting cat eyes. He brought his nose close to her skin, sniffed and cursed badly. He still could sense the slowly evaporating smell of vampire saliva mixed with their venom.

'What's your name?' asked Mark, staring into her unconscious eyes. He patted her cheeks gently, but it didn't help. She stared at him, smiling and humming the same melody. He lifted her from the floor and sat down on the empty chair.

'I need to finish something. The doctor said it's critical. And I'm gorgeous ... and very important...' she sang in the rhythm of the melody. She tried to get up, but Mark pushed her gently back to sitting. He put his hands on her shoulders and held firmly, preventing her from getting up. He knew that vampire's venom would influence humans' mind to the point of being susceptible to suggestion so much that they couldn't distinguish reality from a daydream.

'Of course, you are. I've gave you this order and you've done it all,' insisted Mark, smiling, staring straight into her eyes and stroking her cheek.

'Are you the new doctor? You're so handsome. I'm in love with you. I love you...' she said, fixing her eyes on him with everlasting bliss.

'Please, close your eyes and imagine your perfect wedding day,' said Mark, changing his voice into soft theatrical whisper. She smiled, following his instruction but still singing quietly. He slowly freed his hands from hers, but he couldn't resist slightly squeezing her breast and grinning broadly.

Mark was focused. He noticed that the door was slightly opened and was letting in a smudge of light from the corridor. He sensed someone's presence there. He walked silently towards the entrance, listening to the voices from the corridor and hiding himself in the corner behind the door. He totally muted the sound of his breath, but all his body was tense in anticipation to take rapid action.

The handle moved softly, and the door started to open slowly. Mark was waiting; focused and alert. He had shape-shifted his hands in a matter of seconds. They were more muscular, covered with short fur and ended with sharp and long cat's claws. His face had a feline lineament.

The man entered unsteadily and looked around. He stood in the patch of light from the corridor without making any sudden or intense movements. Mark was literally two steps behind him observing. He immediately recognised the intruder, Draco, by his scent and body movement.

'Mark, I know you're here, but before you jump on me with your warrior attitude let me talk to you first. I won't fight. I'm here to save Gary's life. I own too much to his father,' said Draco, raising his hands in a surrender gesture. He was waiting. Mark came closer, shortened to half his claws but didn't hide them completely. He put his pointing finger on Draco's neck in a place where he could cut his jugular in one sharp pull. A small drop of dark blood appeared in a place where the sharp tip of Mark's claw pressed against Draco's skin. Draco remained still without any movement.

'I knew it was you when I saw her eyes. Only old vamp could compel humans that deep as you did. Sean told me a lot about what you're capable of. I won't let you change him,' said Mark with anger nodding into Gary's directions.

'I know. I don't want to either, but I desperately need him. Not only my life depends on Gary's life but many others as well. Now he's more connected to our world that we all could ever imagine,' said Draco and without any trace of fear, grabbed Mark's finger and gently pushed it away from his neck entirely effortlessly. Mark didn't oppose. Draco peeped at Mark and moved slowly towards Gary's bed, still holding his arms above head.

Mark knew the fight with more than a five-hundred-year-old vampire would be extremely difficult now. He lost the best advantage when he didn't attack by surprise, and his chance to win was minimal. Draco was one of the oldest vampires that Mark knew personally, and he knew that absolutely nobody sane would ever attack him in open combat.

'What makes you sure he won't become a vamp?' asked Mark, surprised by Draco's assumption but followed him to Gary's bed.

'I gave my blood to Gary's father, George. He saved my life, and I saved his. It's not possible to change witch hunters. Erick tried once, but instead he created a perfect killing machine. Many died before Erick's dynasty finally slayed the thing that day,' said Draco staring at Mark without any fear.

Mark started to consider that maybe Draco's blood was the best solution in this stalemate. But what if the vamp's blood wouldn't work on Gary, thought Mark, still not sure what to do. There was the possibility something might go even worse than it was now. Mark was calculating all the pros and cons, and he couldn't find an easy solution. Every decision had a possible adverse side effect. Mark knew that the strongest and the most effective substance for perfect healing was vampire's blood, but there were always unknown consequences for everyone who was using it.

'But Gary never showed any signs of being a witch hunter like his father. He's only a human. That was a reason why he was separated from the rest of our family after the accident,' said Mark impassively.

'He has recessive genes. You can't remove them. It'll work anyway,' replied Draco confidently.

Mark calmed down. He couldn't deny the logic in Draco's arguments. But the unknown results of such old and robust vampire's blood still worried him. Yes, Gary would be definitely healed, but he would never be the same. Mark felt like he was losing his little brother. The pictures of their life together, so very normal, mundane and sometimes boring were running in his mind with a double of speed. The funny, usual life, full of small issues and right now so non-significant and out-of-date would end this instance. The sadness returned once more. Mark sighed deeply, looked at motionless Draco, hid his claws and modified his hands into normal human shape.

'Three syringes? Seriously? You can change at least five humans with it,' snorted Mark. Draco lowered his arms with relief and looked around searching for the last syringes containing his blood. He spotted it laying under the chair, now occupied by the woman quietly singing the same tune over and over again.

'Speaking of which, I've never changed anyone. I hope Sean mentioned that as well,' said Draco calmly. He gazed at the nurse, smiled and gently touched her head making her fall into deep sleep. Draco picked up the syringe and came closer to Gary's bed.

'There is something fishy in you. No vamp hangs out with hunters and ferals without a reason. I'll found out what it is,' said Mark sitting on Gary's bed.

'Perhaps, but now Gary is first. His body is too damaged for only one dosage,' replied Draco offering the last syringe to Mark.

'You don't have a choice, Gary doesn't have a choice, and I don't have one either,' continued Draco waiting with his hand stretched passing syringe. Mark looked at it, still weighing up in his mind the consequences of his decision. But he took the syringe and put the needle directly into the cannula. He was watching the vampire blood slowly going into Gary's flesh and colouring his veins dark.

'The unknown consequences are on you, remember that. You'll have to deal with it like rest of my family,' warned Mark. Draco smiled and nodded with agreement. They both knew that something long forgotten was coming back in the speed of flowing blood inside Gary's damaged body.

'What do you want from him?' asked Mark curiously.

'Sean knows everything, and we'll explain it to you in time, but Gary needs to wake up first,' declared Draco softly because seeing Mark doing the injection relieved massive tension in him.

'Is it connected to London's riot ten years ago? Answer me,' demanded Mark, but couldn't take his eyes off the dark lines under

Gary's skin indicating flowing and mixing contents from the syringe. He stopped pouring the liquid into his brother's flesh for a few seconds but then he realised it was too late to reverse the course of destiny. Draco was observing him silently till all liquid was pumped into Gary's veins.

'It has everything to do with your family and what really caused the mess ten years ago-' Draco didn't finish his sentence, inspecting the colour of Gary's arms that were changing from normal into grey ash-like hue.

Draco jumped closer to the bed and grabbed Gary's quickly cooling arm. Draco's face expressed utter surprise mingled with fright. He looked into Mark's eyes with fear. They both knew that something was wrong with Gary. Gary's skin started turning into grey colour, more like frozen body than somebody alive. The shaking spasm ran from Gary's fingertips through his entire body down to his feet, making them bounce very fast on the bed. The whites in his eyes changed to red and started to bleed. Gary was choking with the tube taped to his mouth. His teeth clenched on plastic pipe and his lips closed tightly around it. His hands waved in an unsynchronised way hitting not only the bed but also standing near individuals. Gary was moving vigorously in such intensity that the whole bed and all the medical equipment attached to his body was wobbling. Mark and Draco glimpsed at each other and threw themselves to catch and immobilise him. They barely managed to hold him down, but this seizure vanished as suddenly as it started. Gary's body was grey, and it recalled a nerveless rag-doll. His eyes became normal, but he had bloody tears on his cheeks.

'He's alive. He'll heal. That matters,' declared Draco.

'But we don't know who he'll become,' said Mark, lifting up Gary's eyelid and checking the pupil's reaction to his phone's flashlight.

Draco sent away the nurse and left Mark alone nodding only as the way to say goodbye. Mark called Sean and told him about everything that had happened. He left when Gary's condition seemed for him stable and his skin looked normal again.

After a few hours Gary's condition didn't change and he remained unconscious but there were a few seconds when yellow patches appeared on the surface of his skin but vanished unnoticed.

*

Gary was observing the whole event, but he couldn't do anything. He saw what had happened with syringes and his injections of a dark liquid. Gary didn't know who the man was, but he looked different than anyone Gary saw so far in his entire life. Gary felt uneasy in his presence. He was stunned about the fact that Draco's aura wasn't as the ghosts he met in the corridor. It looked more like a dark, cold and thick crust without any radiance on a surface but with many thin golden lines all over. It seemed like it was a light that was hidden inside the shell and was prevented from shining out. Draco's eyes had the same golden colour as the lines. Gary felt threatened by his presence like he was standing near an overwhelming source of power. He could sense danger and something unearthly form Draco, but he couldn't define what exactly it was.

Gary was angry at Mark when he noticed his brother didn't defend him against the intruder. He saw the injection process and tried to stop it, but he met sharp, hostile Draco's gaze that scared Gary without any words. It seemed like Draco could perfectly see Gary, because every time Gary moved, Draco's eyes followed him. Gary stepped back, feeling pinned down by the vision that he just saw a vampire from the spiritual world, and he didn't like it.

In the same moment, when the liquid started flowing inside his veins, Gary had a vision of his future entangled for the rest of his life with this completely unknown creepy man. When the black fluid touched Gary's heart, he felt tremendous pain not only in his body but in the entire soul, like his being was turned upside down. But the worst was he couldn't pass out to the blissful and painless unconscious. The vampire's blood embossed an agonising imprint inside Gary's genes. He felt so unusual that he couldn't name the state he was now in. Gary saw on the brink of his consciousness how much his own aura had changed before he fell into a long and nightmarish dream.

CHAPTER 4

20th June - Her Blood

Patric was tall and slim. His Mediterranean origin gave him black wavy hair, tanned skin, dark eyes, a soft smile and made him irresistibly charming. He valued his manners, impeccable expensive clothing and his money more than anything else. Even his casual garments had to be from top brands, or he wouldn't bother looking at them at all.

Today was his re-birthday. He didn't remember the date of his birthday as a normal human as he didn't want to keep in mind the names of his lowlife parents. But today passed one year more of being the person he desired to become since he saw vampires roaming among those who were too weak to fight with them. And every 20th June he recalled the muggy night and the place where he was living back then and all those people who passed away so long ago, even though he didn't want to remember them. This day was a threshold for his new life and he wanted to cherish it for centuries to come. But after so many years, the memory of the town was slowly fading alongside with faces of his parents and all human relatives. However, the picture of this precise night was still sharp like it happened a few hours ago. His new life as an Upir had started somewhere in the middle of the slum and the place where he grew up, precisely one hundred twenty-three years ago during a beautiful night at Rome.

Patric smiled to himself. He kept in his mind the rush, the thrill, the burning emotions of desire for power that was so close to reach, if only he was one of the night children. But for vampires he was nobody. They only accepted into their ranks nobles, artists, highly qualify specialists and those breathtakingly beautiful. Although Patric was handsome, he was still not good enough. Roseanne, the love of Patric's life, was a member of a secret society of vampires living among rich nobles in Rome back then. But he only could observe her from a distance and daydreamed about touching her hand. He wanted badly to be the man she desired, not some blood-bag worm, as humans were for her.

Today was the anniversary of the most significant event of his life, the day when he saw the way out from his wretched existence. It was the day when he met his Upir-father. Only once in his life Patric begged for something, and he begged on his knees to be changed.

Patric loved every single second of being the special type of vampire. Moreover, knowing that he was unique because only rumours about Upirs could cause panic attack among many regular vampires, made him feel superior and gave him the arrogant self-confidence so helpful in his way up inside their society. He liked to celebrate it in an exceptional way, but this year, his plan was destroyed by an old unresolved issue from ten years ago that was coming back suddenly like a long forgotten and an unpaid bill. That made him feel frustrated. He felt threatened by the uncertainty that was lurking around. If there was something Patric hated the most, it was an obstacle destroying his perfect plan and making him worry. And because it was sporadic, it annoyed him even more. That kind of situation always triggered his irritation and led to him being impatient, pushing him to the edge of making wrong decisions. Like this case in Boyle's farm. He should have sent some of his boys, but he was so highly agitated that he ran there himself.

He expected to find the coffin with his old vampire enemy – Erick – but he was too late and that stirred his mind and plans up to the point of losing his nerves. The farm was the last location that showed the position of one of the mobile numbers from Adam's phone, which was the one nearest to London before it had been disconnected completely. The only success of Patric's action was the information that Draco hid something inside a rented self-storage shipping container that was probably leading to Erick's whereabouts. Now, Patric wasn't sure if the story about the coffin and Erick trapped there was even real. After all, Adam had a perfect reason to lie. But Patric knew whatever it was that is hidden there, the messages triggered something into motion, and it was only matter of time that all would eventually come back to light.

The second phone number was logged in Canada, but his track was lost just after the message to Adam was sent. Although Patric combed the storage and found nothing significant other than a few plastic boxes with some meaningless bits and bobs inside, there were signs on the ground that someone took something from their big enough to fit a van.

Even though his deed was a terrible political mistake because of the whole investigation in the Guild that was now being undertaken, Patric kept smiling as he recalled the torture he had immense pleasure to perform on the family who lived in the farm. They told him that a few men in a van came only an hour before Patric and removed something from one container. The owner couldn't refuse them as they knew the password but he wasn't allowed to assist the loading. Apparently, Draco left instruction in case he might send someone for his belongings to open the storage. One of those men from the van had both the password and the three keys to unlock the container. Patric felt mad at himself for making stupid decisions like waiting too long after receiving back texts, and he loathed himself for it.

He was strolling to and fro in his office, thinking intensively what to do next. There were two cameras around the farm, but it didn't help at all. Although the car registration number, shown on footage from CCTV, was from London the licence plate was fake. Patric had to admit, Draco and his associates were pretty well-prepared and smoothly organised. He sat back on a massive, luxurious chair behind his modern glassy desk, closed his eyes and tried to calm himself down. He knew if he would stay so emotionally unstable he might make more bad moves.

Patric's office space was ample and had a stylish design in black, grey and red colours. There were a few contemporary paintings overflowing with a spectrum of red stains shaped like blood drops. His enormous desk was neatly arranged. Only one picture of a woman was a sign of a personal life that he had. Even the door to his private bathroom didn't differ from the rest of the walls. The office was located on one of the skyscraper top floor with magnificent view of the river Thames.

Patric was deep in his mind thinking about all possibilities and consequences of his choices that he might have to make soon when the main door abruptly opened, unnerving him. Patric slowly looked up in the direction of the noise. He knew who had entered. One person was bold enough to meet his anger and just the only one he was in love with. He loved watching her graceful, catlike gait when she was walking. The perfect combinations of fast pace with hips swings acted on his senses like an aphrodisiac. She was wearing a classy, elegant black dress and bright red high heels. Even now, when he was feeling frustrated and stressed about the unknown future, Patric couldn't stop smiling when he saw her.

'Roseanne, darling. What are you doing here so early in the morning?' he asked softly.

'While you're hiding and planning new mischievous political games, what to buy on stock market or whose to kill next, I'm doing all dirty jobs collecting rumours and investigating them. Guess who is in London?' she asked, smiling and using her seductive voice that always turned him on.

She sat on the desk in front of him, putting her feet on his hips and ramming heels into his flesh. She started moving up her dress, exposing her shapely calf and staring at him with an alluring smile that he couldn't ignore. Patric looked at her without any grimes of pain, gently touching her ankle with only his fingertips and slowly started moving his hand up her leg. She smiled broadly, and before he finished on her upper hip, she sat on his knees and kissed him passionately. He hugged her tightly, and after intense, deep kissing, he pecked gently at her neck. He started feeling when the blissful hopefulness of overcoming his troubles was grown in his mind, pushing the blue mood out. Only her presence could calm him down so quickly.

He closed his eyes, and the memories of the taste of her blood made him want her now more than ever before. For him it was like divine ambrosia, the perfect mixture of sweetness and the best old, dark rum he loved the most. No other vampire's blood gave him so much energy and put him on an emotional high than hers. He would never resist making passionate love with her and drinking her blood during this time. The emotions were skyrocketing for both of them, fuelled by the chemicals from his venom that intensify the experience to the highest level. The energetic thrill, goosebumps and all of those sensations started crawling under his skin now, woken up by such a vivid reminiscence of many colourfully and exciting moments from their mutual past as a couple for almost ten years. His hands started wandering over her perfectly shaped body faster and more courageously. Patric's desire and hunger for excitement was boiling inside his veins. He stood up, holding her tightly. She wrapped her legs around his waist, still kissing him. He swept all those things from his desk that might be disturbing the lust and laid on the top of her. He couldn't resist kissing her neck with more fervour. He put his elongated fangs, dripping with venom, on her skin, smearing it, licking her neck and allowing neurotoxins to be absorbed through the skin into her bloodstream. He waited for all those delightful pheromones rushing in her flesh to escalate to the maximum. He wanted to taste them like a child unwrapping Christmas gifts. The Upir's toxins worked like a drug on ordinary vampires regardless of their age. It stimulated feelings most present in the moment and making their mind hugely receptive to manipulation.

He had to use all his control and discipline to not pierce his fangs into her skin too quickly. The time was an essence in this act. He didn't want her to know or remember about the fact that he was drinking her blood. That might ruin his cover, sending not only hunters for his head but every possible vampire dynasty in the whole of London. After all, the Upir was a predator to regular vampires, in the same way vampires were hunting humans to survive.

He was waiting for intoxication signs in her eyes to appear. When she started acting more provocative, when her fever and lust skyrocketing, when she unfastened his belt making her hands busy on his skin under clothes, her eyes showed how deeply drugged she was. He saw a similar reaction many times, and he knew it was time for drinking her sweet blood.

His fangs pierced her neck in the perfect place where visible veins were pumping blood with high speed. He took one sip but choked with disgust. He spat it on the desk and quickly licked the puncture on her skin for immediate healing. She seemed to not have noticed any changes, still under the profound influence of neurotoxin. He barely mastered himself because the taste and smell of something rotten pulled him back to reality from the bliss. He was shocked. What had happened that affected her taste so badly, he was thinking and analysing the last couple of days. Patric knew that the days when she was experimenting with new drugs was over a long time ago and she seemed perfectly normal, but still something was terribly wrong. He took a deep breath, trying to play normal, but had an uncontrolled retching reflex that he didn't want to show. He clenched his jaw and sighed, still lying on her and hugging her tightly. He still was feeling the desire, but after a minute of a very intensive stench from her, everything was gone, slowly dimming away in his memory. He felt like a spoilt child, one who wasn't getting any sweets that were in his reach and who was on the edge of throwing the biggest tantrum in his life. When the taste of her blood became bitter, he realised he couldn't drink from her for at least some time until he would discover and remove the reason. Unfortunately, suppressing his feelings was making him even more wrathful, temperamental and unpredictable. Patric knew that his tantrum wouldn't finish on screaming, yelling and hitting the ground with tight fists but more likely he would fall into an uncontrollable killing rage, leaving in random locations a bloodbath around the city. Taste of her body, so sweet and arousing for him for so many years, became bitter and musty like perishable meat. He was breathing profoundly to try and calm himself down, but it was challenging. Only holding her in his arms stopped him from destroying some casual furniture like he used to do before.

He stood up and pulled her up. He hugged her and reciprocated kisses, but he knew the fire in him was gone. She looked utterly surprised and shocked. She was never rejected, as a woman, by a man in the middle of a physical act. It had never happened between them either. He hugged her even more tightly, brushing her back and saying some apology with made up excuses about how there was a stressful situation in business that he had to face now. At first, she seemed not to know how to react, but after a minute she pushed him away, hit his face and dashed out, without a word, crying. She ran away without looking back.

After she left the room, he took the phone from the desk and threw it, smashing it on the wall. His rage was so immense that the phone smashed on the surface. He wanted to destroy something else, but one of his spies appeared in the door. His presence, like bad news, not only restrained Patric but made him focused and alert.

CHAPTER 5

17th June - The Moon Ritual

'Stop knocking so loud,' said Sean, widely opening the door and making a silencing gesture. Strong light from the corridor behind him was illuminating a person standing at the entrance of a fairly large, two-storey detached Victorian house, located on the peripheries of London. The house was surrounded by a line of old, wide trees growing on the outskirts of the garden alongside a high, brick fence in the same dark red colour as walls of the house. A path leading from a metal gate was built with flat black stones adhering tightly to each other. The path was encircling the house from both sides and was running through green, well-groomed grass. The property seemed well maintain but some signs of the passing time were visible, such as large ivy reaching the roof on one side or flaking paints on windowsills. The site was lit by a few strong LED lamps located on the corners of the house. The lights were switching on by itself, activated by a motion sensor that reacted just after someone passed the main gate.

Robert walked through the doorstep, snorting something incomprehensibly more to himself than to the people watching his arrival. He was limping and leaning on a walking stick a bit more today than normally. He gasped with pain loud enough to get attention from everyone inside the corridor. Sean rolled his eyes with a 'not again' expression on his face. Mark was standing just behind him emotionlessly, but his half-closed eyes followed every move of the guest. They all were sizing each other up when one more person showed up in a hallway.

'Him?!' asked Robert aggressively, staring at Sean and pointing at the person standing near the kitchen entrance.

'Oh, don't mind me, brother. I'll observe your pitfall without any comments,' said a tall male smiling arrogantly. He was a well-built man in his fifties with almost white hair, sun-burnt face and a few visible deep wrinkles near his grey eyes. He was dressed in a well-lying grey suit, colour-matched shirt and a white tie. Sean sighed, covering his eyes with his hand and shaking head with disapproval.

'At least you should have warned me, Sean, that my beloved, mischievous, older brother James will be included in our little soiree,' concluded Robert after a moment of total silence and casting his hostile sight directly to the new man.

'I don't care about your family drama, Robert. This meeting isn't a party with a striper as the highlight of the programme. Simon's life is at risk. You haven't seen him yet. You don't know how bad it is now. So, shut up and work nicely with us,' Sean called him down, raising his voice. He turned around and walked upstairs without looking back.

James walked past Robert, patted him on his back and whispered 'Welcome to your nightmare.' Robert caught his hand, squeezed and rejected it with a wave of anger. James smiled, shrugged and then followed Sean resiliently. Robert walked reluctantly after them but was hobbling step by step on the stairs. Mark locked the door and walked behind all of them upstairs.

The corridor on the first floor was poorly lit with semi-circular coffers hanging near doors to three bedrooms. There was a bathroom next to the stairs to the converted attic. One bedroom door was half open and some bizarre noises resounded from the inside. Mark was the last who walked there, closing the door behind him. The room was vast but cluttered with a huge, vintage canopy bed with massive carved columns and heavy, weathered, brown curtains. There was a massive wooden chest standing at the end of the bed covered by large pillows with pillowcases made of the same material as the bed's drapery. All other furniture matched the bed in size and colours. It seemed like they were made by the same hands as a set and left here like a museum's exhibits from the last century. There was an enormous oriental carpet lying in the middle of the room but shamelessly showing shabby holes in a few worn out places.

Simon was lying on one side of this bed. He was wearing only boxers, and his naked, chocolate-colour body was partially covered by a white sheet, already torn in several places, with blood stains on it. He was tied to the bed pillars with a nylon rope. Each of his hands and legs were bound to a separate column. He was sweating all over his body, shaking, and there were visible signs of rapid changes inside his flesh that were happening now. Muscles spasms were moving chaotically in many places in his body, causing more sweat with tiny bloody drops on his skin. He was in pain, but his screams were repressed by a wooden stick, with marks of his bites alongside. He moaned and sometimes was choking, trying to spit out white foam that was building up in his mouth. His eyes were closed but there were rapid movements under the eyelids and drops of tears ran down his cheeks. On his bald head and the rest of his body started to grow long, white, straight hair. His hands were partially changed. His fingers had lengthened, thickened and ended with sharp claws, but the middle of the hand remained human-like. The skin in some places of his body was broken. The open wounds were showing living tissues under. The cuts were healing quickly but were opening again after every new major muscle spasm attack. His legs slowly started changing into a more massive shape. Under the skin, there were impulsive movements that were broadening the entire limbs up and expanding his feet.

Near Simon, a woman was sitting on his bed, holding a tremendous syringe with yellow liquid and slowly injecting it into his abdomen.

'Sean, the mixture should hold up his transformation for at least two hours. If his body can't change into full feral form during this time, the spasms will tear him into pieces,' she said with sadness in her voice. She didn't look at those who entered but incessantly was watching every one of Simon's movements. She pressed the pump a bit harder, observing his body reactions. The spasms quietened but didn't cease completely. Simon sighed deeply and fell asleep. His wounds were finally fully closed, but they were covered only with a thin, pink membrane.

'If only I could …' she didn't finish but choked the sentence inside her throat. She was wiping sweat from Simon's forehead with a large towel.

'They're here,' Sean put his hand on her shoulder and squeezed gently. She turned and glared from one person to another, wiping tears from her face with a fast hand movement. She wore a dark blue nurse uniform with a logo of the hospital she was working for. James and Robert came closer without a word, only staring at the sleeping Simon.

'Guys, do you understand the consequences of including him in your pack?' asked Sean, looking at the silent Robert and James. Robert was purposely avoiding eye-contact, not only with his brother but with everyone.

'Do we have to do it? There is no other way? Or you just don't want to find out?' asked Robert in a very quarrelsome tone but with his eyes staring at the floor.

'We don't have time to find another way,' replied James with a smirk on his face emphasising the last two words.

'Shut up! You won't drag me to your den using him,' cried Robert, pointing at Simon but gazing straight to James' eyes.

'Oh, yes, I will, my little brother. You have no idea how this ritual works, do you?' answered James firmly.

Robert said nothing but the tension between them was so intense that only Sean standing between was preventing the escalation of the conflict that was starting to grow in the first moment when Robert saw his brother downstairs.

'How does it work?' he growled through clenched teeth, with his eyes fixed on his brother. Sean pushed him back and nodded to the nurse giving her permission to explain the whole procedure and its meaning.

'London is a big city, and similar accidents happen every month, but this one is different. To survive the change, one has to have a warrior's mark inside the soul and want it to take over. Every full moon gives unusual features to all new converted into ferals but there is a price for it as for everything in life. Simon is fighting a battle between his human nature supported by ancestor's genetic memories against the new structural prints of a werewolf, not only in his body but in his whole being. He has to accept on a deep spiritual level that the world is not what he thinks it is, and what his previous generations believed it was. In normal cases, the surviving rate is about seventy per cent to become a new werewolf. Now, due to Red Moon, his chances are less than one per cent. But he is a warrior, otherwise he would be dead not long after you bit him, Robert. You don't get it yet, how lucky you are,' she said, staring at him. The silence between them was interrupted only by the loud breathing of a sleeping Simon. Sean leaned against the bed's column with clenched fists. He looked at Simon and Robert with a body expression of long-held anger mixed with a hurry.

'I believe my dear brother will finally have to face the consequences of his impetuosity and it doesn't matter if he likes it or not. So, can we proceed? I don't have the whole evening to waste to save your arse again, Robert. You owe me more than once from now on,' declared James, coming closer to the bed, taking Simon's hand. He reached out his other hand towards Robert and nodded giving him a sign for catching. Robert looked at him with a frown.

'The ritual is kind of a spiritual adoption,' the nurse continued explaining, but Robert interrupted, shouting at her with high pitch tone.

'What! Wait a minute! What do you mean by 'adoption'?' yelled Robert, shocked.

'Well, it means he'll be your son…' she didn't finish.

'No! I hate children,' shouted Robert, furiously.

'You have a sixteen-year-old daughter,' interjected James, calmly.

'Don't you dare talk about her,' Robert's rage reached the top of his nerves. He launched at James with clenched fists. But Mark was faster. He jumped straight between them, catching and immobilising Robert's hands. James backed off, raising both of his hands in a submission gesture.

'Why not? She belongs to the pack just as you do. Just because you're dodging to introduce her, doesn't mean she's unwanted among us. You've never been banished from our group, so one day she'll find the way without your permission. It's in her blood. Every wolf needs its pack,' James declared, putting stress on 'you' and 'she' purposely and staring at his bother very intensively.

It took a while for Robert to calm down. It seemed like he was battling inside his head and the only visible sign of it was his changing facial expression form anger to acceptance. He was walking to and fro with a bowed head avoiding eye contact with everyone in the room.

After a while, Sean grunted, giving the nurse a silent gesture to continue with the task. She still was sitting on the bed, but now she was whispering something soundlessly with a soft self-satisfied smirk and watching how the atmosphere had changed.

'Shall we continue?' she asked, waiting for Robert's approval.

He glanced at her and just nodded, still having his head down and keeping his eyes away from the rest. He came closer to the bed, looked reluctantly at Simon and stretched his one hand towards the nurse.

'So, where were we? The spiritual adoption will bind you both in this life. You'll have to take care of him every full moon. Your whole pack will help a lot. Without you, he might fall into uncontrolled wildness and start randomly killing those who will stand in his way,' she said, calmly staring into Robert's horrified face.

'And in that way, my dear brother, you'll have to bring him and your stubborn arse to our headquarter for a couple of days. See, I told you, you'll be back. Can't wait to tell our folks about it,' said James, clearly pleased with the pictures running in his head. Robert was visibly getting angrier, gritting his teeth and trying to throw himself at his brother but the strong grip of Mark's hands on his arms prevented the fight.

'Stop right now. It's time to hide your pride, Robert,' said a nurse decisively. Everyone stared at her.

'You have to understand, if Simon dies, you'll face the trial for breaking the law of complete ban for changing humans into ferals during the Red Moon. This is our oldest and the most important legalisation for all Viviters living behind the veil. Every single child knows about it. I don't care what you've been doing in the forest, but you shouldn't have been running in the ferox form at all. You knew the consequences,' said Sean to Robert with a clearly raised voice. Robert nodded, letting all them know that he knew the legal repercussions. There was a silence between them for a moment, interrupted only by the muffled voice of Simon's moan. Robert opened his mouth, trying to say something, but one look at his brother and Sean's fierce faces discouraged him completely. He sighed, shrugged and made a gesture with hands giving them all the permission to continue the ritual.

The nurse sat closer to Simon, making way more space for the brothers to stand much closer to her. She took Simon's hand and passed it to Robert's. Robert took James' hand, turning his head and closing his eyes. James, Robert and Simon created a circle closed by their hands with the nurse sitting in the middle of it. James smiled widely and nodded to indicate the start of the whole ceremony. She put her hand on Simon's chest and the other on the brothers' entwined fingers. The nurse closed her eyes, took a deep breath and started humming softly.

Sean was the one who was the most curious about what she was doing. He was staring at them but couldn't see any effects at first. When she started singing in a low voice a song in a language not recognisable for Sean, he had an impression that more light was in the room, although no additional lamp was switched on. Slowly the temperature rose to the point when Sean felt hot and had to take off his sweater. They all looked like people deep in mind with a blissful and gentle smile on their faces. Simon's body went back to be fully normal human form, completely healing all cuts without leaving any visible scars.

In the same moment, Robert felt the tingling sensation of a delicate energy that came to him from the nurse. Every second the heat around them was rising. In his mind, Robert saw the circle made by their hands as a white light and connecting all of them into one. First, it was like a single thread, but the light started increasing its volume in the rhythm of the song. And then, Robert felt the presence of someone standing right behind him. Somehow Robert knew the being had observed him since he was born. It made Robert shiver out of fear. He saw the exact moment when many new energetic, colourful lines from the outside joined to the light circle and had changed it into a rainbow. He started to hear whispers all around that came alongside with the other energy lines. He had the impression that his whole soul was shaking to the core, but his body was motionless. He saw a white spirit evolving from the lines and emerge in the middle of the circle. It had a werewolf feral form built with streams of energy lines that were running inside its ethereal body, creating pictographs of animals, humans, trees, plants and even water waves, stars and clouds. Some symbols, that reminded scratched by claws glyphs, were woven into those pictures and emanated as slightly flashing lights. The spirit stared at Robert with his piercing eyes that went through his soul like a knife exposing all deeds he had made in his life, even those he was ashamed of and regretted the most and was avoiding remembering. Robert couldn't move. He was still alive, but he knew this was his judgement day. The werewolf spirit put his hand on Simon's chest, clenching his massive claws on his heart and whispering an incantation. The energy lines from the Spirit influenced Simon's, mixed with and affected its colours. Simon's body was shaking like it was being tugged by a power that was far beyond human scale.

Robert felt the moment when his aura was connecting with Simon's and concatenating their lives so deeply that it would never be broken. It had flown from him throughout the werewolf spirit straight to Simon's. Robert saw when the tides of their both destinies were taking control in his own future, redirecting everything into a dangerous path. The running pictures in his mind of this new destiny scared him. It was like a movie on fast forward, but he could only catch a glimpse of a few of the most horrifying events. Robert saw fights, blood and death around, and the overwhelming feeling of being helpless when he was trying to prevent something that was doomed to destruction. Their fate was now like a small snowball thrown on a mountain slope, forming an avalanche that would destroy everything in its way. Robert tried to break the circle, but his body was totally immobilised. And then suddenly, everything was over. He heard the voice of the nurse calling to him, but he wasn't able to understand the meaning of it.

The scars on Simon's hands slowly opened up afresh and started pouring flesh blood on the bed. Simon was moving and moaning, but this time it was more intense than before. Robert opened his eyes and looked dazedly at the nurse.

'Stop rejecting him! You're making everything worse. Look! It'll continue spreading all over his body. Now he has to fight even with you. He'll be dead in less than five minutes,' she shouted angrily, emphasising the last sentence and gazing at the brothers. She looked like someone who was in a hurry and knew very well that no matter how fast they would be, it was already too late.

The silence was broken by Simon choking on screams of pain suppressed by a stick in his mouth. His body started shaking with visible waves of muscle spasms going under his skin. His feet began to grow fast, changing shape into wolf's paws ending with short claws. On his slowly increasing torso, white mixed with black fur appeared. His tights enlarged very fast to the point that he looked like a grotesque cartoon compared with his still about normal size chest and arms. Stretched skin on his legs started splitting up along showing flesh and overgrowing muscles. The room was filled with the smell of blood and the strangled screams of a tortured Simon. His wounds didn't heal this time but only broadened slowly.

Everyone was looking at each other with dismay, parallelised by the sudden turn of events. Sean covered his lips and moved first. He ran away from the room to the toilet. The woman was running right behind him, and the view of Sean's vomiting in the toilet bowl made her feel even worse. She fell on her knees right by the bathtub to puke inside.

Meanwhile, in the room, James was still holding Robert's hand by force with dread on his face. Robert stared in dismay at what was happening, feeling powerless and useless with every passing nanosecond. Mark was the only one person who didn't panic and didn't freeze in shock. He moved quickly towards them, caught the flabbergasted Robert and hit him in the face with all his might.

'Give me the serum now! I know you have it,' shouted Mark as loud as he could.

'Serum?' asked Robert, still dizzy with a half-unconscious voice.

'The VS1. Where do you have it?!' yelled Mark, scrabbling around in Robert's jacket pockets. Robert was unsure what to do but one look at Simon writhing in convulsions hurried him. He pulled out from the inside pocket of his jacket something looking like an injection pen and gave it to Mark. Mark opened it, turning the dosage adjustment dial to the maximum and gave a shot into Simon's leg exactly in the middle of an open wound. He repeated this action several times in different places on Simon's body until the whole cartridge was empty.

Robert was looking at all Mark's action trying not to catch James' eyesight. He was curious how the serum would work on half-human flesh. He knew it wouldn't be long when James would start asking uncomfortable questions and demanding serious answers. Robert's problems would be not only the answers about the serum but about money for it as well and it wasn't the bottom of the pit he was in now. He knew he wouldn't be able to avoid challenging questions about how he got VS1 - the purest and the most expensive serum on the black market. But the most crucial issue for Robert was how Mark knew about the pen.

Everyone in the room was staring at the excruciated Simon in silence. They all felt overwhelming helplessness and did only what was left to do; watch Simon's last earthy battle for life. His body shook one last time in a big wave of muscles spasm, and then he passed out with his eyes opened.

Robert felt extremely weak, like the whole process drained him of all energy. He staggered and leaned against the bed's column. James caught him on time and helped him to sit on the chest that was standing at the end of the bed. Robert cried soundlessly. His face was hidden inside James' arms sitting next to him and hugging his head. James knew his younger brother would never be the same after this evening. Mark sat on the bed next to Simon and hid his face in hands.

They all assumed Simon death prematurely. But it didn't take too long to see the effects made by serum. The first sign was a big gasp of breath taken by Simon, like someone suddenly emerging from the water. The second sign was the fact that his blood stopped pouring from the cuts, and the wounds began to cover with a pink membrane. It took a minute to close all open skin places and convert him into a perfectly built werewolf battle-feral form, but it made all of them happy. Even Robert hugged not only Mark but his brother James as well. Simon was breathing deeply with his eyes closed. His massive body was covered with black fur. He was growling quietly revealing his white, long and sharp fangs. Mark jumped, smiling broadly, ran to the bathroom and dragged Sean and the nurse back to the room.

James was staring at Simon like he had just seen a new-born child. But, at the same time, James was interested in observing his brother tightly. He couldn't hide the utter surprise on his face. Robert watched as his stock of the serum for the whole month disappeared as it flowed through Simon's blood but at least it healed him entirely and made the transformation into feral utterly easy and painless. He didn't know if the ritual was completed, but he didn't care as long as the problem with accidental biting was out of his mind.

Robert looked in a soft way at his brother for the first time since almost twenty years ago when the long family drama created the private war between them. James helped him to stand up and passed his walking stick. They came nearby to the bed, looking at the new perfectly built werewolf lying there, with facial expressions like mothers glaring at infants.

All people present in the room were staring at Simon and didn't know what to do. Sean was first to come closer and dare to touch Simon's chest with one finger. Simon opened his eyes and snarled menacingly. Sean stepped back, but he was smiling like someone who had just won the lottery. Simon tugged the cords that were binding his hands to the bed, but he couldn't break it.

'Keep calm, please. Nobody wants to hurt you, buddy. We're here to help you,' said Sean, looking around and giving everyone the signal to stand still without any abrupt movement. Simon gnarled. He looked at his fastened body and snarled even louder tugging at all his limbs.

'Easy, easy. Before I remove those lines from you, please listen very carefully. Nod if you understand what I am saying,' continued Sean, coming slowly closer to the bed but observing carefully every one of Simon's movement. Simon nodded and stop moving. Sean smiled and made a thumbs-up gesture to the others with the meaning 'it's working'. He continued with evident satisfaction in his voice.

'I will tell a few names. Please nod if you recognise your own.'

Simon gave a sign of understanding. They came closer to the bed, but now with curiosity on their faces rather than fear.

'Adam, Brian, Colin, David, Glenn,' Sean spoke every name clearly, looking for any evidence of an emotional reaction from Simon.

'Lee, Paul, Simon …' he didn't finish the full length of the last name. Simon turned his head in Sean's direction and indicated by snarling vigorously like a little dog that the last one was his name. They all sighed with relief. Even Robert didn't react with his usual loathing when James patted his back.

'Okay, now. Just relax, close your eyes, start breathing very deep, think about going on holiday or something very nice,' Sean was observing Simon's reactions.

'You should know that changing from your current form to human is easy. Think about being a human again. You'll feel tickling on your skin. It's not painful. It might be uncomfortable at the begging, but you'll get used to it,' said Robert, braking into Sean's instruction and continuing with soft talk like a teacher to a small child. He was cutting off the cords from Simon's massive paws with a big hunter's knife he got from Mark. Mark was standing on the opposite side of the bed doing the same with a similar shaped knife he found underneath the bed. Simon closed his eyes and was breathing according to the given order. The nurse checked Simon condition and nodded with approval. Simon seemed in good health. After a few minutes of joy among them, Sean made a 'get out' gesture to everyone but the nurse. They all went downstairs, closing the door behind.

Simon had changed his forms a few times from human to werewolf and back to human without any problems, instructed by Sean and every time checked over by nurse. Simon in his human form was aware of what was happening to him. His body became more muscular and buoyant. The nurse gave Simon one more shot with some vitamins cocktail, and then, for the first time since the biting, he fell into a deep and very calm sleep.

Sean and the woman left the room. They stood in silence watching the brothers talking silently downstairs near the main entrance.

'I haven't finished the ritual,' she caught Sean by the hand and whispered in fear. He said nothing but glanced one more time towards the closed door to Simon's bedroom and sighed. Sean silently showed the nurse the direction of the next bedroom where Jessica was lying in a coma.

CHAPTER 6

17th June - Spirits

The corridor was poorly lit, leaving the place in gloomy shades. The silence was filling the entire floor. Sean and the nurse were standing in front of the door to the room where an unconscious Jessica was waiting for something that might help her wrecked mind to cope with a new reality. Sean grabbed the handle but hesitated to open it.

'May I assist you?' he said quietly, without looking at the nurse like a little boy who was too shy to ask.

'Sure, you can. Your curiosity is written all over your face,' she replied, smiling.

They both walked to the room in silence, turning on the main light.

The room was much smaller than the previous one, where Simon was now sleeping peacefully, and it was furnished in a more modern design. There was only one single bed with Jessica lying in it. She looked like someone deep in a pleasant dream rather than someone who had had a traumatic experience. Her mouth was moving soundlessly, and she was smiling broadly.

'Is she okay?' asked Sean, coming closer and bringing two chairs. The nurse sat on one of them at the height of the girl's head.

'I hope she will be. She is the worst case of all three of them.'

'Why?' asked Sean, perplexed.

'You see, there's nothing more stressful for a normal human mind than a traumatic accident. Unfortunately for her, the changes, like with Simon, have to reshape her on the deepest level of soul's existence,' answered the nurse, taking Jessica's hand and lifting up a bit of her eyelids. Jessica's eye was moving very fast, and most of the white part was visible. The nurse took a deep breath, put one hand on Jessica's chest and looked attentively on her face. Sean was observing every movement, eager to ask the next questions. The nurse turned to him with the biggest grin she had had this evening.

'Don't stare at me like that. Just ask. It'll be faster to feed your inquisitiveness,' she said, putting one hand on his arm.

'Have you started the ritual yet? Why don't you sing like you did with Simon?' asked Sean, smiling like a little boy.

'Yes, I've already started. And I was singing something I heard today on a radio that I like it. The ritual doesn't need any music or humming, and we don't have any incantations either. It was only for them to mark the beginning and help them focus in the moment. Robert's mind was going crazy like a drunk monkey, so I needed something for him to hold on to,' she explained with ease. Sean opened his eyes wider, looking like someone touched by divine revelation.

'But why is Jessica the worst case?' Sean stood up and started pacing to and fro around the room and gesturing with excitement. He smoothed his hair several times, but it kept being in disarray. He removed the hair-band and loosened up the ponytail he had. He was jerking hair impatiently, trying to correct them, but he was too distracted by the shaman. He wanted to curse, but he stopped in the middle of the word seeing her careful look. She nodded and pointed to the empty chair. He sat in silence.

'You see, as you know, we have three kinds of human minds in this world. First, are all born behind the veil, second is all of those who are not aware that there is a veil and any so-called supernaturals that are roaming around. The third is the one living on the outskirts of humankind and hanging between the two of those extremely different worlds,' she continued, without paying any attention to him. She turned into Jessica and was petting her cheeks.

'Yes, I know but…' Sean interrupted. He was sitting on the chair wiggling like an unruly little boy.

'Let me finish, please,' she put stress in this sentence to indicate her slight impatience and continued her lecture.

'The first are born with the veil imprinted already in their souls, or like Gary, have potential abilities inside passive genes so they can be awakened. The second group, like Simon, is one of the one per cent of the human population who apparently doesn't have delirium. They are normal people, but they just can see our ferox forms without their brain firing up. They could be turned if they survived a very painful transition. But third one are all those who react with delirium. Their mind can't process information about everything that is going beyond their fixed side of logic and reasoning. That's why in the moment when they see something outside so-called normality, their mind is automatically switching into delirium mode. For many of them, the exposition is too short to even make any changes, so it's not a problem. They will have so-called 'blind moments' or just don't remember a few minutes in a day. But if they can't avoid the confrontation, as Jessica was exposed to, their mind will turn into useless mash. Basically, they'll never be normal again...' she couldn't finish as she was interrupted by Sean.

'I know but, if Simon could see our true form why it works so late in his life. Do you really think it was the first time for him?'

Sean stood up again and started pacing around the room, gesticulating. His black T-shirt with a logo of his favourite metal music band was marked with patches of sweat. His beard, usually elegantly braided with silver braids, was dishevelled. Even his long, greying hair, always well groomed, waved in chaos. He looked like a person deeply concerned about academic issues in this whole situation.

'I don't know. Every human brain works in its own bizarre way. There is nothing certain about it. Maybe he never saw any feral before, or the whole incident was too close and too intensive for him, and he just snapped,' she replied, softly staring at him and shrugging.

'But why is he...' he didn't finish the question because her sharp voice interrupted him.

'Look, don't get me wrong but I have to help her now. You'll have to find out the answers about Simon all by yourself. Maybe there is no explanation for why he reacted like he did. Some things just happen with people. Maybe the reason is so trivial that you'll not see it at all if you'd continue with some bookish reasoning. There's no logic in life that you can use for every situation. Now, where were we?' she replied, turning to Jessica and checking her eyes one more time.

'But what about her?' Sean continued with new questions like someone who wouldn't take no for an answer. He put the free chair closer to the nurse and sat on it.

'She is just a normal person. Her mind was exposed for far too long to see a werewolf in a ferox form and she can't deal with it. If she'd awake now, she'll definitely go crazy like a person possessed or with severe schizophrenia,' the nurse replied automatically, without looking into his direction.

'But why?'

'You'll never give up searching for answers, will you?'

'No, I won't. It's the first time I'm assisting in a neoshaman ritual. I've read a lot about you folks, but it's not the same as fieldwork. I always saw only the results of your touch,' he said, grinning very broadly.

'Okay, let me show you then,' she said, touching his chest.

In this moment, Sean started feeling a tingling sensation that was warming up the place and spreading all over his body. After the heat, there came exciting emotions like a flooding wave of pleasure that was pouring into his mind. He closed his eyes, drifting away to the daydreams full of hot baths, candles, music, good wines and overwhelming thrills about artefacts from a long-forgotten past that he wanted to find so badly. But he couldn't stay long in this fairyland because her soft calling voice brought him back to reality. He opened his eyes and saw it for the first time in his life, the subtle light of aura surrounding all human body.

'Can you see it?' she asked, waiting for his response. Sean nodded.

'Everything is alive, aware and responsive because it has its own spirit. Humans have a truly intensive one. But you have to be spiritually awake on some level to feel and see the energy beyond the material body,' she waved her hand just once, and bright, visible ethereal energy appeared in front of Sean who wildly opened his eyes.

It was a sphere with an approximate breadth of diameter that was surrounding Jessica's body. It was clearly noticeable; it had a different density depending on the location. The aura that was closest to her body was more colourful, shining and consistent. At the last brink of the aura, the colours seemed faded and thin.

'I'll imprint in her soul a few skills to help see beyond the veil without nasty consequences and even to help her control energies on a low level. This is all that I can do for her now,' she said, making a few hands gesture. It looked like the nurse drew a few symbols out of intense blue energies using only her fingers inside Jessica's body sphere. The lines intertwined with each other creating shapes and patterns absorbed by Jessica's whole body. The last one was an image of a flying bird which disappeared at her heart with all seeable colours. It took only a few minutes for the nurse to finish the whole ritual. There was nothing dramatic that might change neither in Jessica's appearance nor in her behaviour. She simply fell into a deep, calm sleep. The nurse snapped her fingers close to Sean's face which caused him to come back from his deep-thinking zone. It took him a while to come back to full consciousness, but the ritual crated even more questions.

'That's it? What will happen to her now?' he asked.

'We wait. She has to a accept it,' the nurse replied.

'What if she doesn't?'

'She'll die today. Don't worry, it'll be peaceful and merciful, like a dream. Okay, I've done enough. It's a long day. I need a cup of tea,' she said calmly, getting up and stretching her whole body. Sean was still thinking, and his face expressed surprise mixed with curiosity.

'Hold on! This is it? But …' he continued, looking more puzzled than before.

'Yes, it's finished. But don't be fooled. It looks simple but is not so easy as it seems.'

'Could you wake her completely with all those skills you have?' he asked.

'No, I can't. Only she can do it if she'll be determined enough to seek her power. And even we shamans don't know where the limits are. Maybe we don't have any? I'm not the wisest one, so I can't give you all the answers,' she replied, putting both chairs near a desk and switching on a small lamp standing there. She took Sean's hand and led him gently out of the room, turning off the main light from the ceiling on the way.

A few minutes after they left Jessica suddenly sat straight, but her eyes were still closed. One of her hands started drawing in the air similar symbols like the nurse did before but hers were imprinted on her skin like red-inked tattoos that disappeared just after she drew their full shape. She not only re-sketched them all but started to draw many new ones, much more complicated and different than the nurse did. Some of them were elementary symbols, other were more complexed and looked like paintings. But the most intensely shining ones were those which were moving like a movie cartoon on her skin all over her body. When she finished, everything returned to normal, and she looked exactly the same as though nothing unusual had happened. During the whole process, the three ethereal figures were standing near Jessica's bed watching her actions. They all disappeared with the last drawing at the same time as she fell asleep.

CHAPTER 7

16th June - The Stairs to Hell

The hot summer night was loud near almost every pub and club in London. The delicate breeze and cloudless sky, dotted with a thousand stars, gave people a good mood. Like every weekend, many humans were searching for attention, emotional thrill and short romances in every possible way around the city. And that was the best time for predators to hunt and prey on those hungry for excitement and the intoxicating feelings of 'being loved' even if it was for only one night. Weekends were the most comfortable time for vampires to feed on blood and soak in all emotions running in people veins alongside with alcohol and drugs. And vampires were always members of every large gathering in public places.

The most popular club for Viviters was 'The Stairs to Hell'. It was created inside one of the biggest abandoned tube stations in the middle of London. The name was taken from the original, vast and round staircase leading to deep levels of the underground. The club had many subsurface floors, corridors and rooms for different purposes. There was a platform with quiet private spaces for sophisticated clients and their shady businesses. There were discotheques and strip clubs separately for men and women on the other floors. The whole construction had a few exits and entrances including lifts that were located around the surrounding area. The remaining old station building had been restored and remodelled with new architecturally fitting extensions. Inside the multilevel aboveground construction there was a quite large pub on the ground level and offices on higher floors that belonged to the company running this business. There was one place separated by a massive wall that belonged to the club. The wall had a wide gate for delivery trucks and the back-door for personnel. It all could be opened by magnetic fobs only.

In front of the main entrance, next to the pub, there was a large square. There were a few benches and tables that were occupied now by very merry people drinking alcohol and smoking not only cigarettes.

Two men were observing the back doorway for employees, sitting at one of the tables that was standing farther from the pub's bright lights. They were barely talking with each other, and they were drinking only tea. Robert was one of them. He seemed upset. He had black pilot glasses put on the top of his head. He was wearing a T-shirt and faded jeans, but his black leather jacket was brand new. The second man was wearing more modern clothes in light colours. He had black, short hair and a charming smile on his smoothly shaved Japanese face.

'Calm down, Robert. You're attracting too much attention,' whispered the Japanese man. He looked at his companion without any visible emotion, barely glancing at him. Robert was clearly agitated. He straightened his injured leg, the one that was stiff in the knee due to accident that happened a long time ago, but the other leg was twitching nervously under the table. Moreover, he was tapping his fingers on the surface making too loud a noise. Although he kept this damaged leg straight, his foot was moving to and fro.

'They're here. I can sense their presence. Don't you patronise me, Lee. I'm not going to calm down because you want me to,' replied Robert, not looking at his companion. He was observing intensely all of those who were coming in and out to the pub or to the club. Lee was silent for a few minutes, glaring at Robert with a smile. He shrugged and finished his tea in one gulp.

'I'd love to kill them all one by one,' said Robert quite angrily.

'No, you won't. You love to hunt them. There is no fun without the prey for you,' Lee emphasised the last words. He started to be irritated by Robert's grumbling.

'I hate the idea about the peace with vamps. Who the fuck agreed to it?' Robert hissed out through clenched teeth.

'Some dopers, vamp lovers, I guess,' said Lee calmly.

'That always puzzled me, how the hell some humans can drink their blood without changing into those leeches?' Robert asked more to himself than to his comrade.

'Some can, some can't. And yet, still people are missing regardless the ban for making new vamps. But we'd be very bored if we couldn't hunt those rogues,' laughed Lee.

'Don't forget about the money you have from it,' a woman's voice came from behind Robert. He turned and smiled but didn't reply. It seemed that Lee saw her before she came nearer but didn't say anything about it to Robert.

'What took you so long?' asked Lee, taking his backpack from one free additional chair that was standing near their table.

'Guild business,' answered the woman sitting on the empty chair. She was a plump, middle-aged attractive lady wearing a modern and exquisite suit. She opened her fashionable, massive, leather handbag and pulled out a black plastic case similar to those used for carrying glasses. She opened it and showed them what was inside. There were two injection pens with a blue liquid inside. The liquid had some sparkling lines if it was shaken too much. Robert smiled seeing it and seemed very happy. He took one of the containers, shook it, turned the dosage scale, opened the needle's lid and jabbed himself into his stiff knee through his jeans. He sighed and sat more relaxed in his chair.

'It's a brand-new line of VS1 serum. Here's instruction on how to use it and forms. Try to fill them all but not that sloppy like you did before or I'll not give you any more …' she didn't finish because Robert interrupted her.

'Okay, I get it. The lab-rat will fill the forms as commanded,' he replied in a quarrelsome way. He took the envelope and the pen case from her hands and hid them inside his leather jacket. Robert looked relaxed and less tense than before but at the same time more alert and focused.

'Did you bring markers?' asked Lee, lowering his voice. She didn't reply but opened her bag again and pulled out two plastic boxes. She opened it showing the contents of them. There were small darts with containers built in the middle of them and full of white liquid. They looked similar to those used to tranquilise animals.

'Only three months left and the open season for vamps hunt will begin again. I'll need more of those darts soon,' said Robert with obvious pleasure written on his face.

'If only Erick, or any other vampire ambassador appointed by him, won't prolong the contract with the Guild before the time runs out, we might have a war in London, that's true. But do you think they'll allow for new chaos?' asked the woman, lowering her voice and leaning into Robert's direction.

'Nothing is for sure. Draco's back and he's appointed as Erick's deputy. But there's Patric, the scum calling himself The Vampire Prince and he so unpredictable,' replied Robert, taking a long cigarette from Lee's pack. Lee passed her the pack and a lighter and went to bar to order more drinks for them. She took one cigarette but hesitated to light it up.

'Erick was their leader ten years ago, and he'd made that peace for all eight vamp's dynasties. Where are they now? Three of them are completely eradicated, and the rest are hiding. Only the Acheron's are left with any power at all. But why has this scumbag not made any contact with you yet? I bet The Guild sent their requests time after time, but he just ignored them completely. Why?' Robert whispered angrily.

'How do you know that?' she asked, shocked.

'I'm a detective. I have my way to know what's going on around. Patric doesn't want a peace. We'll have war, mark my words,' said Robert.

'No, war's a terrible idea. I think you're taking it too personally. You want it, so you could finally have your revenge on him for your wife's death ...' she didn't finish. She glanced at Robert just once and knew she went way too far. She forgot how sensitive Robert was about the day when his wife was murdered by an unknown vampire. There was an obvious deep hatred inside Robert's eyes, but he was usually holding it under control. Now those feelings were barely restrained. Robert's hand was slowly changing into a werewolf's massive paw. She covered it with hers, holding tight but she couldn't stop the shifting. Robert rallied and just stared at her with fury, clenching his fist. She held his gaze with ease and gave him the sign with her head that they just dragged attention from neighbouring tables.

'I'm sorry. I should've shut up ...' she started to apologise.

'Don't! You're right. The best revenge is planned with cold blood,' replied Robert. His hand was still in werewolf-feral shape, but the progress stopped.

Robert looked around, surprised by the prevailing silence. He realised that some people were acting frantically at the moment when their eyes glanced upon his half-transformed hand. Those who were sitting in the nearest location turned their backs and pretended that they didn't see anything strange and supernatural such as a werewolf hand with massive claws lying on the neighbouring table. But one man was behaving more nervously than others. He didn't know what to do with his hands, putting them in many different places, nor how to sit calmly. Although Robert hid both of his hands under the table, the mans' gaze was coming back to Robert, but couldn't hold his focus on him. Suddenly, the man accidentally hit the bottle of beer standing on the glass table and spilled it on the surface. He jumped and, without any words, ran into the building and disappeared in the crowd. Those who were sitting with him were making themselves busy, pretending that they didn't see anything unusual what was happening a few steps away.

It took a quite long time for Robert to calm down completely. Although his both hands were normal again, he kept hiding them under the table. Lee brought a few pints of beer and cigarettes with marijuana. The neighbours disappeared after the werewolf's hand incident, searching inside the pub for their lost companion.

'Any other news?' asked Robert with his eyes directed at the gate.

'Only bad ones,' she replied and shook her head with disapproval.

'So?' asked Lee.

'We've lost three of our informants last week,' she was whispering in such a way that those who were standing near couldn't hear the conversation.

'That's horrible news,' said Robert.

They were talking about The Guild politics till late at night.

It started to get darker. There were more and more emptied glasses standing on their table. Robert lost count of how many beers he had drank. Lee still was sipping the second one and pretending to drink more than it seemed. After a while, they looked like all regular folks spending the evening in a good company. Slowly, the surroundings swarmed with noisy people standing in groups chatting, telling jokes and laughing loudly. So far nobody opened the big gate, and no one drove into the private part of the club premises behind the wall. Only a few workers entered, but they were already known to Robert and Lee.

CHAPTER 8

1st July - The New Life

Gary woke up. It took him a while to recognise where he was. He was lying in his bed in a house where he was renting a room, covered by his own blanket and clasping his big pillow. The curtain on the window was moved away, and sunlight was shining into the room. Gary didn't remember how he got here, what day it was and where he was yesterday. He tried to sit up on the bed, but as he was turning, the pillowcase hooked and pulled something attached to an upper surface of his hand, causing a stabbing pain for him. That made Gary come to his senses instantly. He sat straight and looked at his sore hand. There was a cannula stuck into his vein and fixed with a white plaster to skin. Gary hissed. He was stunned by the view of the medical equipment he had on. That puzzled him and created a lot of 'what's happened' questions in his mind. He looked at his chest, searching for more unusual things on his body, but there was none. He was wearing boxers and an old worn-off T-shirt he didn't remember belonging to him. Slowly the memory of this place came back to him. A few times, he heard his own voice in his head saying the name Gary. He assumed it should be his own or someone significant. The room looked the same as he remembered it should be. He was feeling now all his muscles aching and twitching like he had just finished a very exhausting marathon.

The familiar surroundings made him feel safe and that brought him back to reality. The large desk with two big, flat screens was untidy as he thought he had left it. He could hear the soft noise of devices that were cooling his computer, and he knew it was used recently by someone, despite black screens now. He glanced at the big poster of the Star Wars original trilogy and smiled. At least he could recognise those faces, he thought. There were other posters from many different movies, and there were Gary's pictures he glued to many of them himself. He felt thirsty, so he took a bottle of water standing on the nightstand and drank greedily, but it wasn't enough for him.

At least nothing drastically changed in my room, he thought. The same shelves were full of games, books and figures of characters from sci-fi and fantasy movies. The same closet with a broken locker with half-closed doors showing his essential clothes. And the same single inflatable mattress used by his nomadic half-brother Mark who was treating Gary's room as a part-time shelter. The pictures of his brother unleashed the rest of the concealed memory of who Gary was.

On the mattress there was a thick sleeping bag and a stuffed backpack partially opened and covered by Mark's clothes. Official-looking papers were protruding from the inside of the bag and that caught Gary's attention. It was rare for Mark to have anything important written on paper, as far as Gary remembered him. Mark relied on two smart-phones, a tablet and laptop in almost everything he was doing. Gary couldn't stop wondering how he managed to buy such expensive items and yet living like a gypsy without a permanent address.

Gary stood up and stretched his whole body. Although he tried to move slowly, he felt weak. He fell to his knees on the floor feeling dizzy, so he pulled out the documents from Mark's bag and laid down on the mattress with his eyes closed. He needed a long moment to get to a normal state, but this small incident got him worried. After a few minutes, when he finally could open his eyes and concentrate, he started reading the paperwork he found in brother's bag. The document he was holding in his hands was the discharge from the hospital with Gary's name as a patient. For a moment, his mind froze, paralysed by the vision of being in such an institution. On some deep level, he felt that something had happened there to him, something that changed his life for good, but he couldn't remember what it was.

He turned the pages to the part where the diagnosis was written. The report stated that Gary was utterly paralysed due to a broken neck and severe internal bleeding causing pressure on the brain. Gary didn't understand more than half of those medical terms, but it seemed serious. He didn't believe it was true at all, so he started to wonder why Mark had them here. He assumed that all those documents might be some joke made by his brother as a prank. Moreover, at the end of discharging papers, it was only one sentence describing Gary as someone in an absolutely perfect health condition when he was leaving the hospital.

It couldn't be true, thought Gary, rereading it. No one with those severe injuries could recover so quickly to the point where there was no sign of any accident at all. Gary thought, maybe it was written for the next gig during the next company's event, as a part of a mystery to unravel. The papers looked very convincing, but only medics could really distinguish fake and real one, thought Gary, trying to logically rationalise what he was reading. Moreover, thinking about gigs gave him some flashbacks about running in the woods at night time triggering anxiety and fear in Gary. Suddenly in his mind, he saw a werewolf standing near him and those pictures causing pulsating pain. He tried to ignore it, but the images were flowing without a break.

He saw himself running through the forest, wearing a military outfit, holding a rifle and had the thrilling feeling that someone was following him. That pictures brought back all his lost memories, but he still couldn't figure out why he had the impression about a werewolf being part of it. He couldn't recognise if what he saw in his mind really had happened or if it was only some kind of weird fantasy he was dreaming about before he woke up. His stream of thoughts was interrupted by Simon's sharp and loud laugh coming from downstairs. Gary got up slowly and walked towards the door, holding onto pieces of furniture to keep his balance but still with the documents in one of his hands.

*

It was a bright sunny Saturday morning. The kitchen was usually empty this time, but today was occupied by everyone who was living in this house including Mark. Simon, half-naked, wearing only trousers, was singing out loud one of his favourite songs and it was very out of tune.

The kitchen was reasonably spacious, with a wide window showing an average size, well-kept garden. Usually tidy and quiet, the place was experiencing a cooking and baking event that could feed a squad of the scouts. Today both Simon and Mark were chefs making the biggest mess there had ever been here. Food ingredients were placed all around the kitchen, some even were lying on the floor in bags or plastic boxes. A few large and small bowls, full of half-processed food, were standing on every possible flat surface that could hold any containers with half-prepared dishes. The loud rock music was in the air from one of the most famous London radio stations of the kind.

Simon was frying thick steaks and there was a large round plate full of already-made meat. One of them had a fork stick in the middle and was half-eaten. Gary stood for a minute in a doorway completely taken-aback. Simon, the most rational and sensible person living here, the one who was sometimes too serious to laugh from jokes but never from mistakes, the one whose pictures had to be taken from the perfect angle, was singing and giggling like a little boy. He couldn't stop staring at Simon's chest. Gary was wondering since when did Simon get so well-built and muscly. Simon was somewhat reluctant to gyms, as far as Gary knew him for the last three years living together as house-mates. Gary had heard many times his complains about possible bacteria and viruses that could be left by users on standard equipment in every public gym. But now, Simon looked like he was literally an Olympic athlete. He seemed even a bit taller, definitely had broader corpus and behaved more spirited. Something changed, Gary couldn't name what it was exactly, but it was written all over Simon's personality.

*

Gary stared for a while at Mark and Jessica who were busy decorating a huge chocolate cake with little sugar fairies and sticking them randomly into pile of strawberries on the top. The cake was standing on the long kitchen counter among boxed ingredients and a few unwashed baking trays. Mark was smiling widely. He was wearing a cooking apron with his name printed on it and stained with chocolate and butter. They both were closer to each other than usual and that puzzled Gary. Jessica was talking about something but loud rock music prevented them from hearing what she was saying. Surprisingly for Gary, she was wearing a light summer dress, not her usual jeans. Her bushy, curly, red hair was unbanned but had a few hair-grips matching the colour of her cloth. Gary frowned at seeing them working together. Gary didn't want to interrupt them by revealing his presence in the kitchen, but he still felt a bit weak as he moved slowly towards the nearest chairs that were standing around the large square table. He tripped over his foot and fell onto Simon's back to catch his own balance.

Simon jumped and shouted, utterly surprised by the sudden unexpected touch. The steak he was turning over on the pan with a long fork had flown high and landed on the cake on a pile of strawberries, messing them and destroying the sugar fairy's composition. Simon caught the falling Gary, but the impact made by his friend's body pushed him back on the cooker. He hooked the pan handle by his arm and threw it in the air. The pan landed on his shoulder covering Simon with hot oil and the rest of the frying meat. He yelled in pain but it was more of a deep growl than a human sound. Jessica and Mark had turned, hearing the noise behind. Gary bounced off Simon and fell on the floor. Simon's face started to develop a werewolf shape. Gary was staring at his friend who was partially shapeshifting into a werewolf, but he wasn't scared. His mind started to analyse the situation with a cold and calculated logic including the nearest location of long kitchen knives. Despite still feeling uneasy, he slipped out as far as he could from Simon and got up on his feet. But he stood up way too fast for his condition so he wobbled. Jessica helped him to sit on the chair and then she hugged him tightly like she never did before. But Gary was busy watching Mark who was holding Simon's arms, giving him commands about controlling the transformation. After a minute of struggles with his body, Simon finally calmed down. Gary was watching it with amazement, not only what was happening but the speed of regeneration from oil burns.

'Are you a werewolf?' asked Gary excitingly.

'How do you feel, bro?' asked Mark, rolling his eyes and sitting next to Gary on a chair before Simon could say anything. Mark put his hands on Gary's chin, lifted it up, raised the eyelid and was staring into his eyes like a doctor. Gary leaned back and put the folded hospital documents into Mark's hand. Mark only took it and without looking at it hid them inside his jeans pocket. He started asking, with concern, about common facts from Gary's life.

'It's not a joke. You had a serious accident. Tell me, do you know who we are? Who are you? And what's the address of this place?' Mark kept asking. Gary replied, telling all the well-known information, not only about himself, and the answers pleased his half-brother. Mark patted Gary's back and asked more inquisitive questions about Gary's health this time. It sounded more like a medical interview in a hospital than a friendly discussion by a family member. Gary gave only brief answers that he was fine, mainly because he felt a bit embarrassed by the number of intrusive issues, including Gary's virility that Mark was asking in front of his friends. Simon was the one who saved the moment by serving freshly fried steaks. He stabbed one and passed it to Gary, silently saying that he indeed was a werewolf.

'Welcome on the other side of the veil,' said Mark, indicating that it was time to have the conversation.

Simon sat on a free chair next to Gary with a plate full of steaks on his knees. He jabbed with a knife the thickest one, and with an encouraging gesture, pointed in Gary's direction. Gary looked surprised, mainly because he didn't remember Simon eating any steaks at all nor such an excessive amount of meat. Mark took the steak in his bare hands, the one that Simon had proposed to Gary seconds ago. Simon looked indignant about it. He muttered something vaguely and hid the plate under his hands. The smell and sight of food increased Gary's hunger, so he followed Mark and helped himself to some meat by hand. Simon didn't oppose this time. Gary couldn't stop watching his friend, who was now biting his next substantial chunk of the meat. Simon glanced at Mark, searching for any sign of him wanting to steal one more chop, nodding and giving the impression he wouldn't tolerate that kind of behaviour any more. Mark smiled and made some stupid face gestures with his half-eaten steak as a prop.

'I was bitten, and my hand should be disabled, but apparently werewolves have great regeneration. Look at my scars,' declared Simon, showing his hands and all the long cuts made by a wolf's fangs. Even though Simon's hand was fully regenerated, including his heavy shattered bones, somehow the first wounds made by a werewolf on his body had left wide marks. Simon was the first to tell his side of the story of what had happened to him in the woods during the Airsoft competition. Mark mentioned the changing ritual and Simon's adoption to the werewolf's pack, but it was only brief information.

'Oh, man. I'm a werewolf. I can't transform myself alone yet, I'm a newbie. But I'm in training so one day I'll show you how big a bad-ass I am now,' said Simon, excited like a child with a new toy.

Gary was listening, awed by the tale of how Simon was bitten, how painful the transition was, how little he remembered and how he felt fantastic when he woke up the next morning. Gary still hardly believed in this story, but he couldn't deny the fact that he saw the partial shape-shifting process that had happened to Simon a few minutes ago.

'What happened to you, Jessica? I know something terrible was going on with you there,' asked Gary, gazing at her with an expectation.

'I don't remember anything after the werewolf appeared in the shed. Sean told me that some neo-shaman had taken care of my wretched mind. The only new thing is, I can see the ferals without totally freaking out,' she declared, shrugging and shaking her head.

'So, Sean is involved as well?' Gary dropped the question.

'Indeed, he is, and I am, and Peter, and a few other members of the family,' declared Mark, who was listening in silence to the last conversation. Gary couldn't look more astonished. Not only were his friends were dragged in this insanely new reality, but his half-brothers and some others Gary knew for his entire life were already there. Gary had no idea how to react to that news. Inside Gary's mind there was a parade of cousins, grandparents, aunts, uncles, other distant relatives and even some people he knew. He was trying to guess who was and who wasn't living on the other side of supernatural veil, but he didn't have any clue how to distinguish one from another. They all looked like average and very normal human beings. The thoughts made him feel uneasy, and it started to build up stress that was too much to handle at one time. The slight glimpse of panic was crawling under his skin giving him goosebumps.

It took some time for Gary to adapt to the news that there was a world behind the invisible, spiritual veil and werewolves were as usual as green trees behind the window that Gary could see now. Mark said they had fully functional society they called themselves Viviters.

'What are you?' asked Gary staring at Mark's calm and impassive face.

'I'm lynx, as most of our family from my father's side. It's time to tell you the truth about your roots,' declare Mark, without any emotions like he was talking about fast changing weather in London. Mark wanted this conversation to be over as soon as possible. Mark thought that adapting fast to the new world was inevitable for everyone who crossed the mystic line, but for Gary, it would always be more difficult than for his friends. The fact that most of his own family was already living behind the veil, including his deceased parents, made Gary even more an outsider than he ever was. Mark was ready to see some kind of tantrum with screaming and shouting, but Gary's rather mild reaction was something unexpected. He started to think that maybe the vampire blood affected Gary on a much deeper level. What if, Mark wondered, the healing Gary's body not only initiated the modification that might lead to unforeseen occurrences, but it triggered brand new behaviour in him that was beyond anyone's recognition. Mark couldn't find any records in a library about other cases when the passive genes were re-moulded unnaturally by something from the outside and transformed the whole human flesh into something new. Gary's insisting questions brought him back to reality.

'Why did I never know about it?' asked Gary with demanding tone.

'Because when you were a child, you'd never shown any sign that you're one of us. After our mother died in the accident, you were given to Hectorian grandparents. The Hectorian's are all those normal people who can see shape-shifters or ferals without freaking out completely. It's only some small percentage in the whole human population that have this ability. They could still keep an eye on you and inform us if something would change in your behaviour. Legally, you were not allowed to live with us. There was a huge possibility you'd see someone shifting and your brain would change into mash. That's the law. I'll show you something,' Mark finished explaining, stood up straight, reached out his hand and started the changing. He knew the days of hiding it from Gary were over. He also knew Gary needed to adapt very quickly to the world he had to live in from now on.

Mark's hand lengthened, at least twenty centimetres, from the elbow up. All muscles increased and were more visible. On his tight skin a half-long grey-white-red fur had grown up very fast. His hand had evolved into a massive cat's paws and ended with long and sharp claws. He hid the claws a few times inside his body, and extended them again, exactly like all cats could do at ease. Everyone was staring at him with open mouths. Mark controlled the change without any effort like it was as easy as combing his hair. He laid his paw on Gary's shoulder. When he saw that Gary didn't withdraw his head, but stayed put without any sign of a fear, Mark gently brushed his cheek with his sharp claws. It was such a subtle movement that not even one mark was left on Gary's skin. Gary slowly put his hand on Mark's furry forearm, he stroked it as if it was a small cat. Mark was speechless. Not even one blink from Gary, he thought. Not even a slight sign of fear in his eyes, Mark thought with astonishment. He was staring straight into brother's eyes looking for a glimpse of restrained panic. But all that he saw was nothing more than childish curiosity.

'Who was our mum then, my dad, yours?' asked Gary, putting strong stress on every family member he mentioned. Gary thought how the strange and unknown the story of his youth and the people who he loved the most was now emerging and looking more like a twisted cheap horror movie. Maybe he suppressed in his mind the evidence about the truth about them. Maybe he always knew there was something different about his parents, but he didn't want to acknowledge it. His thoughts were wandering through many events he remembered. He was trying to find any signs about the other world in his ordinary life he had had together with them many years ago. Unfortunately, he didn't find anything unusual or mysterious inside his memory lane. It was even harder to accept that his parents weren't as he recalled them.

Mark didn't seem confused. He made a quick glance around but held his gaze on Jessica's face and smiled gently. He took a deep breath and started the hidden story of their family.

'Our mum, Helen, was Hectorian. You see, ferals need humans to have children. We can have them between us, but there is a risk they'd be unpredictable, wild and more animal-like with their behaviour. They'd have problems in adapting to the modern world.

So, for our own sake, we're bound to have human partners. Mine and Peter's father was a lynx. He was Helen's first husband who was killed by vampires. And then she met your dad. He wasn't a feral, nor Hectorian. He was a witch hunter, a special human from an ancient family with genetically rare skills and abilities specific only for them …'

'Wait a minute! Are you telling me that there are witches in this world?' exclaimed Gary anxiously. Simon and Jessica followed, asking too many questions all at once.

'Stop guys! I'm not going to explain everything right now. I don't have time for it, but one day you'll know everything that you need. So, let me finish first with the most important,' declared Mark, looking at his brother with expectations. Gary only nodded and gave a sign to continue.

'So, your father was a witch hunter, Gary. Sad to say but not everyone in his family inherits all those rare talents, which he had. And unfortunately, you didn't get any of them. You still have passive genes so your next generations could inherit them, but I'm afraid, it's not you, Gary. Personally, I think it's the best what had had happened to you. They tend not to live a long and happy life. Anyway, your father tested you, and he discovered that you are a normal human. Helen was quite happy with this news…'

'Are you trying to say there are species other than ferals!?' asked Gary, opening his mouth with astonishment.

'Yes, a lot more than you can imagine. There are many ferals, like I am. We have only two forms: humans and battle-form sometimes called ferox. The feral, or ferox, is a human-like shape but mixed with a specific animal. We don't change into a full animal. We just have a vast part of their abilities and skills. But behind the veil there are shamans, mages, witches, ghosts, spirits, demons, witch-hunters, vampires, you name it, they are there. You'll learn about them but one step at the time, guys,' said Mark, changing his hand into normal human shape.

They all started to ask him questions at once, and it sounded like a cacophony of a frenzied crowd. Mark covered his ears, pretending to not to hear anything.

'What really happened to me in woods? Don't lie. I saw the

hospital's documents. I should have been seriously crippled or even dead by now. But here I am in perfect health. A bit tired, weak and hungry but still, I can walk,' Gary enquired insistently about the past. Everyone was gazing at Mark, and he knew there was no option to skip that question.

'Okay. Let me explain this to all of you,' said Mark but it was obvious that he prolonged the answers.

'Yes, you're right, Gary. You should've been paralysed from the neck down. The feral in its battle form is very strong, especially werewolves. Robert, the werewolf who's bitten Simon, hit you hard. You landed on the wall and that broke your spine. You had a hematoma in your head and the probability that you'd die in a matter of weeks was extremely high. I didn't know what to do so I let one ancient vampire inject his blood into you. That healed you completely in a couple of hours,' said Mark with a low voice.

'What!?' shouted Gary

'Is he turning into a vampire?' asked Jessica anxiously.

'Vampires are on a loose?' shouted Simon with a high-pitched voice looking behind his back, like he was expecting some of them to just jump and suck blood from everyone here this instant.

'Am I vampire now?' shouted Gary, even louder than before.

'Don't be absurd. His blood only healed you. It's not that easy to make a new vampire. It needs some kind of ritual but I've no idea about the process. And there's the law written up by the Guild regulating how many vamps can live in a town and who can create them…' Mark didn't finish due to a new explosion of questions about what they just heard. They didn't seem frightened at all. Mark could understand Simon and Jessica, they were infected by the vital energy from behind the veil, but not Gary.

'It's getting even more interesting,' said Gary smiling.

'Guys, it's a long story. I'm not going to explain everything at once. Be patient…' Mark's answer was interrupted by the loud ringing phone. He answered, walking out from the kitchen.

Simon left the place in fast pace, running to his room upstairs when he realised he should have called Robert. Jessica and Gary started cleaning up the mess in the kitchen. Gary was cleaning up the dishes when Mark came back.

'Gary, listen, I hope you don't mind having vampire's blood, do you?' he said, entering the kitchen. Mark was wearing his usual straight, blue, worn-off jeans, tight, red T-shirt and small men's bag that was hanging over his shoulder.

'Are you kidding me? This is the best that could ever happen to me so far. By the way, what about cameras? Do they record all those supernaturals if they aren't in human shape?' Gary grinned, and looked more excited than upset.

'Yes, every camera can record ferals and others but there's a catch. You have to draw a special symbol on it to see their forms. Otherwise, they will look like blurred shapes, or there'll be some glitches. And there's a time limit. It's connected to the moon. If you don't put the mark on till the last day of full moon, you won't get the pictures…' Mark couldn't finish.

'What?! Do you mean, my recordings from the event can show the ferals?' exclaimed Gary.

'Yes and no…' Mark hesitated with the answer. This time he didn't finish deliberately.

'It's like living in a movie, or in a game,' shouted Gary excitedly. He laughed and hugged his brother. Mark looked utterly surprised. He tried to pat Gary's back, but it came out quite artificially and weird, mainly because Gary was in a hurry. Gary ran out of the kitchen, as fast as he could, to his room upstairs still wearing cleaning gloves.

Mark waited to be sure that Gary shut the door behind with a loud bang, and then he turned and came closer to Jessica. She was busy setting up the dishwasher so she didn't see him. Mark could approach almost everyone as silently as every cat could, even wearing boots. When she finished, she turned around and jumped from surprise, losing her balance because Mark was standing just right behind her. He caught her, wrapped his arms around her waist and hugged her tightly. She was so startled that all she could do was stammer something unintelligible.

'So, now you know who I am. I'm not going to pretend any longer that there's nothing between us. I've a crush on you,' whispered Mark, straight into Jessica's ear but it sounded like a cat's purr. First, she didn't move due to feeling parallelised by his overwhelming closeness. His tall and muscular body, pressed against her, made her shiver from unrecognisable emotions that were running through her.

He leaned his head and gently touched her cheek with his lips. But she pulled back her head, regaining confidence.

'What? You're so nagging and sometimes unbearable to me. How it's even possible?' she asked, frowning and putting stress on the negative features of his behaviour.

'Before the accident, it was really hard for me to be around you and constantly hiding my true nature…' he didn't finish. He was searching for the right word, but he got stuck and didn't continue. Instead, he hugged her a bit more and started stroking her back. Jessica shook off the pleasure of his nearness, trying to push him away.

'Mark, I like you, but I'm afraid I'm not on the same page with my feelings,' she whispered back. She turned her head in such a way that it exposed her neck. He kissed her gently just under her ear. It gave her a ravishing thrill which ran throughout her entire body like waves of heat. She pushed him a bit more but couldn't hide the blushing on her face. He wasn't confused and still held her but made more space between them.

'Oh, yes, you do. You're just afraid because I'm Gary's brother, so you don't want a mess between me and him, do you?' he asked, staring at her and grinning widely.

'Look, it's very complicated,' she stuttered, lowering her head and covering her face under long, curly, red hair.

'But of course, it is. You don't want to lose Gary as a friend, and you can't get rid of me because you have feelings for me. I'm more intuitive than you can imagine with my cat's senses. Don't worry. I'm not going to bother you again. Oh, well. It was worth trying,' he said, still smiling. They stood for a while, only just staring at each. The air around them was overflowing with an unspoken erotic tension.

'Hey! Mark! I need your help,' shouted Gary, standing halfway up the stairs and holding a small camera. Mark and Jessica jumped quickly away from each other, pretending that nothing had happened between them ten seconds ago. She turned and started to wipe again the already cleaned kitchen counter. Mark rotated toward the corridor, hoping that Gary wouldn't see the gentle blush on his face and sparkling eyes he couldn't hide.

Jessica was alone in the kitchen, still blushing, making herself busy with cleaning in places she didn't touch for a long time. She still could feel his hands on her body and the exciting thrill connected to his warm breath. Her mind was busy imagining with vivid details what could have happened between them if Gary wouldn't interrupt. *Well, I could kiss him*, that idea struck her mind, but she scolded herself for it. Regardless, her daydream came back stronger than before, with a chain of pictures that created powerful arousing emotions. But the fantasy was interrupted by tattoos appearing unexpectedly on her arms. The tattoos were moving like cartoons showing animals changing into humans and humans changing to unnamed shapes and figures. Everything was drowned in the palette of colours, and after a minute they all disappeared as suddenly as it revealed itself. But Jessica didn't see the end of this. She fainted in the middle of the show just after she realised that she had moving tattoos on her whole body.

CHAPTER 9

2nd July - The Blood Connection

Mark opened the door to Gary's room without knocking. He sneaked into the house so silently that nobody could hear any sound. Gary didn't notice him and didn't realise the fact that he wasn't alone any more. It was just after midnight and the room was pretty dark. There was a flashing light from two computer screens that were standing on his large desk. A fresh breeze of humid air was entering the room through the curtain, lifting it up and making some unnatural forms from it. It created creepy scenery suggesting that someone was standing behind it.

Gary was sitting at the desk with his headset on, listening to his favourite metal band, and waiting to be connected to the online battleground in one of the most popular Internet games. There were various types of cameras lying on the top of drawers and shelves near him. They were rather small, more like amateur cameras, but still could shoot quite good images, so they did the work well in documenting the whole paintball competition. Gary was very pleased about the shots made by Jessica's drone. Even her obsessive care about the equipment, yelling at him and not letting Gary fly the thing for longer than five minutes, was now worth the effort.

All night long Gary had watched the recorded material; cutting it, processing and making four different movies for three different groups of participants and for the company who organised the whole tournament. It all would be finished in a few weeks, but he had catalogued it to make his work easier. He had saved all of those original pictures on his PC and now was waiting for his brother and feeling excited about the possibility of seeing some supernaturals that might be recorded alongside the Airsoft event. He needed Mark to draw Theo's symbol on memory cards form the cameras as he promised. Gary wondered how it was possible that one small emblem would make visible all ferals or even other supernaturals on all recordings but that was the world he was living in. Gary was hoping to discover the thing that scared him away on the path to camp. Somehow, he had a hunch that something was wandering around the woods and he really wanted to know and see what it was. Gary thought that it wasn't only Robert present there but something else. He wondered how many of those competition's partakers weren't regular humans, assuming there were any. He was impatient and couldn't wait so the only way he could pass the time was by being occupied in a fast-paced game.

Mark put his hand on Gary's shoulder, making him jump and shout out in surprise. Mark laughed silently, showing the sign of being quiet. He sat on an additional chair next to Gary, opened a picture of the sign that he had on his phone and drew it with a pencil on every memory card Gary had collected from the cameras on the desk. Nothing spectacular had happen so the brothers just stared at each other.

'How long should we wait?' asked Gary.

'No idea. I've never done it before. Shall we try?' asked Mark and he put the first card into the slot in the PC. Gary downloaded the recordings to a new catalogue and started watching the first one on fast forward.

'What's wrong between you and Jessica?' asked Gary, not looking at Mark and after a few minutes of sitting in silence. The question was dropped with a tone of voice pretending to be casual, but Mark could hear the slight of nervousness somewhere deep inside the sentence.

'Nothing. I found out that she doesn't like me, imagine that. Why do you ask? Did she say something?' Mark asked with obvious awkwardness, trying to hide unwanted emotions that were growing inside him.

'Oh, yes. She doesn't like you. That's the fact …' Gary stopped his sentence, pausing the recording, reversed and started watching on normal speed.

And there he was, inside the forest, straight in front of the camera, the werewolf in his full feral-battle form, sniffing around some bushes. It was Robert, the same werewolf who ended up in the shed making mayhem in Gary's and his friends' lives.

Gary never before felt so happy seeing the raw recorded material. His mind went wild. He knew that after finishing the usual custom-made movies from the event he was doing for money's sake, he would definitely spend time watching thoroughly the recordings and searching for supernatural beings among normal humans. The pictures were good enough, and he could use them if only he could have some short story to match. Gary was so absorbed in the pictures that the issues with Jessica and the questions he wanted to ask his brother vanished from his mind. He grabbed Mark's hand and squeezed, smiling like a little boy who just got a brand-new toy. He was cheering, making his waves of happiness by hands that everyone in this house were familiar with. He did it with maximum silence, but in his head he screamed out of delight. For the first time since he moved to London, he started to feel the wind of luck in the sails. The thought appeared in this mind that the accident might just turn in to Gary's long-life career advantage. Mark helped him to download the material from those cameras, and when they finished he rubbed out the mark from all memory cards.

'You can't keep the sign?' asked Gary, taking a picture of the sign with his phone as well as drawing it on pieces of paper and hiding it inside a very stuffed drawer in his desk. The sign was a glyph, the draw of crossing few lines similar to claws marks scratched by animal rather than any known written alphabet.

'You can keep it only for three days or it'll destroy the device. It has something to do with a high frequency of ethereal energy but it's all that I know off,' answered Mark.

They were busy watching the recordings together until the early morning lights of the rising sun shone through the window. Gary was enchanted by the new reality that was waiting for him to be discovered. He was asking a lot of question about Mark's life as a lynx and especially about their family. Mark had never felt so close to his younger brother than this night. They had sat in this room together many times, but today he finally didn't have to pretend to be someone other than who he really was. Moreover, the truth was finally told and there was no reason to hide anything from Gary anymore. Mark knew he couldn't tell everything at once, but this was his deepest and the most desirable dream that came true.

Gary went to bed when he heard Simon and Jessica waking up and starting their normal daily routine. After all, regardless what had had happened to all of them, they still kept their lives going as normal as it might seem. It would never be the same but at least they pretended that nothing had changed for all of those regular folks who they had known but were living without any acknowledgement of supernatural beings walking on the streets.

Simon was fast, rushing through the house in fifteen minutes to catch the tube and be on time for work at New Scotland Yard. Jessica was ready in forty minutes, and for many of her friends, it might be considered as quite slow compared to her abilities to rush. She felt surprisingly well after yesterday's incident in the kitchen when the mysterious tattoos were coming into view and freaking her out to the point when she fainted. Although she was a freelance engineer working with many companies and her knowledge was based on solid facts and scientific measurements, somehow the new world didn't collide with her beliefs as much as she might have expected.

*

When the house was quiet again, Gary fell asleep, feeling exhausted but very pleased. But after a few hours, he was suddenly awake due to Mark tugging his arm and saying something hastily. Gary barely opened his eyes, hoping that his brother would stop and let him go back to sleep, but he had a problem with breathing through his nose. He had blocked nostrils by scabs of dried blood. He could feel the taste of it deep in his throat with a bit of unusual bitterness that made Gary feel sick. That woke him up instantly. He sat on the bed, putting a hand around his mouth. Now he could recognise what Mark was saying.

'Hey, Gary, something dark is oozing from your nose. How do you feel?' asked Mark nervously. He put his hands on Gary's shoulders and sat next to him on the bed. At the beginning Gary didn't feel anything, but when he tried to stand up, he collapsed back on the bed with a severe headache. It was so painful that he cried for a few minutes, holding his head. Mark took his phone and was searching for Sean's number when Sean called at the same moment.

'I was just trying to call you. Something is happening to Gary. What shall I do?' yelled Mark, hustling Sean with questions.

'Listen! Calm down!' replied Sean with a demanding tone.

'No, I'm not going to. Gary is not okay, and I have to do something now!' shouted Mark, clearly irritated.

'Does his nose seep out dark mucus?' cried Sean, so loud that Gary could hear.

'How do you know?' asked Mark, so taken aback that he asked the question in a much lower tone, looking more stunned than angry.

'Because it's happening to Draco right now. I'm in the museum dragging his half-conscious body out of view. They're both connected. I have a nasty feeling about it. Stay put. I'm on my way to you,' he exclaimed and cut off the conversation.

Mark started feeling anxious. He had decided to let Draco inject his blood into Gary's body. He had known that the consequences of it might be far worse than he could ever imagine, and he didn't have to wait long for first symptoms to occur. Mark justified to himself that he didn't have any other option, but now, when he was thinking about all that had happened back in the hospital, he felt guilty because he had never checked if there were any other solutions.

'I'm fine now,' said Gary at ease, staring at Mark who was walking to and fro in the bedroom. Gary got up without any problems or more bleeding. He took new clothes from the wardrobe and went to the bathroom, ignoring Mark's insisting to stay in bed.

*

'What took you so long?' Mark was asking nervously while opening the front door to let Sean and Draco in. Draco looked rather well, but he had stains on his clothes, marking places where a dark ooze was dripping. He was wearing his usual jeans and a plain T-shirt. His face was paler than normal, but he walked by himself. Sean, on the other hand, looked agitated. His long hair was tousled, and his beard had lost its silver rings. He was wearing a light shirt, polka-dotted red tie and well-tailored suit. But his normal neat clothing was now creased and soiled. Gary was standing just right behind Mark, feeling a bit weird and unnatural seeing one of his beloved uncles for the first time not as regular human. Sean entered and hugged Gary tightly.

'How are you, Gary?' he asked, patting Gary's back. Sean took off his jacket and rolled up his shirt's sleeves, showing colourful tattoos on both of his arms. Gary never paid too much attention to those pictures, but today, he looked at them from a very different perspective.

'Gary, this is Draco. I hope Mark told you a bit about the accident,' Sean directed the last sentence towards Mark, and it sounded more like a question than a statement. Mark nodded in agreement. He opened his mouth trying to say something, but Sean didn't let him.

'Okay, so you know he's a vampire. Unfortunately, it seems you're both connected by his blood that healed you,' said Sean pointing out into Draco's direction. This time only Gary nodded.

Draco looked pale, but his behaviour didn't show that he might be feeling unwell. Gary couldn't stop staring at him and felt a weird tingling sensation inside his guts, like he sensed a subtle threat with unknown power. Waves of shivering and goosebumps were going through his body making Gary feel tense. Somehow, he felt like he knew Draco for a very long time, like he had just met a long-forgotten friend from childhood. The tiny voice in Gary's head whispered two different commands. One of them created the vision of dangerous bloodshed and the feeling of wanting to run away as fast as he could. The second, on the contrary, was extremely pleasant, making him feel like he was in a warm home of his own with a cosy fireplace in the living-room. At first, Gary was overwhelmed and didn't know what to do or what to say. He couldn't believe he was facing a real vampire and not some fake movie character from a cosplay party. Gary always imagined that vamps were more like the monsters from horrors based on Bram Stoker novel, cold-hearted killers of humankind for the sake of sucking blood so vital for their existence. But Draco looked more like some friend of Mark who he met in a pub, maybe a bit weird, but still a human-like chap. At the end of Gary's battle of thoughts, his usual curiosity took over, so he sat on a couch in the living-room eager to, at least, listen to what they had to say.

'Gary, you're connected with Draco and because of your father's passive genes, the blood affects you differently than others I know of. The worst thing is, nobody knows how it works on you. But whatever would happen to Draco, will affect you as well. So, to the point, if Draco dies your hours are counted,' declared Sean calmly, like someone who had to face a hard and unwanted conversation that he lost already. Mark tried to say something, but Sean gave the sign that he hadn't finished yet.

'And now we have a problem because Draco will certainly die, give or take, in a month…' Sean held the sentence, watching their reactions. Mark looked at Gary, shocked. He couldn't articulate what was going through his mind. Gary didn't react at this news. He was frozen in a panic.

'But there is something we can do to stop it,' Sean continued, causing Mark and Gary's faces to light up with hope.

'Well, well, well,' a jeering voice surprised everyone in the living-room. They turned around and saw Robert standing in the doorway with Simon, who was right behind him. Robert was leaning on his black cane, limping with every step. He was wearing his usual worn-of jeans, plain T-shirt, black leather jacket and heavy boots. He sat in an armchair, looking very pleased. He stretched out his crippled leg and started gently massaging his injured knee. His face expressed the confidence of a person who had just caught someone in some mischievous action or found out what the long-hidden secrets were all about.

'What's going on here?' asked Simon, leaning against the door frame.

'What are you doing here? Shouldn't you be at work now?' asked Sean, but his eyes were fixed on Robert.

'It just happens that I live here and I'm working right now. It appears, after the accident, my department has been changed in a matter of hours. Now, I'll have to 'make a coffee' for him,' said Simon sarcastically, nodding into Robert's direction, making an inverted comma hand sign and emphasising the 'making a coffee' phrase with a fake theatrical smile. Gary looked at him astonished. For the first time since they both started living under one roof, Gary heard Simon saying something with such a rough voice.

'And you suck at it. How does it make you feel with all your superior computer knowledge? How many hours of Internet research do you need to find out how to make 'good coffee'?' asked Robert, mimicking Simon and mocking his tone. He also did a similar fake smile, stressed 'good coffee' and showed it in inverted comma hand sign. Mark laughed but others stayed calm and rather concerned.

'It'll be fun watching you lot working together. How does it feel, Robert, having an adopted son? Aren't you the 'lonely wolf'? How is your 'babysitting' going so far?' asked Sean, imitating Robert, taunting him, making the sign and accentuating the sentence with a funny face. An expression of anger appeared on Robert's face, but he swallowed it without a blink and didn't reply. Gary quickly realised that the quarrel could break out any time so he felt like he needed to prevent it from exaggerating to the point where they both would do or say something very nasty. He was surprised how all those grown-up men reacted at each other's presence like some suppressed tension couldn't be held under control any longer. Gary guessed that the bitterness was rather on Robert's side that on Sean or Simon. Sean said directly to Simon the warning that the issue of rejecting his adoption by Robert didn't disappear and it might come back in a strange way. Robert put his head down, hearing this comment.

'Okay, enough!' shouted Gary. His loud tone made them all turn to him and stare. Gary didn't see this scene as funny at all, as it seemed for Mark and Sean. He looked annoyed rather than amused.

'Who are you exactly?' Gary stood up and asked Robert, pointing at him, looking straight in a defiant manner. Sean hid his smile under his long hair and just made a hand gesture, giving Robert permission to speak for himself. Robert hesitated for a moment.

'May I introduce myself? My name is Robert Leclaire. I'm a werewolf,' he said it calmly.

'And? Is there anything you would like to add?' asked Sean. Robert didn't answer. There was a silence full of unkindness around the room. Gary was staring at Robert, expecting something more than those few words, but nothing more was said by him.

'Gary, let me represent you. Robert is the werewolf who caused an accident that had broken your neck,' declared Sean, very officially. It sounded like an induction to a court case than an accidental meeting in a small house somewhere in London in this sunny afternoon.

'Oh, so you are the guy who owes me life then?' asked Gary,

indicating in Robert's direction and frowning.

'Well, you looked surprisingly good for someone so badly smashed. Draco helped you with a very good vintage of vampire's blood, I reckon. How close are you to becoming one of them?' Robert regained his confidence. He smiled broadly as he gazed at all of them with a pinch of contempt in his look.

'Robert, you know very well you need the ritual to create a vampire. A drop of blood won't change Gary,' said Draco for the first time since he came to this house. Although his voice was quiet, it had something deeply penetrating into everyone's mind. Gary shivered. Some uneasy feelings were crawling under Gary's skin, like a slow, wavy movement of a snake, and his low and mesmerizingly poisonous hissing was piercing through souls.

'Okay, Robert, you are kind of not welcome here. Whatever you have to do with Simon, please go to his room and make yourself busy, however weird it might sound. We have essential things to discuss, so please leave,' said Sean angrily, showing him the door. Robert didn't react at first and looked rather busy with his thoughts.

'No, I'd heard what you said about Gary's life being at stake, and he mentioned clear that I owe him a life. I don't want to have any unfinished business for my mistakes any more. So, I'm in, whatever you'll do, for good or bad. So … what's the plan?' asked Robert very seriously. Although he was sitting, he looked at them with superiority, observing everyone's reaction with a faint sneer.

There was a silence so deep that it seemed like nobody was there. Gary glared at them from one face to the other thinking what would happen next. His life was going in a very complicated direction, whether he liked it or not. He felt like a leaf in the wind, pushed by unknown forces to places and situations way beyond his comfort zone. At that moment, he knew he would do absolutely everything to get out of this mess however difficult it might seem. He was sure that between Robert and rest of those here, there would always be some arguments and they would never be friends. The dislike was obvious like the hatred he could see in Robert's eyes when he glared at Draco. How vivid this twist of fate, or bad karma, was unfolding right at this moment, thought Gary. But he couldn't stop smiling to himself. He always wished to have a colourful life full of adventures, like in action movies or games. But he never thought it would emerge so fast and in such an unexpected way, with new people entering into his life making an impact like an avalanche.

'We need to talk,' said Sean, nodding to Draco and Mark. They left and walked to the kitchen, closing door behind.

Gary felt a bit awkward being left alone, so he started asking Simon questions about his adoption as a werewolf and people in his pack just to kill some time and to avoid an embarrassing silence in the room. He didn't pay too much attention to Simon's stories because he wanted to go to the kitchen and listen to Sean, Draco and Mark talk about the crucial decision about Gary's future. That thought made him a bit angry. He wasn't a child, and he wanted to know what was going on. He jumped and ran to the kitchen without any explanation. When he was in the corridor, the entrance door opened, and Jessica walked in.

In the same moment, Gary met them leaving the kitchen, so he followed back to the living-room without asking questions. Jessica peeped at the parade, glanced at the meeting in the living-room and walked after them like she belonged to the gathering since it happened. She wasn't shocked by the number of people being there. She greeted everyone, introduced herself, and sat on the couch drinking water from the bottle she took from her bag.

'I sense some exciting meeting according to your facial expressions, so what's up guys?' she asked, smiling. It was so light and cheery that it seemed like she was asking about party preparations on a girl's night out.

'Robert, we've decided, you can't join...' started Sean but was interrupted by an angry Gary.

'Hold on! You can't decide without me. It's about my life, and I want him on board,' declared Gary. He sounded more aggressive than ever, maybe that was why people who knew him stared at him speechlessly, especially Jessica. But inside Gary felt strange, like he had got some peculiar new confidence that was popping out of his control. Gary felt uneasy that he crossed good-manners boundaries and he should make apologies for this outburst. But, some tiny voice inside his head kept whispering encouragement to push the situation even more and to force his will, even if he was wrong.

'He might be useful, whatever we'll have to face,' continued Gary with a normal voice this time. He took a deep breath but didn't break eye contact with Sean. Sean shrugged and gave a hand gesture with the meaning that he gave up. But Gary didn't feel like he had won the argument. Somehow, deep down inside his guts, he knew that having a werewolf as an ally might be beneficial for the sake of safety. Nobody knew what kind of horror they would have to face next. Gary thought Sean was driven only by his antipathy towards Robert, but such selfish behaviour would make more mayhem than it already had done.

'I don't mind,' said Draco, calmly breaking the way the awkward silence was hanging in the air. He didn't ask around but gave the signal to Gary that he was standing on Gary's side. Nobody opposed. Surprisingly, Sean smiled faintly, shook Robert's hand and was greeting him in as a member of a team.

The living room was quite spacious, but not everyone had a place to sit. Draco and Sean went to the kitchen for additional chairs, but Gary knew it was only an excuse, probably to cover their need to privately discuss some issues. But the atmosphere among those who stayed inside the living-room was much lighter. Even Robert seemed more relaxed. He was asking questions about how Gary and Jessica were feeling with the new supernatural reality that was unfolding ahead of them. It wasn't a philosophical conversation about what was going on deep inside the core of their beings, but Gary was content that the overwhelming stiffness was replaced with a friendlier attitude between all of them.

'Okay, let me start,' said Sean, with his voice accustomed to student's lectures. He looked at them as a professor would look at his pupils, regardless of their age. He waited till they sat and got quiet.

'Draco and Gary are connected by Draco's blood. It's a fact, but it's not all. Draco is the vampire's son of Frederick, aka Erick, one of the oldest vampires known worldwide. For those who don't know, Erick is the father of The Acherons dynasty, the one classified as the most powerful and influential probably in the world,' Sean stopped and glared from face to face, smiling like he knew how big an impact this news would make on Gary and his friends. Gary only slightly opened his mouth and kept his gaze fixed at Draco.

'If something bad happened to Erick, it will affect not only Draco's life but the whole of Erick's bloodline including you, Gary.

And this is it. Erick is dying, trapped in one of the most powerful artefacts created by witch hunters …' Sean didn't finish his sentence. He was interrupted abruptly by Robert's question.

'Erick is alive?' asked Robert, sitting straight and suddenly looking very interested in having the answer.

'Kind of,' said Sean, slowly weighing every word.

'Where is he then?' asked Robert, smiling like a child seeing sweets.

'He is inside a coffin called the Tritus' End. It's an artefact to trap powerful beings and to strip them from powers before they can be killed,' Sean spoke with his lecturer-like voice, carefully watching everyone's reaction.

'Isn't this illegal, after signing the Vamp's Covenant to do any harm to him without some trial and the Guild permission?' asked Robert, but the answer was written clearly on his face like he knew it before even articulated the question out loud.

'It is for you, but not for me. I did it,' said Draco with his cold, emotionless voice.

'Maybe yes, maybe not, but you'd have known about it. You just admit it,' continued Robert with a bit of a mischievous smirk, staring straight at Sean. Although he was sitting, Gary had an impression that Robert was looking at Sean and Draco from above without hiding his arrogant approach to them.

Sean started to pace around the room combing his hair. He peeped at Gary and shook his head. Gary had never before saw his uncle in such despair. Sean seemed devastated by Robert's comment, and Gary intuitively knew that Sean was in huge trouble. And the thought that Robert knew about it, and maybe enjoy seeing Sean struggling, stuck in Gary's head like an annoying buzz that couldn't be switched off by anything. Thank goodness Sean was standing with his back turned to Robert, thought Gary, thinking about doing something, or saying something that might put an end to this obnoxious situation.

'And the plot thickens. I don't care if it's legal or not, or who did it and when. I want my life back. One problem at the time, please. Focus first on how to get him out of there and save not only my arse,' demanded Gary, with a dictating tone staring straight into

Robert's eyes.

There was a murmur of consent around, and it seemed that everyone was supporting the project. Sean sighed deeply with relief and even smiled gently. He looked at Gary, nodding in agreement mixed with gratefulness.

Gary was observing how quickly their moods changed and the whole atmosphere cleared up from the tension. The first who got back to himself was of course Sean. He said that everyone needed a break, to get fresh air, a cup of tea and biscuits. He revived completely and almost ran to the kitchen, organising early tea time.

Mark and Jessica went after him. They were walking quite close to one other and even accidentally bumping into each other. They were doing more disorder with the tea preparations by having mini-quarrels, which they both enjoyed, than helping Sean. Sean looked like someone deep in his thoughts and wasn't listening to what they were talking about, but he seemed pleased to have their company.

*

After a while, when tea was drank and all biscuits had been eaten, mainly by Gary, Mark and Robert. Small-talks made them friendlier to one another. Sean said that the task with Erick would be challenging and they would probably be exposed to some level of danger. The story about Erick was unclear not only to Gary and his two friends but for Mark and Robert as well. Gary kept asking questions, but neither Draco nor Sean were willing to give him clear answers. Gary thought that there were reasons why they omitted the full story, and one was the blue elephant in the room called Robert.

Sean was a member of the Guild and his knowledge about Erick's whereabouts was making him a suspect. Although Gary was puzzled that Sean might ever put himself in some dodgy errands, on the other hand, Gary found that the issue was something that was giving him the thrill of exposing a new exciting supernatural story with a vampire as the leading role. Gary started thinking how he could use this event to make a movie about it. He somehow knew that the key to all the history of events behind Erick's imprisonment was hidden inside Draco's head.

Gary smiled to himself, thinking that in the best-written horror tales, demons were always hidden inside people they least expected.

Although Gary had very mixed feelings, he walked towards Draco willingly for the first time since they met. There was some strange connection between them on a subconscious level, and he could feel it. Draco seemed to know what Gary wanted to ask and before the question was spoken, he stood up, walked into the middle of the room and start talking with his low and piercing voice.

'Okay guys let's get started. I'll explain very briefly what I know, especially to the three of you,' he said and pointed at Gary, Simon and Jessica. He patted Gary's back and showed him to a seat.

'Erick is one of the oldest vampires known worldwide. For centuries there was a war between humans, vampires, ferals, lycans and others until the Guild was created. It had begun in ancient times, first as a cease-fire in capital cities but the idea spread and developed around the world. It gave background to the society we live in now and the rules that all of us are bound to obey. The Guild is governing in every country by their divisions. Its headquarter is moving every five years and now is in London. Different groups, like for example werewolves, have their representatives inside the institution and therefore they can decide about politics and privileges. Unfortunately, there are groups like witches or vampires that had never had their deputies or even invitations for an armistice. The deepest desire of Erick was to be part of the new order and be treated not like a hunting animal but with respect as one of the beings that is living behind the veil. We all have differences, but we can learn how to live in peace. For many centuries, he built his influence among vampire's dynasties, and I have to admit, not everything was clear and honest, but that's politics. Anyway, he was chosen as the one and only representative for the most influential and significant bloodlines. He made a covenant with the Guild to have a seat in the council and finally move us out of the margins of society. But the side effect for vampires was the vow to obey legal regulations written for our kind. Not everyone was happy with it. But the main point is that hunting for vamps, members of the dynasties under oath, is illegal. Those who have not been sworn are outcasts; therefore, everyone can kill them. One more thing you should know about us, when the new vamp is created, the whole ritual makes a special parenting bond. The blood is connected on such a deep level that if the maker would die, the whole line would cease to exist. There is one exception to it, but it's too complicated to talk about now. Anyway, going to the point.

The witch hunters were trying to catch Erick for more than five hundred years without success. Ten years ago, I helped them, that's why he is trapped in this bloody coffin,' Draco finished his long talk and sat on his former seat on the last free armchair standing near the artificial fireplace, now cold and black. Almost everyone was listening intensely, and even Robert seemed curious about his tale. But Sean looked like someone who knew much more and wanted to add some details but had to restrain himself to not interrupt Draco's speech. Gary's imagination had gone wild, and question after question was bombarding his mind. He wanted to know more and to ask more, but the number of topics overwhelmed him a bit. He made a decision that he needed to spend more time with his family if they succeed with the task.

Mark sat near Jessica on the couch in such a way that back of his body touched hers. She flinched and blushed when his leg touched her hip, but she didn't retreat. There was nothing more, but Gary frowned.

'So, you are behind the mayhem in London and a riot on streets ten years ago, aren't you? Was it the same night Erick signed the official documents with the Guild?' asked Robert inquisitively. Draco froze and held his breath. He looked at Sean, sighed deeply and turned straight in Robert's direction. His face didn't express any emotions.

'Yes and no. Maybe one day you'll know the full story, but now we need to discuss how to get Erick out of the artefact, that's the issue for today,' continued Draco.

'It's no biggie to open it. You didn't leave it in Buckingham Palace for ten years, did you, Draco?' asked Gary, smiling.

'Oh no, in Buckingham Palace there is ...' but Draco didn't finish.

'Whoa, whoa, whoa ... stop right now,' shouted Sean abruptly, grabbing Draco's arm and squeezing. It seemed they had known each other for years and their past was entangled in a mysteriously bizarre way. Gary thought about how little he really knew about his own family.

'Can we stay in the present moment, please? Now, The Tritus' End - the coffin with trapped Erick is standing in the middle of Great Court in The British Museum as a part of the exhibition I'm organising. I won't explain how it got there. The clock is ticking so …' Sean sounded annoyed.

'So, what's the problem? You're working there, and as a curator you have access to every place, I believe,' said Gary.

'Well, yes, theoretically I can but …' Sean hesitated for a while.

All present in the living room were glaring at him intensely.

'But you can't because to open it you need to trigger some kind of official procedure with witnesses, documents, and all those crappy forms to fill. And you'll have to have an excellent reason to move it from display during the exhibition. That might get you even more attention, and that's the last thing you want,' said Jessica leisurely.

Mark turned his head in her direction, leaned closer to her ear and said something silently that made her blush. She was hiding her red face under the bush of ginger and curly hair. Mark put his hand on her head and stroked it tenderly but only once before he caught Gary's startled gaze. Gary frowned again.

'How?' Sean tried to ask a question, but he had at least three different versions of it and couldn't decide which one is more important. He was pointing on Jessica with amazement on his face.

'It's going better and better every minute. I'm sure your boss doesn't even know that the coffin is kind of an unmarked item in the museum, standing in the middle, so it's not easy to move or to hide,' said Robert, chuckling and very pleased.

'Because if it belongs to the museum, therefore it might be easy to open, so you'd not have to ask for help. Am I right?' asked Gary and started to giggle a bit, imitating Robert. Sean was silent. He looked confused like a chastened dog.

'Okay, okay smart asses. There is something more,' Sean proclaimed, looking in Draco's direction. He started talking very fast in case someone would pop out with more uncomfortable ideas.

'The coffin was put there in a hurry because Patric Vence, aka The Vampire Prince of London, is chasing it with the intention of killing Erick,' said Draco.

'Wait a minute. Why did you help to trap Erick? You don't want him dead?' Gary asked him straight.

'Oh, not that fast. In some legends it is said some items can help to bypass the bloodline connection. I believe, Draco wants not only to kill Erick but to take over the whole dynasty, so he needs him alive for ritual proposes. Pretty cunning plan you're cooking,' laughed Robert, gazing at Draco with specific admiration.

'Everyone has to die one day,' declared Draco, shrugging and smiling like he didn't care about keeping secret his ill-intention.

Gary thought that would be a great story idea in a movie, but he couldn't believe that was happening now in real life. Draco seemed pretty normal while talking about his plans to kill his vampire father, as though he was organising a child's birthday party. But Gary felt an impulse to run and hide that was kicking in his mind in the moment when Draco admitted his plan. Gary shivered out of fear but stayed put in the living-room. He promised himself he would try to avoid being alone with Draco as much as it was possible. Gary barely heard what the others were talking about.

'It just so happens that some of the relics collected in the museum influenced something in the coffin to kill whoever is inside quickly. Erick's still alive only because nobody really knows how old he is. Rumour has it that he's more than a thousand years old so he can survive longer than any other known species. There is very little knowledge about Tritus' End around...' Sean's speech was suddenly interrupted by a loud shout from Simon.

'Vampires have a Prince?'

'No, he called himself one. One day you'll all regret not being normal humans with all those easy lives,' said Robert, smiling broadly and pointing towards Simon, Gary and Jessica with his cane.

Simon, who until now was standing in the doorway, sat down on the couch, pushing Mark even more closely to Jessica. Mark took the opportunity and moved as close as he possibly could. His body was touching the full length of her side, and he even put his arm around her on the top of the couch. Jessica blushed even more, but this time she didn't hide her face but drank only a few more sips of her mineral water.

'And you're one of the creeps that are living there, Robert, stop over-dramatizing! It doesn't help at all,' Sean scolded him.

'So, basically, the story goes like this: you – Draco, with some of your mates – trapped Erick in the Tritus' End. He has been lying hidden for ten years without anyone knowing where, until the vampire Prince called Patric forced you to change the location because he somehow found out the whereabouts of the artefact. So, Sean helped you for an unknown reason. And the museum was the safest place to put it back then, but you didn't predict it would have such a deadly effect on Erick's health. Moreover, keeping Erick there is illegal, and we have to take him out because I'll die along with Draco very soon. Did I miss something?' asked Gary, summarising all that he knew so far. Gary was stunned by the fact it all was true and was happening to him right now. Moreover, the death threat was real.

'Yes, that's it in a nutshell,' said Draco, smiling very gently.

'Well, there was a factor of my boss accidentally walking in the precise moment when we were unloading the coffin. It was late evening, and she shouldn't be there. I wanted to put it in a basement, but she saw us and … I had to … for goodness sake she is a normal human …' Sean was trying to explain but had problems articulating his thoughts. Gary sensed that Sean was stammering because he didn't know what he could say without blurting too much out.

'So, you lied and had to play the role of having a new item for collection. When the display started?' asked Robert.

'Yep, pretty much it was like that. It started two weeks ago, but the coffin arrived just before the accident day.' Sean took the whole plate full of biscuits and started eating without asking if anyone else wanted one. It seemed he had said everything that was important to say and now he was waiting for them to digest the news.

The atmosphere in the room relaxed. Even Robert and Simon looked less touchy. Somehow the tension inside Sean about the coffin was gone, and it did affect everyone.

'Why does the Prince want to kill Erick?' asked Jessica.

'Good question,' said Draco, 'Erick always had enemies. I think Patric knows that Erick is very vulnerable, even a few months after being taken out from the trap. If Erick would be back, Patric's position will be questioned, making him powerless among vampire dynasties in England.'

'How did he find out where the coffin was hidden?' asked Gary.

'I don't know that yet. We all have to remember, Patric has money, resource and not only vampires to his dispositions. We really need to hurry. It's only matter of time until he learns about the new location,' continued Draco, but this time his voice didn't sound like a hissing snake. It was more natural and pleasant. Gary felt like he was immersed in a warm bath with relaxing music after long and hard work.

'Why do I smile at all?' Gary asked out loud, but more to himself than to others.

'It's a probable reaction for too much weirdness going on now,' replied, Jessica smiling broadly like the others.

'No, actually is not, I just feel …' Gary couldn't describe the emotions boiling inside him. He held his sentence not knowing how to qualify what he was feeling right now.

'It's a call for adventure, Gary. Now, officially you're a member of our family. Don't look so happy, bro. It's a curse from father's side. I'll explain to you later,' said Mark with a grave voice. He touched Jessica's hair again, but this time it was so gently that she could hardly notice.

'So, what are we going to do? It's so exciting just to think about it. Do we break into the museum at night?' Gary asked with glaring eyes like a child waiting for Christmas.

'No, Gary. We can't break in there. Firstly, we'll be criminals, and secondly, the cameras will show that there was something hidden inside. We have to do it in a way that nobody else, other than us, will ever know about Erick being there,' said Sean, stuffing whole round biscuits inside his mouth.

'That'll be very difficult. What is it? Mission Impossible sequel?' asked Gary, snorting loudly.

'Okay, guys. We have work to do with Simon in our pack,' interrupted Robert, nodding to Simon and preparing his crippled leg for standing up.

'You can't leave now. We don't have any ideas yet,' demanded Gary.

'Oh yes, I can. I believe you'll come out with something crazy. But if you want me to contribute to this brainstorming session, I'll tell you what I think about it. First, completely forget about opening the coffin at night time. Second, you'll have to do it during the day, when the pick of museum visitors is the highest. Third, you have to make distractions like con artists or pickpockets do. I've no idea how but redirect the crowd focus while opening the relic. I'm in. I can't stay away while you do some mischievous to Patric. This is the best part of the plan so far. I want to be at every meeting that this group will have. If you don't call me, I'll be mad, and that's the last thing you want. That's all for today,' announced Robert with a manner of giving orders to them.

Simon came closer, trying to help Robert to stand up, but Robert glanced at him with a look of indignation. He stood up very fast using his cane and moved vigorously. Simon shrugged, turned back and went upstairs to his room. Robert nodded his goodbye to everyone, even to Draco, gave Gary his business card and hobbled after Simon.

'So, the team is set with a task. Why does it seem to me more like organising a new LARP than rescue mission?' asked Gary, visibly very cheerful.

'Maybe we should do it this way,' said Jessica.

'It sounds like directing a movie,' cried Gary enthusiastically.

'Don't forget about unpredictable vamps and put them into this scenario. They don't need weapons. Have you ever seen fighting vampires, Gary?' Mark scolded him. He stood up and walked around for a while. Jessica was observing his every move.

'Now that they are gone, tell us why you helped to catch Erick in the first place? I need to know if we all can trust you,' said Mark, rather agitated, as he stared at Draco. Draco peeped once at Sean, sighed and shook his head.

'Okay, I'll tell you briefly. Erick told me that he saw me only once when the desire to make me as his son struck him to the core. He can move so fast, that I didn't know he attacked me. I woke up during the transition as it's excruciating that's why not all can make it. Do you know that only less than fifty per-cent of humans can survive the whole process?' said Draco calmly.

'What? It's not like in a movie? One vamp's bit, death and you are brand new 'child of the dark' to suck blood from a stupid passer-by?'

asked a shocked Gary, putting the inverted comma sign and stressing the last part of the sentence.

'No, it's not that easy, and technically, we are not dead. Vampires are creatures between life and death. Anyway, back to Erick, I never wanted to become one of them, and I have hated this life since the beginning. For many years of self-loathing, I met someone who gave me the tiny light of hope in the black pitch of my life. His name is Adam. He's a vampire from Erick's bloodline, and on the contrary to me, he enjoys being one of them. But the main trait of Adam is his passionate interest about vampires' abilities and skills, one might call magic. He told me about a ritual which could reverse it all. Do you understand what that meant to me, Gary? I have a chance to become a human again, and I want it so badly. Unfortunately, I can't do it without breaking the bond with Erick. Normally, it's not possible to cut off the blood link between parent and the vamp child. But the ritual can do it. The point is that Erick has to be present during the revoking vampirism. He doesn't have to be conscious or do anything or even have his powers. Only his still living body matters. It took me a hundred years to find the Tritus' End. It was like chasing the myth of the Golden Fleece itself. Adam and I travelled a lot for a long time, but we found it. Your parents helped me, Gary. Your father was one of the most skilled witch hunters who was walking in the world at that time. Even now there is none who can match his mastery...'

'What?' asked Gary, shocked. He sat near Jessica, feeling weak and very confused.

'Let me finish. So, your parents helped me trapped Erick in this artefact. It supposed to be easy, but in the same night, somehow Patric - young vamp, who wasn't even well-known, found out that Erick was gone, made a riot and killed a lot from Erick's bloodline. He didn't stop cleaning up only among us. He did it to werewolves and others who were in his way. That was the night when your parents died, Gary. He killed them. I saw it...'

'What?!' shouted Gary, interrupting him.

'Please, calm down, or I'm not going to continue,' said Draco with his low, piercing voice. At that moment, Gary felt like a big bucket of icy water was thrown on him. The cold sensation went throughout him like an electric wave making goosebumps along his flesh.

Everyone in the room felt something similar. Silence hung like stuffy air, giving them all the unpleasant impression that they are not welcome here and the best that they can do is to leave the house and never come back. The atmosphere stayed for a few seconds. The first person who moved and shouted was Sean.

'Stop doing it right now, Draco!'

'Sorry, my bad. It's just a habit,' said Draco in a more friendly tone. The cold was gone, replaced by more amicable emotions.

'What just happened?' asked Jessica, shaking off the distressful experience she just had.

'It's just something that Adam taught me many years ago. It's kind of mood controlling skill by using my voice in a special way. I need to find him. Sorry, Gary, I know it's too much to bear, so I'm not going to talk about your parents now. We'll be back to this conversation if we survive the next few weeks,' said Draco, smiling softly. His appearance changed from grim to look more like a friendly seller of ice-creams in a hot, lazy afternoon.

'Okay, you're right. It's too much for one day. But how did you find out that Erick is dying inside?' asked Gary. Draco hesitated for a while and seemed to be thinking intensely.

'I was on my way to England that time when Sean moved the coffin. Yes, Sean knew where the artefact was hidden. It's too late to keep secrets here, Sean. We're all in this shit now,' declared Draco, talking straight to him. Sean nodded and made a 'go ahead' hand gesture.

'I had an awful dream in my first day in London. You should know, guys, normally vampires don't have dreams. If they have, it always means something is going to happen soon, and it won't be nice. In my dream, I was him, seeing where I am, and had a feeling like I was connected to a big machine sucking up my life bit by bit. I knew I can't escape. I heard his voice calling my name for help. I felt the inevitable death coming for me. I woke up suffocating and for the first time since I became a vamp, I felt petrified. I have this dream every time I close my eyes, and it's going worse. We really need to hurry,' said Draco.

They all were listening to him in calmness, and for quite a long time, nobody said anything.

'Okay, guys. We need a break. Everyone has homework to do on how to open the coffin in a way described by Robert. We'll meet tomorrow evening and start making serious plans,' said Gary, interrupting the unwanted silence. While all were stretching their bodies, Gary couldn't stop smiling. Although it seemed unnatural and very hard to achieve, Gary somehow felt amused, and the vision of a new adventure boosted his energy level to the maximum.

CHAPTER 10

3rd July - Neoshaman

The next day, Jessica woke up an hour before her usual alarm time. She felt very refreshed and deep down had a feeling that something fundamentally important would happen today. Since the accident, her intuition had expanded and she started to know about things or events entirely out of nowhere. She could sense strong human emotions even if they looked like an impassive plastic doll. Moreover, she woke up with this weird tingling intensive sensation that someone was thinking about her. It was so strong that, before Jessica opened her eyes, she could see a shape of the person sitting on her bed and it looked like an astral projection of human being.

Sean told Jessica about what happened with her in the forest, and how damaged her state of mind was after being exposed to such a dramatic life-changing encounter. Sean looked very excited telling her about what his friend, one of the neoshamans, did to save her from madness. Jessica kept asking him what it was precisely, but Sean seemed confused when he tried to explain the whole process. Sean had the mannerism of giving a lecture and clarifying pieces of information, therefore he assured her that one day some shaman would visit Jessica and teach her the new way of living.

But after patiently waiting a couple of days, Jessica forgot about the whole thing. Maybe because there were no episodes with appearing tattoos on her skin, nor any nightmares, visions, voices or pain in any part of her body. That was the reason why she was so surprised when she heard the doorbell ringing just after a few seconds when she opened her eyes this early morning. She dashed downstairs without paying attention to how she looked.

When she opened the door, she saw Robert first and some unrecognisable figures standing behind him. He nodded, murmured something very incomprehensible as his usual way to say morning greetings. And then he walked inside without an invitation like he was living here. He even pushed her a bit to make more space for himself and asked about bringing him a cup of tea upstairs. Jessica opened her mouth but said nothing. She couldn't stop staring at the second figure standing at the door. There was an African lady with a bright sparkle in her eyes and a broad smile showing her straight snow white teeth.

'Morning, sweetheart. Ready for new adventures? Mhmm ...' she murmured, nodding and waiting to be invited in. Jessica stepped back and without words, using only hand gestures, showed her the corridor inside the house. The woman crossed the doorstep, swinging her perfectly rounded body leisurely like a cat. She was wearing a wavy dress in light pastel colours, excellently highlighting her dark chocolate skin. Her hair was straight, with a few red braids, gold beads braided inside and tribal make-up with white dots under her eyes. Jessica saw her for the first time, but she felt a warm, positive aura emanating from her and the strong impression that they had known each other for quite some time.

'Ariana,' she said, stretching her hand. In that moment, when Jessica clutched fingers around her hand, she experienced a gush of high-pitched energy, but it was so subtle and fast that it seemed like gentle pricking of small pins on her skin. It went through Jessica's whole body, leaving goosebumps and even straightening her posture.

'Sweetheart, go upstairs and get ready. I'm afraid I don't have much time for your training today. Don't worry, love. I'll make a special tea for this old buffoon. Mhmm, exceptional tea,' she smiled and headed straight to the kitchen without looking back. Jessica stood for a minute observing her with amazement and trying to recognise the melody Ariana was humming under her nose.

Twenty minutes later, after a shower and all those morning routines, Jessica met Ariana in the corridor walking out from Simon's room. She shook her head with disapproval and said to Jessica,

'This man has serious issues with flexibility. But he'll learn one day, eventually. Everyone has their own karma to bear, no exceptions, in this life or another. Oh, you're fast, love. Now, we're going to start with something simple. Mhmm, no rush, everything in its own time will come to you,' she said walking downstairs towards the kitchen.

Jessica had pleasant feelings being around this woman, like Ariana's aura was a safe harbour before setting off to daily battles.

'You like him a lot, don't you?' asked Jessica, surprised by her own thoughts and boldness. She realised about the content of the question just after she articulated it.

'Mhmm, I do. He is a troublemaker, but I do like him. Unfortunately, he was born with too much of a warrior spirit. You, young lady, caught that up very fast. I'm impressed but shush about it,' said Ariana, putting her finger on her lips and checking if someone else was around. Jessica could feel how utterly surprised Ariana was about exposing her deep affections to someone who seemed totally unaware of it.

'Does he know?' Jessica whispered in a confidential way.

'Robert? Nah, he's blind like a mole digging his tunnels under the lawn. His dramatic past clouds his mind. Keep this to yourself, nobody else has to know,' said Ariana, putting a kettle on and preparing mugs. Although she was talking about having feelings that might never be developed into requited love, she was smiling broadly without any shadows of pain inside her eyes.

After breakfast, tea and small-talk about today's weather, Jessica couldn't hold on any longer and started asking the questions she had wanted to ask since Ariana walked into the house.

'Who are the neoshamans? I want to know everything,' declared Jessica, cleaning up plates.

'I know you do, sweetheart, I know. Let's go then,' said Ariana, putting the rest of food back in the cupboards.

'There are many shamans around the world from many cultures and traditions. They differ in rituals and belief systems, but the core is alike. Neoshamans work with the most creative and yet self-destructive creature on this Earth - human beings living in an urban environment. You see, sweetheart, despite all those visible differences, deep down in our souls we're all similar…'

'But what exactly are you doing?' asked Jessica impatiently.

'Ah, you see, for shamans, everything is built with spiritual energy. And I think some scientists might agree with us, but it's not important to have their acknowledgement. The shamanic system is working regardless if you believe it or not. The material things you can see and touch, are energies, but their density is on different levels. It looks like the amplitude of ocean's waves. Anyway, humans, using their mind, can make the waves go into desired directions. Moreover, those who are well-skilled can also call for things, or people that'll come to you when you need. It's simple but not easy,' she declared and walked out from the house.

Jessica was walking right behind her, processing in her mind what she had just heard. It was a sunny morning with a cloudless sky, and a fresh light breeze was making the walk enjoyable.

'So, it is some kind of mumbo-jumbo from new-age era awareness of spirituality and conditions of human souls, isn't it?' asked Jessica in a quarrelsome way.

'Oh, are you always so judgemental?' asked Ariana without changing her voice tone. They were walking on an empty sidewalk in silence for a while.

'I just don't believe in such things,' said Jessica with a bit of jeer.

'You didn't believe that werewolves are real and yet, one changed your life to the core of your existence,' said Ariana, imitating Jessica's voice. Jessica didn't know what to say. The fact was unbeatable.

'You see, sweetheart, you're an engineer, and this should give you an idea that some things exist and works regardless if you can see them or not, such as atoms. And I'm not talking only about basic physic rules like gravity or friction, but about love, friendship, hate, that our life is spinning around …'

'How can you compare science to beliefs and feelings?' asked Jessica, but this time scoff disappeared from her voice.

'Why can't you?'

'What? What do you mean?'

'Yes, they are both different, but they exist even if we don't like them. Moreover, the next generations, who are coming after us, they'll be using science for building spaceships and they'll be searching for love, get emotional over rumours, have issues with self-acceptance and be scared about death itself,' she said softly. It sounded like she was talking to a child who was afraid of making the first step.

'Some things you just need to accept that they'll always be around. You don't need to prove if they are real or not to use it for your life advantage. Others did it before you, and it worked. See, sweetheart, I'm here to show you the tiny, invisible path of endless possibilities you can use it if you're open enough for it. But you have to walk alone on it to learn because only experience can teach you how to master your mind. But you don't have to. That's the beauty of having free will,' said Ariana, putting her hand on Jessica's shoulder.

'Do you mean I don't have to have any meetings with you?' asked Jessica with a bit of stress in her question.

'Of course, you don't have to. But before you resign, ask yourself, what if it'll work for me? Are you not intrigued as to what you can create? Every great discovery was made through curiosity. So, what kind of 'what if…' will you ask yourself today?'

Ariana knew that was the moment when she got to the essence of Jessica's personality. They were both standing on the crossroad near the stairs to the underground. It was getting late in the morning. More and more people were rushing around, trying to fulfil their busy lives' schedule.

'Where do we start? And do I need any books?' asked Jessica seriously.

'I'll bring you some books. Okay, so let's try something elementary for today,' she said, looking around and thinking about the small and uncomplicated task for Jessica. Ariana was observing people that were passing nearby.

'Can you guess what feelings they have now?' she asked Jessica without pointing into any specific person.

Jessica looked at her very surprised. She expected to have academic lectures all way round without any practice. Ariana didn't speak as she waited for answers.

How am I supposed to know what they are feeling now? thought Jessica, confused. She turned around, glaring at all those passers-by walking near her. They all seemed so regular. Like those two ladies wearing elegant suits, holding cups of coffee and talking about some business meetings. Or those three teenage girls in school uniforms making faces and taking selfies. Or this postman, standing near her own house, that she knew, who was delivering letters. Mind reading on the first lesson was pretty scary for Jessica and she felt totally unprepared. How could she recognise stranger's emotions when sometimes she couldn't see the stress written straight on her friend's faces, nor Mark's affection to her? The thoughts about him made her blush and entirely knocked out her focus on the shamanic task. She glanced around from face to face, feeling more and more uneasy. They all appeared so normal. Jessica was skimming their postures, the way they walked, how they talked, but nothing even slightly was suggesting or revealing anything about their thoughts or state of emotions. It was a picture of a typical morning run to work, like Jessica used to see every day in London.

'Let me help you a bit. It's not about you, it's about them. Just close your eyes and feel the energy flowing around,' whispered Ariana.

Jessica closed her eyes and tried to concentrate, but all she could sense was the motion of people moving near her. She heard the clatter of boots, and it was all she could hold her focus on. She stood for quite a while, but nothing cropped out to her mind. A few pictures and flashes of energy, which might have be fear or joy, from some of those people popped up in her head, but then again it might have been her imagination.

'I can't feel anything,' murmured Jessica with resignation, opening her eyes. She was standing alone, and that made her a bit more nervous. She had to search the crowd for a few minutes before she saw Ariana's standing a few metres away. She was chatting with two women like they were well-known friends. In this precise moment, when Jessica saw her, Ariana turned around and waved, inviting Jessica to join in the group conversation. That confused Jessica even more. It should be the first training session for her but was now slightly turning into a woman's social gathering. Jessica went over to them, hesitantly. She couldn't understand the meaning of this event.

They just were standing in the middle of the sidewalk babbling about how to make a perfect lasagne. It didn't make any sense, thought Jessica. How was she supposed to learn about energies without any books, assessments, lectures, video training programs and making notes when her teacher was ignoring her, thought Jessica, angrily. She felt left alone and very insecure. Ariana smiled, nodded to those ladies and left them alone.

'Have you seen your own bias now, Jessica? Focus, please.'

Jessica sighed and took a deep breath when the enlightening struck her like a thunderbolt.

'You can't see or feel if you don't trust yourself. I believe your intuition gives you a hint like a picture or little sensation, but you ignore it or kill it with your 'it can't be true, or it doesn't exist' opinion bombing everything new and strange that's appearing in your mind,' Ariana smiled and continued. Jessica had to admit she had exactly the same monologue in her mind as described by Ariana. She said nothing only nodded, agreeing.

'Sweetheart, if you don't trust yourself, no one else will. This is you, who marks your own progress and give the desired A+. The information was there. It got through your mind, but you filtered it through your insecurities. Don't worry, love. There are books and people who might inspire you, but there's only you who is doing the work. Only real experience will examine your skills and show how effective you are,' said Ariana, hugging her.

Jessica had never thought about herself in that way. She felt more confused than she was before, maybe because nobody deciphered her thinking so fast and so accurately without even asking questions. Ariana hugged her tightly and patted her back gently, without any words.

'But how am I supposed to read someone mind?' asked Jessica with slight irritation in her tone.

'You don't read minds. You just can feel emotions the person radiates,' replied Ariana, smiling broadly.

'But what if I can't tell apart what is mine and what is theirs?' Jessica was clearly irritated, not only by her lack of shamanic knowledge but by impossibility of clearly distinguish between energies.

'Oh, that's an excellent question,' answered Ariana.

'So…'

'You might ask for help,' continued Ariana.

'From whom?'

'Spirits. You see, as a shaman you can call on them to work with you,' replied Ariana, coming closer to Jessica, grabbing her arm and squeezing gently. On Jessica's bare skin, in a place where Ariana's fingers clutched her arm, pictures of tattoos that she had seen before started to appear and disappear on the surface. Jessica was staring at the show speechlessly but for the first time it didn't shock her to the point of fainting. Instead, she felt something warm and familiar like she knew what it was but forgot some time ago.

'What shall I do?' asked Jessica, smiling.

'Call them,' said Ariana. She was looking intensely into Jessica's eyes. The light thrill went down Jessica's spine. She felt like she had just got an invitation for the best adventure of her life. She didn't know where it all could lead but she knew she was willing to follow, regardless of consequences.

'Does it always work?' she asked with her old habitual scepticism that was still well ingrained deep inside her personality. She knew the new path she saw wouldn't be easy, but she wanted to experiment with her own mind like she had never done before.

'No, it doesn't,' replied Ariana, without any remorse.

'Why?'

'We don't know that. Maybe there is deeper meaning to how things have to happen, and you can't change it even if you really want it. Maybe it's karma, or maybe something else. You have to just accept the things as they are if you can't influence them,' said Ariana. Jessica didn't answer. She didn't know what to say, she was overwhelmed by the new point of view that she had explored today. Ariana hugged her tightly, patting gently on her back. They stayed for some time in this position, irrespective of the rushing crowd of people passing nearby.

'Sweetheart, don't be hard on yourself, just move on. You've made tremendous progress today. Correcting ourselves is how we grow. Your first lesson is finished, but it's not over,' said Ariana.

'When is the next one?' asked Jessica.

'I'll know when you're ready. In the meantime, this is my phone number, if you have any questions, just ask,' said Ariana, passing a card with only one number written on it.

'Who were those ladies?' asked Jessica.

'Just someone I had befriended a few minutes ago. I had to keep my mind occupied and let you wander alone. So, I asked spirits if there is anyone who needs some simple help, and then I heard the voice of one of the women. She was telling her friend how desperate she wanted to impress her boyfriend's parents with an upcoming diner. So, I just cut in and started talking,' replied Ariana, smiling.

There was nothing more today. They both went to the underground talking about Ariana's recipe for the perfect lasagne.

CHAPTER 11

4th July - The Tavern

The next day, Simon woke up too late and it was out of his routine. He usually had a well-scheduled day and morning habits were essential. It always gave him the certainty of being under control at almost every situation. But since the accident, his regular grooves were slightly replaced by something new. Like his sudden urge to join a gym, when he saw a reflection of his naked body in a foggy glassy shower cubicle in a bathroom. Or the taste of red meat he discovered he loved so much, that he could eat half-fried on a daily basis in an amount that could feed a regular person for a couple of days. But the most significant modification that everyone who knew him could see, was while entering his room. Although nothing drastically changed inside, his stiff regime to a level of cleanliness had been broken. He had never before left plates with some leftovers through the night but now it was his new habit. He started wearing the same trousers for a few days, as long as there were no visible stains on it. Some new items appeared, like books about ancient mythology lying on the floor near his bed. A new figure of an angry werewolf was standing just next to the screen on his desk. It was only a cheap, plastic imitation of the true feral-battle form of the beast that was made by someone who had never seen real angry werewolf, but for Simon it was a rare gem in his room. And so today, he stayed a few minutes longer in bed. He didn't jaw himself for being late as he used to do but pretended like nothing abnormal happened.

He was renting one of the rooms at the three-bedroom house that belonged to Jessica and was located on a small street in Greenwich in

London. He moved here more than three years ago and never had any problems keeping his privacy. There was no drama around and he even thought that it was too ordinary to be true. After a year of living here, Gary asked him if he knew about some nice place to stay for a longer time. Back then, Gary was just some guy that Simon had known through mutual friends and who was doing cheap clips for an amateur rock and metal bands. Simon was a member of one of them, playing only covers on small stages in busy pubs on some weekends. This was his dream when he was a teenager, to be the best drummer in the world, but, unfortunately, artistic success wasn't Simon's destiny. And that was the story how they both met.

At the beginning, Simon didn't like Gary. For him, Gary was a wishful-thinking dreamer whose ideas annoyed most people. But after two years of living together, it appeared they became very close friends. Gary still was doing movies, not only music clips, but also the company's events, weddings or birthday parties. Simon couldn't understand why Gary was complaining about this. Deep down Simon was a bit jealous about how creative Gary was. There was something magical in this kind of lifestyle with flexible work and lack of a querulous manager. Simon saw how sometimes Gary transformed poorly made shots into exciting short films. Although Simon was working in the computer's field mostly, he liked helping Gary when the real action was needed so they did film quite a lot of parties together. But Simon knew he could never fit in Gary's world. He liked stability and clear rules. That was the reason why he chose to work for the police. It wasn't a dream job, but he did enjoy the environment.

He could have easy work and a simple life till retirement if it wasn't for Robert. Simon remembered well the moment he was bitten by him. Back then, Simon didn't think but only acted in a matter of seconds. He didn't feel fear either, only some kind of astonishment mixed with anger. It all happened so fast that his usual logical thinking didn't question the werewolf appearance whatsoever. The shock that came after he hit Robert's nose made him realise that the beast was real. The transformation that came after was torture. Sometimes when Simon tried to focus on a slight memory of that night's endless hours, he started shaking uncontrollably out of fear. He didn't remember exactly how he got through it, but he had the feeling inside that there was someone who helped him. Every day

Simon felt the change that he couldn't name, that was soaking into his soul slowly like drizzle but making him wet after some time. It was growing inside him and he had to admit he started to like this new self. If only he could get rid of Robert and just be part of the pack, he thought. But unfortunately, it wouldn't happen, at least not soon. Robert was like a painful ulcer on Simon buttocks which he couldn't remove. And the worst was to come, thought Simon, about his first upcoming meeting with the leader and group of other werewolves in his new pack.

*

Although it was late, Simon was still lying in bed thinking about how this meeting would go wrong in any possible way. He imagined Robert in the middle of causing his private hell. He knew he had to rush to catch the tube, but he sensed something bizarre around. With his eyes still closed and pretending that he was still asleep, he could feel someone presence in the room. He didn't hear anything but somehow he knew someone was gazing at him. He never had any situation, as long as he was living here, that somebody was watching him sleep. Sometimes Gary or Robert walked in even without knocking, but it never happened when Simon was in bed.

Simon's senses sharpened to the maximum. He felt the moment when adrenaline started to raise his blood pressure and began preparing his body for action. Recently, he discovered that in stressful situations his muscles were tenser and clearly visible under his skin.

'Okay, that's it! Get up from the bed! I know you are not sleeping. Chop, chop, little one.'

That was the nightmarish voice of the devil itself coming true, even before the day had started for Simon. Robert's sarcastic voice just struck the chord in Simon mind, evoking anger to the edge of madness. He jumped from bed, straight over to Robert and tried to hit him, but in a few seconds, he was lying on the floor. Robert was pointing at him with a long thin but very sharp sword he drew from his cane. Despite his injured knee, Robert overpowered him so fast that Simon was more surprised finding himself in this beaten position than scared of the deadly weapon touching his throat. Instinctively, he held his hand"s palms up in a surrender gesture. He felt his heart pumping up blood at high speed and started to feel some unknown sensation inside his muscles that he had never experienced before.

'Whoa, whoa, easy man. What're you doing?' asked Simon with a high-pitched voice, breathing really quickly. Small drops of sweat appeared on his face.

'I'm supposed to train you to be a warrior, but you're such a wuss that I doubt it'll ever happen,' said Robert, putting the sword back to the cane and giving a hand to Simon to help him get up. Simon didn't grab his out-stretched hand but was slowly standing up by himself. Robert shrugged, but he didn't back off and now was standing close to Simon in such a way that Simon had to step back to prevent clashing into him.

'I've never signed up to be a warrior. I'm not going to fight to make you happy. I don't care what you want. So, forget it. I'll find my pack without you. Get lost and out of my room,' Simon articulated through clenched teeth and tried to push Robert away. Robert leaned on his cane, preventing him from losing his balance. He stared at Simon with anger and determination on his face. Simon turned back and walked to his wardrobe, opened it and start searching through neatly ironed and hanged clothes.

'Oh, yes, you will be. You're a wimp for an arena, but you'll have to learn to fight. You're a werewolf, and we have natural enemies. Vampires are one of many...'

'I thought we're at peace with them,' declared Simon, interrupting angrily. He was extremely annoyed. He picked up fresh clothes and was heading towards the bathroom outside the room. He went around Robert, omitting his eyes and pretending that Robert wasn't there.

'And you still believe in Santa Clause, don't you?' sneered Robert after Simon left with a loud bang of the door behind him.

Robert sat on a large office chair near a large and tidily maintained desk, looking at everything collected in this room. He saw for the first time how the room was organised. On a white wall, there were only a few photos of Simon with his family in tropical places. Two tall shelves full of games, programs and some technical books were perfectly arranged according to type and size. Although almost everything here had its own place and was kept clean, some things didn't fit into the interior design of the whole room. The plate with crumbs was spoiling the neatness of the room and was evidence of Simon's night eating. Or the werewolf statue that seemed more suitable to boy's bedroom that twenty-eight-year-old man. Robert couldn't avoid peeping into the drawers standing near the desk, but he found what he expected, more systematic orderliness.

*

Taking cold shower calmed Simon down. The presence of this old rat was enough to get him to the edge of losing his temper like no one ever did. When Simon was back in his room, the first thing he saw was Robert drinking tea with delight on his face. That was the last view he wanted to see. Nevertheless, it was a good sign that it wouldn't be more fighting here, at least for now. Simon had to admit; he felt a bit embarrassed about the fact that in Robert's eyes he was a defenceless child. He had never thought he would ever need any skills to protect himself on that level. It was all happening way too fast for Simon, but on the other hand, life always was writing its own scenarios. Deep inside his mind, Simon agreed with Robert, but he would never say it out loud. Being a werewolf had its personal consequences, and it seemed that fighting with vampires or other unknown, yet for him, supernatural, creatures was the bad side of this new world. He desperately needed to learn how to fight, but he didn't want Robert as a teacher. He wanted to find the pack alone and get along well with them. Who knew what sort of monsters were lurking around in shadows, concluded Simon, secretly observing Robert.

*

They walked outside in silence. There was a car parked up in front of the house. One man was standing near and waiting for them. Simon turned and started walking towards the underground, but Robert clutched his elbow.

'Piss off. I'm going to work alone, and I'll resign from my post,' shouted Simon at Robert. He didn't remember the last time he was so angry. The view of Robert was enough to trigger aggression in Simon. Only thinking about having to spend more time with this old rat was more than Simon could bear. He started to feel on the edge of losing his temper. At that moment something started to happen in his body. He looked at his hands and saw fur growing slowly in a few places. He was breathing fast and observing delicate muscle movements under the skin on his hands. Robert looked at it with fear. He came close,

147

grabbed Simon's hand and whispered in a low voice.

'Look, I'm sorry. I'm obnoxious to everyone. I'm your boss at work, remember, so basically, you're working now. I'll help you get your old workplace. But please, we have a meeting in our pack's headquarter and I don't want to be late. James is bonkers about being on time as you are about organising your living space. Calm down for goodness sake. You don't know how to control the beast yet,' hissed Robert, leaning so close to him that Simon had to deflect himself otherwise Robert's lips would touch his cheek. But this time Robert didn't sound as arrogant as he usually did, and that surprised Simon. He looked at Robert, and for the first time, he saw a tiny blink of caring for him inside Robert's eyes, something so unusual that it seemed to be a small miracle. Simon sighed deeply and only nodded for agreement. They didn't talk for a while.

*

Robert sat in the front seat next to the driver, his close associate, Lee Nakano, and introduced Simon to him. They both only nodded to each other but remained silent to the end of the journey.

The headquarter was located on the far outskirts of London in an old, massive Victorian mansion surrounded by more than a hectare field. The land was fenced by high brick-walls with barbed wire on the top. The walls had pillars with strong lights and cameras installed on the top. The house was standing at the beginning of the property, leaving plenty of space in the back for old trees growing around and looked like a small park. There were a couple of alleys with benches and lanterns that were giving splendid light on those narrow paths.

The building was very well maintained with two long extensions and two large conservatories on the sides. The most significant extension was on the left side of the mansion, and it was twice as big as the main building itself. It looked like the property belonged to wealthy family from generation to generation mainly because all those enlargements were made in such a way that they kept the first architectural design unchanged.

The car entered through an already opened gate and parked on an empty lane not far from the main entrance.

Robert walked towards the mansion first without looking at his companions. Simon followed him, discouraged, hoping that this day was soon over. Robert didn't knock on the massive door but just grabbed the handle and opened it. But James was standing only a few steps upfront in a corridor like he was waiting for them. He was smiling broadly as though he was expecting a very dear guest.

'There you are, my little brother,' he said, hugging Robert without his consent.

'Okay, okay, enough of these pleasantries. I really don't have time for chit-chat with you. Let's get to the point,' said Robert, pushing James aside and heading straight towards the open stairs leading down to a basement. Robert looked around like he was seeing the design for the first time, shrugged and walked away.

'Your charm will never fade, Robert,' said James, turning towards the still open door. Simon stood on a doorstep observing both of them. It seemed Robert characterised himself very accurately, thought Simon, he was just a grumpy old man. Simon's opinion about Robert softened a bit when he saw a picture of his coldness towards the host.

Although the mansion was old, it had modern interiors. In the hall, stairs were leading to the next level above, a staircase going to the basement, a few closed doors on the side and a bright, spacious living area with an entrance to one of the large conservatories used as a dining room.

'Simon, nice to see you safe and sound. We haven't met yet officially. I'm James Leclaire, and I have the honour to be a leader of the werewolf pack called Night Reapers. Come on in, let me show you The Tavern, our clan headquarter. It's the name we use for calling this premises …'

'You've changed it. Nobody likes it,' shouted Robert, standing halfway down.

'Just ignore him. It works for me. Everyone loves that name but him,' said James, lowering his voice.

'I heard you, James. Simon, please hurry! We need to go back to the office asap,' shouted Robert from downstairs. James rolled his eyes, shook Simon's hand, nodded, smiled and followed Robert. Simon took a deep breath and walked behind him, feeling safer with every step like he had just entered his own home.

*

The basement had a similar modern design like the ground floor and the rest of the rooms in the property. There were a few long windows just under the ceiling and above the ground. There were two wide glass-doors on the opposite side of this massive room that was leading to an outside platform with brick walls and stairs up to the garden. The main space was converted into a vast living room with a couple of sofas, small tables, large TV set and even a projector which one was able to show movies on a white screen that was now rolled up.

James explained there was enough space in the premises to accommodate more than sixty people at the same time. In the added wings there were many bedrooms, and even lofts were converted into living spaces. He laughed, mentioning that there were traditional clan events when the mansion looked more like a hotel than a privet estate. He said that they had a few large tents in case there was no more room inside the mansion for more guests.

James was asking Simon about his health and overall condition. He mentioned that he was present during Simon's first shifting and the fact that it was very dramatic, but he didn't dwell on any details. Meanwhile, when they were walking downstairs, Robert was opening the door to the next room at the end of this spacious living-room and left it that way. The next chamber was a gym with similar oblong windows near the ceiling, two shower-rooms and toilets. Two exits were leading outside and were built similar to the ones in the first room and located on similar opposite sides to each other. Two men were lifting some weights on benches; they peeped at James, nodded and went back to their activities.

A young woman was standing in the middle. She was wearing clothing emphasising her sporty body shape. She had long, light blond hair tied in a ponytail. Simon was surprised at seeing Robert, who was laughing, standing close to her, talking and behaving like he was boozed at a party. She saw James and Simon arrive and waved to them.

After an official introduction, Simon learnt that she was James's daughter - Maya.

'I'm going to leave you now, Simon. Maya will do tattoos on your skin to help you adjust to new life. It's our clan's imprint glyphs, and everyone has to have them with no exceptions. When you finish, just shout, I'll show you around. By the way, we'll have an official barbecue at the weekend. You'll be introduced to other members. Robert, you don't have to be present …' declared James, nodding to Robert. He couldn't finish because Robert's challenging voice disrupted him.

'When do you stop kicking me out, James?' asked Robert, quite angrily.

'When did I do it? You said you don't want to be in a pack, but you still have a key to the main door. The locker is the same. You're just doing fuss over and over again about something that happened twenty years ago and can't let go,' said James in similar tone to Robert.

'Oh, fuss about it! Don't get me started, bro…' he didn't finish, mainly because he caught a glimpse of Maya's disapproving gaze. He shrugged and waved his hand, giving the sign that it was the time to abandon the quarrel. Simon was shocked. He had never thought that Robert would give up a fight. But now, it seemed he didn't want to do it in front of this young lady.

Both brothers went towards one more door at the end of the gym. Simon didn't see it before but when he looked now in this direction it was clear why. The full door structure was flat and in the same colour as walls that it made it hardly recognisable from the rest of surroundings. It didn't have a door-nob but only an electronic panel on the side to type in a code and open it. James did it, but his attempt to hide the number's sequence from Robert's eyes was unsuccessful. Robert not only was standing very close to James, but he leaned on his brother's shoulder to see it more clearly. He asked James to say out loud the combination, and he even typed the code inside his mobile notes. James rolled his eyes at least twice but to avoid the next wrangle with Robert he gave up and revealed the cypher.

'So, you're the new blood, aren't you? The first time someone survived Robert's bite. I hope he told you?' said Maya, sitting behind the small desk located on the corner not far from the glass-door that was leading outside.

She showed him to a chair standing on the opposite side and took a little kit case from the first drawer, unfolded it and picked one of the silver claws that were there. She opened the top of the claw, poured inside a dark liquid from a silver container shaped like a fang and closed it. She put the claw on her right forefinger and checked if the black ink was flowing. Simon sat on the other side of the table but couldn't stop staring at her. She took his right hand, put it palm down and clasped inside two leather belts attached to the desk's surface, one on a wrist and second on the height of his elbow. Simon watched what she was doing like he was enchanted. For a minute he couldn't say anything, observing her shapely fingers working fast.

'So, how did it happen? Tell me everything. How my favourite uncle finally ruined his so-called lone-wolf life?' she asked curiously but didn't stop her work. The odour of strong alcohol spread around when she took a small bottle from the kit, opened it, poured a bit on a cotton pad and wiped the skin on his trapped forearm. Simon stuttered, not knowing how to start the story. She didn't look at him but leaned over his hand and touched his skin with the silver claw she was wearing on her finger. The claw was large enough to hide her entire finger inside. It had engraved symbols that reminded him more of animal scratching than any known human language. At the moment, when metal had been laid on Simon's skin surface, he shouted out of pain but wasn't able to withdraw his tightly fastened hand.

'Yeah, I forgot to tell you. It might hurt a bit, but the liquid will numb your skin soon, just hold on for a second. Don't worry, you'll survive,' she said, smiling broadly. They were staring at each other longer than it was needed.

Simon gasped with pain again and withdrew his hand instinctively. Maya smiled, but she didn't stop making burnt marks on his skin. Simon barely could hold back the tears. He wanted to wail like a banshee out of suffering, but one look into her eyes made him swallow his cry. He was clenching his teeth and moaning quietly out of misery. For some period of time, cold chills and hot flashes circulated throughout his body like waves on a rough ocean. He was parallelised, and bizarrely, he could feel like the symbols were burning deep inside his guts. It felt like his core of existence was painfully bonding and shifting in the rhythm of the silver claw moving on the surface of his skin. The time stopped for him. Simon was so focused on the sensations he felt now that he didn't hear Maya's voice at all. She paused for a second when she realised that he wasn't listening. But she continued asking him questions after a few minutes of a break from the unnatural silence that was hanging between them. In this extended moment, they looked at each other without blinking. For him, it was like staring into a bliss, the tranquillity he couldn't reach because of the soreness that was weighing him down to the painful reality. He put his head on the desk and prayed for it to be over soon.

'So, I heard it happened to you when the red moon was the highest. Dude, it's a miracle you're alive,' she was carrying on the conversation, shaking her head in unconcealed admiration. Simon raised his head, quite taken aback with her comments. He still didn't know what to say, so she went back to work in silence. *Get a grip, man,* he chided himself inside his head. He cleared his throat and started telling the story when the pain in his hand was finally gone.

'I punched him straight in his nose. I remember it very clearly…' Simon sighed with relief and felt relaxed when his confidence was back. He felt only her small fingers working on his hand but what he saw was more dreadful. Every time when she drew a line on the skin, the moving silver claw was leaving a black mark with a bit of smoke and horrid smell of burned meat that was floating in the air. The pictures made by the claw were simple. There were symbols resembling patterns that were inscribed on the claw. Simon noticed when she finished drawing on his skin, she touched it with a similar image from the silver claw but after that, the burned glyph disappeared from the surface of his skin like it was absorbed by his body. There were no visible scars or any other marks proving that he had it at all. She was drawing a couple of different signs and in the meantime asking him questions about the event in the woods, the whole idea about filming it by Gary till the time of Simon's first transformation. Simon told her everything he had remembered, but unfortunately, the transition night was too blurry for him. When she finished, all the images from the silver claw were embossed onto his skin, but not even a small scratch was left as a proof.

'What's the meaning of those symbols?' asked Simon, finally rubbing the place where she drew just a few seconds ago. Although there was nothing there, he still had feelings of the tingling sensation on his skin. She gently unfastened belts form his forearm, giving the sign that the clan's marking was officially over.

'Oh, sorry, I should have explained it to you earlier. They're just basics to faster and painless changes into ferox, and for keeping your clothes, so you don't have to undress before you're going to feral; otherwise, all would be torn to pieces. That one is for faster regeneration, but this funny one is for a connection with us so you can find your way here, or if you need the phone number will appear in your head to call for help from The Tavern. There's always someone here, but don't call with trivial things. You really don't want to piss off James,' she replied, smiling broadly. She was showing him the symbols on the silver claw and explaining what they were for when the door opened and a four-year-old boy ran inside screaming with a joy.

'Honey bunny!' shouted Maya, jumping from behind the desk, kneeling and stretching her arms ready to hug him. The joy of their reunion could be heard far in the garden. The boy was telling some stories about animals in the Zoo. She was asking question after question making him laugh and relive the same moments once again that he experienced with other children. Simon was so absorbed in watching them that he didn't see when a well-dressd woman sat on Maya's chair. She touched his arm so gently that it made him jump out of surprise.

'It's her son, Alexander. I'm Dorothy, James's wife and you must be Simon, right?' she asked softly. She was slim, wearing glasses and dressed elegantly in a bright suit. She had a few high-quality pieces of jewellery and perfectly arranged longish hair. Although she was middle-aged, she looked like time was merciful for her, leaving only a few wrinkles near her green eyes that were emphasising her maturity. Simon greeted her officially and answered the questions she asked about him when the loud bang suddenly interrupted this pleasant time.

*

The last door, with the cypher locker on a side, was suddenly smashed so hard that it was torn out from the doorway and flew a few metres to the centre of the gym. The door was hit by James's unconscious bleeding body lying on the top. The hole in the wall showed the next room and some figures fighting inside. Someone was screaming there, and a loud animal-like growl mixed with a hysterical laugh was coming from there. Maya looked at Simon and Dorothy with a panic. She grabbed her son and hugged him tightly, turning herself in such a way that he couldn't see what was happening there.

'Vamps! Run!' shouted Dorothy at the same time. She stood up and walked towards her daughter. Maya turned and ran as fast as she could into the direction of one of the doors that were leading outside from the basement into the garden.

In the meantime, two human-shaped figures came out from the gap moving much faster than anyone that Simon had ever seen before. One of them was climbing on the wall and running fast on the ceiling like a spider. The second leaned his body forward and walked quickly with his hands dangling around. They both looked similar. They were quite bulky but dressed in rag-clothes torn in many places and covered with dark stains. Their skin had an ash-like colour with eyes entirely black, including the skin around them. They both had fresh blood all over their body. Their mouths were distorted in a grimace of rage that made them look more like demons than humans. They were showing long fangs with drops of toxins falling down from the tips like from a snake's jaw. Their fingers ended with a more than twenty-five centimetres long, dark and sharp as razors, nails. They saw Maya first, attracted to her by Alexander's cry and her rapid movement. Simon stood motionlessly, paralysed by their presence. Deep down in the bottom of his conscious, he knew how deadly the creatures were and how useless he was right now. The one on the ceiling was just above Maya's head, ready to jump when the voice from behind stopped him.

'Hey! You! Life-sucking scumbag! Over here morons,' Robert shouted loudly. He was standing in the broken doorway, holding onto the wall and leaving red marks on it. He was in werewolf feral-battle form, covered in bleeding, parallel line cuts all over his body. He barely kept his balance. He held the sword in one hand, breathing heavily. Blood with saliva was dribbling from his mouth. His voice was a mixture of barking and human words, but Simon understood everything entirely.

The vamps turned their heads into his direction, hissing. They started licking their lips at the sight of his blood. They looked at each other in a silent agreement about their next attack. The one standing on the floor jumped in one leap a few metres distance between him and Robert. He swung his claws, trying to cut off Robert's head. Robert blocked him with the sword. When the long vampire nails touched the blade, there was a sudden noise like something wet was thrown into high fire. The vampire screamed out of pain when his nails were cut off by the blade. Robert used the element of surprise and clasped the vamp chest with his claws on his free hand. He tried to pierce through his ribs but couldn't go deeper to rip out his heart.

The other vamp jumped from the ceiling straight on to Maya and the child, knocking them both down. Maya fell on the floor, still hugging her son. She was trying to turn over and cover Alexander with her body, but the vamp was sat on her feet, not allowing her to move. She grabbed her son and with all her strength pushed him away as far as she physically could. He landed a few metres from her, crying and calling her name. Dorothy grabbed him and backed off towards the backside exits. The vamp was sitting on top of Maya's body, raising his hand and preparing razors to puncture her but he was stopped. Simon, now fully transformed into a feral-battle werewolf, gripped his wrist, jerked and pulled him off.

Everything was happening in such a quick pace that Simon didn't know what to do or how to help at first. He started feeling the rage growing in him every second since he saw them walking through the gap in the wall. He felt the change coming, but he didn't have any conscious to take control over it. He could see his hands growing and covering in a black fur, claws that could split open a car like a carton box, feeling the thrill of adrenalin pushing his muscles into action.

The vamp had several straight, bleeding lines on his arms that were made by werewolf claws. And although they were closing and healing rapidly, the cuts were still deep enough to drip with a dark blood, leaving stains all over the floor. Simon squeezed the vamp's arm with so much strength that he could feel the moment he crushed the vamp's bones into pieces. Simon, without much thinking, pulled the vamp's arm, ripping off part of his forearm and leaving it holding only on to a piece of skin with dark blood pouring down under his feet. But the vamp, screaming with anger and pain, was pointing his razors-nails from his second hand to Simon's head and puncturing the skin on his cheek. Simon was blocking the vamp's hand but couldn't stop the nails going deeper into his skin. Surprisingly, Simon noticed that he didn't feel any fear but was moving instinctively like his body knew exactly what to do. He clutched the vamp's neck in less than a second and tore his head off in one fast move. Simon dropped the vamp's body and turned to Robert. He saw him lying on the floor with the second vamp kneeling on his chest.

Robert was holding the vamp's wrists, but the razors-like nails were touching his throat and face. The vamp was laughing maniacally, piercing Robert's skin slowly. Robert was snarling from pain, trying to repulse the enemy but he was weaker and weaker in every second, letting the vamp's nails get deeper inside his body.

Simon jumped to Robert in two lunges, grabbed the vamp's arm and with one tug dragged him out. The vamp turned and leapt at Simon, piercing his razors through Simon's shoulder. Simon shouted out in pain but didn't withdraw his body. He seized the vamp's hand and pushed the nails deeper into his shoulder, making them go into his flesh until they pierced through the skin to the other side. He caught the second vampire's hand in his wrist and squeezed as much as he could, immobilising him almost completely. Simon could feel and hear when he broke the vamp's bones, similar to the first one. But the pain was so intense that Simon knelt on one leg without freeing his hands. He held the vamp's second hand in his wrist, but his nails were puncturing Simon's throat, flooding his gut with blood. Simon was choking and gasping for breath. The surroundings became blurred. He had dark spots in front of his eyes. He felt weak but didn't stop clutching the vamp's hands. All of the sudden everything was over. The razors disappeared, and Simon slumped over to the floor. He saw a white feral werewolf standing over him asking some question that he couldn't understand. He passed out with the thought that they won the fight and he was the one who made it.

*

Simon woke up lying on the floor in the gym. He felt peaceful and painless. He took a deep breath, rubbed his eyes, looked around and tried to recall what had happened. He sat up straight and was slowly getting back his senses.

A few people were standing near, but he couldn't hear what they were talking about. Simon recognised James and Dorothy but there were three other male figures, and one of them had clothes covered in blood. Maya and Alexander were nowhere to be seen. Although Robert was still in his feral-battle form lying with his eyes closed, he was steadily breathing. His fur was covered with blood stains, but he didn't have any open wounds. It seemed that they were healed without leaving any visible scars.

Simon was surprised seeing James's clothes with fighting signs. His perfect suit was torn apart, he had a black eye and bruises on his cheeks. He was walking back and forth in silence with a grimace of anger on his face. Two muscular men were holding between them one man who was wearing ragged and blood-stained clothes and who could barely stay on his feet. Suddenly, James ran closer to them and punched the man in the middle, giving him a new bruise on his face and making him faint. The two men let him fall to the floor and left him like that.

Dorothy was the first who saw that Simon was awake. She came to him, smiling.

'How are you feeling?' she asked, kneeling near Simon and looking into his eyes like a doctor checking brain reactions.

'Normal, I think,' replied Simon, and for a moment he was trying to find any painful signals from his body.

'You're healing faster than we expected. That's a good sign,' she continued, inspecting places where the vampire punctured Simon's body.

'You've just had an unexpected introduction to the werewolf's world. We owe you not only an apology but true explanations. Let me show you something,' she said, standing up and giving a hand to help him get up. Simon grabbed her and stood up rapidly, but it was way too fast. He lost his balance and was struck by a feeling of dizziness. His knees were soft like jelly. But she held him firmly. Simon was surprised she could do it despite her fragile appearance. James came closer to them. He didn't look happy. She nodded to him, gave a hands gesture that only could mean she would take care of everything and sent him away.

'Those two creatures you were fighting with, were vampires in their battle-form. The worst variation that can exist. It seems you've won the ticket to see the most unwanted depth of our world in your first day here,' she said smiling, letting him go slowly, continually watching his body reaction, ready to support him in need.

After a few minutes, Simon was feeling much better. He admitted to himself, he loved the thrill of the change and the werewolf's power that could only come from being in a full feral form. He followed her, shook hands with those two men that he saw with James. Simon wasn't surprised they knew about him but was lost for words that they were very interested in meeting him. Apparently, he became some kind of a legend by surviving Robert's bite. That was weird for Simon. He started feeling some pressure inside and asked himself if he would ever be worthy enough to meet the legend's demand. His stream of thoughts was disturbed by seeing what it was on the other side of the plucked off door.

There was another room built in a similar way, including now closed windows and two outside exits. But the ceiling of the room was situated much higher than in those previous, and the chamber was visibly wider. The whole construction looked like it was a new extension to the existing wing made for one purpose. Simon was speechless at the view of this place. It wasn't a room, but a small sport's hall with an arena and benches built in.

Dorothy was walking first with a fast pace straight through the hall. Simon was following her, but he stopped a couple of times, interested in the construction that was standing inside. In the middle of the room, there was a form of an octagon arena shaped like a massive fighting-cage. It was three metres tall with a metal net on top. There was no way out from within, other than through one of two gates. There was one door leading straight from the hall and situated among three-stage benches surrounding the cage in a semi-circle. But the second entrance was more like a hatch with a flap leading from a built-up metal tunnel. The whole construction was giving the impression that it was stable enough to hold big and heavy creatures inside. There were marks on the pillars and the rods indicating the fierce fights that this place wasn't only witnessing, but it was built for.

The door from the audience side was destroyed as well. Many items had cut marks on a surface and blood stains indicating the last incident that had happened. Some of them were broken or entirely destroyed. One vampire was lying on the top benches. His blood was still dripping down between planks, making puddles of black liquid on the floor level. He seemed barely moving, but he was still alive. His hands were cuffed on his back. There were two feral werewolves keeping watch over him.

On the wall, where the barred-tunnel was attached, there was a door made from a similar metal, now opened and showing one more chamber.

Simon entered the last room, and at that moment he felt sick. He had to cover his nose because the sight and smell of blood were too strong for him to hold.

At the end of this space, there were two prison cells. There were separated by a brick wall, but the front of both of them were made with thick metal rods. On the tunnel side, there was a human-size metal box with a hatch leading through a passage into the arena to the previous room.

There was one cubicle toilet built in the corner large enough to have a small sink inside that was partially smashed now. Although the whole chamber didn't have any windows, there was a ventilation system under the ceiling, currently working in double speed. There were two cameras installed near the entrances to the cells. In the far corner, there was a standing-height black fridge with a torn off door. It showed that its hideous contents were in a horrible state. The fridge's purpose was to keep plastic bags filled with blood in an untouched, chilled condition. But now, all of them were torn-apart, scattered around the whole place and covering the floor with red liquid, leaving it in a total mess.

'This is the place where we keep vampire's outlaws. We are allowed to catch them for training...'

'What? All vamps are like those I was fighting with?' asked Simon, concerned.

'Not exactly...' answered Dorothy. Perplexity was painted on her face but only for a slight moment.

'You see, vampires don't feed only on human blood. They need emotion energy to survive. All those feelings, all those endorphins and hormones from sexual titillation to fear that are produced in humans they crave because they don't have their own. It's exactly like we need water and sun for our basic existence. That's why they have toxins in their fangs. When they bite you, it multiplies and exaggerates every strong sensation you have inside your body at that precise moment. Vamps are addicted to it. Some people can't live without the venom as well. Unfortunately for many, it works like a dope. It's a downward spiral, and it always cost humans lives…'

'Do you mean that vamps drug people and feed on emotions?' asked Simon, raising his voice with curiosity.

'Basically, yes,' replied Dorothy, smiling.

'Holly mother of God,' yelled Simon. He was trying to walk to investigate the cells inside, but she held his elbow, and just by nodding her head, she pointed to blood pools.

'We had seven here,' she declared with a bit of sadness.

'Where are the bodies?' requested Simon firmly.

'When vamps die, their bodies just disperse into atoms. There is absolutely nothing left after them, not even dust,' she said calmly.

There was a silence for a while between them. Simon was thinking and walking around the place trying to omit the blood. Dorothy knew it was a hard lesson for him, but he was adjusting faster than any other newly transformed werewolf she saw during many years. What else new would he bring to the pack, she was speculating and watching him closely.

'How does delirium work with vamps?' asked Simon. For her, he seemed to behave like a little child in a museum full of wonders, instead of being frightened.

'Like with others. But they are really very fast and strong. They can kill before delirium switches on. Fighting with vamps is extremely difficult, especially for humans,' she said, taking pictures of the scene with her mobile.

'Why didn't you guys, I mean werewolves and others, kill them all?'

'Trust me, we tried for centuries, but it's not that easy either. The bond between the parent-vamp and the newly created child of darkness works like magic glue. The head of their dynasty is treated like a saint or a pope, extremely untouchable. The whole bloodline will always protect them. Sometimes I think they move like a swarm.

You kill one, three others will appear out of nowhere. Every ecosystem has its own parasites,' Dorothy declared with a trace of bitterness in her voice.

'And now, they're part of the Guild so we can't kill them without permission?' Simon said in the same voice tone as she did.

'I can see you're one of us already,' she said, smiling. Simon looked at her and shivered. The grimace of her face, the mysterious smile and inscrutable blink in her eyes, made an impression that he encountered the true head of the pack, the silent one, always standing on a side and whispering the orders in a sweet voice that nobody could ignore. At this moment, Simon knew if he would ever want something from them, he should ask her for help.

'Now, you've seen what had happened when they were fed on animal's blood,' she said and went back to taking zoomed in pictures of damaged places.

'So, if I'm correct, animal's blood turns them into beasts, and you use them for cage fighting?' asked Simon, jumping between puddles of blood towards the metal box direction.

'Yes, this is correct. And I'm really sorry that your introduction was so unpredictable and dramatic. We don't push anyone to fight. We have specially trained warriors, and they're absolutely dedicated to it. But believe me, Simon, those vamps are a piece of cake regarding some other savage creatures that the pack have to deal with. You see, there are many lycans, not only werewolves, to protect the whole society...'

'But why do you protect humans?' Simon asked, perplexed. Dorothy looked at him puzzled. She had never heard that kind of question, and that was weird for her.

'Because they depend on us. I'm human, called Hectorian, with a rare immunity for delirium like you are, otherwise you couldn't hit Robert when he was changed. If lycans have children between themselves, they'll be very beastly tempered and sooner or later cause a lot of trouble. To keep balance and peace, they should have kids with normal humans...' she didn't finish.

'What? How can I find a wife?' asked Simon, astonished.

'You're adorable. Don't worry. It's between one and three per cent of the population that has this ability so it's not high, but it's not that low. There are special places to meet ladies who'd like to have a werewolf as a husband, however difficult a life they'll have together,' said Dorothy, smiling broadly. Simon peeped at her and wanted to ask how she met James, but before he had any chance to articulate the question, she continued to talk.

'Anyway, Simon, I know Robert very well. He'll do everything to push you to be a warrior, but you don't have to. You see, he never had a son of his own, and now he has you. Neoshamans bounded you with him by spiritual adoption to save you and if Robert refused to do it, he'd lose all his werewolf powers and abilities...' she couldn't finish.

'He'd become a normal human?'

'No, it's not possible. But he could never change into ferox again and that's the worst punishment ever created for ferals.'

CHAPTER 12

7th July - Movies

For many reasons, they all couldn't meet on the same day. When Robert discovered this, he threw a tantrum and demanded that everyone, including himself, be present at every meeting; no exceptions. Gary had no choice but to postpone the gathering for the next few days and let everyone schedule in the meeting. In the meantime, Gary requested that everyone did some homework by emailing him ideas and solutions for the problem called 'how to save Gary's life'. Unfortunately, nobody replied so Gary didn't receive even a slight hint on how to do it. Therefore, he started feeling that the whole project was on his shoulders.

After the first shock of oozing black blood, Gary felt pretty well for the next days. He called to Draco and asked how it was possible, but Draco was only guessing that Erick started fighting back for his life. After all, he was an ancient vampire and had skills that were way beyond Draco's knowledge. Gary presumed that Draco had more terrible dreams that were keeping him constantly awake, mainly because of his sleepy voice, losing focus and lack of detailed answers. But at least nothing more dramatic had happened and Gary was hoping it would stay like that for the next few weeks.

Gary was quite happy to stay alone for some time, but the lack of Mark's cooking put him on survival mode of eating fast-foods and homemade sandwiches. He made himself busy with things to do, like making event's movies as fast as it was possible, keeping him occupied and preventing his mind from harmful thinking about his blood connection with a dying vampire.

He finished those four official videos and, quite content with his work, sent DVDs via a courier service to the office of the company he had a contract with. Amanda, the director of this business, was so happy with the material, she sent a new proposition for next events but located in a distant island off the coast of Scotland. Gary smiled and thought that it was a great idea, if he would be still alive about that time. Regardless of his own insecurities about still being among the living, he answered positively for the new job opportunity.

But the real excitement impacted him in the precise first seconds he started to watch the same material but with Theo's sign written on them to reveal the hidden secrets behind the veil life of all of those creatures that were described in myths and legends for centuries. Sometimes Gary couldn't believe not only that they existed, as Sean and others ensured him, but that they all had a well-developed society with legal regulations and a community perfectly blended in normal cities all over the world.

Gary was a bit disappointed that the pictures didn't show as much as he would like to have to make a full-length movie. He was wondering what possible short story he could create from it. It wasn't much so he didn't have too many options about the plot, he could only make something out of what he had. That was quite a difficult and challenging process for him. But he needed this second project as a break from the main problem he tried to sort out such as finding a way to secretly open the coffin that was standing in the middle of the British Museum. Gary made a few notes but wasn't content with it. He was throwing one more crumpled page into the bin when his brother came in to the room without knocking.

'What's up, bro?' asked Mark sitting on the second office chair standing just next to Gary's. He threw his rucksack to the corner and didn't only sit, but he adjusted chair's back horizontally in a way so that he was practically laying on it.

Gary looked at his few days beard, wavy ragged hair, tight, worn-off jeans and naked torso showing Mark's perfectly shaped muscles with a few long scars giving him even more sex appeal, and felt a tiny prick of jealousy prodding to the wrong button of Gary's personality. Instinctively, Gary ran his finger through his hair and tied it in a ponytail. Without looking at his brother, he corrected his old, stained T-shirt as much as he could on his bit too rounded belly. But deep down inside Gary's mind, the annoying voice was laughing at him, telling him that he would never be good enough to compete with Mark.

'You stink. Go and take a shower!' Gary expressed his irritation, lowering his voice.

'Whoa! Why you so tense? What's wrong?' asked Mark, sitting straight, putting his hands on Gary's chair and turning it into his direction.

'I'll tell you what's wrong! Stop parading half naked in this house. I forbid you from hitting on Jessica. She's my best friend, but for you, she is only the next chewing gum to use for short pleasure. You're a womaniser. Go hunt pussies somewhere else. Not here, not with her. Am I clear?!' Gary shouted the last sentence, pushing Mark's hands away. Mark just stared at him in silence. There was a slight moment when Gary could see the pain in Mark's eyes, but it disappeared in one blink.

Mark stood up slowly and with a low voice said; 'You're very wrong about me, bro. I'll try to keep distance. She doesn't want me anyway. Are we good now?' asked Mark in a way that suggested Gary's winning position. Gary nodded and went back to his previous task. He was angry. He kept rewinding the pictures as a distraction. It was meaningless but gave him time to calm down. He didn't pay too much attention to what his brother was doing.

Mark took out some fresh clothes from Gary's wardrobe and emptied his bag of dirty ones. He piled it up on one arm, and on his way to the bathroom, he came closer to the desk and put three small spying cameras just in front of his brother. Gary looked surprised, staring from Mark to the cameras and back. He recognised the newest type that he could never afford to buy, and Theo's sign was already written on them. Moreover, the cameras were the size of a thumb and part of their design was a removable little drone shaped like a dragonfly. Regardless of how tiny they were, they still could catch very sharp pictures with great sound.

'How did you get that? These are military type so you can only buy them on the black market,' asked Gary, forgetting to be angry at his brother.

'I have my ways. Don't show anyone. We need to talk,' said Mark walking out from the room.

Gary couldn't believe what was recorded on them. The whole meeting they had a few days ago in the living-room was there, shot from three different angles. Although the cameras looked like toys the pictures and sound from them were sharp and clear. He downloaded the material on to his PC and checked it briefly. He put it all in a specially created folder named 'flowers' encrypting it with one of his usual passwords which was also known to his brother. Gary had a peculiar way for naming things that mattered to him. Before he finished watching the pictures on fast forward from the last camera, Mark was back. Gary peeped at him and admitted, but only in his head, that his brother looked even better when he was shaved and well-groomed.

'Why did you record the meeting and where did you hide it?' asked Gary inquisitively.

'First, I don't trust Robert and Draco. Both of them are coming here for some egoistic reason. They're not for you. Never trust a vampire, bro. That was the first rule of your father that I heard. Our mother trusted him, and she's dead now. We don't have much choice now other than to cooperate with them. But we don't know what the future might bring and when those pictures could come in handy,' said Mark and passed a bottle of beer to Gary. He brought not only drinks but a huge plate full of well-made sandwiches. Gary glared at him a bit longer than before and started wondering again, how it was possible to have a so perfectly shaped body and eat like a horse on a daily basis.

Mark said nothing. He put the best three pieces up in front of Gary and continued to devour food quite fast until the plate was empty.

'What about Robert?' Gary asked with a friendlier attitude towards Mark. After all, Mark was his brother and Gary would die for him. Gary was tearing away a piece of bread and putting it in his mouth like a connoisseur just to enjoy the food for longer.

'I don't know yet, but he was too eager to help and his demands to know everything are suspicious. Moreover, as far as I know, he didn't go to his pack's meetings for years and now, suddenly out of the blue, he's changed?' Mark declared the last sentence lowering his voice and whispering.

'How do you know that?' asked Gary with slight disbelief in his tone.

'Because his pack has the best warriors in England, and a few are my buddies. Robert's brother, James, is an Alfa, and trust me, they never do things that don't benefit the pack. Robert might play lone-wolf, but he'll never leave them. It's just a hunch. How are the cameras?' Mark asked, taking one of his mobiles with a large screen, he switched it on, found the application to control one of the drones and started flying it around the room. They both were engaged in this activity for some time, but unfortunately, the battery ran out and the drone plummeted on to Gary's head. They laughed, drank more beers and were watching the recorded pictures. Mark installed on Gary's PC a program to control drones and to have instant access to recorded films.

Mark saw Gary's notes about making a movie from the material filmed in the forest and was quite interested in the ideas. Gary didn't have any new concept for it, but he confirmed his will to make something that could push his career into new paths.

'What if you'd do only a short movie first time?' asked Mark.

'Well, that makes sense. I could write a story, but the problem is sound and dialogues. They just can't fit,' replied Gary with a bit of sadness.

'What if you'll write different dialogues and replace the originals?'

'It wouldn't match to the lips movement. I thought about it already.'

'Don't focus on roadblocks, Gary. Just switch off the original sound completely…'

'And make like a silent movie from the 20s…' Gary interrupted him suddenly. He had a facial expression showing that the idea hit him like rapid thunder.

Gary was stunned by his own thoughts so much so that he was speechless for minutes. He leaned back on his chair, put his hands behind his head and closed his eyes. His mind was running wildly, connecting flashing images, notions, and ideas into one concept. This was the enlightening moment when the brand-new vision was created in his brain. He saw it. He saw the whole film from the beginning to the end frame by frame in slow motion like he was watching it in a cinema.

'In sepia's, like a faded photograph…' Gary was talking more to himself than to brother.

Mark opened a new bottle of beer and put one on the desk near Gary's. He knew that was the moment when Gary's brain works with its full capacity and if someone would interrupt, it might trigger his anger. Mark also knew he couldn't have any more conversations with his brother until the stage of outlining the idea was over, and Gary would write all of it on paper with every small detail he had in his head.

Mark didn't like being bored, so he went to the kitchen with his own small projects of baking chocolate cake with strawberries on the top that he knew was Jessica's favourite.

After a couple of hours, Mark came back to Gary's room with a few muffins on a plate.

'What's up, bro?' he asked, poking Gary's arm with a cup of coffee.

Gary looked at him smiling broadly. He took the mug in one hand and one muffin to the other.

'You wanted to talk about something with me, have you?' asked Gary, biting half of the cake at once.

'Well, I want you to record all meetings. I might not be able to be here all the time, but that is important to me.'

'Oh, I certainly will do it, that I can promise easily. Just show me where did you hide it the first time. And when I should give them back.'

'It's a present for you. I don't want them back. I just need records.'

'Man, are you kidding me? They're very expensive.'

'Don't worry. Just promise to record something for me from time to time. So, how's the project going so far?' asked Mark.

'Never better. By the way, do you remember what Robert said about opening the coffin?'

'Vaguely, why?

'Because, I just got an idea on how we can do it exactly how he advised,' declared Gary, showing a few pages with something passionately scribbled on them.

CHAPTER 13

8th July - The Plan

The evening was bright this time of a year. Reddish sunset shone through opened windows into the living-room, making this place look like something from a fairy tale.

Gary was walking to and fro, thinking about every possible problem they had to discuss with the group. But despite the fast pace and the death threat following him like a pet on a very short leash, somehow deep down in guts, Gary felt excited. It was the same thrill as he had before going to a paintball competition, mainly because the blazing intensity of upcoming new adventures always made him willing to work without a break. He took one blueberry muffin from the pile that Mark baked and started eating. He wasn't hungry, but the taste of his brother's pastries was something he could never resist, even if he was full to the maximum.

Gary was on his third one when they all started coming in, almost in the same moment like a bunch of well-synchronised watches. The last one who crossed the doorstep was Draco, looking differently this time. He was wearing light-blue T-shirt and white trousers matching his blond hair perfectly. He wasn't as pale as before, and not only appeared more alive but even walked more briskly.

Gary watched him with amazement, and he couldn't resist asking the question.

'Sunlight doesn't burn you?'

'No,' Draco laughed.

For the first time Gary saw him smiling so broadly. Gary was thinking, if he didn't know who Draco was, he could never guess that he was a vampire whose existence was depending on human blood. Moreover, it wasn't only blood he needed but a variety of emotions as well. Gary admitted it was bizarre when he first heard from Simon the story about the fight in his werewolves' mansion and all those descriptions, picturing vampires as vicious predators. The story of Simon's fight was clashing with the view of a polite and well-mannered Draco they all had met. Gary didn't take Simon's news too seriously, so he called to Draco to confirm it, and was no less astonished hearing the same from the old vampire himself.

Today Draco looked healthy, even charming, but maybe his warm expression and elegant style was the trap luring naive people to become his feast, thought Gary, surprised by his new outlook.

'If it was as easy to burn vamps by using only sunlight, we'd have utterly eradicated them all centuries ago,' said Robert sarcastically, walking from the kitchen with a plate full of a big piece of chocolate cake surrounded with strawberries and fork sticking out of the top of it.

'And you are already helping yourself, aren't you?' asked Mark, waving his hands with disapproval on this view.

All participants of the meeting were standing in the hall, but they all came here from different directions.

'I couldn't resist. Some bastard might be faster and eat it all. See, I'm crippled so I can't win the race for food,' declared Robert sarcastically, making his walk even more limping and hitting the floor much louder with his black walking-stick. He stopped near Draco with a challenging gaze.

'Gary, check his skin behind the earlobes. He should have reddish dots. I bet you'll find five of them there, one for every hundred years of his sucking life. The first dot gives them immunity for sun. If you want to kill any vamp, ask me. I'm an expert of hunting them,' stated Robert, not looking at Gary but staring straight into Draco's eyes. Draco didn't react at all.

'Your threat doesn't work on me. I've heard it a million times centuries before your grandparents were born. But I'm still standing here safe and sound. And yes, Gary, I'm immune to the sun,' Draco pronounced his sentences clearly, almost emotionless, and also not looking at Gary.

'Guys, can we finally start? We've lost a couple of days, so we need to speed up everything,' said Gary, accenting the last part, and interrupting this way too toxic atmosphere that might develop into something more verbally abusive if not violent.

*

They all sat comfortably in the living-room, taking seats in similar places as they had before. However, Gary noticed that Mark didn't sit next to Jessica but brought a chair from the kitchen and put it near one of the windows. He situated his position in such a way that he could easily see what was happening on the street near the house's entrance. Jessica and Simon were sitting on the couch whispering something with the lowest voices possible making the conversation understood only by them.

Sean, with his academic manners, came to the meeting well-prepared. He hanged a large white screen board, entirely covering the TV set attached to the wall. He put a projector on the small coffee table and adjusted its position to the screen. He had notes and was well-groomed like he walked to class to lecture his students. Despite the hot weather, he was the only one in the room wearing a bright jacket.

Gary waited until everyone was quiet, especially for Robert to finish eating the cake.

'Evening, guys. This meeting is set for one purpose as we all already know. Let's recap our task briefly. So, we need to find a way how to open the coffin that is standing in the middle of the well-secured property in The British Museum. We have to remove an ancient vampire trapped inside it. It has to be done legally without converting ourselves into criminals. The errand is pretty challenging because, according to Draco's nightmares, we have limited time until I and Draco die horribly very soon. I hope everyone has some ideas but before we will brainstorm the plan, let Sean show us the depth of shit we're all in,' said Gary, pointed at Sean giving him permission to start.

Mark covered the windows with the curtains and that made the room pretty dim. Sean stood up, straightened his suit, sipped black coffee from a large mug and pressed the button of the remote control to start the projector. The picture of the Great Court of The British Museum appeared first. The coffin was standing on the platform between two stairs going around outside the white, circular Reading Room. Two huge banners were hanging on the wall advertising the new exhibition called 'Supernaturals in myths and legends throughout the centuries' with images of werewolves and hunters that were drawn sometime in the Middle Ages.

'Why did you put it there? You couldn't find a less centred place?' snorted Robert sarcastically, pointing at it with his walking-stick.

'No, if I could, I'd do it,' answered Sean without any emotions like he was talking to badly-behaved school-boy.

'Does anyone have any ideas on how to do it?' asked Gary, preventing this dispute to exaggerate. He paused for a few seconds waiting for answers, but nobody said anything.

Sean interrupted the uncomfortable silence by showing more pictures of the museum taken not only in the exhibit halls but also a few from conservation rooms. He was explaining the locations, but it didn't help to find any solution to the problem.

'Well, last time we met I mentioned already I can't move the coffin until the exhibition is over. That means waiting for the next two months, but this option is of the table, as we all know…' Sean wanted to say something more, but his lecture was interrupted by Gary jumping from his place so excitedly like he just had won lottery ticket.

'I know how to do it in the middle of the day with all visitors and your co-workers watching it,' said Gary smiling broadly. Nobody reacted. They all were waiting for him to finish. They were more surprised by Gary's happy outburst than the news itself.

'We'll do a show, like a street theatre, and opening the coffin will be the culmination of this performance…' Gary continued excitedly and was only slightly confused by their lack of cheerfulness.

'What? How?' asked Sean with disbelief. Almost everyone responded similarly but not Robert who grinned with the broadest smile Gary had seen so far on his face.

'I don't know how yet, but I'll figure it out,' said Gary, very enthusiastically.

'I want the main role,' Robert stated and rose his hand high like a child in a classroom reserving the best place in a theatrical activity.

'You can't have it,' said Sean.

'Why?' asked Robert, quite offended.

'Because only Gary can open the coffin,' declared Draco, staring at Robert in a challenging way.

'Why me? Is there anything I don't know yet?' asked Gary, perplexed, staring at Sean. Gary didn't predict the scenario that he might have to play the main role, maybe because he never played any character on any stage. He considered himself as being too clumsy and stressed out to be an actor. It started in primary school in drama classes when all that he was doing back there was sitting on a chair and watching the rehearsals, praying not to be asked to be a more productive participant of the show.

'Because the Tritus' End is made by witch hunters and your father was one of them. It's in your blood…' Sean didn't finish.

'So, how am I going to do it? Just stand near, put my hands on and it'll magically open itself?' Gary looked puzzled. He didn't expect that outcome when he first got the idea about a theatrical performance. He was thinking that while the group would be doing the show, he would be standing behind the camera and recording it.

'No, it doesn't work like that. You need to use the key to open it,' said Sean with a bit of sadness.

'So, I'll play as support and just turn the key, what's the problem?' asked Gary.

'The problem is, we don't have a key…' said Sean reluctantly.

'What?' almost everyone asked at the same time, even Draco. Robert's voice could be heard on the street. He had the loudest tone.

'It burned with your parents. Your father had the key on the day of their car accident. There was never a spare one,' expressed Sean, with a bit of anger accenting the last sentence.

'Why you didn't tell me that?' asked Draco directly and looking utterly surprised.

'When I found out about it, you were already out of London avoiding any contacts. I'm telling you now,' Sean's voice rose, and angry flashes passed throughout his face. For a minute nobody said anything. They all just looked at each other not knowing what to say or what to do.

'So, it seems you both knew about the coffin before Erick was closed in there,' said Robert, pointing at Sean and Draco and observing them closely.

'Of course, I knew. I helped them to find this artefact,' replied Sean, quite snappily.

'Sean didn't know for whom we were going to use it,' continued Draco, glaring from Sean to Robert. Sean only nodded in agreement with him.

Gary was looking at them and had a firm decision of investigating the case of his parent's death after saving his own life.

'Oh, come on guys! Nobody can see the simple solution? We can make a new key,' said Jessica, as if she were talking about something incredibly easy. She interrupted the silence in a perfect moment, redirecting their focus to more present issues.

'What?' this time only Sean asked the question.

'Look, just connect the facts. First, the coffin was made centuries ago so we'll not deal with very complicated electronic locks created nowadays. The keys used in those times aren't small. The whole opening mechanism inside has to be pretty big due to the size of the coffin itself,' she affirmed confidently. Gary gazed at her with astonishment.

'But how will we know what kind of shape the key has to make a new one?' asked Sean, perplexed.

'Well, the second, I have a small camera on a wire with a light. I can record how the mechanism looks on the inside. I'll re-create the plans and ta-da - brand new key printed in 3D ready to use,' she said that with such lightness in her voice like she was buying tickets to the cinema.

'That might work. I'll arrange a photo session before opening times,' said Sean with enthusiasm. It seemed the tension was gone and everyone around looked more relaxed.

'I'll go,' said Gary eagerly.

'Me too, just in case something might happen to you near the coffin like it did to Draco last time,' declared Mark in a voice that cut off any possible objection.

*

They had a short break with tea and cake made and served by Mark. He tried to omit Robert, justified by the chunk of the pastry he ate already, but the werewolf took Simon's plate, licked the cream very wildly and with a smile watched Mark's disappointment. Simon was speechless. Before he realised what was going on, the last pieces of cakes were possessed by Robert who looked perfectly happy with his behaviour. There was no more cake left so it seemed like Simon was the one who wouldn't taste it. But Jessica brought the second fork from the kitchen, gave it to Simon, and they both ate the one from her plate.

*

The atmosphere relaxed. Gary thought that there was something magical about how good food could ease social tension, drastically changing how things stand, especially for improvement of teamwork. Suddenly, the task seemed for all of them more funny than scary. They started chatting about what kind of theatrical performance they could do and how long it might take to complete the opening. Sean said he could have permission for the show but not longer than half an hour which was too short for any act already written. They all agreed it had to be something new, but the story had to match the exhibition theme, and the coffin had to be used as a prop at the end. They brainstormed ideas for next hour, creating a few ridiculous stories from parallel universes, with crooked characters, but none of it was interesting enough for Gary to be happy with. Nevertheless, he did make notes and promises to write some simple acts but catchy enough to make a good impression on Sean's manager. They knew that the unexpected pace of the performance might jeopardise the whole event, but Sean assured them he would do whatever it might take to have the permission for the show. But that wasn't the worst problem they had to face. Gary saw the issue coming way before the meeting started.

'Guys, it doesn't matter if the play is modern or not. The critical question is, what we are going to do after the coffin is opened?' he asked and saw the strike of this vision paralysing not only him but everyone else.

There it was. He said it out loud. The answer, he didn't want to see in his vision, what would happen after the performance was done.

'Sean, do you know in what kind of condition Erick might be after we set him from the trap?' Gary wanted to know more, because suddenly he realised that everything they were planning now, could go very, very wrong.

'Well…' Sean had a problem to articulate his own doubts. He didn't have an answer, and that was the moment when the lack of knowledge he hated so much was the most stressful part of this day. He knew there was no time for research and even if he found witch hunters, and they agreed to talk with him about their artefacts, with enormous luck, all those endeavours bordered on miraculous, and would take years to achieve. Moreover, there was nothing certain in it.

He remembered a similar conversation he had had ten years ago about The Tritus' End with Draco and Gary's father - George Roger. They found the coffin with a strike of luck. They didn't have any written instructions and everything they had was some unproven pieces of information mentioned in legends and a few guesses that Sean could decipher from reliefs and words inscribed on the coffin surface. Sean, not once, came across the issue about old artefacts and facts that the knowledge about how to use them was buried under the blooded dust from wars that were rolling over and over through Europe for centuries, like never-ending ocean waves. But he knew he could never show how unsure he was about what they were trying to do. Because for Sean, it wasn't only about Gary, Draco and trapped Erick, but also about the weak peace between vampires, humans, lycanthropes and other creatures living in this world, that the Guild established with such a persistent effort only ten years ago.

Sean sighed deeply; he corrected his clothes while keeping his usual poker face.

'The coffin itself is created to stun and slow down some creatures trapped there. So, I believe Erick should not be able to walk on his own feet but need to be taken out by us,' said Sean calmly and quite confidently, accenting the last sentence.

But the tiny voice inside Sean's head was mocking him. It was saying that he might be wrong and the angry, hungry, overpowering vampire would jump out with a killing rage, so long fuelled by his survival instinct enhanced by a long time of slow tortures, and vent the anger by slaughtering those present not only in the museum but exceeding his hunt to London streets. Sean shivered when he was thinking about the possible outcome. Who would catch Erick if this scenario came to life? And what kind of consequences would they all would have to face after it? Sean thoughts ran like a storm giving him only the most horrible vision of failure. The concept stuck inside Sean like a sword of Damocles hanging over his head.

'Are you sure about it?' asked Robert.

'Yes, I had time to study the reliefs on the coffin. It was made in times when written language was reserved for the rich only, and witch hunters were folks from many different backgrounds. So, they showed the basics features on the surface of coffin. I'll do zoomed pictures of them to show you,' at least that was true, thought Sean answering calmly. But still, the reliefs didn't answer every question he had. There was no certainty about how the whole item worked on such an old vampire trapped inside. And how one of the largest collection of artefacts from around the world was influencing the coffin itself. Sean looked around, saw trust in their eyes and he shivered again. Although Sean was pleased to see how it calmed not only Gary but his half-brother Mark, the fear of the unknown grew even stronger in him.

'Okay, I think we have to trust you. After all, you're the expert in that field. So, what are we going to do after it's open?' asked Gary, only to redirect his focus from own doubts to something he could hold on to, something that sounded a bit more optimistic.

'We can make him look like Juliet and pull him out of the coffin like she got out of the crypt after faking her death,' said Robert, smiling.

Gary wasn't sure if he was mocking them or was trying to help. Everyone laughed, even Robert himself.

'And you should be the Romeo waking her up from eternal sleep by a romantic and passionate kiss. That's your leading role,' said Draco, still laughing. Robert made a crooked face and showed a rude hand gesture to him. This looked more like comical mocking than open hatred between werewolf and vampire.

Gary was laughing with the others, but inside his head, the little sparkle of the new concept started to emerge. He admitted that was a pretty good idea, putting Erick as one of the characters in the act. He took his notes and start writing fast.

'Gary, you aren't taking this seriously, are you?' asked Sean with his serious lecturer gaze.

'Why not?' Gary looked around and saw puzzlement in their eyes.

'How are you going to connect Shakespeare with a vampire, I wonder?' asked Robert, perplexed.

'Why can't you? They have something in common,' answered Gary, smiling.

'What's that?' asked Draco.

'A lot of freshly cut wounds and flowing blood' declared Robert, sarcastically.

'That too, but I was thinking more about the amount of dead bodies that we can be used for the show's sake...' Gary couldn't finish as he was interrupted by Simon question.

'Like a zombie?'

'Zombies weren't seen for a century,' said Sean with his academic lecturer tone.

'No! No zombies. I hate zombies. Zombie-free zone in this play,' Gary continued the conversation but didn't stop making notes.

'Okay, let's focus on the scenario. The coffin is open, Erick is half conscious; we are taking him out and then what? Don't forget where we'll all be standing,' said Sean clicking on a remote control to find the first picture of the Great Court in the museum.

'You haven't mentioned that we'll be surrounded by a cheering crowd, probably more than a hundred people staring at us. And, I bet there'll be some vamps among them,' said Robert, very cheerfully.

'We can't leave the stage and walk away with him. Someone else has to do it. We need some diversion,' said Mark.

'We can't make more mayhem in the museum. Our show is the distraction already,' said Sean with a high-pitched voice, indicating his irritation.

'So, after taking Erick's body out, we need to replace him with someone who can get up and keep playing the role,' said Gary writing notes and not looking at anyone.

'Like a magic trick in a cartoon. Snapped fingers, loud bang and there, it is a brand new person replacing Erick. I love the idea. Who has the wizard powers in this group?' asked Robert, very amused.

'Or, we need to create an illusion trick like magicians do. Puff, and the mechanism hidden in a stage's floor is triggered by stepping on it and someone will disappear. I'd love to build it. Finally, something that can make my brain go wild,' said Jessica in such manners as if she was talking about changing a lightbulb. This time nobody laughed and even Robert was calmly staring at her. Gary, with his mouth half open, glared at her the longest and then searched for approval in Sean's eyes.

'Well, as you can see the coffin is standing on the podium about one and a half metres high above the floor. There is a possibility we can build the scene around,' said Sean, zooming in on the picture of the coffin and encircling the surroundings, showing the empty space they could use.

'That might work pretty well,' said Gary and everyone agreed but Robert.

'Okay, let say we'll somehow exchange Erick's body with her,' said Robert, pointing out at Jessica.

'Why me?' she asked.

'Because if I play Romeo, I'd rather kiss you than him,' declared Robert, waving his hand into Draco's direction with a rude hand gesture and distorted face expression like he did before. But this time Draco didn't respond to this provocation.

'What makes you think you'll play?' asked Mark.

'Oh, I'm sure I will. You need to keep the crowd occupied for about half an hour, and nowadays you'll need some good action otherwise they'd be bored, especially teenagers. We all need to play,' said Robert, very pleased with his comments.

'He's right. It's only seven of us, so basically we need, at least, ten more people for help with this venture,' said Sean. There was a silence after his declaration.

'I'll ask my pack for help,' said Simon, raising his hand.

'No way!' shouted Robert, sitting straight.

'Why not? Maya said I can do it, if I need. And I need it now. Do you have any problems with that?' asked Simon confidently. After their last visit in the Tavern and all that happened there, the relation between Robert and Simon had changed for better.

'Oh, really? You've been there once, and you demand something from them already?' asked Robert, quite annoyed.

'No, I don't demand. I'll ask for help. I don't have any unresolved problems from twenty years ago like you do. And as you mentioned, there might be a lot of vampires waiting to snatch Erick, that's why we need protection. Do you know anyone better than a pack of warriors for it?' asked Simon, staring at Robert. Robert said nothing but nodded with agreement. He didn't look happy with this news, but he didn't oppose any more.

'The bottom line of our meeting today is: Gary will write the script and prepare cameras, Jessica will recreate the key and adjust the stage for our purpose...' Sean didn't finish again.

'I'll help her. I have access to 3D printing, and I know people from whom we can borrow the stage and other equipment,' declared Mark, raising his hand. Jessica smiled and blushed but said nothing.

'Simon will bring help from the pack as our support...' said Gary.

'You, Robert, need to figure out what to do with Erick after getting him out from the museum,' said Sean but he didn't finish as he was interrupted by Robert.

'What he's doing?' asked Robert, provocatively pointing at Draco.

'I'm paying for everything,' stated Draco confidently.

There it was, the big elephant of this meeting that was lurking behind everyone's back was finally let out. About half an hour ago, Gary started to think that the project was growing with every matter they had to deal with, and the question about money was banging inside his head louder and louder with every question they asked. He couldn't stop asking himself, who would pay for it? Gary's job was based on money he earned from gig to gig so sometimes he didn't have enough to pay for himself and had to depend on his brother's cash. He felt ashamed thinking about asking for more money from Mark and felt even more uneasy about the vision that he would have to borrow from his friends. Draco's declaration relaxed Gary completely.

'Just please note, guys, don't be afraid to ask for it. And I really don't care how much things will cost. I'm not going to argue about it…' Draco didn't finish due to Robert's laugh.

'I want one million,' he said scornfully.

'You're not a professional actor but an amateur. Your wages will be on the minimum level, but yep, I'll pay you,' replied Draco seriously and that made Robert feel very uncomfortable.

'Okay, it's all settled. We'll meet in a couple of days and revise our progress,' said Sean and he switched off the projector, giving the official sign to end the meeting.

CHAPTER 14

9th July - The Coffin

'It's 8.40 already. Why are you so late?' asked Sean angrily while walking very fast through the Great Court of the British Museum this sunny morning.

'Seven o'clock is middle of the night for Gary. He often is going to sleep at this time and the traffic was horrible. We couldn't make it anyway,' said Mark, making excuses for them all.

Sean snorted incomprehensibly, rolling his eyes. Mark wanted to add more comments about the apparent fact about living in busy London, but he only sighed and waved a hand with resignation.

'If I can be on time by the Tube, you too can. No excuses...' but Sean didn't finish his sentence. He peeked at his watch again, turned around and continued walking with double the pace, grumbling something under his nose. Fortunately for those who were walking behind him, nobody understood what he was saying. Gary, Jessica, and Mark were following him trying to keep up with his speed. It was that time in the museum when the staff started preparing for the work day ahead, and some of them were already walking around the Court solving current problems.

Gary was stunned and amazed by the view of the casket. There was something magnificent in it, but he couldn't name what exactly it was. It wasn't only the enormous size, much larger than a standard human coffin, nor all those reliefs and inscriptions covering every possible place on the surface, but it was more of the splendour that was emanating with gentle vibrations a subtle energy that could be felt all around. Gary felt a sudden shudder going through his whole body, like low electrical shock-waves, leaving goosebumps on his skin. He looked around and wasn't sure if they all were as highly impressed or felt a similar sensation.

'The casket was made around 50 A.D. from about a thousand-year-old olive tree. It's covered with black wax from an unknown source,' Sean sounded like a tour-guide, pulling out a professional camera from a special bag and started taking zoomed photos.

'But why did they call it a coffin?' asked Gary curiously.

'Because whoever, or whatever, was put there, never meant to get out. They were left to die in a very slow torture. They could suffer for years inside. It was specially designed for ancient vampires, the ones you can't kill so easily, as far as I could decipher from some notes on it,' replied Sean, not interrupting his activity.

The casket was nothing like any ordinary coffin for humans. It was a black, rectangular, massive box which could contain quite a large creature inside. It was more than two and a half meter long, about a metre in width and height. It didn't have a standard lid, but there was a line indicating that the box was split at exactly half of the heights. On most of the sidewalls surface and on the top there were the bas-reliefs that were picturing stories of hunting monsters. There were werewolves figures, vampires with long claws and fangs coloured in bright red, other shape-shifter creatures standing over human's mutilated bodies, fighting among themselves or with human warriors. There were groups of knights wearing silver armour with long swords who were protecting cities. There were witch hunters torturing non-humans in all sorts of ways and killing them using strange looking types of equipment. There were inquisitors tormenting witches and burning them on stakes. There were symbols, moon phases, short notes, and even sketches of some herbs or liquids that were picturing deadly methods of the fastest way to eliminate the monsters. All figures, written words and symbols were perfectly formed in silver. The bodies were built very proportionally and detailed. Their faces were expressing all sorts of emotions from happiness on humans who were torturing their enemies, and to fear and panic on non-humans fighting for their last breath. There were three massive hinges on the opposite side-wall to the locker. Although the whole box looked very well-preserved, there were a few places where figures were partially broken or even wholly destroyed leaving only their shapes on a surface and showing the colour of the wood under the wax. However, there was one place on the corner that had claw marks that were cut deep into the surface and left the area wrecked.

'Guys, you need to hurry,' said Sean, much calmer than a few minutes ago. He continued taking pictures, zooming closely at every scene.

Gary, Mark, and Jessica reacted similarly. They all were wowed by the magnificence and mastery of the casket creation. They walked around it with amazement, pointing at figures, showing the scenes to each other and making loud comments. They stopped at the spot where the keyhole was placed. It was surrounded by three knights in full, gold armour riding on white horses. Their swords were made from red stones shinning now in the intense morning light. That was only one place on the whole coffin where gold colour was used, and the figures were sitting on horses. They looked different compared to other which hunters that were pictured on the surface. There were some descriptions, some symbols near the knights and silver crescent moon among stellar constellations.

The keyhole was round, and that confused all of them, even Sean, who came close to their group. They were taking pictures with mobiles wondering about the unusual shape of the key. Sean gave his camera to Gary and was ready to depart when suddenly a warm woman's voice that came from behind made him freeze in one place.

'Sean, are you giving a private tour to your family?'

Gary, who was standing with the camera pointed directly to the locker, turned around fast, looking so perplexed like a teenage boy peeping through a small window into the ladies' bathroom. They all were taken aback by her gentle voice and abrupt question.

'Morning, Nora. You're early today. I'm just showing them around my new exhibition,' answered Sean, disconcerted.

'Hello, Mark. You're handsome as usual and Gary is here. It's so unusual when you're both visiting uncle at work. That's very nice that you finally came along. Who's that lovely young lady? Are you the girlfriend of one of them?' asked Nora, staring at Jessica and pointing between Mark and Gary. They looked at each other, not having a clue how to answer.

'I'm only their friend,' Jessica replied, smiling. Mark tried to say something but resigned in articulating his thoughts after Jessica's statement. Nora turned to Sean without any comments. She came closer, gazing at him with a kind of admiration.

'I bet you're very proud of yourself. It took ages to make that exhibition happen. Speaking of which, I can't find this casket's documents. You said it's from a private collector, but from whom exactly?' she asked with the same warm voice. She was standing a bit too close to Sean, and her nearness made him blush.

Sean peeped at them, waved a hand to Gary in a gesture that might only mean to continue the task of taking pictures, turned and with a soft voice, so unusual for him, said to her; 'Let's go to my office and try to find it together. I'm sure it's on my desk. I haven't seen you for a while. How was your trip to China?' Sean continued the conversation with her. Gary noticed that Sean's voice was trembling when he stammered twice, trying to hide his insecurities. But he covered it fast by coughing up and pretending that something was scratching his throat. They walked away from the group without looking back.

Gary was the one most surprised here. For him, Sean was always single. Gary didn't remember him being involved in any romantic relationship or even mentioned that he was dating someone. But this was too obvious to ignore without any words.

'Am I wrong or is there something going on between them?'

Gary was asking Mark while directing his hand towards Sean and his companion and their slowly disappearing silhouettes behind the museum shop. Mark looked a bit surprised as well, but he didn't follow the discussion but only shrugged and turned towards the coffin.

'Why are you surprised? For some women, Sean's really hot,' said Jessica, like it was an apparent fact for everyone. Mark looked at her with a frown but didn't comment on it.

Just after Sean left, there was a large group of visitors emerging from a side interior entrance. They stopped near the collection shop that was now opening. Jessica, Gary, and Mark looked at the group, then looked at each other and in silent agreement started to speed up everything that they were doing. It was one of the early morning private tours that was roaming in the almost empty museum, following the tour-guide. Gary, with a low voice, whispered loudly enough to be heard by Jessica and Mark that they had to hurry because there was another tour walking around the Great Court just behind the first one, and they all would definitely come to see the casket in a matter of minutes. He said he would keep watching their positions and movements, so he walked back a few steps to see the groups better.

'Watch out!' whispered Mark to Jessica, slightly nodding in the direction of the museum's cameras installed high in the corners. She looked distressed but he was calm. He came closer, took her underarm and pulled her near to the casket's locker. Jessica blushed under his touch but didn't retreat. She took a tiny camera on a wire and a tablet from the small rucksack that she had on her shoulder. The camera had a LED light installed alongside, and on the opposite end there was a USB plug that Jessica inserted into the tablet. The light immediately switched on, leaving quite a strong beam on Mark's T-shirt. The camera showed a sharp view in the tablet application. Jessica pressed a button and started recording everything caught by it.

At this moment, a bunch of people appeared behind the first tour-group that was now standing in the shop. It was the third group of tourists in the central court and they were heading pretty quickly towards the casket.

'Hurry, we have less than a minute,' said Gary with a hasty voice, coming close to them and then stepping back to keep watching every movement of the group. He combed his hair a few times with both hands and made a new ponytail. Jessica's hands were shaking and making the light from the camera dance around but Mark was focused and fast. He covered the light by one hand, put his second arm around her waist and pulled her against his body. She felt the tiny kick of thrill at the moment when he put his hand on her. Mark leaned in gently and smelled her hair. She blushed and stuck the camera inside the lock and pushed it more in-depth and recorded it all clearly. Jessica stared at the tablet, watching the recorded pictures and busying herself with the devices mainly because she didn't want to look into his eyes. But on the contrary, Mark was pleased holding her close and observing her face. He felt confident despite his brother's presence.

Gary grunted and frowned but said nothing at seeing how close they were stood together. He didn't like what he saw but could do nothing about it. Gary knew it wasn't the moment to have an argument with Mark, but he promised himself to warn Jessica about Mark's womanising approach to ladies. Gary admitted to himself that they looked like a happy couple who just stopped to admire the museum exhibit and that was a perfect cover for the real purpose of their trip here.

Mark was gently holding Jessica's shaking hand and helping to direct the camera to record all possible insides that were needed to re-create the key. It was totally unnecessary because it wasn't much of the mechanism to shoot and she was capable of holding the wire and tablet under her control. But, nonetheless, she let him do it and was pretty pleased with his closeness. It didn't take long to finish the recordings. After it, Mark hid the camera and tablet under his T-shirt, inserting them partially inside his trousers. Gary warned them almost in the same moment when the tour came near the displayed coffin.

'Guys, could you give us more room, please,' said the man with a 'tour-guide' badge to Gary, Mark, and Jessica. He asked if they missed their tour, but Mark showed him a badge with his name on it that he pulled out from his pocket. The man stopped asking them uncomfortable questions and started telling information to his group about the casket, that could exist only in a legend.

Jessica was curious what kind of badge Mark had so she forced him to show it. There was 'curator assistant' written on it, and it really had Mark's picture with his name on it. She asked if he was working here, but Mark didn't answer that question. Instead, he nodded towards the guide direction and put his finger on her lips giving the sign for silence.

'Please came closer, but don't touch the casket,' said the tour-guide loudly, in a tone accustomed to giving orders to group of people. Mark pulled Jessica even closer to him than before, but this time he held both his hands on her waist. Gary stood on the opposite side of him and prodded Mark with his elbow. Mark shuddered an took his hands off Jessica, but only because he started typing news to Sean about achieving the goal for filming the locker inside.

'This is our first stop…' the tour leader continued.

'We should go,' whispered Mark.

'Wait. I want to know what he'll say about it,' said Jessica, grabbing Marks' wrist and stopping him from walking away. Gary gestured with approval and came closer to the man to hear better the official story about this object. He wondered how much information Sean was able to give to the public.

'This object is one of the most mysterious in our supernatural exhibition. According to my notes, we don't have any solid knowledge about it. The Museum didn't have a chance to examine it thoroughly because it came to us at the last minute from a private collection. The owner wishes to remain unknown. Our curator, Sean Miller, who for many years was searching around the world for objects to fill this exhibition said that everything that we know about it is based mainly on legends. My dear visitors, let me take you on a trip, where deeply buried myths will rise like a phoenix from the ashes to amaze us with their stories.'

This guy knew how to make a dramatic entrance, thought Gary, intrigued by the speech. Mark, Jessica, and Gary got mixed among tourists. People were whispering comments about the brutal content showed on the reliefs.

'As stated by legends, for centuries there were groups of people hunting those who were classified as monsters such as lycanthropes, vampires and witches. The word 'lycanthropy' doesn't refer only to werewolves, but to others who could shape-shift into more animalistic forms. The hunters were working as kings' agents, but their existence shouldn't have been known to the public. We don't know what the reason was, maybe political, religious or just a fear of using against the crown all the creatures that were lurking in the shadows. Nevertheless, the presence of hunters was hidden from the rest of society and making them one of the most secretive organisations established in the ancient world. According to my notes, they were still operating until the First World War, but all we know is only that they existed, so no names of members or locations of their headquarters...' he didn't finish his tale because he was interrupted by one of the young visitors.

'Do you mean that they were still hunting something...'

'Oh, it's pure hogwash just to suck money from kings or government,' said a woman's voice from the centre of the group. People were whispering their theories about what they just heard.

'What we have here, is their artefact. It was used as punishment for the most vicious and dangerous non-humans known to them. They called it the coffin, despite the fact that the trapped creature was still alive. They put the casket into the stone sarcophagus and left it for months or even years. The creatures were slowly dying inside, suffering tremendous tortures of unstoppable pain, not only physical, but tormenting their mind with twisted visions like in the worst nightmares…' the high pitch of a shout broke the tour-guide's tale.

One young girl dropped on the floor, writhing in agony of pain, screaming and crying. People were shocked. Some of them tried to help, but every small touch of her body made her scream even louder. She started yelling that she saw something going out and it was so terrible that no words could describe. She started saying something, but the words weren't recognisable and sounded more like not related to each other syllables. People were moved away from her by the tour-guide, who called for help and paramedics.

Jessica noticed that Mark secretly recorded the whole event on his phone. In the same moment when the girl fell to the floor, Gary felt Erick's presence like he was standing just behind Gary. He didn't know how, but Gary knew it was Erick. He felt the freezing cold going on his skin and the horrible sensation that Erick was holding Gary's arm, squeezing so fiercely that it caused frozen marks on Gary's skin, making him feel real pain. He heard a voice in his head that was begging for help. The voice was deeply piercing Gary's mind to the point when Gary got a severe headache, blurred vision and his nose start oozing dark blood.

Mark saw it and reacted instantly. He took Gary under the arm from one side, Jessica did it from the other, and all walked out from the museum through the main entrance.

CHAPTER 15

10th July - The Key Shape

'Hey Gary, I need your help,' said Jessica, entering into the kitchen and holding the open laptop with a frozen picture of the casket on the screen.

'Sure, what's up?' asked Gary, taking out three plastic containers from the fridge with food in it. He opened them and put veggies and meat on a large plate and heated it in the microwave. Jessica put the laptop in the middle of the table, took the largest container, smelt it, and tried a few small bits on the top of teaspoon.

'I love Mark's cooking,' she said.

Gary muttered in agreement with a mouth full of leftovers from yesterday's lunch. She took a small plate from the cupboard and put what was left of the meal on it.

'God bless, he's always doing it when he's here, otherwise I'd starve to death. He should open his own restaurant instead of working as a taxi driver. Why does it taste so good?' said Gary with a face expressing delight.

'No way. Don't say that idea to him. He might do it and then you'll have to pay a lot of money for his cooking,' declared Jessica, smiling broadly.

They sat at the table and ate it in silence.

'Nah, he'll never stay in one place for long. Speaking of which, please be careful. He'll break your heart, he's a womaniser...' Gary didn't know how to tell Jessica his concerns about the close relationship between her and his brother that was growing pretty fast.

Gary felt uneasy ratting out the brother he loved to his friend he valued so much.

'Don't worry, I know. But thanks for the heads up about him,' she replied softly. Gary sighed with relief, feeling happy that this uncomfortable topic was over. *At least, I had done something to prevent eventual drama that might occur in-house,* thought Gary.

'So, what's the problem?' asked Gary, changing topic to a more pleasant one.

They both stayed in the kitchen to watch the recorded material after they finished eating and cleaning up dirty dishes.

'Look at this video and tell me what you see,' said Jessica, switching on the keyhole footage from the museum. Gary sat and watched the recording three times while he sipped his tea. Meanwhile, she was looking carefully at the printed images of the coffin's reliefs that were taken near the keyhole.

'Okay, it's quite shaky, but I can adjust it to have better quality pictures. Besides, they're solving our technical issues, not for entertainment and so for that reason, I think the recording's pretty good as it is,' said Gary with a professional tone.

Jessica took a few folded pages from her jeans pocket, smoothed them out and passed them to Gary. There were images of old-fashioned keys with sketches of their locks from sizes of small jewel cases to huge city gate keys. Gary flipped the pages and realised that the constructions of locks from past centuries were nothing like the inside of the one installed in the coffin. They both watched the video again in slow motion, trying to figure out what kind of shape the key could possibly have but nothing had matched the blueprints from the past.

The loud knock to the front door interrupted them. Jessica ran fast to open it and was surprised to see Robert standing behind the door. He looked like someone pensive and a bit sad. This time he said nice evening greetings and waited to be invited in. Jessica let him in with the information that Simon wasn't at home yet. Robert shrugged and answered that he would wait for him and then passed the doorstep. They both went to the kitchen. Robert asked where was the food that he could smell and who cooked it. When Jessica said it was Mark's, he opened the fridge searching for some leftovers, but nothing had been left. He found a few chocolate muffins in a clear, plastic bag so he took it without asking for permission. He even started making his own tea, but Jessica offered help, so he sat at the table on her chair near Gary. He was eating muffins and apparently that cheered him up as a soft smile appeared on his face. He put the bag with rest of them on his knees and didn't ask anyone if they would like to eat some. But Gary couldn't resist and snatched the bag and took two muffins, one for him and one for Jessica. Robert smiled and that reaction confused Gary. Jessica put a large mug with milky tea for Robert on a table, brought a new chair for herself and sat close to both of them.

'Could you help us, Robert? Just have a look, maybe you'll have some idea how the lock is built,' she said and switched on the recording of the keyhole from the beginning in slow motion. Despite Robert's injured leg, he changed his sitting posture quite fast. He sat deeper in the chair, bending both his knees with a slight grimace of soreness, but smiled and said nothing. He straightened himself and pulled the laptop closer to him. He watched the movie only once and said that he knew what kind of key would be the perfect match for it. He asked about all the casket's pictures, suggesting that maybe there was some shape of the key hidden among figures just to be sure about his concept.

'What makes you think there's any key pattern among all those brutal scenes?' asked Gary.

'It's simple logic. Most of those ancient people couldn't read. They had to have some way to pass the knowledge otherwise it'd cease to exist in next generations. But as we all know, they're still operating somewhere,' said Robert with a tone sounding more like a good uncle teaching children about the sky and without any trace of his usual sarcasm.

Jessica opened another file on her laptop and showed the gallery with images from the coffin. They were watching them and discussing the eerie stories behind the bas-reliefs. All of the time, Robert wasn't obnoxious and that was the first situation when Gary and Jessica were not only positively surprised about his behaviour but kind of amazed by his reasoning.

'It's here,' said Robert, pointing at shape left by a torn-out figure. It was a place on a casket on the side of the hinges on the bottom corner. There were figures of warriors on horses escorting the image of the coffin that was laying on the open waggon. There was one much bigger knight who was looking like he was their leader. He was standing next to the cart holding the horse's reins in one hand and in the other was a shape that resembled a flail more than anything that might slightly look like any keys used throughout the centuries. Moreover, it was the only one place where the casket itself was part of the hunter's story. Robert showed the places where marks on the surface gave a pretty clear idea that someone intentionally removed the key-shape from the surface. Robert drew a model of it on a piece of paper.

'Are you kidding? It's not a key,' cried Jessica.

'Oh, yes, it is. My granddad used to have a similar metal-rod to lock the house and chicken-coop back then in France during World War Two. It was so effective in preventing burglary that he was accused of witchcraft by a whole village. My family had something similar on a farm installed in a house and a barn when I was a child. Look at the video again, and you'll see that I'm right,' contradicted Robert but this time with a bit of sarcasm in his voice.

They watched the recording twice to be sure not to miss anything important. They paused when the camera turned and dropped into the vertical tunnel at the end of the lock. There were two black spikes that looked exactly like part of the toothed-gear mechanism. Jessica wasn't very keen, but she had to agree with him at the end.

'But it doesn't look like a key,' said Gary.

'That's the point. Nobody would ever expect that a metal-rod which one bends in one quarter, with a sharp ending like a screwdriver, can open anything,' affirmed Jessica, making a brief sketch of the item and writing notes about approximate sizes of it.

'See, sometimes simplicity is the best solution,' declared Robert, smiling.

'So, everything that we have to do is to stick the rod and push those spikes hoping that it'll move the mechanism?' asked Gary, staring from Robert to Jessica.

'Or you'll die if it doesn't...' replied Robert seriously.

'How will I know which side is opening the lock and which side is closing it?' asked Gary, staring at Robert.

'I don't know. I guess you'll have to figure that out yourself. Don't forget to smile to the audiences in the museum. You'll be participating in an ongoing show…' Robert's black sense of humour came back like a boomerang and hit with double the force but he didn't finish because a new voice interrupted him.

'What are you doing here so late?' the question surprised everyone. It was Simon standing in the kitchen doorway, looking very tired.

'Waiting for you and solving the mystery of the key. Why are you so tense?' asked Robert, raising his voice a bit.

'I'm hungry and…' Simon tried to explain, but Robert stopped him.

'Stop, I really don't want to know. It was a rhetorical question. You'll need this for tomorrow at work,' replied Robert as he passed Simon a grey envelop that he pulled out from the insides of a pocket in his leather jacket. Simon grabbed and opened it. There was a new badge for him and some official-looking documents from his work. Simon skimmed the pages briefly, put all of it into the envelope and passed it back to Robert.

'No way, I'm not going anywhere from S.C.D. Stop pushing me around like a yo-yo, or I'll challenge you in the arena!' yelled Simon angrily, and that puzzled Robert.

'You can't challenge …'

'Oh, yes, I can.'

'But you said you don't want to work with me. There is only one S.C.D. department in London …'

'I've changed my mind.'

'When?'

'In the moment when I saw those hideous vamps attacking us in The Tavern…' replied Simon, much softer this time. Robert smiled faintly.

'What department? What kind of arena?' asked Gary loudly, indicating that there were two other people present in the kitchen. Simon looked at them like he just realised he wasn't alone.

'There's a police's branch officially called The Special Cases Department, but the real name is The Supernatural Cases Department. And they have cases you'd never imagined existing even in the worst horror movies.'

'What? There's a special department for lycans?' asked Gary, staring at Robert.

'If there were only lycans, I wouldn't be bothered…' said Simon, opening the fridge and searching for something he wanted to eat.

'Well, someone has to clean up the mess,' said Robert, shrugging but with the broadest smile he could possibly have.

'And I want you to teach me the fight,' declared Simon in quite demanding tone, gazing at Robert.

'What?' asked Robert with astonishment.

'You always wanted …' Simon didn't finish.

'No, I wanted you to learn but not from me. I'm banned,' said Robert defensively.

'You're banned from a professional fight for imprinting illegal tattoos on your body but not for teaching. By the way, you can still be challenged. I've checked the law. You haven't been for so many years because James took all your fights on him. And, yes, he can do it. He's the Alfa for a good reason.'

'How do you know about my tattoos?' asked Robert, totally surprised.

'You have no idea what kind of magic a bottle of scotch can do to a human mind. Besides, I'm not that antisocial as you are so I talk to the pack, not barking at them,' said Simon, smiling. Gary admitted to himself that it was really amusing to watch the utterly confused Robert and his face expression that he couldn't hide.

'What are you talking about?' asked Jessica.

'Sorry guys, I'm too tired. I'll explain tomorrow. Good night,' said Simon, who was carrying a bag with half a loaf of bread in one hand and a plate with a fried meat in the other and went to his room upstairs without looking back. Jessica frowned and looked a bit too astonished, thought Gary staring at a speechless Robert, but on the other hand, he never saw Simon verbally neither aggressive nor eating without fork and knife either.

'Seriously, there is a special department in the police created only for all those living behind the veil?' asked Jessica with a bit of disbelief in her voice.

'Yes, indeed…'

'You really were fighting in the arena?

'I was the best back then…'

'What kind of illegal tattoos?' asked Gary, clearly more and more inquisitive about Robert's past.

'Okay, enough. That was while ago and I was too young and too stupid. I'm out. Good night,' replied Robert nervously, and despite his injured leg, he left the house pretty fast. Jessica locked the door behind him and joined Gary in the kitchen for the next cup of tea.

'You know what, this new life's getting more and more interesting every single day,' said Jessica, smiling.

'Tell me about it. I'm feeling like I'm living in one big role-playing game,' replayed Gary, still watching the pictures of the coffin on the laptop.

'Moreover, it seems there's underground in it, and I can't stop wondering what's there…' said Jessica curiously.

'And some other secret organisations and gangs that lives inside this underground,' said Gary with a specific sparkle in his eyes that he always had when his imagination was going wild.

CHAPTER 16

10th July - Draco

'I've got Adam! I know you're looking for him. I've recorded a few hours of his torture. Fancy watching it?' yelled Roseanne hatefully in to phone.

There was a silence, like she was talking to an empty line that confused her and pushed her to the edge of uncertainty. She glared at her mobile, checking if the call was still on. It was, but the silence suggested that nobody was listening on the other side. She put it back to her ear and softly enquired.

'Draco are you there?' she asked this question four times before she heard Draco's calm and firm voice.

'Yes, I'm here, now listen very carefully, I'm not going to repeat it. If you, or your scumbag lover Patric harm Adam in any way, I'll find you with an army of my witch hunter friends. I'll not kill you, my dear sis. Oh, no. That'll be too good for you, but you know what happens next. They'll make you suffer for fun, day after day, keeping you alive for a decade. Trust me, they mastered it. Are we clear?' Draco's calm authoritative voice scared her.

She knew that Draco was mentally stronger than her due to skills that were passed to him by Erick as a gift to his beloved night-child. She was always dreaming of being in Draco's place as a favourite child, but it was never granted to her. She suspected Draco's involvement in Erick's disappearance from day one. Although she couldn't prove it, something inside her guts told her that Draco was the mastermind behind the whole abduction. Logically, that was easy blame she put on Erick's pet child, Draco. But she excused herself, knowing that Draco was hated by many others in their dynasty, as much as by her, without any solid facts and reasons. Moreover, she didn't care about evidence and explanations at all. Draco's errands were always obscure and hidden, even from Erick himself, so unusual for Acheron's dynasty.

But his calm, categorical and piercing tone left her speechless for a while. She was walking to and fro in Patric's office with a fast pace, thinking about how to play this conversation.

'I want Erick in exchange,' she stated after a few deep breaths and a large sip of vodka with tonic she was carrying. She desperately wanted her vampire father to return, and she wanted to be the saviour, earning his attention and gratitude. There was nothing more important for her than winning Erick's love again.

She came closer to Patric, who was leaning on window-wall with his gaze fixed at the thick fog rising over the river Thames this morning. She looked at his tall, slim body, wearing perfect clothing, at his wavy dark hair and typical Italian shape of face and a flash of warm emotions ran through her. She admitted to herself that she had pleasant feelings for him. Moreover, they both had a lot in common, but that wasn't the crazy, overwhelming love she felt for Erick when they first met and she wanted it back so much. With Patric, everything was too easy for her. Their relations were mostly based on lust and fun they had together, but there was nothing beneath the facade of sweet promises, professional acting and empty lyrics, at least she perceived their relationship like that. For her, Patric was only a companion to keep her occupied and to fill the emptiness she felt so often. But sometimes, when she was alone, she felt like she was somehow addicted to him when she unconsciously started searching for his closeness. But she always killed those thoughts with her own confidence and constantly denied the obvious facts that she might be in love with him.

Despite the fact that Patric was only a bit more than one hundred years old, he was as remorseless as she was. She never stopped wondering what kind of emotions he had for her as he never showed anything deeper than liking her. And maybe only the one thing that kept her near for so long was his aura of mystery and some kind of authority that was emanating from him, but she couldn't figure out what exactly was it.

'Are you kidding me? Adam isn't worth that much. All you can have is only Erick's whereabouts ...' Draco's rising voice made her even more nervous. If only Draco were near her, she would kill him with pleasure, despite the possibility of facing Erick's rage after it.

But even though the conversation wasn't on speaker, they both could hear Draco's loud laughter. Roseanne put her hand on Patric's arm and squeezed gently. He covered her hand with his, smoothing her soft skin, but he kept his eyes on a far distant object on the other side of the river.

'You're a moron! I've never understood why you're so attached to Adam. He's trash. He's alive only because you back him up ...' she raised her voice, feeling more confident this time.

'If so, why are you so jealous of him? Why are you dragging the family drama over and over again? You can't stand him because he reminds you how ruthless, cruel and spoiled you are!' Draco shouted with rage.

'Erick gave you everything!' Roseanne shouted at the top of her lungs. Small drops of tears appeared in her eyes. Her face became more aggressive, showing long fangs, dark eyes and blackened skin around them. She hated Draco now more than ever. Patric turned his head, raising one of his eyebrows. He grinned mischievously but she couldn't see it. She walked to the massive desk and the cabinet standing behind it, full of bottles, to refill her crystal glass with another alcoholic drink.

'Everything you wanted?! He changed me because you're his biggest disappointment. I'm a fucking vampire because of you! He doesn't want to kill you out of sentiment only. He loved you once, way too much, when you were human, and he paid the price for changing you. He could never understand your desire to watch the pain of those going through the transition. Your obsession to keep making new vamps, watching the process, even torturing to increase the suffering, didn't impress him at all. But you kept doing this for centuries, dreaming that one day he'll come back to you ...' Draco's low hissing voice showed maximum anger.

'All I wanted was to have a strong family for him and you ...'

'Bullshit! Keep lying to yourself. I'm not buying this shit, nor is he ...'

'But you betrayed him!'

'Oh, yes. I waited for that pleasure for more than five hundred years, and I'll do it again, and again, and again until he's dead …' Draco sounded furious.

'If he dies, you'll die with him …' she was yelling on an equal level as Draco.

'Maybe I want to die and take the whole dynasty with me!' Draco's rage reached the top. He was shouting like she had never heard before. The only one calm and smiling person in this room was Patric. He still was standing near the window, pretending he was lost in his thoughts, but he was watching, calculating and creating every possible scenario in his head based on the information he just heard and wanted to use it for his advantage.

'But why? Why?!' she asked softly, like she didn't have any more strength to fight with Draco. Tears in her eyes were dropping, leaving small, wet brooks on her cheeks.

'Because I hate being one of you. I hate every hour of my life as a vampire.'

Draco's statement confused not only her but Patric as well. That was rare but not unusual for old vampires to feel tired after so many years when their essential role was to lie and pretend to be normal humans. Long life never suited any humans well, and regardless the power that vampires had, they had more memories and feelings than any average person possible as well. If they didn't drink blood that contained people's recollections and emotions, they would decline into vicious monsters in a matter of days. Although human excitement kept them entirely sane for a long time, it also slowly affected their own personality for the worse.

Roseanne was lost for words and didn't know what to say for a quite long time. Only the fast pace of Draco's breathing was interrupting the silence between them.

'You can kill yourself. That's pretty normal for depressed and sick-minded vamps,' she said calmly when she finally shook off the shock that she had after his statement.

'I don't have to. I found the way to kill him without any effect on me,' Draco's voice was almost cheerful, and that caught Patric's attention immediately.

'What?! You found, what?' she asked, startled.

'There's an ancient witch hunter's ritual I'm going to use on him that allows me to survive but eradicates the whole of Erick's family,' Draco laughed. It was an angry, nervous and malignant laugh that made goosebumps all over her body. But on the contrary to her despair, Patric was intrigued. He was gazing at the scene with a frown.

'You're bluffing?!'

'Do you want to bet who'll be the last man standing? Just use your little knowledge about me it'll tell you that I never bluff. Besides, I had a few centuries to get ready, as I am now,' he laughed maniacally.

She was speechless. Patric came closer to her, put a hand on her shoulder and nodded like he agreed to something known only to him and Roseanne.

'I don't need Adam, but I like him. He's the only one leverage for you, if you want to see Erick for the last time before your sick vampire dynasty turn into dust. So, my little princess, how's it gonna be?' Draco claimed furiously, with a voice of a tyrant who had just crushed his last enemies.

Patric was calm and focused. But she looked utterly terrified, like a little child watching the worst horror movie for the first time. She knew Draco was going to do it. He always got what he wanted, no matter the cost. She saw him killing kings who were stupid enough to cross him way too much, like the riot he made later called The French Revolution.

Patric shook her arms again. He was nodding and soundlessly saying the word 'yes'. She understood that it was the agreement to Draco's ultimatum.

'Okay. I'll do it. I'll bring him to you,' her voice was shaky and stammering. It was all that she could pronounce. Patric hugged her from behind, brushed aside her long, black hair and kissed her neck. She sighed, putting her free hand on his forearms.

'So, bring him to my pub at my favourite hour and you better be alone or no deal,' Draco disconnected without a goodbye.

Patric smiled mischievously, even more broadly than before, but again, she couldn't see it.

*

London streets were well-lighted but empty this time of night. The pub was already closed. It was situated on the corner of a three-street crossroad under the name of The Bridge End.

Roseanne was walking to and fro nervously, peeking on her mobile every few seconds. She was wearing a light-tight dress, classy and expensive and sewed in a purpose to draw attention to her slim figure. She parked her brand new, red cabriolet a few steps away, not caring about the red line on the street.

Draco watched her for a while. He checked the surrounding streets fast and silent like a ghost. He wanted to be sure that she really was alone as she supposed to be. He didn't see or feel any other vampires nearby, but he didn't trust her. He knew her too well to be fooled. Draco was suspicious about her fast agreement with him, but he was too impatient and was worried about Adam's life. Draco knew that without Adam his plans were more likely to be completely ruined. He also knew that Roseanne was always abrupt with her decisions and actions, so there was a huge possibility she might kill Adam just for fun or for some sick revenge.

Maybe it was the rapidity, or perhaps the fact that Draco started feeling unwell again, that lowered his patience and carefulness. He noticed his loss of focus when he started to have more intense nightmares that began three days ago. There were now not only pictures of Erick's suffering but his voice that was calling for help and which one Draco could hear as a whispering even through the day. He needed Adam more than ever and wanted all of it to be over, he was thinking about it while strolling towards her.

She rang again like she did a dozen times in a last ten minutes.

'I feel a bit disappointed, I thought you wouldn't show up, my dear sis,' said Draco, with courtesy mixed with sarcasm, emerging from the shady corner opposite the pub. He crossed the street with his hand stretched like he wanted to give her a warm hug. She stood observing him closely but put his hands down, avoiding the hug, even taking two steps back to distance herself and making more space between them.

'Don't come any closer. You disgust me,' she announced with a crooked face. His politeness was always a trap, she was cautious of him and so she watched his every move, maybe because she suspected any kind of backstabbing actions from him. She never liked him and couldn't find what was so special about Draco that Erick loved. He was very mediocre and never showed any talents or even good social skills to be accepted in to high society, she thought, looking at him with detestation. The question, why he was changed into a vampire, so noble distinction for selected ones, would never cease to exist in her mind.

'How so? Am I not too savage? You like more rough men, don't you?' he asked with a seductive voice.

'Get to the point,' she replied with a sharp, imperative voice.

'Where is Adam?' Draco voice was cold this time.

'In the trunk,' she replied, walking to the car, opening the trunk and showing the body that was lying inside.

'It's not him,' replied Draco, laughing and staring over the body of the unknown person, but he checked his pulse and listened to his breath. The man's clothes were slashed in many places and heavily stained with drained, dark blood. He was a young vampire who looked similar to Adam. Draco uncovered this man's earlobe, searching for the reddish dots that would indicate his mature age, but he didn't find any. His face was almost unrecognisable. Despite being a vampire, whose natural ability was fast healing that was inherited with his blood connection, this unknown young lad had large bruises on his skin alongside barely closed cutting wounds. Draco knew it was a sign of a merciless beating and torturing for days without a drop of blood that was so crucial for a full healthy recovery, but at least he was still alive.

'You don't know where Adam is, do you Rose?' Draco stared straight into her eyes. Draco smiled, knowing that Adam was still alive and hiding somewhere because Draco would definitely have sensed if something bad had happened to him. He stepped back, observing her closely. Although he was a much better fighter than Roseanne, she was cunning and was using it remorselessly to achieve what she wanted. Draco looked around cautiously, switching on his alertness to the maximum.

'Where is Erick? Speak, you ...' she couldn't finish because

Draco's loud laugh interrupted her.

He took his mobile from his trousers, found and dialled a number. He didn't wait long for an answer. Somebody picked up silently and without any words put the phone down.

'If you think I'm going to tell you all, you're very naive. Adam knows where the 'Tritus' End is, the artefact where your beloved Erick is trapped and slowly dying,' said Draco, turning to her, grinning broadly. He was observing her and slowly walking back, taking small steps. He never saw her so shocked like at this moment.

'What's that? Where is it? Tell me!' the panic was easily recognisable in her voice. She ran to Draco and grabbed his hand.

Draco reacted instinctively, lengthening his black, razor-sharp nails and putting them on her chest, right over her heart. She froze but didn't show any fear on her face. Draco pulled a gun with a silencer that he had had hidden on his back but now aimed it straight at her head.

'Silver bullets, sis. It's a merciful death. We had a deal, but you …' Draco didn't finish and couldn't pull the trigger either because he was shot in his neck by the dart with a liquid inside specially created to drowse vampires. He caught the dart, but it was too late. The sedative was working and had dazed him already. He leaned on Roseanne with all his body weight, knocking her down. She fell on the ground with him.

A black SUV appeared on the corner and pulled over behind Roseanne's car. Patric Vance was the person who was getting out from the passenger's side. He was holding a tranquiliser gun, ready to make another shot if the first one wouldn't work as expected.

'You?' asked Roseanne, getting up.

'Missed me?' Patric looked pleased.

'Did you plan that?'

'Yep.'

Patric knocked to the driver's window and without waiting for him, went to pick up Draco's body. He squatted, handcuffed Draco and threw him into the trunk of his black SUV.

'Do you know where Erick is?' asked Roseanne, opening her small cabriolet and getting inside.

'No. But I know where to find Adam,' said Patric, going back into the SUV.

CHAPTER 17

11th July - The Werewolve's Pack

'Get up! My granny is moving faster than you. Gods help me! Why do I have to teach the most clumsy guy here,' declared Robert loudly, standing in the middle of the arena with his arms widely stretched, his head pointing up like he was talking to a higher power that was hanging under the ceiling, and with a mischievous smile, was watching his efforts.

'Because you agreed, and you have bad karma,' shouted James, emerging from behind the gym door, and waving to Simon who was lying on his back, curled up in pain. He understood perfectly the language used by werewolves in their full feral-battle form, as Simon and Robert were now shaped into, even though for normal humans it might sound like a mixture of barking with some words.

'Why do I have to teach at all,' continued Robert with an even more theatrically pose and dramatic voice.

'Because finally you can be on the arena to show off,' said James, smiling and clapping his hands as loud as he could to be heard at the end of this large chamber. A few other members of the pack, who were sitting on the benches watching this lesson, joined him with applause.

'See, you're famous again,' James continued, came closer to the arena and pointed into the audience.

Robert shrugged and walked towards Simon. Before he reached the place, he transformed into a fully dressed human. He looked happy, even his steps were less limping and more briskly. Robert shook Simon's hand and patted his shoulder, waved to the viewers by making a funny gesture with his hand, imitating taking off an invisible hat from his head.

Simon didn't look joyful but more like someone tired and downcast. He had a few bruises on his arms and naked torso, which were slowly disappearing as an effect of fast healing. He was silent, quite the opposite to Robert who couldn't stop talking about tactics, those fighting positions he used, kicks and dodges he knew so well. He knew a lot nowadays about teams and participants in all tournaments available to watch, not only online, but even on a specially coded television channel accessible for Viviters all over the world.

They got out in time when the next four players were preparing to take their place inside the ring. Robert nodded to them when they were showed gestures meaning 'good sparring'. Simon didn't smile at their approval. He didn't feel well losing so easy. Moreover, some stubborn voice in his head kept demanding fast improvements in his fighting skills. Sometimes Simon couldn't recognise himself. Only a month ago, that kind of thought would never have crossed his mind. But today he realised that his primary goal was to defeat Robert. Moreover, the middle-aged man who looked like a coach and arena veteran patted Simon's shoulder and said that holding the fight for more than fifteen minutes with Robert was a great achievement for some inexperienced newbie. It didn't improve Simon's mood at all.

After a shower and some small talk with other members of the pack, they both headed towards the main hall. Simon was still not in the mood, but he smiled anyway, only because he saw Maya, wearing a flowery, short, summer dress, who was entering to the mansion from the garden through the back-side door. She left the door open, letting a fresh, late afternoon breeze whiff in to the chamber. They met in a middle point quite far from the others pack's members.

'How is my peculiar uncle treating you?' she asked, smiling at Simon and hugging Robert at the same time. Simon waved his hand with a 'don't ask' gesture and just shrugged.

'So, Simon, you asked for help. Can Robert be present or is it more of a personal issue?' asked James, who walked from the lounge side and showed them all the direction to his office.

'I'm not going anywhere. I'm a significant part of it,' declared

Robert, without looking at Simon, walking first like he knew exactly where the leader's office was located. Simon nodded, rolled his eyes, showing this way that Robert was truly irremovable from the case.

James's office was spacious and elegant. Despite the modern design of rest of the house, this room had large and heavy antiques made from dark mahogany that looked alike as a set. They sat at a round table and ate late lunch brought in by the cook. Simon tried to explain the whole request as much as he could, but he was interrupted over and over by Robert, who was talking like it was his idea to ask James for help with the performance in the British Museum. They told the story about Erick, the casket and the need to open it. James was listening to both of them without a word, but Maya asked a lot of additional questions, unfortunately for some of them, they didn't have answers. The whole idea of doing the show was fascinating for her, but James was quite sceptical.

'I can't approve this event, and officially I prohibit you all to participate. It's very dubious. Night Reapers can't be involved in this errand for political reasons. I'm sorry, Simon, but my decision is definite,' said James with a serious facial expression.

'But …' started Simon, trying to convince James to change his mind, when someone kicked him under the table. He looked from Maya to Robert to James, trying to figure out who was it, but their faces didn't express anything new. He went silent, frowned, grunted and stared at them all. He didn't know how to react, so he didn't drag the topic of the museum any more. But he couldn't stop feeling sad and disappointed. Even Maya tried to convince her father, but James stuck with his statement and didn't want to continue this topic. Instead, he asked about Simon's opinion about Robert's lessons and his health in general. He invited them to spend a weekend in the Tavern, but Simon refused politely. Robert didn't comment on his brother's verdict but only once peeped to his niece, and that made Simon wonder. Robert always had his own strong opinion about everything, so his silence seemed very suspicious.

After their meal, James led them to the main hall and open the front door. But he was suddenly pushed inside by a man who was leaning on them vertically on the other side. He fell flat on the floor moaning in pain.

'You?' said Maya through clenched teeth and kneeling near the fallen man.

'Dylan, drunk and stoned again,' declared James with a disapproving glare at him.

'We're out. The family drama arrived,' said Robert and he left the mansion without looking back. Simon followed him but turned back twice, staring at Maya. She waved to Simon, trying to explain something soundlessly, but he didn't understand what it was all about.

CHAPTER 18

10th July - The Prison

'Anne! Stop!' shouted Patric, entering his private prison.

The prison was located in a closed London underground station in one of unused tunnels deep under the streets. One of the tunnels was converted into this place, where Patric Vance could hide his dark affairs and punish those who crossed his plans. There was one hidden entrance to it, from the side of 'The Stairs to Hell' club owned by Patric and one as a backside exit that was going through closed corridors of the Tube and partially in old sewers.

The prison chamber was wide and still contained a railway truck but now was partially covered by a wooden floor. There was a metal platform dividing the height of the tunnel in two. The bottom part had prison's cells, but the top was reserved for guards and a place used for investigations and torture.

The guards had a long office-counter with a few monitors showing footage from cameras not only from the cells but from the main entrance, sewers and corridors leading to different spaces inside the club. They were wearing black suits, black shirts and white ties with a club logo embroidered on them. Although they were tall and well-built vampires, they all looked slightly confused and uneasy with the whole situation that was going on now between Patric and his lover.

Patric was standing near the entrance to the cells' space gazing at Roseanne with anger on his face. The cells were occupied not only by other vampires but by some humans as well. There was a corridor under the platform leading to inside lockups.

Draco was in the first unit, but on the contrary to other detainees, he had silvered shackles on his wrists and ankles that were chained to the concrete wall. He was lying on the floor in a puddle of dark blood, and with urine covering most of his trousers. The stench was beyond endurance. Roseanne was whipping him mercilessly. She was holding a long whip that was made with black leather and thick silver fibres woven into it. Her elegant, dark-blue suit was covered with drops of his blood mixed with small bits of peeled-off skin and hair. Draco was shouting and crying every time the lash smacked him, leaving dark-red and broken skin. He was shaking uncontrollably, curled up like a small dog, hiding his head under his wrapped up arms.

Patric jumped to her, turned her over, clutched her wrist and pulled out the whip from her hand. He threw it far away hissing in pain. The silver made a few red marks on his skin. He pushed her so fiercely that she landed up on the wall, losing balance. His face changed. His skin was white as snow. He had dark-red marks with thin black lines around eyes. He looked vastly threateningly.

'I told you a few times to leave him alone!' he muttered through clenched teeth. His fangs lengthened visibly. He leapt to her, grabbed her forearm and dragged her out from Draco's cell. She yelled, trying to break away, but surprisingly, she felt like a puppet being pulled by invisible strings. Her mind was frozen like her will was suppressed by some unknown power. It had overwhelmed not only her speech, but it limited her body movements to the minimum. She had an impression that she was watching the whole event from the outside, like something possessed her body, pushing her mind deep inside into hiding. She felt scared and small like a five-year-old girl facing the dark entrance to the basement seeing a pair of green eyes of monster that were staring straight at her. The last thought she had before she fainted was the impression that she wouldn't remember what was happening to her, especially his actions, and she had the overwhelming sensation that it wasn't the first time she had been exposed to this power.

He was abrupt and rough, as much as possible, but he didn't hit her. He ordered to one of the guards to take the unconscious Roseanne to his office inside the old-station building standing above the ground. When the guard left, he looked at the remaining three guards with disapproval but couldn't punish them. She was on the top of Erick's dynasty, so the guards were on her command but only theoretically. He knew that they couldn't prevent or stop whatever she wanted to do here. But they did the only right thing they could do in that kind of situation, they called him. Fortunately, he was upstairs and could interrupt the worst scenario before it happened; watching Draco's body slowly disappearing into molecule dust. It might have happened after she had got into a rage because she didn't get what she demanded.

He smiled faintly to himself, thinking how easy he overtook leadership of this dynasty by manipulating Roseanne's mind, bit by bit for the first two years after Erick's disappearance. And he knew he would do everything what was possible to never lose that position.

He stood up, took a fob from his pocket and went to open the electrical lock to the last cell where two mature humans were being held. He always had someone captured in his prisons. Patric called them 'the snack' just in case he needed to use their emotions for his own pleasure or as a bribe for long-time starving vampires in this prison.

His guards helped him to drag in one of them to Draco. Patric sat on a chair, brought by one guard, and watched Draco who was greedily drinking blood until the human's veins were emptied and he was dead. He sighed, combed his wavy hair, stretched his body and put his head on his laced fingers. He remained in that position for a while, thinking about what kind of questions he had to ask to get the information he needed. Moreover, Patric was considering how Adam's name could be used as the leverage he needed so badly. He gave a sign to the guards to take the body out. He put the chair inside Draco's cell but left the door open.

The cell was very simply decorated. There was one bunk bed with grey blankets and flat pillows, one long bench, sink and small toilet hidden in the corner. Draco took his ragged T-shirt off and laid down on the lower bed. His scars were slowly healing. Even though he had just drunk fresh blood, he was very pale, and his movement was limited. He looked sick. Draco stared at Patric, waiting for whatever he might bring next.

'Shall I thank you or curse your kindness?' asked Draco with a low tired voice.

'It depends on how you'll answer my questions,' Patric answered, emotionless.

'Go on then. I don't have anything else to do other than talk to you,' Draco sounded sarcastic, regardless of his bad situation. He was rubbing the skin on his wrists in a place where the silver shackle had made red-black marks on his skin.

'I know where Adam is …' he paused, pointing at Draco.

'I'm not surprised. He's always around Rosa. By the way, only an Upir, or Erick, could manipulate her so well, as you did. I've heard of your kind, but I've never met them before,' said Draco, who got up from the bed and sat on a bench with his eyes closed.

Some low whispering could be heard from all detained vampires.

'Nice try but weak one. Accusing me of being a predator that feeds on vamps doesn't help you get out from here. Besides, you're so deep underground that nobody cares, and nobody's looking for you,' continued Patric, with a cold voice. His face didn't change after Draco's statement.

Draco looked exhausted, but he was alert.

'What do you want?' Draco asked without looking at him.

'Where is Tritus' End? I know you've helped capture Erick …'

'Why do you want to know? To suck his blood …'

'Don't be ridiculous. On the contrary to you, I don't want him dead. You see, I'd like to extend my influence outside England; therefore, I need him,' declared Patric, using his polite voice that he always had in all his political negotiations.

'You hate Erick more than I do. Why do you want to free him?' asked Draco, sitting back on a bench.

'I don't hate him, I envy him. I want to be adopted by him. His dynasty is the most powerful and influential all over the world …'

'So, you want to be his saviour?'

'If you put it that way. He'll kill you, and he doesn't like Anne. Two of his oldest night-children totally disappointed him …'

'So, there'll be a vacant place after he's back, and in your daydreams, is for you to take?' asked Draco, snorting.

'I'm more than sure it's for me. Besides, the dynasty influence doubled during his missing time and under my command. That's making me the best candidate.'

Draco didn't reply at once. He remained silent for a while and confused Patric this way.

'I can take you to Adam. I know where he is, still alive, but not for long.'

Patric tried for the last time to convince Draco to talk. He knew that despite the physical pain that he might be using to torture Draco, he had minimal chances to get anything from so old and mentally strong a vampire as Draco was. Patric stood up and was slowly walking away from the cell when he heard Draco's voice.

'I'll tell you the location but only when I'm standing free, near Adam, still alive,' Draco sounded tired but calm. Patric smiled to himself. It seemed everything was going as he wanted.

'Going back to the topic; how should it be opened?' asked Patric with the most cheerful tone he had since he entered the prison.

'Like every lock, you need a key,' Draco smiled faintly.

'Okay, let me establish something. You'll tell me everything about the Tritus' End, and you go free, or I'll get it after days of racking you both. I wonder how long Adam will stay alive? Trust me, her whip will look like a summer holiday hammock on a tropical island compared to what I'm capable of,' declared Patric calmly, smiling like he was saying a good joke.

'The key is missing. I don't have it nor anyone I know of. It belonged to the witch-hunter George Rogers and his wife. You killed them an hour after closing the casket. He'd had it with him in the car which you burned and pushed into the river Thames. I saw you doing it from a distance.'

Draco finished his statement, watching every one of Patric's facial reactions. The Prince looked stable, like a marble figure, for a quite long time.

'I don't care about a key. I'll use C4 or some acid. I'll open it anyway,' Patric laughed, but there was false tune inside his tone like he was trying to ineptly hide his emotions. He left the cell and when he was outside; he turned back and said in the same emotionless voice as he had at the beginning.

'I sold Adam for an excellent price to The Blue Fairy's Circus to a death match. I promised I would not harm him under some oath he used on me. Make sure the location is real, or you'll never see Adam before some werewolf tears him apart in an arena.'

Those were the last words Patric said to Draco before he left. He shouted some orders to guards and walked fast upstairs.

CHAPTER 19

10th July - The Secret

Patric entered his private house and tapped the code on the alarm panel hanging on the wall just behind the door. He waited until it was accepted, and the board displayed a green-lighted spot for a fingerprint. Although it was almost pitch black inside due to late night hours, he didn't switch on the lights in the corridor. He not only knew the way to the rooms upstairs, but he had a well-developed sense allowing him to walk like a cat in the shadows.

The property was a rather average size. There were two large bedrooms upstairs and one smaller room that he used as storage. He went straight there knowing exactly what he was looking for. He was thinking about the place where he could find the key while driving here.

Now, most of the elements in the one big jigsaw puzzle from the riot that happened ten years ago became more evident than ever. The Tritus' End was the missing piece to solve most of it. Although Patric could sense that the mystery was slowly unfolding itself, still, there was a lot unknown left to discover. He smiled to memories about his own share in it, but he admitted, he didn't know who started it. He just was in the right place at the right moment and used that for his great advantage.

The storage room was cluttered. There were long, vast shelves from the bottom to the top of two walls and a built-in-wardrobe on the other one. The shelves were packed with cardboard boxes with some descriptions written in small letters on the side. Plastic containers were piling up in the middle of the room. Some books looked like they were taken from museums, standing on shelves and some lying on the floor. There were thick folders with names, not only people but places and politic errands, branded with an alias written in inverted commas just under the real ones.

Patric looked at all those things collected throughout so many years and swore badly in his thoughts. He didn't have any organisation system in his private archives, maybe because he was always too busy doing things rather than a systematised history of his enquirers, and he would never bring anyone here to help him, that was for sure. Despite all the untidiness he had to get through, Patric knew exactly what he was searching for.

It took him more than two hours to finally find the old shabby leather rucksack with some dark stains, as though it was splattered with an exploded ketchup bottle. It belonged to George Rogers, one of the most dangerous witch hunters born in Europe. Patrick took the sack without thinking in a matter of seconds from the back seat of George's car. That was the moment when Patric killed him alongside the woman, apparently his wife, accompanying him, ten years ago during the riot spreading like a fire after Erick's sudden disappearance. Back then, Patric looked just once inside the bag but didn't understand the meaning of notes, ancient books with titles written in ancient languages, mainly because he was afraid to touch it. Rumours were going among all vampire dynasties about hunter's skills and spells that could instantly kill any vamp in a blink of an eye if they touched anything that belonged to witch hunters. Maybe it was only a myth, but he was too afraid to risk his life to check if it was true or not. So, he just put the bag deep inside the cupboard in his storage and forgot about it. It was Draco who triggered the picture of the rucksack in Patric's memory. And now, he had a feeling that the mystery of Tritus' End was hidden inside this bag that fortunately belonged to him.

He brought it to the living room, poured a full glass of old whiskey, sat on one side of the couch, opened the bag and threw its contents near him. He switched on the bright light in the room, but the windows were covered with metal shutters, preventing the light from shining outside the house.

He poked the thick book with his the smallest finger while wearing black, leather glows. Nothing happened. He did it more than ten times, in different places with the same results, before he decided to grab it by full hand. Nothing happened either. The book was a size of a large atlas but much thicker. The book-cover was made with black leather, but it looked like the skin of a fish with golden scale reflections that appeared and disappeared under a varied light angle. The paint of the title was mostly worn off, but it could still be read from the shape of pressed letters.

Patric put the book on a couch, clutched the first lid and slowly opened it. Nothing happened at all. He couldn't understand what was written due to some unknown language for him. He flipped some pages and went to the middle of the book, intrigued by the content. It was like an album showing many different animals, but the specimens looked far worse than the ones in an ordinary zoo on display.

Moreover, there were pictures of plants, weapons, artefacts or even traps used to hunt and kill the monsters including witches and any kind of shape-shifters. Patrick was astonished. He never thought that kind of creatures had ever existed. Thank goodness hunters were dealing with them, thought Patric about what was drawn in ink on the pages. And one of next thoughts he had was that the guidebook was definitely very valuable for hunters but explaining to anyone how he got into possession of something that supposed to stay as a secret might be very uncomfortable for him. Almost at the end, there was copper book-mark as long as the whole handbook. Patrick opened it and smiled. That was marked at the first of three pages dedicated only how to catch and kill vampires.

There was a very brief note about Upirs being the worst breed of them all, but it didn't give any pieces of information regarding the method of killing or anything describing their skills. There was one note on a margin written in red ink, visibly in somebody else's handwriting and telling that vampires had a separate notebook dedicated only to them. This book included the rituals of stripping off their powers before they could be killed. It all could be used by hunters especially for the very old vamps that were hard to deal with.

There was nothing more in this guide about vampires, but Patric was turning page after page for more than an hour. He put it back awestruck when no more creatures were left to be seen.

The next thing he took from the hunter's rucksack was a large envelope bent in half. Patric opened it and drew out a few pictures of the Trius' End with one handwritten letter addressed to George and signed by Draco. Draco wrote information about the casket but not only. This stunned Patric and made him really alert.

According to his and Adam's study through antique books and scripts about a vampire, there was one ancient ritual they found after one of the Guild informants helped them decipher the text correctly. Draco only briefly described the method as taking control over Erick's mind, possesing all of his power, and in that way, reversing the process of becoming a vampire. Moreover, there were two possible endings of this act; both could be made by anyone, not only from the same dynasty. First would have reverted the conversion into a vampire and make the participant human again. The second allowed any vamp performing the ceremony to take all of Erick's powers and become the head of the dynasty without completely eradicating the bloodline. In both cases, Erick would die. Draco wanted to become human again, but he needed hunters to help to catch Erick and to make the ritual possible, by using the Tritus' End. He needed their help in exchange for turning into dust more than thirty per cent of the vampire's population from all over the world in one shot. There were no more descriptions or any notes about how to perform the ceremony and what was needed for it, other than the record about the key for the casket included in this envelope. Draco wrote, at last, no one could open the coffin but witch hunters; therefore he passed the key to George as a token of good will and co-operation.

The last line in the letter contained information about Adam as an expert in the field of vampire's occultism and his significant role in this operation.

Patrick cursed out loud. He stood up, poured whiskey to the top of his empty now glass and drank it all at once. He squeezed it after and felt a sharp pain when the glass broke, piercing his skin through the glove. He took the bottle and smashed it on the wall so fiercely that it stuck in a hole made by it there. For the first time in his life, he regretted the decision of selling Adam to the circus. He didn't care about Draco, but he had to have Adam back. And he knew that there was no way to reverse the transaction or even repurchase him for a pile of large, rare diamonds.

CHAPTER 20

12th July - News

'Gary, Gary, Gary wake up, please!' Jessica was yelling and tugging Gary's shoulder. There was desperation and anxiety in her tone. Gary slowly opened his eyes but his face expressed a sleepy state with a lack of surroundings recognition. She was sitting on the edge of his bed, but on the contrary to him, her face represented agitation mixed with fear. She was wearing a nightdress with her favourite cartoon theme. She had ruffled hair and her hands were shaking.

'Something terrible happened to Draco. I had a nightmare so scary that I woke up screaming. I have to do something, but I've no idea what's going on …' she spoke fast like the time was the most important issue now. She couldn't sit still, so she got up and started pacing in his room from the window and back to his bed, breathing rapidly. She opened the curtain and let light enter the room. Early morning sky was covered with stormy clouds indicating incoming heavy rain. Gary looked at her, still drowsy, he moaned, turned back and covered his head with a pillow.

'No, you can't sleep …' she shouted, leaping on him and shaking his body.

'Oh, God help me!' mumbled Gary with his head still partially under the pillow.

'Please, we need to find him. Call Mark now, please …'

There were rush and panic in her voice. She took Gary's phone from a nightstand and put it to his hand. He moaned again but uncovered his head and switched on the device. He called Mark, but his brother didn't answer. Gary tried two more times with the same result.

'Something bad has happened to Mark as well!' she was panicking and exaggerating her worries even more drastically now.

'Nah, he'll call back. He always does,' said Gary with a confident tone.

'Why is he not sleeping here when we need him?' she asked with a bit of resentment.

'Oh, good for me. I can't stand him on a daily basis,' replied Gary, snorting.

'But you're totally lost without him. Listen! I've never had a dream so clear. I've never remembered any dream with so many details. I was inside the dream and I knew that I was dreaming. Everything was so real like I see you now. I was inside a big, circus tent. There were a lot of weird creatures, humans wearing masks, and others I've never seen before, sitting around me. Draco was standing in the middle of arena dressed like a clown from the worst horror movie. He couldn't move. He had chains on his wrists and ankles. Someone was lying on the ground with a head on Draco's boot, crying, curled up like a dog. The crowd was shouting, and then …'

'Maybe it was only a bad dream?' suggested Gary, sitting on the bed wearing only boxers and rubbing his eyes. He interrupted her in attempt to comfort her worries, but it didn't help.

'Listen! No, it wasn't only a dream. I have the feeling that it's real and it'll happen very soon. I've never been so sure.'

'Okay, okay. See, he's calling back,' said Gary, showing Mark's incoming call. Gary answered but wasn't able to say more than a few words with his brother. Jessica poked his arm and soundlessly demanded to talk with Mark. Gary gave her the phone without forewarning him. She told Mark not only the same what Gary already heard, but how the story ended. Gary went to the wardrobe and picked some fresh clothes. He looked at her and admitted that talking to Mark somehow calmed her down. She even smiled faintly. Before leaving the room to take a shower, Gary heard the rest of her nightmare. He pictured it pretty well and shivered. If it were happening somehow, it would be the worst scenario of Draco's and Gary's death.

*

It was raining for most of the day. It started early morning as a storm with a wall of water pouring down, flooding and making huge puddles on streets and sidewalks. That lasted for an hour, but it didn't finish. The rain was coming and going all day long, chased away by a rapid wind. The dark clouds were swarming in the sky ready to drop the water on the ground at any time. But now, it drizzled soundlessly, leaving small drops on passing people's clothes and umbrellas.

The team was sitting in the living room this late afternoon talking about Draco and Mark's absent, museum tasks and what they had done already. Jessica showed the sketch of the key and outline of the stage that would suit the performance. Simon's news about the lack of help from the pack made them feel uneasy. Sean was going through all his friends who could help with the show, writing names on a piece of paper with notes about their capabilities for doing individual tasks. He made sharp comments about Robert who didn't have anyone he could ask for help. Robert replied that he had, but he had to ask them first if they wanted to participate in this endeavour. He promised that next time he would bring them to the meeting, after knowing what exactly had to be done.

They had quite a heated conversation when Mark entered the living-room an hour late. He looked tired and untidy, an unusual appearance for him. Robert asked if Mark had baked some cake and hid it from him and was trying to make a joke about it. But Mark wasn't in a good mood to answer. He only shrugged and sat on the sofa near Jessica, busying himself with reviewing the technical sketches she gave him.

Robert snorted for news about no sweets for today and kept quiet, looking quite unhappy. Nobody knew why Draco wasn't present. Even Sean, who was the closest with him, had no idea why Draco's phone was out of reach. That gave Robert reason to criticise the whole idea of inviting the vamp here at all. He stated that Draco's role should be limited to money only and hoped that nobody would befriend him in a future for their own good.

Gary started the next part of the meeting by giving everyone copies of a script. He looked somewhat unsure about it. Before they had a chance to read it, Gary was explaining that it was only a brief idea and they need to work on it together. Sean interrupted him by asking about having a break to familiarise with the text first and then talk about it.

Gary sat on the edge of the armchair, waiting to be fiercely criticised, especially by Robert. It was the first time he gave something he wrote to people he knew. Although they were his friends, but somehow, he felt like he was standing there completely naked. He knew it that would be the hardest part of today's gathering, but he didn't expect that he might feel so exposed.

But, on the contrary to his expectation, Robert said that he liked the idea of using Shakespeare's plays as a background. Deep inside, Gary felt relief. He thought that Robert would destroy all Gary's effort by his sarcastic comments. He even smiled, feeling more confident about his first written short play.

'Is it your intention to use Shakespeare's name because it's catchier?' asked Jessica, flipping the pages. She still was a bit on an edge since this morning.

'I like that idea. It matches the theme of the exhibition perfectly. I'll get approval tomorrow,' said Sean, reading in the middle of the script.

'Do we have a problem with anything here?' asked Robert, raising his voice one tone higher and showing the script around with his stretched hand.

Suddenly the doorbell rang. Almost everyone was staring at one another surprised. Jessica went to open the door and to check who was buzzing. Mark followed her but stood only in the doorway to the living room, observing what was going on at the main entrance.

'Hi, is Simon Harris living here? Is this the correct address?' a soft woman's voice was heard to those sitting in the living room.

'Yes, he's here,' replied Jessica, and she called Simon's name loudly. Jessica looked at the young lady in her early twenties standing on the doorstep and smiled. It was quite a long time since Simon had invited any girl to a place where he was living, she thought. Jessica wondered if this blond woman belonged to Simon's werewolves pack or she was just a regular human being.

Simon rushed to the hall. He greeted the young woman, asking what she was doing here and apologised because they were busy. Almost everyone followed him to the corridor.

'I know. But you've asked for help, so, here I am. You have a meeting about the show in The British Museum. Am I right?' she asked, leaving Jessica and Gary astonished. Gary and rest of the team gathered in the main hall. Robert nodded to the newly arrived lady and smiled like he just won the jackpot. He didn't stay in the corridor but headed to the kitchen.

'Hi. I'm Maya and a member of Night Reapers werewolves pack,' she said, waving to all of them. Jessica pushed Simon gently aside and with a hand gesture invited Maya to come in.

'Are you alone?' asked Robert, standing in the kitchen's doorway.

'Oh, no. But I'm here alone. I didn't take all of them with me. It might scare you away,' she replied. Robert rolled eyes with a face expression meaning 'obviously' like he was expecting the situation to happen.

'Wait a minute. But James prohibited the whole pack to help us,' said Simon, more like a statement than a question.

'Yes, he did,' she laughed.

'You really don't think that the full pack would obey all his orders, do you?' asked Robert, staring at Simon who didn't know how to react.

'Welcome in a rebel,' said Maya, smiling very broadly.

'Are you always like that?' asked Gary.

'Sometimes, but don't worry. It's not the first time. So, what's the plan?' she asked eagerly.

'They couldn't miss the opportunity to do something out of boredom,' said Robert, going out of the kitchen with a big bag of crisps he found there and now he was eating them loudly. Mark snorted, seeing him but smiled. Simon grinned and asked her if she wanted something to drink and invited her to the living-room.

'See, my cavalry arrived,' said Robert to Sean, pointing at Maya. He walked back to his chair, but on his way, he stopped and ordered coffee for himself and didn't care who would be making it.

During the short break, when Gary and others were organising drinks and snacks, Mark had a few phone calls which made him look even more concerned. Gary asked him what it was, but Mark replied he would tell after the meeting.

After half an hour, when everything was said about the casket and the need of taking out Erick from it just for Maya's briefing, they focused back on the script. Maya looked terrified and excited at the same time. The whole story sounded more like a movie idea than something actually happening in reality, and therefore she wanted to be part of the team even more than before she came here. He wrote his phone number on the script copy that belonged to Mark and gave it to her. Both Robert and Simon glared at him curiously.

The text was a mixed version of Shakespeare's 'Romeo and Juliet', 'A Midsummer Night's Dream' and 'Macbeth' in one mystical story in a quite modern comedic style.

'So, who is playing whom?' asked Robert, giving this question as the sign to begin a very energetic conversation about the show itself. Everyone pointed at Gary to play Romeo's role. Gary blushed but didn't disagree.

'But why Romeo and Juliet?' asked Mark.

'Because it's well-known and there's a crypt at the end,' replied Gary.

'Great idea. Open the coffin and quickly finish the show,' said Sean.

'You have to be Romeo. You'll need to turn the key, open the coffin and save the sweetest girl whose name is Erick,' said Mark, smiling for the first time since he came to the meeting.

'And who is playing Juliet?' asked Gary, glancing from Maya to Jessica.

'Maya. I need to be sure the equipment is working smoothly,' declared Jessica, making a hand gesture to Maya, who reddened and looked a bit confused, but agreed silently.

'No kissing,' said Robert, smiling and wagging his finger at Gary.

'Yep. She's married, and her husband could make even bigger mayhem than we if he was there. So, be careful,' said Simon, without looking at Maya. Gary could have sworn he heard a tone of liking mixed with bitterness inside Simon's voice. He couldn't help but grin broadly. Simon always seemed picky in his choice of women, but he never revealed anything about the type he was attracted to, thought Gary. That was the first time Gary heard him talking with hidden, pleasant emotions about the girl sitting next to him. They both were staring at one another a bit longer than was needed, and then Simon peeped back to Gary, giving him a look that only men could understand perfectly.

'But how will we replace Erick with Juliet?' asked Jessica and puzzled everyone this way. Sean grounded and said that this was a technical problem that had to be solved pretty quickly.

'What might happen after we open the coffin?' asked Gary and perplexed them all even more, staring at Sean like he was an expert about vampire's well-being after lying in this unusual artefact for so long.

'I don't know,' replied Sean but his short answer made everyone worried.

'I'll give you a tranquiliser,' stated Robert, supporting Sean this way. He didn't want to explain what it was, but Maya backed him up saying they had special liquid to calm or made very sleepy almost every vampire when they were hunting for outlaws. Robert suggested increasing the dosage to about five hundred per cent because that should only stun Erick and not kill him. Robert said it should help keep him unconscious but didn't know for how long it would last. After all, Erick was one of the oldest vampires known in the world. Nothing that might work well, even on Draco, might be as effective on Erick as it would be on others. Sean said that he would take care of Erick after releasing him, but he didn't say any details how.

For the next hour, there was a hot debate about roles to play. They all started to re-write the script, making dialogues longer and the story more complicated. Everyone had something to do but Robert. His typical reaction for any proposed character was only his laugh and the word 'no'. In this brainstorming time that was roaming throughout the living-room, the drama was rising to a three acts play that could make a good show in a professional theatre.

'We can't play that,' Sean's cold voice interrupted them.

'Why not?' asked Gary.

'It's too long. Look, I have to show the script to my boss to get approval. What we just did, it's great to a full stage, but we are amateurs. Don't get me wrong, Gary, but it's too much. We have to even shorten the first version,' replied Sean with saddens in his voice. Gary lingered for a while, trying to convince him for this new vision, but Sean was immovable.

'What if we skip most of those dialogues and introduce the narrator? That way we can shorten the time of the whole story and keep only the most important talks,' asked Gary, waiting for an answer. Sean was thinking a bit longer than Gary expected but accepted the new idea.

'You'll be the storyteller,' Sean was pointing at Robert with his teacher voice. And to all surprise, Robert greeted that news with a happy face. He nodded, agreeing with a bit of a mischievous smirk.

'What's the plan B?' asked Robert.

'We don't have it and our plan A is not ready,' responded Mark who wasn't as active in the debate as he usually was.

'I think total improvisation is the best as plan B,' implied Gary.

'So, we know what to do, is there anything else for today?' asked Sean in his lecturer's voice.

'I have horrible news,' claimed Mark and without waiting for their response, he continued. 'Draco was captured by someone and sold for deathmatch to thc Bluc Fairy's Circus.'

'Hahaha! Really?' asked Robert, laughing.

Mark didn't answer but showed them the news on his phone. He opened the application with a picture of Draco, which one was filling up most of the space on the large screen of the newest phone model that Mark bought recently.

'How did it happen?' asked Sean, raising his voice with recognisable panic in it.

'No idea. I'll find out, but without him, everything is lost,' replied Mark angrily.

Almost everyone was concerned, but not Robert. They all had a lot of questions, but nobody knew how it had happened without any solid answers based on facts. Moreover, Mark said that his colleagues he asked about it didn't know either, regardless of their streetwise knowledge about illegal, underground arenas. But it left suppositions about the unknown third part being involved in this incident. At least they all agreed, it had to be some dark business, including a kidnapping theory, behind this. Robert wasn't as active in this debate as he might be. He looked more like someone who was deep in his thoughts analysing information known only to him without sharing with the rest of the group.

'We need to find a way to get him out of there,' declared Gary firmly.

'What? Are you kidding? Nobody ever gets out from The Blue Fairy's Circus before the match. It's impossible,' snorted Robert.

'How do you know he was sold?' asked Jessica.

'Look here. He is on the circus side …' Mark couldn't finish.

'Fairies classify vampires as monsters. The match is monsters versus rest of human-kind, aka - ferals …' continued Robert, interrupting Mark with a calm voice.

'Only those who are captured, or sold to fairies, are fighting on their side,' Mark finished his thought.

'Did you just say fairies?' asked Gary with a frown, interrupting Simon.

'Yes, but they're not fluffy and colourful like from kid's fairy-tales. You don't want to meet them and by any circumstances, never ever make any deal with them …' said Robert, cutting off his sentence like he wanted to avoid blurting some secretes out. He said it with a voice tone indicating some mysterious dangers only well-known to him. Gary couldn't help but think about how those uncanny fairies looked, and the urge to see them, even from afar, was growing in him.

'How we can get him out?' asked Gary, sighing.

'You can't, but I can,' replied Mark, putting his hand on his chest.

'No, I forbid you!' Sean's sharp yell worked like the crack of a whip for the gathered team. Everyone was shocked, probably because that was the first time they had heard Sean shouting with so much wrath in his voice. His face changed drastically and started having features of a lynx. Gary was stunned. He was staring at Sean cat's eyes that were getting more yellow every second, with horizontal pupils. Sean's skin slowly covered with grey fur marked with black streaks. His mouth was open, showing visibly lengthened fangs. Sean was hissing like a scared but still fighting cat. Nobody moved. This sudden change of atmosphere shocked all of them, including Sean himself.

Mark put his hands on Sean's arms, trying to calm him down. Sean sat on the couch breathing deeply, clenching and unclenching his fists.

'I know you're angry, but we don't have any other choice. Draco will die there, you know that …' Mark continued talking to Sean softly, like talking to a small crying child.

'Compared to this shit, the museum issues look like a Christmas show for nursery kids,' said Robert with a hint of sadness.

'Okay, what can we do for Draco, to get him out?' asked Gary, demanding answers. There was only silence around.

'Gary, you have to know something about the circus,' said Sean. He was now calm and focused. The moment of his lost restraint was now only a memory in the meeting's participant's minds.

'The Blue Fairy's Circus is odd. They have only two performances in a year, but there are always cruel and deadly. It originated from Roman gladiator's arenas, and they've survived for centuries. One single ticket for the live-show is worth thousands of pounds. Even if we could buy them, there is no way we could come closer than two meters near the arena. Have I mentioned it's a huge cage?' said Sean bitterly. His anger and agitation start rising again.

'One way to get in the circus and that close to the fighters is by being one of them,' said Robert, staring at Mark. The silence was so deep that it seemed nobody dared to breathe.

'But what if …?' Gary started but was interrupted by Mark.

'I'll do it,' he said. There was no reaction, it was like Mark never said it.

'What do you mean?' Gary asked, smiling gently, but there was confusion mixed with disbelief in his voice.

'It means your brother is going to fight in that arena to try to save Draco. Are you insane?' this time Robert's voice showed rage.

'No, I'm not. If someone has any chance to do it, it's only me. So, no discussion,' declared Mark, accenting his last sentence with an irritation.

'You can't. You're not a warrior,' said Gary, laughing.

'Oh, yes, he is, and a bloody good one,' Robert's comment made Gary, Simon, and Jessica stare at him with open mouths. But, on the contrary to them, Sean and Maya muttered something and nodded with agreement.

'What?' Gary was staring, utterly surprised, at his half-brother.

He couldn't believe what he just heard. He sat next to Sean perplexed. The one thing he could do now was cover his mouth with his hand to prevent very heavy swearing that might come out any time soon. He was shaking his head, disapproving to listen to the ongoing conversation. Jessica was white as a piece of paper with her eyes fixed on Mark. She nudged Gary and half-whispered, 'It's my dream, I told you, something nasty is going to happen.' Her hands were shaking, and she couldn't talk for a while.

'Why have you never told me?' Gary asked angrily, straight to Mark.

'I couldn't …' Mark started explaining himself but was interrupted by Robert.

'One more family drama and I'll be sick. Cut the shit off and get to the point. I'd like to see you fighting there. The bets will be high.'

'But it's a death-match,' said Sean with a trembling voice.

'I know, but I'm not going to die. I'm good,' said Mark.

'You're cocky. I like it,' continued Robert.

'What does it mean, 'death-match'?' asked Gary.

'It means the winner is usually the last man standing,' said Robert.

'Usually?' Gary insisted.

'There is an option, but nobody ever got the chance, nor live that long, to use it,' replied Robert.

'What is it?' asked Jessica.

'After five minutes of the fight, if you are injured, you can use the so-called 'the mercy box'. But the winner is paid money for every dead body lying on the floor. No one inside would ever allow you to get to the box,' said Sean with sadness.

'Jeez! Is it even legal?' asked Gary, annoyed.

'Theoretically, it's not, but nobody would ever stop the fairies from doing it. You have to be a trusted customer to have the true location given, so even if you have a ticket, you might find yourself in the middle of nowhere. You might watch the match online if you pay for it with stacks of money. Fairies are badly secretive,' said Robert.

'How do players know where to go?' asked Simon.

'The location will be sent by text, an hour or two before the match. It's usually on the outskirts of London. Everyone will wait in the city,' replied Mark.

'How does it work to take part in the fight?' Simon was very intrigued by it.

'Well, you just have to put your name on a list …'

'…and wait for the vote to end …' Sean finished Mark's sentence.

'Vote?' asked Simon.

'Two days before the match, there's a list of all fighters who want to participate. Everyone with a ticket can vote. Those with the highest number are chosen. And then you can make a bet,' replied Robert.

'Why are people going there to die?' asked Jessica.

'Because the price for winning is so high, that some would never refuse to try their luck. If the last one dies on the stage, his family get the money. Besides, only the best, already known fighters, can put names on the list.'

'The list is open. I'm on the top there …' Mark couldn't finish, he was interrupted by Gary's sharp voice.

'What? Have you already decided without us?'

'Show me …' said Robert, interrupting Gary's dramatic questions. Mark showed everyone the list of all fighters with his name on the top. Gary was shocked. He turned and ran away from the living-room, but Mark walked fast behind him calling brother's name.

*

'Hey, open the door, or I'll break it,' shouted Mark, knocking loudly on Gary's door. He repeated his demand two more times but without any effect.

'Okay, I'm doing it now. You've asked for it. Back off. I don't want to hit you,' he declared angrily. He made as many steps back as he could in the corridor, but at the moment he was ready to turn into feral and destroy the obstacle, he heard the lock click, leaving the door slightly open.

Mark went inside and found Gary lying on the bed with his head covered by a large pillow. He sat on the edge but didn't know what to do, or what to say. He saw Gary's body shaking, heard the sound of silent sobbing and he felt useless. All he could do was put his hand on Gary's back and pat him for a while. Mark said nothing, but he brought a box of tissues, took a few from it and stuck this bundle into Gary's hand. Gary used them all, still with his head hidden under the pillow. After he used all of them, he reached out his hand with opening and closing fingers and waved to Mark. Mark put the next vast bunch of tissues into Gary's hand and watched, with a faint smile, when all disappeared under his cover. The sound of a blowing nose was long and intense. Mark left the tissue box near Gary's head and put his hand on it. Then, Mark went to the desk and sat on the large office chair he once bought as a present. The computer was working. Mark minimised the opened word processor with the museum's play to the task-bar, switched on his favourite game, put the headset on and started playing in one of the newest battlegrounds. He peeped at his brother when he sensed a slight movement from the bed, but Gary only covered himself with a blanket. Gary, with a pillow still on his head, took his mobile from trousers pocket, stick headphones in ears and put music on. It was audibly enough for Mark to recognise Gary's favourite metal band.

It was late at night, and Mark was so absorbed with the game that he didn't notice when Gary stood up and went to the toilet. He was a bit taken aback when he found his brother sitting on an additional chair next to him, watching how Mark was playing ranking-match with other people online. Gary nodded to him, giving the sign that he was okay. Mark finished the game, put the headset on Gary's head, stood up and mentioned that he was hungry. Gary knew he would bring something specially made for him from the kitchen. Gary thought that cooking wasn't only a hobby, but it was the easiest way for Mark to show that he cares.

Gary played the same game when Mark brought a plate full of sandwiches and a few cans of beers. They ate, drank and talked about the content of a game, maybe because neither of them wanted to start the essential conversation about what happened in the living-room. After the food vanished, all game enemies slain, and achievements points earned, Gary thought that it was the right time to ask the most significant questions.

'Why didn't you tell me who you really are?' asked Gary, who finally dared to end this unnatural, invisible tension hanging between them.

'I wanted, but since the forest accident, everything is going so fast …'

'Everyone knew but me …' said Gary bitterly.

'Sorry bro, but that's bullshit. Simon and Jessica didn't know either,' answered Mark calmly.

'So, your taxi driving is only a cover?' Gary still had resentment in his tone.

'No, I'm a taxi driver and also a cage fighter. People say that I'm good, but I've lost many times …'

'So, you decide to commit suicide?'

'No, but there is no one else who can do it. Remember that Draco is important because you still have his blood in your body, so you're bound to him, and Gods know for how long.'

'Mark, you'll die there!' Gary raised his voice with a rage.

'But, what if … that fight would never happen?' asked Mark with a tiny smile on his face. That perplexed Gary so much; he said nothing and only stared at his brother with an open mouth.

'I've been thinking about all possibilities while playing. As a fighter, I can have access to Draco before the match starts. If only I could manage to drowse him, the fight will be over. It won't matter if they ban me from the circus' fights. I don't care. Besides, it's illegal anyway.'

'Seriously! Could you do it?' asked Gary, less nervous than before.

'Well, I have nothing to lose if I try,' answered Mark, staring straight into his half-brother's eyes.

'What about the fairies?'

'Oh, they're little arseholes, but I'm not going to quit …'

'Do you have a plan?' Gary was more interested in this new idea than scared.

'No clue yet. I guess I'll have to improvise.'

'I want to go with you,' Gary demanded.

Mark didn't answer for a while, just put his hands behind his head, straightened his whole body and sighed.

'There'll be a lot of very dangerous ferals and vamps who can sense you're human. I'm not sure if you can go with me backstage …'

'I'm a dead man walking anyway. What the worst could happen to me? And, I have a plan,' said Gary, switching off the game and clicking on the folder with the website project he was working on.

'Let say, I'm doing the reality show about your career, and it's happened I follow you almost everywhere you go. You said you're known in this sport,' said Gary. Mark looked at him and saw the sparkle in Gary's eyes that was always cropping up when he was excited about something or had a creative idea.

'That might actually work. We can even come close to Draco for that reason, to show the kind of nasty vamp I'm fighting with.'

'But we'll have to take someone else with us, to make it more realistic.'

'Only one, who?'

'I don't know yet. Maybe Robert?'

'Why him?'

'Because, as I've heard, he's still a good warrior, who would be handy if something goes very wrong. And his arrogant boldness can over-talk everyone and make them feel like a piece of shit. Mixing him with a camera and we have a perfect reality TV show,' Gary replied, feeling a bit more confident having some plan to work on.

'You're a genius,' said Mark, happily.

Gary showed Mark his website project. Mark was amazed.

The website was created like the film reel in a black and white frame and a sepia colour inside stills. The name 'The Faded Photograph' was written in old-fashioned font used by the first typewriters.

'What's that?' asked Mark.

'Well, I'm thinking about making movies, like the one from the forest but about ferals and all those Viviters that live around …'

'You can't expose our world!' Mark raised his voice.

'I'm not going to. It'll look like an amateur film-making production of cheap horror movies. No one would ever believe it's real. It'll exist only in the Internet. I'm not even sure if someone will watch it at all. Okay, maybe a few bored freaks, or no-life's trolls, are more likely to see it,' said Gary, and he showed Mark the not finished yet movie he made from the forest paint-ball event but with the werewolf in it. The silent movie was stylised on the 20s-30s in a black frame and sepia colour inside. Boards were telling the story like in the first movies. The characters had dialogues put in white bubbles, like in comic books. The film wasn't finished yet, but Gary looked so happy when he was talking about it and that made Mark pleased at seeing his brother's focus switch to something more positive.

CHAPTER 21

14th July - The Blue Fairy's Circus

'What you're doing here?' asked Mark, astonished, staring at a group of people crowding in the hall right in front of the main door to the house where his half-brother Gary was living, and Mark was sleeping on an air mattress from time to time. It was eleven o'clock at night, and five minutes ago, he got a text about the location of the death-match in the Blue Fairy's Circus. Gary was standing right behind him, grinning broadly. He was holding a mobile and a bag with his camera in his other hand.

'It's show-time, right?' asked Robert, smiling. He was wearing his usual leather jacket and jeans, but this time he had a leather baker-boy hat with sunglasses on a peak.

'I told you to say nothing to them,' said Mark to Gary, with a bit of anger, gesturing towards the figures standing in the hall.

'I swear I didn't do it. I only asked Robert to go with us,' replied Gary, patting himself in the chest in a gesture of telling the truth. His face was showing surprise but mixed with satisfaction. Because, deep down in Gary's heart, there was a tiny little spark of hope that someone else would support them in this outrageous and possibly deadly mission. Gary sighed with relief after seeing his friends, and smiled thinking that however unforeseen, he just classified Robert as one of them. Mark shouldn't have been expecting to keep a secret about such an important issue, thought Gary, staring at all of them, ready to jump to some strange and dangerous event.

'All of you? Simon? Jessica? And who are you?' asked Mark, pointing at a tall man with a perfectly tailored black suit who looked like some gentleman from high society.

'My brother, James, the leader of The Night Reapers werewolves pack,' replied Robert, putting his hand on James's shoulder. James rolled his eyes but nodded to Mark as greetings.

'You didn't seriously think we'll let you go alone, did you?' asked Jessica, glaring at Mark stony-face. She was wearing a purple T-shirt with a vast logo; 'The Triangle 51 television', the same as the rest of the team but James. All of them had plastic ID cards hanging on a green leash with a TV station name printed on it. Most of them hung the badge on their neck, but Jessica tied it to a belt loop with a card near her jeans pocket.

'Ta-da! The cavalry has arrived,' said Robert, spreading his hands and showing everyone his grin. He looked more like someone who was going to a party than to a seriously threatening event.

'Is Sean with you?' asked Gary.

'Nah, he's picking up the stage and the rest of the equipment for the museum. Somebody has to do it. Besides, he doesn't care how badly we screw up in the circus, as long as we come back in one piece,' explained Jessica, smiling.

Gary didn't know what to say, but inside his head the little tiny voice of intuition was teasing him with 'I told you so, they'll do it', repeated over and over again. He smiled, walked closer and shook James's hand, introducing himself more formally. Mark was walking right behind him. He showed the exact location of tonight's circus, saying they should go and discuss the action plan in the car by phone. But Gary and Mark weren't ready for what was waiting for the team outside on the street.

The newest model of a broadcasting television van was parked up in front of the house. It was huge, with a massive satellite TV antenna that was installed on the roof alongside other useful equipment that reporters might need on the way. The white sides of the van were partially covered with a large logo of a television station named 'Triangle 51'. It was the same brand TV name that was printed on all of the ID cards and leashes that the team had. James informed them that this van truly belonged to the international TV station created by ferals and Viviters for all those living with a mark of the veil. The TV was broadcasting in almost every country around the world, including Internet television.

'What? How?' asked Gary, even more surprised.

'What's that?' asked Mark at the same time.

'That's the best show off to stunned stupid fairies,' replied Robert, looking very happy.

'Are we really going as a television team?' Mark kept asking as he couldn't believe what was happening now. It seemed that Gary's idea to film a warrior's biographic story rapidly expanded to a reality show of illegal arena fighting that would be shown around the world in a supernatural television. Gary was stunned by the fact that he might use the event to make a movie that he could put to his own website, if only they succeeded.

'Oh, no. They hate fairies. But, let's say that the CEO of London's branch owes me a lot. So, I pulled strings and borrowed it,' said James, directing his hands into the vehicle.

'He's a bloody good lawyer and he has a mutual hatred for fairies, like many others. That's why he's here. If something could destroy The Circus, James is first in line to help to do it. Don't ask why. Let's go guys. Chop chop,' said Robert, and he went to his car parked up in front of the van, throwing the key to Simon and showing him to the driver's seat. Simon caught it and took the first place without a word.

'These are for you guys,' said James, giving badges to Mark and Gary.

'Is it real?' asked Gary, gazing at the badge. There was his picture and name printed on it, and it looked very professional.

'No, I've made it. The real station has a bit of a different layout, but it's unrecognisable,' said James, opening the van's door, sat behind the wheel, putting his backpack behind and starting the engine.

'But they're original,' said Jessica, and she gave Gary a brand new, purple T-shirt, with the same logo as she had and the TV station trademark on the back. She quickly checked if she packed all she needed, including her drone, additional batteries, two air-screws, and a small laptop.

Gary had one case with his professional camera packed and a few bags with things he needed for filming. Mark helped him put it all in the van. Gary jumped inside and was astonished by all those screens, hardware, and sets that were installed there. He felt like he was in a little heaven, staring at the equipment, as he had never been inside a broadcasting van before. All the equipment installed there was unknown to him. There were many screens, buttons, keys, computers and a chair attached to the floor, and that made Gary feel totally unprepared. He had no idea how to switch on the machines, even just to make an impression to passers-by by pretending to do something professional. Gary wondered if there was any form of manual as he glared at black screens and all the switched off devices.

Gary thought that James was nothing like Robert and looked a bit out of place, dressed like he was, as though he was going to a cocktail party in Buckingham Palace. But instead, he was sitting behind a wheel of a van driving to the place where the cultural dinner party was replaced with bloodshed of gladiators' fights to amuse the audience.

On the other hand, Gary thought, the camera had the magic of converting the long-drawn dirt of life into short fairy-tales. He hoped that the desire of being a television star, even for five minutes, was consuming some of the mysterious fairies on the same level as many humans all over the world. Gary started feeling more confident, seeing all of them going together to the unknown event. He hoped that press had the same almost untouchable status as in the normal world. But at least now, the chance that they might succeed in saving Draco was much higher than an hour before.

Gary left his bags in the back, sat near Jessica on the double front seat and fastened his seatbelt when Mark's phone rang.

'So, what's the plan bro?' asked Gary.

'We have to seriously improvise. We have a problem. The Prince is on the list as one of the fighters. He'll kill Draco first,' replied Mark with a voice tone indicating stress and fear.

CHAPTER 22

14th/15th July - The Fight

Mark's knowledge of London's street's shortcuts saved them driving time. They were at the circus twenty-five minutes before the first gong. The security manager didn't even check the identity cards but just let in the cars through the makeshift gate and showed them the parking space right behind the stage, in the opposite direction than for the rest of the guests. It wasn't the first time when Gary saw a positive reaction about someone holding the professional camera, but the easiness of making an impression on the circus crew members with their TV station branded van surprised him more than ever.

The massive four-masts circus tent was standing on a broad field surrounded by a small forest from one side, a longitudinal lake and two crossing streets from the other. Although the place was lying on the side-lines, there were street lights and houses of the nearest village in the far distance within eye-shot. The whole area was well-lit and secured by a temporary fence made by barbed wires. The guards wore military uniforms, bulletproof vests and full-face helmets all in one black colour, and that made them barely visible in the shadows. They had small machine guns, knives and looked like a private army.

But those few who were standing at the gate entrance were a civilian kind. They were giving orders, checking guests lists and directing the cars' movement towards free parking spaces. They were easy to distinguish from the rest of the crew due to their traditional ringmaster outfits: bright red jackets with tails, white shirts, gold waistcoats, golden embroidery and finishings, black trousers, high boots and tall black hats.

James parked the van a few metres away from the extension of the main tent, where the whole backstage was set. The extension was made from the same material as the huge circus tent, in a deep blue colour like a summer ocean.

He parked the car in a front position to the road-exit, giving them an easy start in case of a quick evacuation. Simon followed him and parked his car behind the van, making it invisible from the tent's hatch. Further down on this field, there were parked trucks, SUVs, and caravans that belonged to the circus personnel. There were plenty of human-shaped figures busy with some important matters, but most of them stopped at the moment when the TV van came into sight. Some of them came closer, staring at the ongoing scene. Gary watched them and was thinking, if they were humans or just someone who only had a similar form? He couldn't stop wondering how fairies looked in their feral-battle form. Were they small, and did they have wings, like those from stories for children? Or did they look more like a giant caricature of kids' toys but in a more ferocious way? But now, as far as Gary could see, there were only human silhouettes with nothing special apparent and certainly nothing that could fit into horror tales.

There were no black guards near the rear entrance, just one short man, like a midget, who was sitting on a camping chair sipping beer from a large plastic cup. His sun-bed was located next to one of the posts that were holding the extension of the main tent. He dropped the cup, spilling the liquid on his clown's outfit, and ran inside wholly shocked by the arrival of the van.

Before Gary's team got out of the cars, a small group of people gathered at the tent's entryway. They all looked surprised and slightly dazed by the TV arrivals. Gary watched their reaction and knew, at least the part of getting inside the circus tent would be quite an uncomplicated task. But the picture of heavily armed guards near the main gate was alarming and stressful, not only for Gary. Nobody had expected that complication to occur and maybe this was one of the biggest mistakes they made so far this evening. On the bottom on his skull, the words *your friends will die, it's your fault, idiot'*, were banging like a loud bell and with an accompaniment of a dark, sarcastic laugh in the most terrifying voice. He knew, even if Mark and the werewolves would be in their feral forms, it might be not enough to stop bullets fired from so many guns that were carried by the heavily armed guards in this place. The tingling sensation that he always had when he sensed trouble made him shiver. Nevertheless, he took his camera and the rest of his equipment from the van and followed James. Somehow, James's coolness and calmness was working on Gary like a bandage on the bleeding wound and was stopping him from having more worries. They all were standing near Robert's car, using the van as a cover from the curious gazing eyes of the circus' staff.

'Guys calm down. It's all under control. Just play arrogant professionals, and everything will be all right. This is the biggest dream of The Blue Fairy's Circus, to have the show on international television. In their eyes, we're doing them a favour. Don't forget about it. They're here for our service. Savvy?' announced James, whispering and giving them all walkie-talkies that he pulled out from his backpack. They nodded, murmured something and adjusted the frequencies in their devices.

They agreed to follow the simple plan they had made during the drive here; the reality show that was broadcasting live one of the most unexpected and highly rated death-matches of the last decade. The fight was between a five-hundred-year-old vampire and his three-hundred-year-old side-kick as the aggressors from the circus' side, against the rest of the world. The betting of who would be the winner of the match was skyrocketing when Patric Vance, the well-known leader of the most prominent vampire dynasty, The Acheron's, put his name on the list as one of the warriors standing against the circus.

In the whole of The Blue Fairies Circus history, a fight where vampires faced other vampires hadn't happened for over two centuries. Moreover, the event was being streamed worldwide, boosting one virtual access to their private internet channel to the price comparable for circus' tickets for a few years.

Mark's role was to be the leading warrior of a TV performance, at least he was introduced to the circus' manager this way. Their plan contained a simple task, to get inside the place where Draco was held, sedate him, take him out, make some disturbance and drive back to London as fast as they could. It was the skeleton of this operation here. They did make the assumption that the fight in the arena would never happen and therefore Mark would leave the place unhurt.

James went first to the tent. With his upright posture, stern face and self-confident attitude, he made the circus' people get out of his way without saying anything to them. He said a few sentences that sounded like an order about the filming process not only to his own team but to the circus' crew as well. Gary watched him, amazed by his lack of fear when James was having uncomfortable conversations with the circus's manager about the TV station's unexpected arrival. Gary and the rest of the group didn't hear what he was talking about, they focused on unpacking the camera, the drone, and any other things that they needed to have in order to start filming.

Gary and Jessica organised the camera's recording as a transmission to their two working laptops inside the van. The van's engine was still on, giving them the power that was necessary to keep all the TV equipment inside switched on. Gary didn't know how to operate it, so he and Jessica just kept pushing random keys until some screens started flashing and emitted a low, electrical working sound. Gary thought that from the outside, it looked professional, gazing at all those lights and the slowly moving satellite plate on the top of the van. Jessica sat on a stool, behind a narrow worktop that could only hold the width of the average laptop. They adjusted the laptop's programs that were operating cameras, checked the connection, pictures, and the pitch of the sound. Jessica tried to fly her new drone that she bought yesterday for the purpose of this event. It was smaller, lighter, had all the possible modern upgrades such as radar, autopilot to the main point, longer-lived batteries and a few others. She started flying it around to the front side of the big tent, recording the entrance with all the guards' positions and most of now arriving guests. She smiled, feeling like a child with a brand-new toy like it was an early gift for her birthday.

The drone was working smoothly, reacting like a dragonfly under her fingers pressing the buttons. The controller had a built-in small screen, giving her great vision of the recordings. Hours of practising flying drones, and even destroying the previous ones, finally paid off. She operated it on a pretty low level and that made the upcoming guests feeling uneasy. Those who noticed the camera started walking faster to the tent, pointing fingers at it. One of the guards aimed his machine gun at the drone, but his attempt to shoot it was prevented by the same man on a charge, who let the fake TV team in.

In the meantime, James had a very vibrant conversation with someone who looked like the leader in the circus. James didn't look happy, but regardless of the topic he was winning it. Gary could read it, based on the manager's body language with his sad face and a red blush on cheeks.

Gary noticed that all of the circus' staff were wearing distinctive, colourful clothes that were fitting to one another like a set. You couldn't miss who was who, based on their outfit. Other than the guards outside the main entrance, there were a bunch of tall and bulky looking men in brown, vintage leather jackets that were working from the rear side of the tent. They also had brown leather trousers, and red ram's skull masks covering their heads. All were similarly tailored and it made them look like members of some special team. They were swarming around a separate place, where, as Gary and the rest expected, Draco and the other captured creatures for the show were held. The places were divided inside by fabric walls made from the same material as the rest of the circus tent.

Gary started recording before they entered the tent. He pointed at Robert and gave him a sign to start the show. Robert, with a professional TV microphone, came closer to Mark, and with his usual confident voice began to talk about the circus and its history, the today's death-match, Mark's fighting achievements and the reason behind this reality show. They both played like old buddies sitting in a pub and discussing the newest holiday destinations, or well-known, effective methods to hitting on women. Gary was surprised at how fast they both adapted to roles in this show. They even laughed at some dirty jokes that Robert was telling, and Gary couldn't distinguish when the laugh was real or well-played only.

Gary was listening to their conversation and thought that he didn't need any script for this show. It appeared that Robert had a lot of knowledge about modern sport's fights, not only official ones but about underground fighting clubs as well. He even mentioned his disappointment about Mark's past failures. Mark kept calm with buoyant sense of humour, even laughing with Robert when he referred to the beating and loss Mark had experienced in some crucial tournaments.

At the beginning, the circus' crew were following them with

astonishment, but they slightly disappeared in the moment when Robert's boldness kicked off, and he dragged Gary with a camera around, asking them too inquisitive questions about fairies, circus, shows, money, bets and how it was possible to catch a vampire as old as Draco was, for the performance sake. And even Mark started feeling restless when Robert was asking them who would win and what the audience expected from the Prince, maybe a well-known vampire leader but without any arena experience as a warrior. He didn't stop examining only the staff but came close to the prisoner's part and questioned the guards wearing the skull masks in an even more spying way. And of course, as Gary predicted, the entrance to the place where Draco was captured, was soon freely open for them.

Gary heard it first and then saw Jessica's drone flying inside above their heads. The guards were shouting in a language Gary had never heard before, pointing at them, the drone, and the place where the captured vamps were held.

Gary thought that he was ready for everything, but one look at the creature inside the cage made him realise how very wrong he was. Because what he saw wasn't Draco any more, but some kind of vicious demon in a human form. Suddenly, he remembered Simon's facial expression when he was talking about the event in the werewolves headquarter. And now he understood why Simon seemed pretty scared about fighting with vampires. Even Mark and Robert, who were familiar with vamps' battle-form, and as they had said that they were seeing them many times before, were stunned at this view.

Draco skin was grey like ash. He was a bit taller, but his body muscles doubled and were visible under his skin. He looked more like a body-builder champion than a regular human. His unnaturally crooked face had white fangs with a slowly dripping venom, blackened eyes and about thirty centimetres long, sharp as razors, nails, that didn't leave anything that might slightly resembled the ordinary Draco that Gary had known. Even Draco's light hair had turned an ashy colour and was thinned out. Gary stood speechless. Mark and Robert said nothing either. Only their faces showed utter shock. Gary thought it had to be very bad if someone like Robert, who was claiming to be the vamps hunting expert, was now standing as frozen.

'I've never seen anything like him before,' said Mark and Robert only nodded, agreeing.

'What's happened to him?' asked Gary, coming closer and lowering his voice.

'A couple of days on animal blood and you can see what's left,' Robert replied, whispering and was strolling towards the cage where Draco was held.

The lockup was made from metal bars covered with silver. Every time Draco touched, even accidentally, the bars, there wasn't only the sound of something burning but the intensive scent of it that was spreading around. Just behind his cage, there was one more cell with another vampire, who, on the contrary to Draco, was lying on the floor, curled up like a sleeping cat. He had a less grey colour but was skinny like a skeleton, with muscles less exposed and noticeable ribs that everyone could see. His body was shaking and a low growl, like that of a scared animal, was coming from him. He had a few bruises and red marks all over his body, now getting yellowish and indicating the slow healing progress.

'Who's that?' asked Robert, walking straight to the second cell. At the point where he was only a step from his goal, Draco jumped furiously in one leap from the opposite side of his cell to the closest place where Robert was standing. Draco pushed his arms between the metal bars trying to scratch Robert, completely ignoring the pain from touching the silver surfaces. He appeared even more vicious, with dripping saliva and venom, licking his lips, and looking at him with a beastly hunger. Two circus guards ran to Robert, caught him under their arms and pulled him a few metres away. Meanwhile, two others, who were holding long sticks buzzing with electricity at the end, kept prodding Draco with it, forcing him to step back deeper into the cage. The tasers were leaving black and bloody marks in a place where they touched Draco's skin. The guards seemed pretty pleased with their work, increasing the voltage and number of hits they were trying to do on Draco, but his dexterity was a bit too good for their low reflexes. They probably could do this for next hour if wasn't for the first gong indicating the beginning of the show.

'Hey! You have five minutes to prepare for a fight,' shouted the short man who was previously sitting outside and sipping beer, but this time, presenting himself in a new costume. He pointed out Mark and made a hand gesture to all of them, showing the direction for fighters' dressing-room. The man was wearing clothes so different than the rest of the circus team. It was in a few shades of green, with black elements, all fashioned like a leprechaun's costume, including a tall, black hat and a golden four-leaf clover pinned to it. He looked rather annoyed, walking quickly towards those vampire's guards and yelling at them. Despite the fact that the guards were as twice as tall as he was, they were confused, showing remorse and obedience with their body posture and voice tone. Mark, Gary, and Robert started walking to the second separated tent space, designed for the fighters and their assistants. Gary didn't stop recording but, for the first time ever, he felt anxious during the filming.

'Guys do something. I can't fight with them, especially so many vamps,' said Mark, sounding desperate and scared. For the first time, as long as Gary could remember, he saw his half-brother really frightened.

'Take this,' said Robert, showing them a small purse containing two things, shaped like insulin-pens, inside. Robert took Mark under his arm and slowly walked towards the fighter's space. He was pretending to discuss with Mark the tactics, movements, dodges, blocks and vulnerable places on the vampire body's, but he was more focused about giving proper instruction on how to use the injection.

'It's easy,' said Robert, taking the pen, shaking the white liquid inside, turning the dosage to the maximum and showing the place to press to release the fluid.

'You have two full dosages in two pens. Usually, one pen has five shots, but what I saw there, you'll need to use the full ampule only for Draco to numb him completely. The second pen is just in case something bad would happen to the first one. I have one more if Gary needs,' said Robert, patting his jacket, where the inside pocket was located. He put the first syringe into Mark's hand and said that the best tactic would be to avoid the fighting as long as he could. He mentioned that he and James would do something dodgy but didn't explain any details. He stuck the second pen inside Mark's pocket, wishing him good luck and promising that they would do everything to take him and Draco out of that arena. Gary was speechless during Robert's monologue. Now he realised that Robert and James came here with a mysterious plan, and now the life and death of Gary,

Mark, and Draco were in werewolves' hands.

'What about Patric?' asked Gary.

'I'll take care of him. Mark, just push him to me,' declared Robert, showing only to them a tranquiliser gun he had hidden under his jacket.

'How?' asked Gary, but he couldn't get an answer because he was interrupted by a loud voice behind.

'Here you are,' said James to them, standing in front of the place arranged as a dressing-room for all warriors. He came closer and gave Mark a hug.

'Mark, the man of the hour. Just hold there for three minutes, it's all we need,' he whispered straight into Mark's ear.

'What are you going to do?' asked Mark in a similar low voice to James.

'Look, I know you're scared. They're much better warriors than you are but …' James continued whispering. He wrapped his hand around Mark's shoulder.

'I know. I'll die there,' replied Mark, not looking at him. He hung his head, and a tiny blush appeared on his checks.

'You won't. Just stick to the plan with Draco. You're not going there to win. Run away if you have to. Three minutes, trust me,' said James, who looked rather happy.

*

'Well, well, well …' someone's voice broke through the buzz of shouting commands by the circus' crew, the fight participants, and their assistants. Gary turned and saw the tall and handsome Patric Vance. He only knew it was him from pictures that Mark had shown him a day ago, when they were discussing the plan for today's night.

'Patric Vance. How is it possible that such a gentleman like yourself, partakes in such a disgusting and low-level competition? Did you lose money on stock again?' James's voice was calm but somehow aggressive.

Patric was wearing a modern, elegant grey suit and looked like James's competitor to the prize for the best-dressed man of the year on the fashion catwalk. Two similarly well-groomed men were accompanying him. Gary didn't stop recording and allowed himself to make some close-ups of the approaching group. He felt more optimistic with a camera in his hands among his friends. He remembered James's advice to play the TV professional camera operator, so he came closer to Patric and gave the hand gesture to Robert to start interviewing the newcomers. Robert couldn't help but grin like a child seeing sweets. He started asking similar questions like he asked many others before, about the fight, bets, chances, money and the motivations behind Patric's participation in this event. At the beginning, Patric looked a bit confused, but when he saw the TV's logo, his voice tone changed, he corrected his body posture and answered with high self-confident manners like he was partaking in a reception after winning the Nobel Prize.

Suddenly, Robert nudged Gary, pointing his cane at one of the figures who appeared in the backstage entrance. Robert cut off the conversation and turned around, completely ignoring Patric. He grabbed Gary's elbow and directed him to those new people. There were two rather characteristic people among others. One, tall, with a body like a small giant wearing shiny, full plate armour, including a shield hung on his back, two axes in hands and a full-face knight's helmet. He was surrounded by his kind of folks, who looked like overgrown humans. The second person was smaller than Gary, wearing a white ninja costume, two swords on his back and two long knives located on his thighs, with his head covered with a leather helmet hiding his face under the mask. Only black eyes could be seen under this outfit.

Gary start walking towards the giant and his assistants, but Robert stopped him abruptly and redirected him to the lonely ninja. Gary kept recording the crowd, not paying too much attention to the small figure, but Robert kept dragging him there murmuring something that Gary couldn't hear due to rush and noise around. The third gong rang, making the uproar in the surroundings more chaotic. The giant shouted something in his language that made his companions yell cheerfully. Robert sped up and called to the ninja, Leith, but his shout was ignored. The ninja kept walking towards the arena, passing close by Gary and Robert.

'Hey, wait. Only one question,' yelled Robert, desperately. He grabbed the ninja's hand and tried to pull him closer, but in one sharp, swift movement the ninja freed himself, staring surprised straight into Gary's camera. In the same moment, Gary saw Robert catching the collapsing ninja's body. Robert put the ninja's arm around his neck and was heading to the far corner of dressing-room without being held up by anyone from the circus crew. Gary followed him, still recording all the hustle around them.

'What happened to him?' asked Gary, watching Robert put the ninja's body gently on one of the large chairs.

'To her, you should say,' said Robert, taking off the mask covering the fighter's face. Gary was stunned. He didn't expect a woman participating in such brutal sport, especially in a death-match. He kept filming her face. He smiled, imagining what if he would meet her in a coffee shop, serving a latte. *I would have definitely kept staring at her*, Gary thought. He felt amazed at how attractive she was. Those thoughts made him feel uneasy around her. He made the last zoom at her light chocolate skin with characteristic Polynesian face shape wishing to meet her in a less hostile environment.

'What did you do?' asked Gary.

'Just sedated,' replied Robert.

Robert took the injection pen from his pocket, changed the needle, put the used one into the pen's small purse, and increased the dosage on a counter.

'That was clever. When you did it?' asked Gary but Robert only shrugged.

'Let's go. Vamps need a higher dosage,' he replied.

'You saved her life,' said Gary.

'No, I saved theirs,' answered Robert, smiling and pointing his finger into arena direction. Gary zoomed in on her face one more time, fascinated and intrigued by Robert's words.

*

Gary and Robert hurried to the main circus tent. On their way, they passed the tunnel going from the cells to the arena, that was made with similar metal bars covered with silver. They saw guards poking Draco and the second vampire towards the entrance to a fighting ring. The vamps were walking fast, growling and hissing.

Draco, who was visibly bigger and more vigorous, was hit more often by guards than his companion. All the time, he was trying to protect the smaller vamp from the stabbing, electrical rods, hiding his companion behind his back. One of the ringmasters, who appeared suddenly, shouted rudely at the guards, forcing them to stop the harassment. Although the vampires were fighting with the sticks, they were pushed to the arena quite fast. Somehow, they both knew what was waiting for them at the end. They sensed death like animals in a slaughterhouse.

The full metal flap dropped with a loud bang, just after Draco and his friend entered the arena. When the tunnel's gate had closed, they looked around, and stood in formation to cover their backs. Meanwhile, when they were waiting for the signal to start the fight, the audience was loud, hooting at them and calling names and throwing some rubbish towards the arena.

Gary had never been inside such a big tent. It had four main metal columns holding the deep blue cover canvas. There were lines and chains on the top joined between the poles and some pinned to the ground and securing the masts upright. In the middle, there was a massive cage that was standing in the place where usually the circus ring was. The cage reached almost to the top of the tent. Inside the construction, there were fitted two quite thick swings like a circus trapeze. There were also loops hanging on chains in different places, some could move, but some were fixed permanently to the cage. There were also about ten heavy planks of various lengths installed randomly. Some were going throughout the whole diameter, but some were dangling, only attached from one side of the cage's metal posts.

About two meters from the cage, there were luxurious cubicles for VIP guests. There was transparent plastic, two-metre-high barrier in front of them that was preventing any blood splashing from fighters to drop on those wealthy clients. Nevertheless, the cubicles weren't built to keep privacy because all walls were only about a meter high, so wealthy spectators could easily see who else was sitting in the neighbourhood close to the arena.

The warriors walked into the arena by only one metal door, before the attacking vamps were pushed inside. The door was closed with a massive gold padlock on. A gold key was shaped like the ones from centuries ago with ornaments and gems on it. It was held by the presenter, the short man wearing a leprechaun outfit and who was standing on the podium holding a wireless microphone in one hand. He introduced himself as Jack Pott and then he introduced all those who were inside the cage, but emphasising the presence of two very old vampires fighting against the rest of the attackers. He mentioned the absence of the ninja, making a joke about her being a wimp with lack of guts and a few more colourfully vulgar epithets. He cited the main reason for this death-match, the ultimate lust for huge money, and as he talked about the big prize, his face became crooked with a mischievous grin and his voice trembled from excitement.

The audience was laughing, shouting some foul-mouthed words, and cheering for their favourite fighters. Most of the spectators were men, but there were women and some of them cheering even louder than the men. One look at all the viewers, and it was apparent for Gary that the circus was creepy entertainment for those who loved being excited by watching bloodbaths.

Gary shivered. He couldn't understand the excitement from not only watching how someone was killed but applauding the show as well. But on the other hand, he thought, he liked horror movies, and the story in many of them was based on methods of torture and strange deaths that were attracting and kept people interested. And there always was some kind of beast or monster who was doing the colourful slaughter.

Gary kept recording, zooming in on faces not only in the crowd, but he was mainly focused on the VIP guests and all those warriors waiting inside the arena with a hope on their faces that they would win their life retirement. Gary was curious about who were all those folks sitting here, even on the cheapest seats. And all those well-dressed, chatting, laughing and behaving like on a cocktail party would be potential characters for Gary's movies. He had imagined them working in offices as officials, managers, directors, or just working class in human society. He thought about all of those privileged and nobles, with old and new money, usually so restrained, self-controlled and undemonstrative, but showing today their dark and aggressive side by participating in this bloody and illegal sport. And now, they were sitting and waiting for the show that was triggering the most primitive instincts, so many times associated with only lowlifes.

In the corner on his eye, he saw Jessica's drone flying to and fro. Good, he thought, the event would still be filmed even if he had to run to puke in one of the portable toilets standing in a row outside the circus tent.

James and Simon went to one of the VIP cubicles, where apparently James's friends were sitting. There was only one seat, and already taken by James, so Simon wasn't invited. But he was more interested in recording on his small tourist-size camera, what was going around, than staying in one place. Apparently, the TV T-shirt he was wearing made an impression on James's associates, so they also wanted to be a part of the recordings. Simon had to spend some time zooming in on their faces and recording their enthusiasm about watching the match. He saw Gary, waved and walked to the place directly opposite the point where Gary and Robert were standing, and was barely seen behind the arena's cage.

Robert was active as a commentator. He was pointing his cane to guests sitting in the VIP location, naming them and telling their position in the Viviter's community. Gary thought that if he would have never known Robert, he would be sure he was a professional reporter enjoying being here. Robert sounded natural, like someone well-prepared for this evening.

The leprechaun on the podium took a drumstick with a padded head and hit the gong standing next to him. The sound was repeated in speakers, giving the sign that the death-match was officially open. The crowd jumped with excitement and joy. Nobody was sitting any more, even in the places for VIP guests.

*

Gary started feeling a bit sick seeing his brother standing among those who were willing to die on the arena for money's sake. All this time, the fighters were waiting patiently for the signal, judging opponents, calculating the chances, planning a tactic and preparing for the first stroke. In the arena, there were eight fighters including Draco and his companion. The leprechaun addressed them all by their already known stage nick-name or something made up for this evening by him.

The biggest one, wearing the full armour like a medieval knight, changed into the battle-form of a bear. He named himself Beartank. He was almost three metres tall, massive, and heavy. He was standing on two legs and was covered with short brown fur. His face was a fusion of human and bear shapes, with its hairiness and long fangs. His hands were giant, and ended with long, bearlike, black claws. At the moment when he was shifting, the armour was absorbed by the body and blended into a thick skin, making it impossible to pierce. The lines of metal elements were still slightly visible on his body, but nothing restrained his movements.

Next one was Mark. His height remained almost unaltered, but he gained muscles and body mass. After the hospital accident, Gary didn't have much time to spend with his half-brother so he didn't have the opportunity to see Mark in his full battle-form, by being busy adjusting to the new reality he was thrown into and sorting out the troubles that were piling up on his head. But now, Gary stood stunned looking at him. Mark's posture was upright, his body covered with half-long reddish fur marked with black dots all over his body, a short tail, soaring, large ears ending with hair jutting out like a paintbrush. His stage name as a warrior was Redshade. And as all cats had, he had extended fangs and long, red, sharp claws.

The third one was a werewolf. He was about two metres tall, bulky with massive muscles, grey fur, long fangs and black claws. His name was Steelclaws. He looked nervous, sniffing around, trampling in place and continuously looking behind his back. Gary was observing all of them with his mouth open. He saw the entirely shaped werewolf for the first time in his life, and he was absolutely flabbergasted. The thought that Simon was definitely looking alike as a feral, made him feel envious. *Maybe, if I would convince Simon, he might bite me, and I would become a werewolf like him,* Gary wondered, staring at the fighters.

Patric Vance was standing next to Mark. Like the vampires fighting on the Blue Fairy Circus side, he looked similar to Draco, but his skin had a more human colour. His naked torso, attractive face, black military trousers, high boots, and muscled body, made some ladies shouted his name quite loud. The one noticeable difference from those two other vampires, other than the skin, was the fact that his nails in one hand were half the length. The leader of the show called him the Prince, as a stage nickname. Gary was sure that those who were cheering for Patric were mostly vampires or someone who was associated with them.

The fifth warrior was the tallest. He had dark skin, a bald head, and some tribal symbols that were burned on his skin all over his body. He was the one person who was standing bare-feet in this place. His name was Solsting, and he transformed into a massive, black, human-like shaped scorpion. He still had a normal person's posture, with two massive legs, but his hands developed pincers, with the left side larger than the other. His whole body reminded a chitin armour, making his skin hard to puncture. The only modification on his face was strengthening the skin by stiffening it, making it impossible for any facial expression and giving the limited ability for moving his lips. He had a two-metre-long thick tail ended with a colossal sting like a spear, that was now dripping green venom, making him look even more deadly.

The last man was short and thin. His dark, long, and thin dreadlocks were braided with silver, wide rings with engraved ancient symbols. His milky chocolate skin had only two tattoos on his shoulders, and both were referring to Star Wars movies. His name was Spikeish. When he changed, his feral form was similar to his normal body size. He was a perfect combination of an African porcupine and a human being. His skin was covered with a dark, short quills on the front side, getting longer on the sides, till being almost a meter of length on the spine line. The colour of the quills was black near the skin but white at the end of them. He had a short, rounded tail covered by the longest thorns that were going through his back to the top of the skull like a brush of deadly needles. The crowd gasped seeing him. Some people started yelling that he shouldn't be allowed to fight, and some, cursing angrily, left the tent rushing away.

The leprechaun finished presenting the show's participant by giving the stage name to the two vampires as mortal enemies, that belonged to the circus. Draco, as the oldest, more than five hundred years old, well-trained in combat, he was called Antique. When the spotlight was directed on him, he was calm and still hiding his companion behind his back. Draco looked like a focused human, only gazing at every movement of those attackers on the arena. He was standing near the flap that he was pushed throughout by the guards, but he turned his head to the left once, checking the distance to the 'mercy box' and localising of all his enemies. Draco comrade was introduced as Bard, due to his occupation as a musician. Although he was about three hundred years old as a vampire, he didn't have any positive ovations from the audience. It sounded more like cussing for being the arena's unworthy weak link, ready to be killed like a cockroach.

One by one, the fighters were shown on four massive screens installed at a certain angle, on the top of the cage. There were four cameras fitted on the same level but inside the cage. Gary pointed at the nearest screen to him and, using a walkie-talkie, asked Simon if it were possible to find the place where the circus was broadcasting for the online viewers. Simon didn't answer, but he gave thumb-up, turned around and disappeared between the circus seats, heading backstage.

In the same second the fight had started, all fighters were jumping to those they wanted to kill first. Solsting ran towards Beartank as fast as he could. He tried twice to jab someone on his way with his sting, but he missed. Steelclaw dodged it, but still kept running towards his aimed goal. Mark, Redshade, avoided the sting in one, rapid, vertical leap. He caught the lowest plank by his claws, climbed up on it, and like every cat, he was observing his enemies from above, waiting for the best opportunity to strike.

Something unusual started happening to Draco, Ancient, at the precise moment when the gong sounded. Yellow spots appeared on his body. There were tiny first but had grown, making his skin and long razor-like nails an ash-yellowish colour. Moreover, Bard looked at him with utter astonishment when he realised he had similar spots on his skin. Both of them were not vicious animals any more, but very human-like vampires. Even their faces eased and had regular features. At first Draco glanced around like he didn't recognise the place he was in. He looked like a person who just woke up from a deep dream, not having a clue where he was and how he had gotten there. He was staring at his companion, when both of their skin converted into a yellowish colour, not understanding what was happening to them, and what was going on inside their bodies. Draco peeped around, heard the cheer from the crowd, turned over and whispered something to the second vampire. After that, they stood together, back to back, ready to fight. It looked like they both knew very well the tactics of fighting with multiple enemies. Draco was staring at Mark longer than the others, and then he slightly nodded, giving the sign that he recognised him and understood the reason why Mark was here. He glanced once at Spikesh. Mark nodded almost imperceptibly towards Steelclaw. And then, Mark fell on his shoulders, when Steelclaw was heading to Prince.

In the same moment when Draco's yellow spots had occurred on his skin, Gary started feeling warm and pleasant sensation inside his guts, and it was growing like a fever all over him. He blushed and drops of sweat appeared on his face and the rest of his body. He touched his forehead when he realised that the drops were running down in small brooks, wetting his T-shirt. He looked at one of his forearms and saw yellow spots, but they were a bit different than Draco's. Gary's were more like uneven marks arising and vanishing randomly but didn't colour his whole skin permanently. Gary stretched out his free hand and couldn't stop staring at his own body. He almost dropped the camera, but he caught it reflexively. He was so absorbed by the phenomenon that he didn't hear Robert shouting at him and didn't see what was happening in the arena. But before Robert came closer to Gary, the marks disappeared utterly, without any trace, leaving him speechless and in shock. Although it was only a few seconds, and he didn't feel the heat inside any more, but somehow something changed but Gary couldn't name it. He felt like a snake that was losing his old skin, or caterpillar transforming into a butterfly.

Robert shook Gary's shoulder and repeated his name three times before Gary reacted. Robert frowned but said nothing. He pointed at Simon's disappearing silhouette and nodded that he had to go after him, because no one should be alone in this hostile environment. Robert called to James and ordered him to look after Gary, and then he walked outside to find Simon.

*

The crowd gasped loudly, and that brought back Gary's attention to the present moment. The Prince was staring at Draco, and that was his mistake. His alertness got out of control, making him vulnerable. He was targeted by Solsting, who pierced him with a sting into his stomach and had thrown far up. Prince bounced off the big cage's wall and landed on his back, on the highest plank running along the arena's radius. He moaned and curled up, trying to bear the agonising pain he was feeling now. One from the top cameras was zooming in on his wound and projected the picture onto the screens, showing how nasty and dangerously poisonous it was. Green ooze, mixed with dark blood, was covering Patric's stomach, flowing on his body, down to the plank and was dripping to the ground. He pressed both hands to the puncture made by the sting, positioned himself face down so that the cameras could record only his naked back and a growing puddle of slime. Some nervous spasms were going throughout his body, but he was still alive.

Meanwhile, on the ground, Solsting caught up with Beartank. He hit him with one massive claw. It did absolutely nothing to the three metre pile of thick bear muscles, but the impact turned Beartank over, exposing his back part of the body. It took two steps for Solsting to climb up on him, straight to the head. Solsting struck again but this time aiming at his outreached hands. Beartank grabbed the wrist of the bigger claw and pulled, trying to rip the scorpion claw off. But Solsting closed the small pincer around Beartank's neck and started squeezing it. The thin line between Beartank's helmet and the rest of his flesh wasn't covered by armour. It was one of the rare places where his body was weak and vulnerable. Beartank roared in pain, he held his hands on the top of it, trying to open the pair of pliers. Blood came out of his clenched fists at the same time, when a few red streams from his neck started running down on to his shoulders, torso, and his back. Beartank curled into a ball and threw himself at Solsting on to the ground, landing on his belly and he crushed the second scorpion pincer under his massive posture. Solsting was grounded, he started kicking but his torso was immobilised by the weight of Beartank. He was squeezing his claw around the bear's neck harder than before, causing the blood brooks to run faster. Beartank was gobbing, pounding his legs on the protruding parts of Solsting's body, trying to loosen the claw that was choking his neck. Its sharp edges were piercing bear flesh deeper and deeper, and flooded the blood on scorpion face. Then Solsting's tail was beating the ground, trying to make more stings to anyone within his range. He hit Beartank a few times, but the melted armour made his skin none pierceable. It left only small punctures overflowing with a dark, green venom. They stayed in this clasp as long as the bear was moving. The last Beartank convulsion was shown in close-up on all four screens. Gary covered his mouth at the moment when the bear's head was cut off, and was casted aside like a ball, hitting one of the planks, bouncing, going through one of the loops, finally landing on the ground splashing blood, a broken skull, and a brain. Part of the audience applauded vigorously. Gary had to cover his mouth due to feeling dizzy. James, who replaced Robert's presence, caught Gary by the waist, held on firmly, and ordered intense deep breathing. Gary still held the camera, but he didn't care anymore about perfectly taken pictures. On the screens, there was a display of a bet that was made at the beginning of the fight, about who would be killed first and numbers were showing how many people wagered on Beartank.

Meanwhile, Mark jumped on the werewolf's shoulders and sank his teeth into his neck just under the skull. The werewolf grabbed Mark's neck with one of his massive claws, making a bloody puncture on the lynx's skin. He yelped trying to remove Mark from his back, piercing the skin deeper and deeper and marking his fur in bloody spots. Suddenly he stopped making any sounds. The spasm went throughout the werewolf's body only once. His torso, neck, and head were covered with a thick layer of thin but long and sharp needles, which were thrown around by Spikish. The longest of the three was sticking out from Steelclaws' mouth, transfixing the cranium through. His massive body prevented Mark from being deadly pierced. Redshade had only two average needles that jabbed him, one in the ear, the second in the arm.

Spikiesh was shivering. He was squatting, he placed his hands on his face and after a quick break, puffed out his quills again like a porcupine, and with one massive spasm, exploded the spikes around in every possible direction. The werewolf body slowly slid to the ground, shielding Mark from the second blast of thorns. This time, Mark got three more needles, but again only as scrapes.

Unfortunately, the spikes didn't stay only inside the arena, but a lot of them had flown through the cage's bars hitting randomly everything and everyone within their range. The yells, screams, and cries resonated around. Only those sitting in the VIP section, shielded by the transparent plastic panel, were free of worries. The rest of spectators weren't so lucky. A dozen thorns hit into the crowd, piercing the bodies of not only participants but those who were the circus's crew. There were at least three deadly casualties of the flying needles and a bunch of injuries, some were wounded terribly but others had only scratches. Gary was pulled down to the ground by James when he saw the first symptom of Spikiesh's blast. Although they both were standing near the VIP section, and therefore covered by a plastic barrier, instinctively they ducked even lower.

Draco curled up and threw himself onto the ground. Bard followed him, making his body smaller and therefore less exposed. After the second round of throwing the quills by Spikeish, they both had a couple of them sticking into their flesh. Draco had more than Bard due to protecting his companion with his own body. There were four metre-long thorns sticking out of Draco's back. They pierced him through, but missed his heart and head, those two vital organs that were fragile enough to cause instant vampire death when injured.

Bard got up first, grabbed, and pulled out a bunch of spikes from Draco who was still observing his enemies. Spikeish was standing upright, he looked around and estimated damages and survivors. He smiled hearing the sound of cries from the audience. He lost the majority of the quills from around his body during two rounds of attacks, but some of the best he still had on the spine line and on his head.

The strength of the spikes explosions was awe-inspiring. Two of the circus' cameras were sparkling with tiny lightning of electrostatic discharges, covered with smoke going from the place where the thorns pierced through the equipment. Only one screen was left untouched and undamaged. The rest of them had the same misfortune as the cameras, now blackened and emitting the burnt smell of plastic.

The leprechaun was coming back to his podium, he had jumped down when the first blast had blown. His meticulous outfit was wrapped up in dirt and dust from the ground. He was holding his high hat, now with three very long quills piercing through it. He had two scratches on his face, one deeper than the other with drops of blood sliding on his cheek. He said nothing but his face expressed his emotions. He grinned from ear to ear, clapped his hands and roared with laughter like a freak. He put his hand on his heart, picked up the microphone and tried to say something that sounded like prising the adrenaline rush that everyone just experienced. But he couldn't articulate his sentence properly due to gasping for breath and laughing like a crank. Some people from the audience followed him, but some were furiously mad.

Spikeish was coming closer to Draco, smiling and holding a few the longest spikes he had torn out from his back and was using as spears. He started throwing the thorns at Draco, but at the same time, he got hit by Solsting's venom inside of the patch free of quills. Spikeish panted, spat out blood, and with a stunned facial expression, first knelt down and then collapsed onto his torso and face. The loud cheer rose around the circus arena. The screen showed, again and again, his death in slow motion.

The scorpion scrambled out from beneath the massive trunk of Beartank who was lying on him, and now was looking to get rid of the nearest opponent. Mark was standing a few metres behind him but farther than his sting could reach. He jumped again on the plank and then caught one of hanging trapezes, held himself by one hand on it, then he swung and was aiming as close as he could to Draco's zone. Solsting attacked Draco with double speed. He lifted up his tail and directed the spike to Bard. Draco and his companion stood in battle-like formation, observing and waiting for his first strike.

But Mark was faster. Solsting peered at him, waiting for the next smooth cat's leap on his back but it never came. Suddenly, on Mark's inner side of the forearm, the one he was holding the trapeze with, a purple light appeared, first vague and shapeless but changing in a matter of seconds into the hilt. He grabbed it and drew out something forming in a samurai sword. It didn't have any physical manifestation but was built from a formed light with visible contours. Although it was solid and three-dimensional, it was transparent like glass.

Mark was swinging above Solsting when he pulled out the sword, and with one stroke, he cut off the top of scorpion's tail. The sting was still dripping with venom when it landed near Bard's feet. A few drops of it splashed on him and Draco, and, like acid, started dissolving their skin, bubbling and emitting a horrid vapour. Solsting screamed in a low, furious tone. He stopped and looked over for Mark's position. But Mark didn't swing back down. He stayed high above the ground with one hand holding the sword, his second hand grasping the trapeze and with one of his legs lying on the plank with pounded claws into wood. The scorpion realised that the lynx was out of his reach, so he turned and attacked Draco. He moved to such a position in the arena, that even if Mark released his anchoring limb, Solsting was too far away from the blade.

Draco and his companion didn't have time to do anything with the acid burning places, but the solution came with their abilities to regenerate their own bodies. The wounds started slowly closing, and before the fight was over, there were no marks on their skin after the acid attack. The same happened to punctured wounds made by spikes, even those which had gone right through Draco's flesh. It took only longer to fully recover, but there were no marks indicating localisation of the hits.

They both, Draco and Bard, were facing Solsting. Draco's nails were much longer than Bard's and had a pure yellow colour. Bard's wounds healed much slower. He still had dots after Spikish's quills punctured him and blackened skin in places where he was bruised, made by many people that had beaten him since he was captured, just after his unfortunate encounter with Patric a few days ago. His nails were black, less than half of the length than Draco's, but still keen-edged like well-sharpened blades. Solsting attacked them with his massive claws which he lifted up, ready to hit. In the same time, Prince landed near the bigger pincer and cut the arm off, on the high of an elbow, in a place where the chitin coating was the thinnest. It landed on the ground at his underfoot, still moving and shaking in convulsion, and sprinkling blood around.

Prince looked sick. The place on his torso that was hit by the scorpion's sting was still visibly large and covered with a thin, red film of his skin. He was soiled by his own blood and the ooze from Spikish's venom. The dark skin around his eyes was more extensive and had much more black lines on his face. He peered only once at Draco, and then kept his gaze on Bard.

He made one step and with a fast stroke, hit once again, but this time puncturing Solsting's head in line where his chin was connected with his neck. Patric's sharp nails punctured though Solsting's skin straight to the brain, breaking the skull from the inside and causing an instant kill. He kicked Solsting's body, pulled his razors from his cranium, and partially tore out the cerebrum. There were pieces of

Solsting's brain and bones on Partic's long nails that he shook off on to the ground. The scorpion fell down, creating a barrier between him and Mark, who swung back on the trapeze, jumped down silently and in two leaps was next to Draco.

Draco peered at Mark, and they both attacked from two sides as one. But Prince bounced and landed behind Draco's smaller companion, he clutched one hand on Bard's neck by putting his claws in a way that he could cut his throat in one swift jerk. It happened at the same moment when Mark threw his sword towards him. Prince dodged it by hitting the blade with his long nails. The sword had flown high, and landed on the opposite side of the arena, far from Mark's reach.

But before anyone was able to make the next move, there were two loud explosions inside, both shook up two main columns holding the circus tent. The columns were slowly slanting but were still held by metal lines, chains and partially by the canvas. The canvas was firm but started to tear apart under the weight and pressure of the unstable and heavy, slowly falling poles. There was loud shout about a fire but there were no signs of flames. A few chains broke up, causing one of the masts to lower down even more and rip off a few metal bars of the cage. There was loud tearing of the tent's canvas above, and a massive gap appeared on the top, letting heavy rain pour down on the broken screens. Next, there was an immense bang, and suddenly all electric power went off, leaving the whole circus and surroundings in pitch-dark.

James changed into his feral form, grabbed Gary under his arm and ran as fast as he could out of this place. Before Gary could react, he was carried like a child by a werewolf, who was pretty massive for its kind. Gary held the plastic handle of the camera firmly and prayed in his head to not lose his precious device. In less than half a minute, Gary and James were standing near the TV truck observing the massively wide-spreading panic. Gary jumped into the car, which, it appeared, was the one only source of light in this area. He switched on all the van's lights, making the place shine like a moon on a very dark night.

'You set bombs there?!' yelled Gary at James, pointing at the circus tent but he still couldn't understand what just happened.

'Shut up, Gary,' replied James, visible annoyed. He sat behind the wheel and pressed the car-horn a few times

'But why?' asked Gary without fear.

'My first son was stupid and arrogant like your brother. He was killed. Three years I've been waiting for it,' continued James through clenched teeth. His face started changing slightly, showing his feral shapes. Gary had an impression he was staring into eyes of a beast so clever and dangerous that he could be dead in a blink of an eye.

'Oh, I'm sorry, but we have to go back!' shouted Gary, regardless of James's anger. He was ready to go and search for the rest of the team. He was staring at James whose eyes were set on the collapsing circus tent. Although he was sitting in a bit of a shady place, Gary could have sworn he saw a delicate smile on James's face, like the picture of the disaster was more pleasing than terrifying for him.

'No, they're warriors. You're not. They'll make it here themselves. Stay!' James ordered with a voice tone that didn't allow any disobedience. He was calm and focused, like a captain who had trust in the skills of his team. Gary stood still in one place and couldn't argue with this fact. Moreover, he found himself not wanting to cross James in any more circumstances. Gary felt a bit useless thinking about his friends and brother that might need some help that he couldn't provide. He turned and made himself busy, praying in his mind, for their fast return to the van. He was so deep in his mind that he missed Jessica who was staring at both of them utterly astonished. Now Gary understood why James ordered her to stay in the van. James's reasoning was that Gary and Jessica were humans, that might attract vampires' attention, and mainly because a human presence was prohibited by the circus, even as spectators during the show. But Gary suspected that was only an excuse to keep them both safe. Now it was obvious for him that keeping an eye on one human inside the tent was much easier than for two of them.

Meanwhile, Jessica had flown the drone through the hole inside the tent's canvas and put it on autopilot back to their base. Gary and Jessica checked the drone and laptops, securing them inside individual bags they had brought here, as fast as they could, expecting their rapid departure very soon. Meanwhile, James was calling by walkie-talkie every member of the team but Mark. Gary and Jessica were nervously glaring at the tent and waiting for rest of the team.

First Simon and Robert came back and headed to the passenger car. James only nodded to Robert silently. Simon was carrying a sack, but as far as Gary remembered, it didn't belong to him. Simon put the sack into the trunk, walked over to Gary and tried to tell him something but he suddenly stopped and looked surprised, staring at Mark's direction.

Mark was walking back in his feral form. He emerged out of the blue from a different direction than he was expected to come. He was carrying Draco's unconscious body, like a firefighter, hanging on his shoulders. Mark was badly injured. He had four long red cuts alongside his chest and few on his arms. He was bleeding heavily. Gary, Simon, and Robert helped him get inside the van, putting Draco at the end of the truck. Mark laid down on a floor, moaning in pain. His fur was coated with blood and some dark ooze. But Draco looked even more injured. He had cuts and places pierced through his body and was still bleeding like Mark.

Jessica was in such a deep shock about what happened to Mark that it took her a minute to react about what was going on around. She puked outside the van and had to sit on the floor inside to cool down.

The chaos was increasing around. There was a lot of yelling, growls, and rifle shots from almost every possible direction. There weren't only human silhouettes running or fighting with one another that made Gary feel horrified. The darkness created the scene, even worse inside Gary's lively imagination, that what might begoing on now. Gary gazed at Draco and started feeling dizzy. He didn't feel well since James carried him out from the circus tent and seeing Draco unconscious caused panic in him. He sat near his brother, who was breathing heavily, with his hands shaking and felt even more useless than he had felt in his entire life. He realised this was the moment when his brother, who he had argued with so many times, might die for real.

Jessica took off her hoodie, knelt down near Mark and tried to cover his wounds, but he refused it. He took her hand, clasped his fingers with hers and pressed them to his cheek. She stroked his furry face and kept trying to put her hoodie on his cuts without losing eye contact with him. He said that he should heal but asked if Gary could bring him the tranquiliser Robert had. Surprisingly, his talk was quite understandable for Gary and Jessica regardless of his meowing tones so typical for cats.

'No! You can't sedate him. Not with those massive wounds. If he doesn't fully heal before changing into human form, he can bleed out,' shouted James, and he ordered them to shut the door. Simon was driving the car with Robert as a passenger. They passed the van and used back lights as a signal to follow him.

In spite of feeling weak, Gary rushed, grabbed the van's door-handle and was wrestling with it when the car started a slow, jerky movement. At the moment, when the door was half opened, a small hand with long fingers caught an edge. It scared Gary so much that he yelled, backed off, and fell onto Jessica, who was sitting next to Mark holding his hand. The leprechaun's head appeared in the gap. Jack Pott lost his long hat, and now, his fanciful outfit was ragged, dirty and stained in a few different types of liquids starting with blood. He didn't smile, and his face had changed into what resembled an old, frustrated toad with all those pimples, blotches, and scabrous skin in a rotten greenish colour.

'You! You did it! You've ruined my show! You'll pay for it!' he shouted, pointing his long finger from Gary to James and making one step into the car.

'Kick him out! Don't let him touch you! Kick him out!' yelled James with panic in his voice.

He honked a few times, put his foot down on the accelerator, and then on the brakes, causing the car to suddenly tug. The door slid back, fully opening the entrance, and the sudden stop helped Jack to get a better balance. The leprechaun held the edge firmly, but this time with his two hands on a car's frame and one foot already inside the van. Gary fell even deeper inside, pushing Jessica on Mark. In the last moment, she stretched her arms trying not land on Mark's wounds with her full body, but the sharp movement was too strong. She fell and hit Mark's chest. He screamed from pain and hissed angrily like a scared cat showing his fangs. A few slowly healing wounds on his chest were opened again, spouting blood on her face. She felt sick, turned around and dashed her head outside the van with the spasm of vomiting. Unfortunately for her, she was a few inches away from the toad and he knew how to use the situation for his advantage. He grabbed her hair and started pulling himself up. She yelled and was leaning half of her body against the car's walls to prevent falling out of the van.

The car stopped abruptly, and that finally gave Gary the opportunity to kick the leprechaun in the stomach. Jack was halfway through to get inside, still holding Jessica's hair from one side, and the van's edge from the other. When the car stopped, everyone got more stable and started moving with more controlled actions, and that included Jack Pott. He jumped inside, pushed Jessica back and threw himself on Gary. Jessica tripped on Mark's legs and collapsed on the floor on the other side of him. Meanwhile, Jack grabbed Gary's wrist and snapped his fingers with his other hand. But nothing happened, so he repeated it several times. And every time he did it, the shock on his face was more visible.

'Witch hunter?! And a fucking Cassian?' he asked and started grumbling something in a language not recognisable to anyone present.

'What?' asked Gary, but he used the leprechaun's utter amazement to his advantage and pushed him out as hard as he could.

Jack landed on two vampires, which were lured by the strong scent of fresh blood and were trying to get inside the van as well. They looked aroused, but only long fangs with dripping venom differentiated them from normal humans. They didn't have any specific marks on the skin, like the older vampires, just some black lines inside their eyes. Gary didn't hesitate any second longer and shut the door with a loud bang. James was watching the whole scene, startled and speechless, but he went back to driving immediately, in the same moment when Gary had thrown out the unwanted guest.

The van moved faster than before without and sharp motions, honking all the time on the way towards the now broken gate and even further up the street. Simon was waiting for them, standing on the side of the road, but he started driving again when he saw the TV van going through the main gate. James didn't allow them to talk much by walkie-talkie or mobile, saying that they would have time for stories in the house, but now they have to focus on escape from this place. He was driving, but it wasn't as fast as he wanted due to the running away crowd and other cars trying to get out. James switched on the strongest lights, blinding the people around and constantly swearing like a grumpy old pirate.

Mark was bleeding again, but this time he didn't moan. He was slowly falling into sleep, and only Jessica's shouts kept him alert. She patted his face a couple of times, but it stopped having any effect on him. Gary knelt near and with tears in his eyes was holding his hand. Jessica was crying and kept telling him to hold on, but nothing changed for the better. The scars were too deep to close on time, and he had already lost too much blood. Gary curled near him, put his face on his brother's shoulder and sobbed. That was all he could do, and he had never hated himself so much for being totally unhelpful. Everything went so wrong, not as it was supposed to be, Gary thought, praying for some miracle to save his brother. But deep down in the core of his mind Gary knew nobody would come with help, and only Mark's own strength was his last hope.

Jessica kept pressing her hoodie on Mark's torso, but it didn't stop the bleeding. His hand got flabby and collapsed under the weight of the massive feral arm. She couldn't hold it any longer by being busy trying to do something. She never felt so desperate as she was feeling in this moment. She saw death itself staring at her from his slowly fading eyes but kept begging for help from whichever God was listening right now and was willing to create something to change Mark's inevitable fate. But nobody answered. She felt like the nano-seconds of time were stretching into hours of her immense pain and agony.

In this precise moment, when she saw his closing eyes and heard his last breath, the time had stopped like the reality speed was paused. And whispers, first unnoticeable, kept repeating *you're not alone* over and over again. It sounded like a large choir of many disembodied voices with a vast scale of tones merging into one sentence. The voices brought the serenity and warm feeling inside her heart that were growing intensely and swiftly took over not only her body but the surroundings. She felt connected to them like an embryo by the umbilical cord with a mother. She saw thousands of lines of different energies entwining into one thick cord and connected with her aura on her heart level.

Somehow for Jessica, the voices felt familiar, like family that was lost a long time ago but had never been forgotten. She felt their spirits near so intensely that she caught herself looking around and expecting someone's physical presence, but nobody physically appeared in the van. The sensation of being part of the world of the shamans' family gave her the courage to look at Mark's face without fear but with a faint smile. She rose her hand, stained with his blood, to her face level and looked at it, like it didn't belong to her. She saw rainbow colours radiating alternately from her whole body and felt eternal happiness. Some symbols started appearing from inside of her flesh, first vague and dimly, but getting many shapes on the skin's surface. They were in constant movement, changing into humans and then into animals, stars, flowers, oceans, waves, and wind and others she couldn't recognise.

Suddenly, the voices started singing only one word: 'ask'. She didn't understand to whom and what she had to ask. But the aura from her hand moved down to Mark's chest, leaving her motionlessly but still connected by a few colour lines with her body. Mark opened his eyes, and she knew, he saw exactly the same spiritual silhouette as she did. He grabbed her hand and that was the answer to the question which she had never asked out loud. The answer that hung between them silently with his response as a little sparkle of joy inside his eyes. She was staring at him, and somehow, she knew, that she touched the core of his existence, letting the ancestors take the lead. The last thing that she remembered before they both passed out was the massive dose of energy she sent to his body with an order for instant healing.

Gary rose his head when he stopped hearing Jessica's desperate callings. He looked at her and didn't understand why she was smiling. He was avoiding glancinig at Mark's face, worried that his nerves could snap without control at seeing his brother's lifeless eyes. Gary was staring at the scene, but he didn't see anything other than Mark grabbing her hand before they both became unconscious.

Although there was nothing visible happening between them, Gary felt a warm thrill coming from Jessica's direction. It was like a slight voltage of an electric wave running through him and causing goosebumps all over his body. Gary shivered, shouted, and kept pulling his brother's shoulder until he realised there weren't feral there anymore but human. Mark changed in a blink of an eye, leaving Gary totally astonished. Mark didn't have any scars. He was healed so fast that only smeared blood on his skin reminded of wounds he had second ago. Gary saw Mark's chest moving, indicating that his brother had regular normal breath. He fainted.

*

After leaving the mayhem in the circus, the rest of the way was very ordinary. When Gary recovered in the moving van, he found Jessica and Mark sitting on the floor and watching on a controller screen the footage from the drone of the last minutes before the blackout. The drone had its own LED lights, but they weren't strong enough to show all what was going on in the ground after the electric went off. But there were a few places near cars or caravans, that had independent lights still on and therefore gave quite good pictures about the panic outburst and its consequences. Gary asked them how they were feeling a few times like he didn't believe that Mark was perfectly fine after seeing him on the edge of death. After one more display of Gary's concern, Mark got annoyed and growled that he didn't remember anything that had happened to him after he sat down inside the van. Jessica just nodded, shrugged, and grinned broadly, replying that she felt like she had just woken up after a good, long sleep, refreshed and ready for action.

That night, they came to Jessica's house exhausted and didn't speak much on the way. They unpacked and set the last meeting for rehearsal before the show in the museum. Gary promised to email them the script and was quite surprised when James asked for it as well. Although James looked normal, with his classy clothes and same perfect manners, Gary had a feeling that something had changed inside him. Maybe it was a bigger smile he had now, or the warmer tone in his voice when he talked to all of them. Or just perhaps the little sparkle of joy in eyes that appeared after destroying the circus, which Gary saw every time he stared at James' face.

Draco didn't wake up at all. His wounds were closed but not fully healed. He still had visible scars covered only by faint bit of ashy skin but his pulse was stable, and he was breathing. Sean was waiting for them near Jessica's house. Simon called him and they both transferred Draco to Sean's car. But the biggest wonderment for Gary was seeing Robert voluntarily helping them. He even gave Sean the injection-pen with a sedative liquid inside that he had in his pocket. Sean took it without any comments and injected a maximum dose to Draco, just in case he might wake up in a blood-thirsty rage during the drive.

Moreover, Sean came well-prepared, bringing with him a bag with blood and set a drip for Draco. He said it wouldn't help for long, but at least it would definitely calm Draco down. He covered Draco completely with a blanket, including his face, and said a few words about show equipment. He drove away looking happier than James when he heard the brief story about destroying the Blue Fairy's Circus.

James remained behind the wheel in the van and he drove away just after Sean's departure. He was nodding and waving goodbye to all of them. Gary was the last he kept extended eye contact with, and Gary could swear, he said 'I owe you one,' soundlessly in the way that only Gary could see it. Gary was smiling faintly, observing the car disappearing on the corner, knowing that whatever comes next, James would always be there for him.

Robert declared that he was staying with them, sleeping in Simon's bed and ordering Simon to sleep on the couch. He explained his decision by his concern about being followed from the circus. He said the smell of fresh human blood was still firm around, and it might attract not only vamps but something even worse. Nobody opposed, not even Simon himself. After all those new creatures they saw in a circus tent, nobody would be stunned at seeing something even more gruesome that might be lurking in shadows. They felt safer knowing that a well-trained werewolf warrior would be sleeping with them under the same roof.

Despite the tiredness, they all sat in the kitchen, ate pancakes they made together, recalling all those emotions, pictures, and actions they were participating in no longer than about hour ago. Now, when the death threat was over, the stories became more like an adventure than a horror, but the rising daylight and good food made them all feel sleepy.

The last thing that Gary thought before he fell into a deep sleep was Jack Pott's snapping fingers, when he was trying to get to the van. He couldn't find any logical answer what it might be, and the name 'Cassains' he called Gary sounded even more mysterious.

*

Sean visited them the next afternoon. Gary was reluctant about telling him the whole story, but he couldn't hide the footage they recorded, so Sean knew about everything. Although the circus was one of the most dangerous events that Gary was partaking in so far, he had never felt so content about the amount of recorded material he had gotten from it. He was pleased when he found an envelope, with just his name written on, that someone dropped by the letterbox. Inside, there was a memory card from the TV van dash cam with a journey footage. Gary, Mark, and Sean were more shocked watching the turmoil that was going on after the panic outbreak than when they experienced it by being there.

'Guys, what's Cassian?' asked Gary suddenly.

'Where did you hear that?' asked Sean, staring at Gary, surprised.

'Well …' Gary didn't know how to explain something that might refer to him and had apparently confused Sean all ready.

'Oh, come on, Sean. Get a grip and tell him,' snarled Mark.

'Your father was one of them. Cassian is an exceptional witch hunter …' Sean didn't finish.

'Cassians are elite among them. You have to be born to be one. The bloodline has skills and abilities that no other can ever have,' said Mark.

'Like what?' Gary was interested even more.

'There are rumours that some of feral's skills can't work around them. Your father was one of the best in Europe,' declared Sean.

'Why do you ask?' asked Mark with a suspicious tone.

'No reason. I've heard the name and was curious what does it mean,' replied Gary and he changed the topic of conversation. But the growing hunger for knowing more about Cassians didn't allow him to forget it.

While they were telling the story and showing the pictures about the death-match, Sean got a phone call from work, so he left Gary's room.

'We've got a problem,' said Sean, coming back to room visibly stirred.

'What's happened?' asked Gary.

'I've just moved the museum's show. We're performing in two days…'

'We can't!' shouted Gary, panicking.

'We have to. Patric Vance, aka The Prince, just booked the whole Great Court for a private hire after the museum closing time,' replied Sean nervously.

'What?!' Gary felt like the ground was shrinking beneath his feet.

'And now, what?' asked Mark, standing from his chair and pacing around the room.

'For that amount of money he just paid, he could have it today if it wasn't for the other corporate bookings,' Sean sigh and rolled eyes.

'Can they organise an event in such a short time?' asked Mark.

'For a private dinner to few people, it's not rocket science,' answered Sean.

'How can he open the casket without the key?' asked Gary perplexed.

'Easy. A small lump of C4 will do the job,' answered Mark, and he peeped at Sean who frowned, nodding with a wrathful gaze.

'And destroy the artefact,' declared Sean, with disgust on his face.

'Maybe there's no other way?' argued Mark, slightly raising his voice.

'There's always another way …' Sean didn't finish. It seemed for Gary that they had never finished a similar dispute since Gary's accident, but maybe they would never close that part of their past.

'Okay, stop! Don't panic. We've been in worse shit-holes,' replied Gary, wiping his nose. He noticed that the bleeding had come back.

'Oh, good to know that my brother has access to explosives. By the way, I've no idea who you are, bro' continued Gary, smiling to both of them. Mark didn't answer but hung his head and covered his eyes with one hand, trying to hide massive grin on his face.

'So, we need to improvise again,' said Gary, taking his phone and notebook with all those important points of the show production that he scheduled.

'It seems we've mastered it. I've changed the show date already,' said Sean.

CHAPTER 23

17th July - The Rehearsal

'You didn't bake anything?' Robert seemed a bit irritable. He was poking around the kitchen and opened not only the fridge but a couple of cupboards as well. Mark smiled, took two cans of beer from the fridge, passed one to Robert and left the kitchen without a word.

Although it was a late afternoon urgent gathering, nobody was surprised by Gary's texts. And now, they all were present at home but Draco. His absence was announced by Sean, but not explained. Everyone welcomed one more member of the team, Maya. Gary warned them about the rush of the show in the British Museum and asked for reports what was already done and what was only as a work in progress.

Most of them still were astonished by such a fast pace of happenings, but nobody questioned the decision itself. Even Robert, instead of his usual sarcastic complains, seemed to be pleased knowing that everything would be done much faster than he expected. Gary presumed it was connected with Robert's open hatred to vampires, but maybe it wasn't only that.

At the beginning, Sean briefly clarified the reason of the hurry. The date for the show was initially scheduled in about two weeks from now, so there was no advert going around about their earlier performance. Sean mentioned his manager had agreed to let them play tomorrow but under one condition. Instead of only one, they had to play the same show twice. The fist would be treated as publicity of the leading performance. They had to record it, making a video from it and put an advertisement on the Internet for the second show. Gary was taken aback about the group's reaction. Nobody moaned, and it looked more like an announcement to the amateur theatre group that was well accustomed to plays. At that moment, Gary noticed how a deep bond had been made between them, after facing together such dangerous situations like they experience in the circus.

'Okay, let's start with what we already have,' declared Gary and got through his list, checking point by point on what kind of level of preparation all the things were. It appeared that the stage, lights, microphones, cameras, and some basic theatrical decorations were ready. But the most crucial element, the actors, weren't at all. Everyone said they weren't prepared with the play itself, and there was no chance to learn by heart the whole written text, nor to have a few good meetings to practice it.

Gary blamed the time for it, but deep down he knew it wasn't true. Even if they would have a few weeks more, they weren't actors, and his idea about the show was one of the worst he had had this year so far. He could sense the total disaster coming, and publicly making fun of himself and them. Just one thought made him bear this situation; the feeling that he didn't have anything to lose because his life was at stake. So, even though the time was running up, Gary was glad that it would be over soon. The waiting for what could happen and how bad the nightmare could be during his sleep put him on the edge of emotional exhaustion. Gary knew he had to find the solution to this stalemate situation.

'I know what to do,' said Gary out loud and interrupting their chattings.

'With what?' asked Mark.

'The show, the dialogue on stage ...' continued Gary, feeling the heat growing like wildfire inside his head. He always felt like that when the creative, often brilliant, ideas started multiplying in his mind.

'Please, share,' said Sean, smiling.

'We don't have to talk at all, or at least, we can limit the dialogue,' replied Gary, he stood up and started walking around the living room.

'What?' asked Robert, staring at him, frowning and surprised like rest of them.

'Do you mean we should play it like a pantomime?' asked Jessica.

'Yes, and no,' Gary was on fire, and everyone could see it on his face.

'First, let's say we have a narrator, like in an ancient Greek theatre, who'll be telling the story. We'll still be playing, but we can cut off most of the dialogue and keep them to the essential minimum ...'

'And, if someone will not follow, we can improvise, just stick to the main story?' asked Sean, smiling broadly.

'They'll be staring at us,' said Simon, like he wanted to warn them.

'That's the main point,' continued Gary.

'So, once again, we throw ourselves in at the deep shit, but it's piece of cake after the circus,' said Robert, sipping the last drops of beer.

'Does anyone have a better idea?' asked Gary, looking around from face to face.

'Who'll be playing the narrator?' asked Sean.

'You,' replied Gary, pointing at Robert, who choked a bit and spilt the last sip of beer on his T-shirt.

'Me? Why?' he asked, shocked.

'Well, in the circus you were very natural among strangers. If someone can interact with the audience and confuse them, it's you. Nobody would make a joke on us as funny as you can. And that'll hide how unprepared we all are,' replied Gary.

Gary knew that Robert's sassy comments and bold movements around people made him feel like a child in a candy shop, if only he could be playing the leading role of a show. And right now, Gary knew how to use him for the team's advantage.

After that, there were a few hours of re-writing, rehearsing and playing the story. Gary made one more amendment to the show about costumes, and that was the last thing before tomorrow's storm.

Late that night, when everyone was asleep but Gary, he was thinking about all those small and significant events that happened in such a short time, he felt like he lived not one month but the whole year. It was so emotionally intense that he had never felt so connected, thrilled and engaged in teamwork in his entire life. Gary laughed silently but continued working on details in his 'The Faded Photograph' website. He didn't want to wake up Mark who was sleeping on an air mattress and snoring like a bear.

CHAPTER 24

18th July - The Show

The Great Court of The British Museum was well-lit. Summer was always an active time for the museum. Groups of private tours started walking around at nine in the morning. They were passing the stage that was built around the mysterious coffin standing on a platform, and a tour guide, with excitement in his voice, announced the midday performance.

Gary smiled, staring at them, but a tinny tone of doubt whispered in his head about a massive failure, raising his anxiety and giving him little shivers.

Gary and Sean were first in the museum. There were show matters to talk about with the manager, so they both came two hours ago. The manager looked rather pleased, not only about the performance idea, and a theme but about filming as well.

Gary set the cameras, one of his own, and two others that belonged to the museum and adjusted small microphones that would be pinned up to actor's clothes. Gary checked the folding screens on wheels, usually used as mobile room dividers by the museum, if there was no problem to manoeuvre them on the stage. Almost all was ready for the spectacle. There were pictures of the scenery such as the house in woods, panorama of the town and a mausoleum printed on the cloth and pinned to the screens.

After ten o'clock Gary sat in one of the cafeterias, eating sweet doughnuts and drinking coffee. He put notes in front of him, going through the text and plans over and over again. He was feeling stressed and tense. More and more tourists started walking around the museum. Gary was watching their smiling faces and felt unreal. Maybe because, for Gary, now was a few crucial hours that would determine his life. Someone touched his back, making him jump.

'Oh, you're freaking me out. Stop jumping up like a Jack in a box,' said Jessica, and she sat next to him. She looked at his now empty paper plate and offered one of her own cakes. Gary took it but ate mechanically without noticing the taste. Soon everyone from the team was present. There were a few people that came with Maya, and apparently, there were more of them, but now roaming around the museum's halls. Gary could swear they looked exactly like a family on a nice museum trip. Time was running fast, and Gary, surrounded by all those known and unknown people, started feeling a bit more confident. Nothing was entirely ready, but like in life, it never was, thought Gary, smiling faintly. They moved closer to the stage, took the cases and boxes that were there waiting prepared under the stage and at the back of the scene. They were hiding behind the high screens on wheels that separated them from the public view and waiting for Robert to start the show. They all were smiling but Gary knew, under the happy mask, the stress and worries were crawling inside their minds, still waiting for the gong.

*

The gong tolled. Tourists, members of the Night Reaper pack, museum's employees, some special guests invited by Sean and his manager were gathering around the empty space, in front of the scene.

The stage was lifted a bit more than one metre from the floor, to level it with the Tritus' End stand. There was a long, two-metre-high screen on wheels that usually was used as a room divider in the museum, standing now on the stage, in front of the coffin. The screen had a painted picture of a Renaissance's town where the play was set, pinned to its frame. There were two other similar screens on the floor, one at each side of the scene, standing behind stairs leading to the platform. The place under the stage was covered by a black, wrinkled, thick material, attached to the edge of the stage.

Sean, alongside with Draco, asked the public to move back and give more room for the performance. He briefly inspected those around, searching for signs of Patric Vance or high-ranked members of the dynasty he was leader of. And then, the second gong tolled twice, announcing the moment for silence and focus on the show from all witnessing the new event in the museum. Sean moved behind-the-scenes after, letting Robert take the narrator's place.

*

Robert walked in a very confident way, tapping his black walking-stick excessively loud on the floor. He behaved like someone who didn't know that stage-fright did exist. He was limping on one side a bit more than usual, and Gary, who was peeping from behind the screens, thought that he was making it up for an unknown theatrical purpose. Robert was wearing his usual jeans and worn-off T-shirt, but he also had an unfastened, burgundy Renaissance coat with a lot of golden ornaments, that were alongside a black fur sewn onto a heavy material that was hanging across of his chest. Moreover, he had a large beret with a long and massive feather, matching not only in colour but the theatrical costume he was wearing. The combination of his outfit looked rather bizarre and made a lot of viewers laugh, but it didn't stress him at all. He stopped in the middle of empty space with a face like a conqueror, looked at his left side, looked at his right side, making the gathering be silent by using only his gaze and one eyebrow frown. He waved to Mark, who was standing behind one of the cameras on a tripod, checking the equipment yet again, and then Robert put the wireless microphone close to his mouth and started the show.

'A long time ago, in high mountains, far, far away, a little witch was living in a small cabin. One day, she stood in front of her house, looked around and said …' he was talking slowly, emphasising some phrases to trigger curiosity around the room. Robert paused, checking up on the audience reaction. He came close to some people, asking questions about what the witch could have possibly said. Some people followed his game by trying to guess the end of the joke, but Robert's disapproving nodding was the answer about their failure. He came back to the middle of the space and continued with a big smile.

'I'm in the wrong story. This is what the witch said,' he laughed alongside some of the more engaged audience members.

'Ladies and Gentlemen let me present a new, truly paranormal story of romance between Romeo and Juliet. The story of love and hatred, greed and lust, that was forced by the spell that was casted on the innocent, pushing their lives not only onto the edge but beyond life and death itself,' he paused, walking around like he owned this place.

A few people came out from behind the scene carrying a small, round table and three chairs. They put the items in the middle of the empty circle, reserved for the performance and went back, but leaving quite a large, closed, black bag under the table. Next, three women came out from behind the screens and sat at the table. One was tall and wearing a long blue dress stylised in Renaissance fashion. The next one had a curvy figure, wearing a short skin-tight red dress and white like snow, high, bushy with a lot of curls, wig as a theatrical element matching the time of the story. But the third one was wearing men's Renaissance clothes, including shoes and a massive, fake, black moustache that was slipping from under her nose and was falling on the table from time to time. The owner put it back on, even helped to keep it under her nose by twisting her mouth. But it kept falling off on the table, so she ripped of one of the ribbons from her coat, tied the moustache from both sides to the string, and then put it around her head. The moustaches finally stayed in the right place. She showed the 'thumbs up' sign to the audience with a happy smile about sorting out her costume problem. People were laughing watching their play, mimics and silent talks about the tarot cards that one of actresses put on the table.

'Far away, in Verona, three witches were living happy, peaceful life among human beings. They were serving to the community by selling the curses and love spells for those who had money. Be aware, because magic always comes with a price, and sometimes money is the last currency,' continued Robert, coming closer to the witches, mixing the cards and causing turmoil. All three witches stood up and in a hilarious way chased him off, showing rude gestures.

'One evening, Lord Capulet knocked on the door,' continued Robert, walking to and fro. The sound of knocking rang around from speakers standing on the scene. Robert saw the incoming actor, stopped him with his hand gesture and continuing playing like in a pantomime, opening an imaginary door and letting him in.

'Oh, a new client,' said the first witch.

'Rich Lord,' declared the second one.

'And the cute one,' said the one dressed like a man.

It was Sean, who was playing Lord Capulet. He was wearing suit trousers, a standard white shirt but he had a long, black, hooded cloak tied across his chest and a sizable rounded hat on his head. The hat had a large red feather attached on one side. Although his outfit looked similar to Robert's, it definitely was more luxurious, showing the character's high position in this Renaissance town's society. He walked like he didn't belong to the place or he was a shy little boy. He took his hat off, bowed himself in exaggerated greetings, and waving the cap in a way that it swept the floor in front of him.

'The witches asked Capulet if he knew about the consequences of casting spells, but seeing his distress they knew he'd sell his own mother to change his inevitable destiny,' Robert was standing near the stage observing Sean kneeling, with hands folded up like in a church's, with his whole body expressing the begging.

'Lord Capulet had lost most of his merchant fleet because of the pirates. He just got the news, and he knew he was bankrupt. But for his luck, nobody in Verona had learnt about it yet,' said Robert with a mischievous tone.

Sean silently was showing his tragedy.

'So, he asked for help, regardless of the price,' continued Robert.

Sean threw himself on the floor, kissing the witches' shoes and crying.

'And the witches agreed to help him.'

The ladies picked up Sean and sat him on one of the chairs. The one that was wearing men's clothes sat on Capulet's lap, put her hands around his neck, hugged him and looked extremely happy. Sean blushed and grinned but didn't stop acting.

'We'll cook you a spell,' whispered the first witch.

'Very powerful,' shouted the second.

'Love perfume' ended the one that was sitting on Sean's lap, talking with a sensual voice and winking to him a few times. Sean blushed even more.

The first witch pulled out a small microwave from the bag that was standing under the table. She placed it in the middle of the table and drew out a box of ready-made food form the bag. She showed it to the audience and to those sitting with her. The witches started making voices that sounded between pleased approval and surprising discovery. She put it inside the microwave and turned the timer. And then, the three witches jumped and danced a wild dance around the table, waving hands, shaking bodies, and making a weird noise. There was music in the background with an evil laugh that could scare the creepiest of ghosts. They sat down back on their chairs, looking very content. The first witch opened the microwave, found a small flask of perfume inside and showed it to the public like a prize. Robert clapped his hands and encouraged the audience to follow him. Some people cheered and clapped, but some only smiled broadly. While the witches were dancing, one figure walked from behind the scene. He was moving in such a way that suggested that he was spying on them, trying to figure out what they were up to. He was hiding behind the imaginary door and was listening to part of their conversation. The witches didn't see him lurking around.

'You can use it twice. Just spray in their faces,' said the first witch.

'They'll fall, very deeply in love, and get married,' said the witch wearing trousers. She looked at Sean with utter admiration and with bliss on her face.

'So, chose wisely the richest, for yourself or your daughter,' continued the one with a white wig.

'Have a big party tomorrow and use it before midnight,' declared the first witch.

'Or the spell will be useless,' said the one sitting on Sean's lap.

They all stood up and walked away behind the scene smiling, dancing, and looking cheerful. The members of the werewolf pack that came to help took back the table and microwave. Their outfits were mix of old-fashioned clothes with a modern twist, but were showing their small-town, middle-class status in this story.

'But, like on every market, there is always a rival who doesn't want you to succeed,' Robert stretched his hand and pointed at the new figure who appeared. It was Draco wearing red leather trousers and a black T-shirt with the words 'no brain, no game' on it. He had a red, peaked gnome's hat, large pointy ears and huge crooked nose made from soft plastic that imitated human skin.

'So, in Verona, Robin Goodfellow, a mischievous hobgoblin is living, also known as Puck among those who are cursing his tricks,' continued Robert, coming closer to Draco and putting his arm around the vamp. Draco grinned with a mean facial expression, an exact copy of the sly grin on Robert's mouth.

'Who couldn't wait for the opportunity to mock the witches he hated so much,' said Robert, smiling broadly, observing Draco rubbing his hands like he was washing them in an invisible soap and behaving in a very prankish way. Robert continued the story after Draco left like he was still spying on the witches.

'The very next day, in the evening, when the party was on,' Robert was waiting for actors to take their places.

Soft and cheerful party music was playing in the background. The actors were wearing combinations of casual clothes mixed with elements of Renaissance costumes in every possible way. Robert introduced the main characters of the story: Sean as Lord Capulet, Jessica as Juliet, Simon as Romeo, Gary as Friar Laurence. There were more than ten other people as citizens of Verona, but they were doing only background acting. They were chatting in groups, laughing, and drinking an imitation of wine from metal chalices. The witches joined the party like it was prepared for them, and the crowd welcomed them in that manner. Just after their arrival, Puck walked in as well but dressed as a jester. He had a face expression like a conqueror and was looking pleased, like the applause was only for him. He was wearing a colourful clown costume, a mask on half of his face, red jester's hat with a jingle bells on many pointy ends. He was following Sean, making ridiculing gestures about guests, but somehow always directing his rudeness towards the witches.

Robert came to Juliet, grabbed her hand and pulled her from the crowd. He left her in the middle of the playing space and walked back to the party guests. He did the same with Romeo, who was busy chatting with one young woman. Robert dragged him and left only one step from Juliet.

'At the beginning of the ball, Romeo and Juliet didn't like each other,' Robert placed them face to face. They both were showing to one other crooked faces and gestures, that could only mean how disgusting it was for them to stand close together, mainly because of their mutual antipathy. Robert put the microphone near Juliet's mouth, but this action didn't help at all. The fear froze her like a statue, making even blinking impossible.

'So, tell me, little flower ...' Robert stopped the sentence and peeped at Jessica, grinning broadly. Jessica was staring at him with an angry frown. She smiled crookedly. It reminded more the pose of an angry, snarling dog than a face of a sweet little girl.

'What do you think about this gentleman,' continued Robert, pointing at Romeo. Robert covered his eyes with one hand and tried to stifle the silent laugh inside. Juliet put a hand on her mouth signalling with her head and hands that she wouldn't give any comments. She looked rather shy and withdrawn in the presence of inquisitive Robert and his microphone. Robert, still laughing, did the same with Romeo but his reaction, which was rather stiff, showed how uninterested they both were to know the other person at all. Juliet pulled out a mobile with a large screen, took a picture of Romeo, and played a person who was busy doing something on her phone. Robert and Romeo looked surprised, but they followed her with checking their own devices. Romeo moved behind Robert's back, peeped over Juliet's shoulder and tried to spy what she was doing.

'Seriously? You're the Internet troll called Nymph, aren't you?' shouted Romeo. She turned to him, hiding the phone inside her bra. She looked shocked but kept denying everything by her posture, expression, and waving head. Romeo looked at her with a detestation. And then, to his astonishment, she snatched his phone from his hand and looked at the screen.

'Holy Wizzard? The well-known hater?' Juliet stared at him with an open mouth. Romeo took back his mobile and switched it off. She made a body gesture imitating vomiting, looked at him with even more disgust than he had on his face when he was looking at her. Robert tried to make her talk, but she ran away as fast as she could. Romeo and Juliet hurried away but didn't stand with other people. They were busy with their phones aside.

'And the war on social media had begun,' continued Robert, walking between guests. He came closer to Lord Capulet, took him underarm and drew him out to the middle of the acting space.

'It was close to midnight when Lord Capulet made a choice that was supposed to give him a fortune and his new wife,' Robert pointed at a woman, thin like a stick but wearing the most expensive dress, with pounds of golden jewellery hanging on her. She was wearing overdo, heavy make-up and had a few younger suitors around. Robert came closer to the lady, kissed her straightened hand in the biggest ring's gem, and walked back with her to the place where Sean was standing. She looked at Sean, Lord Capulet, with a frown sizing him up. He gazed at her like someone hungry looking at a feast. He was rubbing his hands, showing how pleasant it was for him the vision of being even richer than he had ever been in his life. He was searching for the love perfume that the witches advised him to spray on someone, but he couldn't find it anywhere. Lord Capulet turned all his pockets inside out and left them in that position. He started crying, running around searching for the missing magical spray among present guests but it was nowhere to be found.

'But the dark fate named Puck had twisted Lord Capulet destiny,' continued Robert, showing Draco, Puck, who was standing among the biggest group of actors, and making them laugh with jokes he was telling.

Draco jumped when he heard his stage name and ran to Robert, waving the one hand holding the love perfume. Puck patted his forehead like someone who just recalled the forgotten mission, turned around as he began searching for prey to his new prank. He saw that Juliet was typing vigorously on her phone. She was standing aside, quite far from the rest of the party, but she couldn't see that she was alone. Puck came closer and stood behind her back, reading the texts she was typing. He covered his eyes with his hand but peeped through his fingers. His face indicated utter shock mixed with aversion. Puck turned around, searching for other people who were glued to their devices instead of enjoying the real party. He found only Simon, Romeo, who was standing in the exactly the same posture as Juliet. And like with her, Puck stood behind his back, reading the texts that Romeo was typing. And then, once again, he hit his forehead, smiling mischievously, like the worst trick just popped into his mind. He looked at the perfume, made a funny face and sprayed it straight onto Simon's nose. And then, he dashed and sprayed it all over Juliet's face. And then he pulled her to Romeo. She peeped at him once and went back to her previous activity. Romeo did the same, shrugged and said silently 'whatever dude' to Puck. Puck stood perplexed, glanced at the perfume, smelt it, licked, tried to bite, and then shrugged with disappointment. Puck made a funny face, looked at the flask and then put it inside the big, white wig that one of the witches had been wearing all the time. He went back to being the jester of the party, focusing on amusing the most attractive women there. He behaved like nothing had happened to the stolen spray.

'Ladies and gentlemen. It's not the end of the story,' Robert paused, observing the audience.

'Magic always works, but sometimes you need to wait for the effect,' said Robert, giving the sign to end the party.

Actors were leaving the space, playing people that were more merry and friendly to one another than at the beginning of the scene. The jester was surrounded by all partakers, with two women, arm in arm on both his sides. The richest woman was Puck's favourite, clinging on his body like a leech. Lord Capulet left the stage wincing and crying when he looked at the rich lady that was walking with Puck. Sean, Lord Capulet, was accompanied by the witch, the one still wearing men's Renaissance clothes but now more sophisticated.

In the meantime, Romeo and Juliet were standing, still staring intensely at each other. Both had put mobiles to pockets and were walking closer and closer to one another. They stopped when they were just one step away. Robert made a surprised face like he was expecting a bit more of an emotional scene. They stood still for a minute of complete silence, and then they rushed to each other in one fast move. They fell into their arms and tightly hugged one another.

'And there we have the love. The cause of the most significant changes in everyone's lives, for good ...' said Robert, clapping his hands, encouraging the viewers to follow him. The crowd started cheering with a roaring demand for kissing.

'Or for bad ...' he continued, grinning widely and joined in on the 'kiss, kiss, kiss' shout. Jessica, Juliet, blushed and looked around confused. She held a longer glare at Mark and blushed even more. Simon looked calm but he made a quick peep into the stage direction and the place partially covered by screens on wheels where the rest of actors were standing. He saw Maya's face. And then, he turned to Juliet and passionately kissed her. The red colour appeared on Maya's face. She turned and vanished behind the screen. Spectators applauded briskly, cheering on their romantic activity. Robert clapped, smiling from ear to ear, but he changed to be less cheerful when he peeped at Mark's direction. Mark was standing behind the camera, with a frown and rather unhappy, pouty face.

'And you know what happened next, do you guys?' Robert asked the public. Some people shouted their answer about the balcony scene at night time. Simon and Jessica left the acting zone, holding hands. They walked unnaturally fast, like someone who didn't want to stay too long on public view.

'Yes, you're right. They got married and consummated their burning love in the chamber of pleasure. No, we're not going to show you that,' said Robert, laughing along with the audience.

'Meanwhile, after that, there was a conflict in the community and her father, Lord Capulet, arranged her marriage with Count Paris. It seems that Capulet's lust for money would never cease to exist. Blah blah blah. Let's skip it to the part when Juliet visits Friar Laurence, desperately in need of his help,' declared Robert, waving to Gary, Friar Laurence, and Jessica, Juliet, to take place in the middle of the acting space. Juliet was crying on the Friar's shoulder, telling soundlessly about her troubles and begging for some solution. Friar, Gary, was wearing long grey, cleric's robe with a thick white cord on his waist. His long hair, tied in a ponytail, perfectly matched his role.

'Help me, reverend Friar. You're my only hope,' begged Juliet, kneeling and holding Gary's legs in her arms. She hid her face in his long cloth. Her body started shaking like someone who was crying uncontrollably. Gary put his hands on her head, nodding with understanding.

'What would you do, to escape the inevitable destiny of an unwanted marriage, just to feed your father's greed for money?' asked Friar, accenting the phrase about the fate of doom.

'Everything!' shouted Jessica.

'Even life itself?' asked Gary, smiling wickedly.

'I'd rather die than live without my sweet Romeo,' cried Juliet, throwing herself on the ground. Gary grinned from ear to ear showing to everyone long, fake, plastic fangs that he had glued to his teeth. He took Juliet under her arms and lifted her from the floor she was lying on. He grabbed her hair, pulled it back to reveal her neck, and then he bit her. Artificial blood streamed on Jessica's skin, staining her dress.

'And now, you'll witness the creation of new vampire,' said Robert, pointing in the actor's direction. Juliet looked exhausted, but she was still playing an alive person. Gary helped her lie down on a floor, gently caressing her hair and cheeks. He knelt down near her and with one long nail, he cut open his wrist and gave Juliet his dark blood to drink.

'She won't die. That'll be too easy,' continued Robert, staring at the silent audience.

'Vampires are not dead. There are transformed, supernatural creatures of the night. The changing is sometimes so painful, that they have to be tied up, otherwise they might kill themselves to escape the torture. Not every human being can get through the fight inside their bodies and minds. It's like drinking poison and the antidote in the same time,' said Robert slowly. He was walking quite close to the public, observing their reactions and facial expressions.

'But the last stage is the most difficult moment, when they're hibernating. It looks like they're dead, and unfortunately, not everyone will ever wake up to a new kind of life. That's why, in the old days, the changing took place mostly in a graveyard,' said Robert, observing theatrical assistants entering the stage.

Two people unpinned the cloth with a printed picture of the city of Verona attached to the screens-on-wheels that was standing on the stage. The new view beneath depicted a massive mausoleum with a graveyard behind, during night time.

'So, in Verona, Friar Lawrence, hid Juliet's body in a place far away from too inquisitive people,' said Robert, helping Gary take the half-asleep Juliet under her arms and lift her up from the floor.

Gary caught her waist and slowly walked to the stage's stairs. He was hauling Jessica, who was playing a person dazed and barely conscious, to the centre of the stage, and then, he stopped, facing the picture of the entrance to the tomb. He turned his head and waited for Robert to continue telling the story. He was looking at the smiling audience, but his hands started shaking when he realised that the culmination of the whole show, the opening of the casket, was within reach. Theatrical assistants folded the screen exposing the primary prop of this whole show, the Tritus' End, that was standing behind it.

'Because Friar Lawrence was one of the oldest vampires walking on Earth, he had a powerful artefact in his possession. The coffin that could help everyone became a vamp almost painlessly,' continued Robert, pointing at Gary, who was showing his long fangs smiling broadly and nodding to the spectators.

Gary helped Jessica lie down on the floor near the coffin, and he smeared artificial blood on her neck. He put a sizable plastic knife in her hands in such a way that it was seen by the viewers. She smiled gently, watching him through half-opened eyelids. She put her warm hand on his, squeezed and held tightly. Gary heaved a sigh, trying to hide his fear from her, but his trembling and icy hands were illustrating the actual condition of his mind. Gary was scared even more than during the circus show. That was the moment when he had a problem hiding the small plastic bag that was used as a container for the fake blood. She took it from him and hid it inside her bra, smearing even more of the red liquid on her chest and her dress. Gary smiled, took a few deep breaths with his eyes closed, and continued playing his role, like a professional actor.

'But before he put her inside, lovely Friar had faked her suicide and run to her family to tell them about this tragic event,' said Robert, observing Gary running downstairs towards a group of actors walking nearby. There was Sean, as Lord Capulet, who looked very happy, walking arm to arm with one of the witches who was still wearing men's clothes. He was surrounded by people who were guests at the party scene.

'Look at him! He's so happy with this sudden wedding,' exclaimed Robert, pointing at Lord Capulet and the cheerful group orbiting around him. Gary ran fast to them, knelt, grabbed Sean's cape and cried. He was telling about Juliet's death silently, using only his hand's gestures and body language. The group reacted with distress and sorrow. Friar Lawrence was leading them to the tomb where he left Juliet's body. When they entered, Sean threw himself on the floor and seized Juliet's hands and cried deplorably. The rest of his companions started moaning, crying, and hugging one another.

'After a time of grieving, Friar put Juliet's body in the coffin, and left her there until the end of the night,' said Robert, watching the actors surrounding Jessica, kneeling near her.

Gary helped Jessica to stand up. Other actors encircled her in a way that made her invisible for the viewers. They walked from the stage in one squeezed group.

'And the story goes…' said Robert, hesitating.

There was a bit too long a silence when nothing happened, that slightly confused even him. Gary was supposed to stay there just after the crowd left the stage. Robert sighed with relief when he saw Gary, wiping his hands, trying to erase the red colour from his skin, and walking with Simon from behind the screen. They both were playing people deeply engaged in a conversation.

'Romeo learnt about her death and came to Friar Lawrence with the intention of taking poison and finishing his wretched life without his beloved Juliet,' Robert was nodding to Gary and Simon. He pointed at Simon who knelt and begged Friar for the opportunity of ending his suffering in the painless arms of death.

'Friar told him that she is still alive, but Romeo didn't believe it, so he demanded to see her,' Robert was observing Simon and Gary miming the scene. They both went onto the stage and stood in the front of the Tritus' End. Friar showed the coffin indicating that Juliet was lying inside but still alive. Romeo took out the wooden sword, touched Gary's neck and demanded to open the coffin.

*

There was a moment of silence around. Everyone was staring at Gary, even the werewolf pack actors were peeping from behind the screens. Mark left the cameras unsupervised and walked closer to the scene. He was focused and tensed, like a cat observing his prey, but this time his focus was set on Gary.

Gary turned and stood near to the middle of the Tritus' End, where the keyhole was built. His hands were shaking, and small drops of sweat appeared on his forehead. '*Please work*,' Gary was repeating to himself over and over again in his head. He took out the metal rod that Jessica had made for him as instructed by Robert. It was supposed to be a key to this casket, but the sad truth was, they didn't have any time to even try to see if it could fit the mechanism. Gary saw the worst, horror-like scenario in his head. What if Robert's advice was fake and purposely misleading? His deep hatred of vampires was never hidden.

Moreover, his loathing for Draco was shown by him publicly on almost every occasion when they had met. Gary realised now how foolish he was trusting Robert so quickly. The fear growing in Gary was so overwhelming that Gary was breathing like a fish taken out of water. He felt the silence behind, and all those eyes that were tracking every little body movement he was making. He tried to insert the metal key inside the lock, but this simple operation caused more problems than he expected. It was all due to his extensively trembling fingers and all those bass-relief figures carved on the surface of the coffin. He dropped the key, leaned on the lid of the casket feeling weaker with every second. Something inside his mind shouted '*do something, do something for goodness sake*' in nagging, demanding voice of his own.

Simon picked up the key-rod and held Gary by his waist. His firm grip and serious face were like a lighthouse for sailors in dark, stormy weather. Gary had an impression that the time had stopped, stretching nano-seconds into hours. The pictures of his life were running through his memory from yesterday evening, with nervously repeated drama scenario, to images of his toys he had as a six-year-old boy.

All of a sudden, he saw pictures of his mother and father arguing about something that probably was referring to him. He didn't hear what they were shouting about but his mother was pointing at him and his father was intensely staring in his direction, and this was telling more than any words can describe. That was the moment when he felt inadequately not good enough, like a broken toy-car he was holding in his hands. He remembered the awkward feeling when he wet himself and cried, interrupting anything that could have happened between them in those heated moments. That was the first time when Gary saw his father's face in his memory. It scared him even more. It seemed like he was staring at himself in the mirror, and the reflection was the best version of you that you could ever imagine. Like someone from a parallel universe sent by a mischievous ghosts to hunt you down, only to destroy your already lowered self-esteem. Gary saw his own scornful smile and the blink in his eyes, that only tyrants could have, staring at others like they weren't human beings, but some disgusting maggots living on some carcass.

But then, when he saw himself lying on the bottom of his existence, the face of Yoda, one of the most loved characters by Gary from 'Star Wars', appeared in his head, totally out of the blue. And suddenly, Gary was inside the scene of the first meeting between Yoda and Luke Skywalker, on the swamps of Dagobah. *'Wondering I am, why are you here?'* Yoda's question banged in his head a thousand times. Gary was too surprised to say anything. The specific laugh of a small, green plastic figure echoed in Gary's ears over and over again. It did annoy Gary at first, but then, like listening to any other laugh, it started to influence him. There was a moment when Gary heard himself laughing vividly in exactly the same voice as the fictional movie's character. *'Ready is he not'* the sentence said by Yoda cut off the laugh, but it didn't change the cheerful mood that Gary started to have.

And then, Gary asked himself, *'Where is your strength now?'* The question surprised him more than seeing some movie character talking to him in his mind, and the fact that impressing Yoda was more important for Gary than to a living person. *'I am ready, I can do it,'* Gary shouted to the figure with desperation. He knew that he was lying to himself, like he did many times before, to cover his own insecurities. And Gary knew, Yoda, as the creation of his own imagination, was well aware of it. At least he couldn't fake deceiving his own mind. And so, after repeating a thousand times the same *'I can do it'*, he started to feel differently. He didn't yell any more, he was singing in a rhythm of his favourite metal music. *'Fake it until you make it,'* Gary sang alternately after a few *'I'm not afraid'*.

Gary realised now that he didn't feel fear any more. 'I'm not afraid' he exclaimed to himself, positively shocked. He opened his eyes, recalling the place he was standing on. The time didn't move. The battle he was fighting with himself took only a few seconds. He peeped at Simon and grinned broadly. Somehow, he knew what to do and how to do it. Everything seemed easier. He could feel deep down in his soul that this wasn't the day for him to die, not here, not now.

He turned to the audience, rose the hand he was holding the key-rod, and then, with one smooth motion put into the lock. He felt the tiny vibrations in his fingers, the precise moment when the rod bent in two and clicked, sticking in the place inside the casket's gearwheel. Gary tried turning it, but it didn't move at all. He repeated this action more than once. But there was no perceptible effect. Gary was astonished by his own reaction. Instead of becoming nervous and panicking in such a dangerous situation, as was normal for him, he felt optimistically thrilled. Somehow, he knew that it had to be some way to open the artefact. And then, the Yoda character appeared in his mind, laughing in his peculiar way and saying grammatically incorrect sentences, *'use the force can you'*.

Gary felt a bit confused trying to figure out, what kind of force Yoda was talking about. He didn't feel any special energy running through his body, especially the cinematically impressive blue lightning that was shown in Gary's favourite space movies. But at the same time, surprisingly he felt confident with himself. He knew he didn't have anything to lose trying something he had never done before. So, inside his mind, he ordered the lock to open, with the most demanding and confident manner that he could have mastered right now. And then, he rotated the handle one more time, and it worked so easy, like a soft touch of a small finger on a smart-phone screen.

It clicked, causing some audible noises. It reminded him of the sound of rotating wheels inside some steam machine that started pushing and pulling triggers into motion, giving them the permission to remove blockades and therefore allowing the casket to be open. Almost everyone came closer, including Robert, whose silence drew more attention than the opening itself. Even he was staring speechlessly at Gary's broad smile. A few werewolf pack actors came out from behind, trying to play the discussed earlier scene, but they looked slightly baffled without any of Robert's comments and introduction. They walked up to the stage and stood near Gary. Sean was mixed into the crowd, but this time he was wearing different type of clothes to make him more unnoticeable, with a massive judicial wig that the most prominent magistrate would be proud to own. Robert was stunned so much, that if it weren't for Mark, who poked him in the stomach, and raised the one hand holding the microphone so quick that it smacked Robert in his mouth, he might forget entirely about his leading role in the show. Robert cleared his throat, took a deep breath and was grinning like a child in a playground. He started applauding like a person who just watched the climax in the most dangerous stunt, and some of the viewers followed him with a cheering.

'And Friar opened the coffin in the presence of his vampire children. Because, you have to know, vampires are connected by the blood of their creator into dynasty,' said Robert, finally continuing telling the story. He couldn't stay in one place, so he ambled towards the stage. He didn't want to miss anything that might be happening right now.

In the meantime, in the scene, Gary looked at Simon with utter surprise. He even opened wide his mouth but covered it with his hands when he realised that he was supposed to continue playing the role and that the show wasn't over yet.

There was a tiny gap between the coffin's lid and the rest of the casket indicating that the artefact was indeed opened. Sean pushed himself through the crowd and stood next to Gary. He was holding a large sheet of black cloth hidden under his Renaissance cape. Gary put his hands on the edge of the lid and slowly moved it up. It went pretty smoothly without much of an effort that could be expected by briefly estimating of the size and the heavy material that the coffin was made of, including all those figures representing stories of witch hunter's deeds attached to the lid.

Gary didn't know what to expect to find inside the coffin. Somehow, he was always avoiding thinking about it. Maybe because this was one of the scariest moments he had to get through in his life so far. The vision of facing one of the oldest vampires still living on the Earth crossed his mind from time to time, but he couldn't imagine any possible good scenario. But it was happening right now, and the fear came back to Gary, even more powerful that he had before. He almost dropped the lid but couldn't because of so many other hands of his fellow actors that were holding it. Gary looked around and held his gaze on Sean. Somehow his presence calmed down Gary, giving him the courage to continue. Gary noticed that, although all those people put their hands on the lid, for some reason, they couldn't lift it up. It looked amusing for Gary watching them trying without any visible result. They could only hold it on to the level already lifted up by Gary.

Gary smiled, thinking the whole situation looked like he was a superhero in a graphic novel having some kind of invisible, special powers in his body. He frowned, smiling more to himself than to others. He tried to test this new theory and lift up the lid a few more centimetres. It worked, moving up like it didn't have any weight for him. But after that, the specific smell caught Gary's attention and brought him back to action. It was a strong scent of sandalwood mixture with lily-of-the-valley aroma. That was something Gary didn't expect at all. He imagined it could have a scent more like old crypts with rotten corpse's odour, not a smell that might win the prize for fragrances of the year.

And then it happened. The hand popped from inside, grasping Gary's forearm like a pincer. Gary shouted and released the coffin's lid and immobilised the hand under the weight of it. The hand looked like it belonged to someone skinny. The skin was grey with a lot of black dots covering the surface and showing tendons and bones underneath.

'She is alive!' shouted Robert, hobbling fast towards the stage.

Sean and rest of the crew that were standing on the stage stepped back with fear in their eyes. Nobody ever expected that kind of scenario, and nobody was prepared for it. Gary felt when the hand squeezing his own forearm like pincers made from liquid nitrogen was freezing him to the bone. And then, the sensation that someone was sucking up his vitality came just after. Gary felt dizzy, and immediately he saw in his mind an ashy, skinny face with sunken eyes that belonged to the creature suffering inside, and who grabbed the only one chance he had to escape the torture and would do absolutely everything to succeed. Gary heard some whispers, and he knew it was him trying to take control over Gary's mind. When the first shock was over, some rebellious part inside of Gary's head said calmly 'no' to this vampire. Gary started hearing his voice like a noise behind thick glass, like erratic babble in an overcrowded Saturday pub. The dizziness disappeared suddenly, absorbing the face and the coldness in nightmarish memories. Gary opened his eyes and the first thing that he saw was Simon's hand with an injecting-pen, stabbing the vampire's hand and pumping all the blue liquid into the vamp's flesh. Simon pressed the button on the top of the pen and kept it until the whole dose was gone. The hand loosened its grip but didn't release Gary's arm completely.

'But this is not the end of the story. Now, Romeo's desire was to be reconnected with his beloved wife, Juliet,' declared Robert, putting a solid accent on Romeo's name. It sounded more like crying for attention, and it worked well. Simon, playing Romeo's role, turned around and looked at Robert with a frown and 'what?' question on his face. Robert didn't explain, but instead, he threw to Simon a similar injection-pen with even more intense blue colour.

But it was Gary who caught it, in the last moment, when the pen bounced from Simon's chest and was flying out of the scene. Gary turned back and made one more shot of sedative fluid into the grey hand, that was jutting out from under the casket's lid. The hand eased off completely, so Gary could finally free himself from its cold, frightening fingers. He sighed with relief, looked at Simon, and then at Sean, who nodded in such a way that Gary understood as pushing to speed up all actions.

Gary lifted up the lid and revealed the insides of the casket. And there he was, Frederick, the ancient vampire whose blood saved Gary's life. And the one who errands and politics had caused a lot of turmoil, not only inside vampire dynasties. The one whose faith to live peacefully alongside other supernaturals made him unite the most influential vampires families into one group and get a trial contract with the Guild, for the first time in history. He was the one, known worldwide, that give all vampires legal protection from the hunt, in exchange for a packet of obligations that all of the dynasties agreed to restrictively obey. But this created more enemies than he had got during centuries of his life, not only among his kind, but also those Viviters who were already members of the Guild. And the most unexpected foe was Draco, Erick's beloved son. Draco was the one who got too friendly with witch hunters, the most vicious enemies of vampires and witches, and who helped catch and close Erick inside the mysterious artefact called the Tritus' End.

But now, Erick reminded him of more like some spooky figure used as part of the decoration in Halloween theme park. His ashy skin was hanging on him like thin, plastic foil covering a visible skeleton. His clothes, still elegant and classy, were much too baggy.

Sean just peeped at Erick's face, and then he threw on him the large black cloth he was hiding under the theatrical cape.

'While she was still asleep, they had to take her out, once the coffin had been open,' Robert continued the story, walking around and staring at the audience. He was searching for all unusual movements or people that he classified as suspicious.

At the stage, the group of actors covered Erick's body completely by cloth, slowly lifted him up and then put him on the floor just next to the casket. They corrected the cloth on him in such a way that his body was lying directly on the stage floor.

'Nobody ever survives being closed a second time in the casket, so Friar told Romeo that if Juliet dies, it'll be his fault. All they could now do was wait till dawn and hope that she'll wake up,' Robert was observing the actors, who sat on the floor in front of Erick, holding hands and murmuring a melancholy melody.

'When daylight broke the night darkness, she came back to life. Well, it's more like a different being, but we won't be conducting any philosophical discussion about the core of a vampire's existence,' said Robert, observing the actors. There was still a shape of a body covered by black cloth that was lying behind all those people on a stage. Everything was exactly the same as it was, before they sat on the floor. Simon, with one sharp pull, uncovered the body of a person who was lying beneath. It was Jessica wearing Juliet's dress covered with red paint that was used to imitate blood. She sat, rubbed her eyes, yawned, stretched her hands like a person who just woke up from a long and refreshing sleep. Jessica and Simon fell into each other's arms. All those actors around that were playing Friar's vampire family cheered happily and welcomed a brand-new member of their dynasty.

'But if you think the story has a happy ending, don't be fooled by these short joyful moments. Changing to a vampire leaves a stigma on their souls, twisting them into bloodthirsty creatures,' continued Robert, watching the moment when Juliet changed from a lovely girl into a predator. Jessica put a half-mask on her face with a picture of a red devil and then attacked Simon by biting his neck.

'So, poor Romeo was the first meal for the love of his life. And now, it sounds pretty sarcastic the romantic saying 'I'll die for you', as so he did,' Robert pointed at the scene where other vamps joined to feast on Simon.

'This is the end of the story. Who knows, maybe vampires really exist, or they're only legends in old folk tales and myths. And maybe, somewhere out there, Juliet is roaming the Earth, hunting for the sweet love of the next Romeo before she'll drink the blood from his veins,' said Robert, pointed at actors who were walking down from the stage, coming closer to him and the cheering audience. The public was applauding vigorously, and all of those actors who were present made a bow to the viewers.

'Ladies and Gentlemen. Welcome to The British Museum. I'm proud to announce that our exhibition 'Supernaturals throughout centuries' is officially opened. I hope you've enjoyed this short show. Human history is full of mysterious creatures, demi-gods, demons, and fairies. Please, take leaflets from those stands and have a tour around the museum, searching for listed exhibits. On our website, you can find an extended version of their history with accompanying legends. Thank you for your attention and enjoy your time here,' said Sean, standing up in front of the audience, holding one of the leaflets in his outstretched hand.

Jessica and a few actors from the werewolf pack, still in their costumes, were handing out flyers around to people who were watching the show, explaining some of the content and showing directions. Mark abandoned the show and left the museum at the moment when he saw Jessica rising from under the black cloth. The cameras were recording by themselves, until Jessica switched them off after giving away all the museum's maps with all those mysterious objects located around exhibit halls.

Gary, Simon, and Robert left just after waving goodbye to the public. They undressed the theatrical clothes behind the screens and went out in a hurry through a back entrance, heading to their assembly place on the street behind the museum property.

*

'I have to admit, Gary, that was pretty clever how you arranged to open the artefact,' said James, getting out from a new luxury car. He was holding a mobile with large screen, waving to Gary's group that came out of the museum by the back exit. He was wearing his usual elegant and classy suit, like he was attending to the meeting with high officials.

The car was parked on the Montague Place, a small street just right behind the museum, not far from a crossing with Mallet Street. A few busses were standing on designed places for them, alongside the street, and waiting for tourists. A large group just got out from the bus that had parked minutes ago, a few metres from James' car.

Robert and Simon seemed perplexed seeing him, but Gary somehow presumed that James would be here. Maybe because

Maya's agreement to help them, with so many pack's members, was way too eager, to not have any hidden intention. Well, a brilliant move, thought Gary about James's political game. In case Gary's group couldn't succeed, James would behave like he had nothing to do with their actions. But they made it, and that changed his approach.

'What are you doing here?' asked Robert, coming closer to his brother. Robert's emotions were skyrocketing now, and it was easily seen on his face.

'Saving your all arses. Careful guys, we're surrounded by vamps,' announced James calmly, like he was talking about an invitation for dinner.

'Where is Mark?' asked Gary, passing the street near some bike's stands with a few of them chained to it. Gary felt rising anger in him. He didn't know yet if he should be glad or curse James's presence, maybe because Gary didn't see any vampires around, but on the other hand, he didn't think thoroughly about anything that would definitely happen after the show. He was so absorbed with all those major and little issues connected to the performance itself, that he skipped facts of consequences that it had.

'Where are they, Maya and the others? Where is Erick? Did you take him?' demanded Robert, with a pressing tone.

Gary peeped at him and admitted, if Gary was angry, Robert was definitely pissed-off. That made Gary feel a bit more confident. At least he wasn't alone on that waggon, Gary thought, trying to suppress the little smile that started rising on his lips.

'Hey, relax. Everything is under control,' continued James with a calm voice and his usual charming smile.

'I'm afraid of it. Under your control, you mean?' asked Robert, coming closer to his brother with something that could be recognised as low growling.

'Where is Mark?' Gary repeated this question, looking around for a sign of his brother, who was supposed to help Maya and others to hide Erick in his taxi and wait for the rest in this exact location. But neither Mark nor his car were anywhere to seen. James nodded slightly in a way that pointed towards one of the tall trees growing alongside the street. Gary glanced there, but he had to focus a bit longer to distinguish Mark's body from the shadow and shapes of the tree. Gary turned back to Mark and lowered his head down. He didn't want to give any sign that might reveal his brother's position, just in case someone really was observing them right now.

'You didn't come here out of mercy. What do you have from it?' asked Gary, staring straight into James's eyes without a blink. He snorted in a way that Gary saw once when James had played vabanque in a risky situation, such as entering an illegal circus show only to destroy it. James shrugged arrogantly without any answer. His reaction infuriated Robert even more.

'Where is Erick?' insisted Robert through clenched teeth.

'Safe and sound. You didn't expect me to let you guys keep him captured, did you?' asked James. The silence between them was the clearest unspoken answer.

'Oh, I get it now! You didn't have any plans, did you?' asked James like he was talking to children that had made a mess and now was the time to face the consequences of cleaning up.

'Yes, we have. Stop playing your usual know-it-all pose and tell us where he is!' Robert came way too close to his brother. James stepped back but didn't change his confident body language.

'Oh, please tell. I'd like to know, what did you do to my father?' a woman's soft voice came from behind the nearest bus. Gary turned in her direction but wasn't sure to whom the voice belonged. There were loads of tourists that got out from the bus and were crossing the street in small numbers to get to an assembly point near the tour-guide with a board and a name of the group on it.

Robert and Simon looked in the same direction but couldn't distinguish the owner of the voice from the crowd. None of them knew who she was, but the word 'father' did the job, indicating her connection to Erick and therefore being a vampire.

'Roseanne! Your ability to appear with such a charm will never cease to surprise me,' said James with a diplomatic courtesy, smiling and behaving like he was waiting for party guests.

Roseanne was wearing a light, tight summer dress, large sunglasses and a black purse hanging across her chest. Her long, black hair was uptight in a ponytail. Although she looked beautiful, having the most innocent smile, that nobody would differentiate her from average human beings, Gary knew that she was a dangerous predator that was hunting humans for blood, and was able of killing them without any remorse. Her skin colour was tanned with a rosy blush on her cheeks. Somehow, Gary didn't feel frightened by her presence. It was more like a sweet, holiday encounter with the cute, giggling girl and all that he wanted to do now was spend some time in her company in romantic scenery, overflown by thrilling emotions. Gary felt it for a few seconds before an evil laugh in his head turned those dreamy pictures to bloodbaths nightmare.

'Cut the crap out, James. Tell me where you've taken Erick or I'll kill all those maggots on this street,' she declared with a tone that could freeze hell in seconds. It made Gary alert. He looked around and started gazing at the passing people more carefully, searching if they had some suspicious behaviour and doubtful movements, any signs and symptoms, that may reveal their vampire's nature.

'I have no idea. The Guild took him...' replied James submissively, having bliss on his face. But he didn't finish, because he was interrupted by Gary.

'The Guild? Is that good for him?' Gary's question astonished her. It wasn't the content of the enquiry, but the fact of saying it, that made her perplexed. She stared at Gary, utterly surprised.

Gary now realised that Robert, Simon, and James had a specifically blissful expression in their eyes, like a person under a drug's influence, or someone very deep in love in a honeymoon phase. It hit Gary immediately, reminding him about one of the phone conversations he had with Draco when he was asking about vampire's skills. Back then, Draco mentioned some abilities to influence human's mind by the oldest, for a short period, usually used for hunting to gain the trust of the prey. But this power could only be learnt if they had the luck to meet the appropriate mentor willing to share their knowledge with. Gary knew that she couldn't affect his mind so easily, like she probably was doing to most of humans or shape-shifters. She had lost focus, and therefore the control over those that she tried to dominate around through her manipulating aura.

'You? Bloody Cassian!' she shouted. Her appearance changed from a sweet girl into a dangerous beast. There were dark marks around her eyes, with thin black lines going down on cheeks. Her nails had grown, reaching about thirty centimetres in length and looking like black, sharp, razor blades. She hissed and jumped into Gary's place, who was standing a few meters from her, slightly behind Robert's back.

Her shout woke up James, Robert, and Simon from their daydreaming romance, demanding to respond to the fast-changing reality. She passed Robert just a few centimetres from him. She probably assumed that he would be still under her influence, but that was her mistake. Robert reacted with remarkable speed. With one sharp hand movement, he grabbed her hair and pulled down as fast as he could, changing into feral-form as he did so. Although Gary stepped back, she scratched his chest, leaving shallow bleeding cuts. If it wasn't for Robert's action, she might have pierced Gary's torso like a needle a light fabric. Everything that came next was like in a movie on fast forward.

James, Robert, and Simon changed into ferals regardless of all the bystanders around. Robert's pull was so fierce for her, that it knocked her down, throwing her a few metres away from him. She cut one of her thighs and tore her dress on the pavement. Blood splattered around, intensifying the smell of it, already made by Gary's wounds. She didn't stand up yet when five other vampires came suddenly from nowhere and helped her to get up. They didn't attack the werewolves, but they were standing and estimating how the event would play out, waiting for her instruction. She ordered to attack without any hesitation, but they were too astonished by her demands. She shouted the attack command to her comrades. She had to repeat it three times before they started to draw out their own nail blades.

Gary was in shock. It was first time in his entire life when he saw his own blood flowing from so long wounds on his torso. He had three, parallel cuts that were bleeding much too intensely for his nerve. He started feeling dizzy. His vision blurred, and he had some high-pitch sound in ears. He knelt on the ground when more vampires come into view. Although they looked like any other ordinary people on the street, Gary somehow knew they were vamps. With his half-closed eyelids, he could see a slight reflection of aura surrounding human silhouettes. He fast skimmed all present figures nearby, and noticed the significant differences in aura intensity, between normal humans, ferals, and vampires. Maybe it was the fuzzy sight he had now, but the vamp's aura seemed dim and gloomy comparing to much lighter and cheerful energy that was emanating from tourists, and the very dynamic colours from the ferals.

Suddenly, he felt a bump near him, like something heavy fell from above. The impact shook Gary's body, dictating his instinct reaction to cover his head in fear of attack. He peeped at the shape, but it took him a while to recognise the feral form of his half-brother Mark. He was hissing and growling like all angry cats do. His back was curved, fur erected, face grimaced showing long fangs and sharp claws at the end of his ready to strike hands.

Meanwhile, there were screams on the street just after Roseanne attacked Gary, from the direction of the nearest tourist group. The shouts started incising and spreading like a fire, just after werewolves occurred in their feral-battle forms. Some humans turned their head around pretending that they didn't see anything. Their reaction was to cut off mind from the scary reality so well, that even the sound of the fight couldn't force them to look at the scene. They walked away, or ran, very fast out of this place. Most of them went to the museum without any conscious recognition what they were doing, and just after a few minutes of being inside, when they felt safe, they went back to their minds like nothing had happened. They didn't have any memories of the event, or, even if their mind recorded it, they blocked the pictures to such an extent that they could have sworn nothing strange or unusual had happened around them. Most of the bystanders on the street reacted in this way, running in all possible directions, but surprisingly, they were silent. People with that kind of backlash were called 'snowers' in a society living behind the veil and were classified as less problematic to deal with.

The second group was called 'insaners' due to the severe madness their mind would fall into, in case of seeing something that differs from their very stiff and fixed vision of reality. The supernatural encounter would always make a profound stigma on their mental life that would never be recovered to the previous state.

The third group were called 'Hectorians', and they could see everything without any serious mental effect on them. Although, they were able to see shape-shifters in their feral forms, it sometimes took a while for them to adjust to the brand-new reality, after having the shock of discovering that the world they were living in was much more colourful than what most people perceived.

That was what Gary remembered from Mark's lectures about the actual place he started living in, just after the accident in the forest about a month ago. And now, Gary could see how it worked in an authentic situation. Majority of humans ran away as expected. But there were quite a lot of screaming around from those who were exposed to the danger of coming across living legends or arising nightmares. They too, ran away, but it wasn't peaceful, but somewhat chaotic, and it was attracting attention all passers-by further down the streets. Gary was sure he could hear a car accident just on the corner that might cause someone's death. At this moment, Gary understood why it was so important to keep the ferals world hidden behind legal regulations made by The Guild, and he was glad to whoever did it the deep past, it made humankind life so much easier.

Gary's wounds weren't deep, but he never had such long cuts in his life. Although his body was shaking after the first shock, he stayed alert and started moving. He was amazed at how sharp his mind was now, and the tiny details he could perceive, when he was watching what was going on around. He was even more astonished when he realised he didn't feel fear at all. He thought that watching movies seemed to trigger more emotions inside him than this severe and life-threatening event he was experiencing now.

The fight was getting to the point of no return. Gary was sure it was only a matter of seconds until someone would be killed. He hoped there would be only vampire's casualties. They looked like humans, talked like humans, even lived and dressed like Gary's kind, but now, they were for him like bloodsucking leeches or fleas on dogs.

This was the first time Gary saw fighting werewolves in a group. He guessed that Simon was the one with entirely black fur. James and Robert looked similar with black-grey coating; it was whiter on their chest side. They were standing in formation to cover their backs, not allowing to be encircled by vampires. Robert drew out the sword from his black cane and with two smooth flicks, he cut off the nails of both the hands of the first vampire. There were a hissing sound and a smell like rotten eggs spreading around. It was coming out from the severed fingernails lying on the ground. There was a smoke emitted from the nails that were slowly turning into ashes. The vampire who had lost his weapon stepped back and walked to the side, trying to get to Gary. Although the endings of his hands were smouldering similarly like the ones on the pavement, he still could do harm to a human by using his fangs. The vamp realised that the little embers at the end of his nails didn't cease but transferred to his fingers, causing enormous pain. He shouted, trying to put out the heat by tapping hands against his body, but it didn't make any positive effect.

That made all of the vampires behave more careful. They automatically stepped back and tried to attack someone who didn't have any weapon in their hands. But Robert was waving his sword so forcefully, boldly attacking them as much as he could, regardless of being restrained by his crippled leg, that they had to dodge most of the time. James tried to borrow the sword, but Robert wasn't eager to share it.

Roseanne jumped but only a few centimetres from the ground. She landed on her feet but wobbled on her high heels and collapsed on the pavement. She looked at Gary with an utter hatred, showing long fangs sticking out from her twisted mouth. The vamp standing next to her helped her to get up. The vampires stopped attacking. This stalemate situation could have lasted much longer if it wasn't for a new vampire who had just arrived in this place. He pulled out a gun from under the light suit he was wearing and started shooting into the werewolves' directions. He didn't seem worried about injuring or even killing some civilians present on the street. The first two bullets hit James in his torso. He fell on the ground, heavily bleeding, and it looked pretty bad. This made Robert furious. He roared and leapt at this vamp, aiming his sword straight at his body. There were two more gunshots at the same time. One bullet missed Robert, but the last one hit him in a stomach. Robert collapsed, howling in pain but managed to pierce his chest with his sword. A similar hissing noise and the smell of decaying meat spread around. They both fell down flat on the pavement, with a vamp lying on the bottom, covered by werewolf.

There were only Simon and Mark standing up against six vampires, who decided to attack at once. Mark jumped at the speed of a rushing cat. He moved faster than them, dodging their razors with his well-trained flexibility. He drew out the purple blade enchanted into his skin and cut off the head of one of them. He did one swift manoeuvre and punctured the nearest vamp straight in the heart. The first wounded vampire, the one with cut-off razors by, knelt down and was screaming like a banshee. His fingers and hands were crumbling and turning into dark ashes. But it wasn't the end. The ash never fell on the ground but evaporated to nothing, leaving no physical evidence that the vampire ever existed. The same happened to the bodies of those vamps already killed. They all vanished, even with clothes they were wearing, and things that they had when the process of disintegration touched their surface.

Simon, who didn't have much experience fighting with someone that had a real weapon, especially so sharp and deadly like the vampire razors, spent most of the time avoiding being hit. He had a few scratches, but it healed pretty quick leaving no marks on his body.

Gary stood up and watched the whole scene, more excited than scared. But on the other hand, he felt useless. He didn't have any skills or weapons that he was aware of to fight the vampires or even humans, and that made him feel angry. He couldn't stop admiring the bodies of ferals. Compared to him, they were massive, much taller, heavier, with muscles like a professional bodybuilder that could be easily seen in some places under short fur. Gary knew that every one of them could tear him apart with one sharp hit. Even Simon, now with his fully black fur, looked terrific. Gary felt a pang of envy, and a tiny voice inside his head was wishing to be bitten by Robert in the forest, instead of Simon, in exchange of being infected by vampire blood that only healed him. Naming him Cassian by some strangers didn't make any difference in his life; at least nothing that he might use now, thought Gary, wishing to be more productive now.

He was so absorbed watching the fight, especially Mark's, that he didn't notice Roseanne when she was only about two metres from him. One step more and she would be able to strike again with her razors. Gary stepped back when he heard Robert calling his name. He peeped into Robert's direction and saw the sword flying to him. Everything was happening in a matter of nano-seconds. Roseanne jumped in the same time when Gary caught the blade with his bare hand. The intense pain from the sword cutting his skin went through his body like lightning, waking up fury and some unknown energy deep inside his being. And then, he saw the yellowish marks on his skin, the same he had in the circus. Gary didn't think or aim. He just reacted instinctively, throwing the sword into her. The sword hit Roseanne's eye, piercing her head through, and killing her instantly. Gary stood still, just staring at the scene of this vampire disintegrating into atoms, with his mouth wide open.

The fight was over. It took maybe about two minutes, but Gary felt as if half an hour had passed. Only a gun lying, on the street, was a reminder of the whole incident.

Gary thought that James and Robert were dead when he saw the shots they both had taken. But it seemed it wasn't that easy to shoot werewolves in battle-form using only a few regular bullets. Robert and James's wounds were healed in the next five minutes, but they had to stay as ferals as long as their skin was broken. The bullets were pushed outside their bodies by the healing flesh, and all that they had to do was pull it out like thorns to help the skin close completely.

Gary picked up the sword from the ground where Roseanne's body disappeared utterly and gave it back to Robert. The blade was thin and flexible, but surprisingly firm. It was shining like it was made from pure silver and had little blue runes engraved on the surface.

Gary had two scars on his palm in the places where the blade had touched his skin. They weren't deep but hurt him more than the wounds on his torso. Surprisingly he felt quite well, compared to the beginning of his first fight with vampires.

Before Gary completely cooled down after the encounter, there were a few cars that came immediately after Robert's call. But Gary just sat down, leaned against the nearest tree and waited for an ambulance, as his brother directed him to do. In this full of actions and emotions day, Gary met officials from The Guild. He found himself being served by Viveter's paramedics in a special ambulance, which took him to a separate hospital ward that was for all those wounded that were living in the supernatural world.

CHAPTER 25

18th July - The Guild

Gary left the hospital on the same day, patched up and bandaged, carrying a paper bag full of medications and instruction on how to take care of all those wounds. It took a few hours of treatment, but it was a remarkable experience for him. Gary saw the hospital wards built separately for supernaturals, including humans injured by them. He saw almost all of those panicking tourists from behind the museum, brought one by one to the ward. Most of them were sedated, but some of them had delirium with unpredictable behaviour. Gary felt pity seeing them. He was sure, not long ago, he was one of those ordinary folks, and he could end up here, if he didn't have any relatives living behind the veil. And he could finish like them, with a twisted mind, being not able to think straight to the rest of his life, if it wasn't for Draco's blood.

In the hospital, Gary promised himself, he had to find who Cassians were and why he was called this name by two Viviters, totally not related with each other, including one vampire. Somehow, Gary sensed that Draco's blood not only healed him but triggered something hidden deep inside Gary's. Despite success in the museum with Erick's rescue, and preventing his death, Gary still could sense a bond, a kind of connection he had with Draco on a subconscious level. Gary felt it in those two moments when the yellow marks appeared on his skin. Sean and Draco tried to ensure him that the link with vampire dynasty would disappear in time, like it was for all normal humans after vamp's blood healed their bodies, but Gary doubt it.

Mark was assisting him all the time after the fight, but they barely talked. They both were too tired and unsure about what would might happen next, after The Guild had entered the scene behind the British Museum. After all, they had broken a lot of rules and legal regulations that would definitely bring some consequences. Gary admitted, all could end much worse than it really was, and for this, Gary was immensely grateful.

It seemed Gary's team had pushed the Guild's actions in motion, that would definitely change a lot in London, or even in the whole of Europe. But Gary just wanted to go home, eat something good and watch some easy movies that he didn't have to think too much about.

He felt tired, but couldn't stop smiling thinking that, at the end of the day, it all worked out faultlessly. The show went perfectly, the actors played beautifully, the swapping of Erick's body with Jessica's went flawless. Only the last part, the incident behind the museum, was utterly unforeseen. Gary kept smiling when he admitted in his mind that his first work as a director of a show, with a public that applauded it, went great, even on an amateur level. Moreover, he had recorded it on a few cameras. Gary started thinking about creating a movie with a story of the show itself, of course without showing the actual reason that it was created for.

*

It was late evening when they both, Gary and Mark, went back to home carrying bags with hot pizzas they had bought on the way.

'The purple blade you used, what is it?' asked Gary, interrupting silence between them. He wanted to ask about it after circus, but there was no opportunity for it.

'It's kind of an energetic weapon. Prohibited in professional sports, but very handy in situations like we had today,' explained Mark. He sounded weary but was still walking quite briskly.

'Does everyone have it?' asked Gary, thinking about himself. If only he could have such a blade, he wouldn't feel so useless next time he might have to fight with some kind of monster.

'No, it's not possible. First, you need to find the right neo-shaman who can do it for you,' answered Mark, but he was interrupted by Gary's inquisitive questions.

'Shamans? Why?'

'Because it's made from energy of your own body. Only shamans know how. There are maybe four around the world who are able to do it,' explained Mark.

'But you know one,' Gary's pressing tone made Mark smile.

'She passed away a few months ago. She was your grandma, Stefanie, from your father's side. You met her a few times when you were a child, but she never told who she really was, for your own good…'

'I had a grandmother who was a shaman?' asked Gary, astonished, interrupting Mark's talk. They were standing near the front door to the house. Mark found the key inside his trousers but didn't put it into the lock yet.

'Sorry, bro, I wish I could help you …' Mark's sentence was disturbed by Jessica. She opened the door, shouted joyfully and jumped on Mark's back, hugging him tightly and kissing his head.

'We've made it!' yelled Jessica. She repeated it a few times, ruffling Mark's hair. It looked funny for Gary watching Mark's happy face while carrying her on his back. Gary took the bags with food from him, pushed the door and entered the house.

He went straight to the living room, guided by loud voices coming from there. But he stopped in the doorway, a bit taken aback, when he saw couple of unfamiliar faces wearing dark suits as he entered the room. Although all people inside seemed relaxed, some of them looked like officials from movies about FBI agents, and that made Gary feel uneasy. Sean, holding a glass of Scotch, had a ruddy face indicating that it wasn't his first drink. Sean ran to Gary and offered help to put the boxes with pizzas on a central table.

Sean introduced all of those new people as members of the Guild, who just arrived a few minutes ago. Gary didn't remember their names or positions but only what was important from a legal point of view. It appeared that the team's action in the museum was working for good, by securing peace between the species. Gary knew Erick's story partially and didn't mind when one of them told it once again, while he was eating pizza.

Ten years ago, Frederick, in short known as Erick, united the most powerful vampire dynasties around the world by a legally binding document with him as a representative from all of them. The paper was a contract between the Guild and the vampire's dynasties about peace between them, especially ending the war with ferals that was going on for centuries. It gave vampires legal protection and made hunting and excessive killing of them, illegal. But in return, vamps had to obey a rigorous set of rules, such as vampires' population regulations with an obligation to register every single one living in the country, in a specially created division for them in Guild. But the rule of creating only one new vampire every thirty years, made Erick unpopular among some groups of his own kind. Moreover, putting vampires on the same level as any other members of the Guild, which one was automatically protected by Viviter's law, infuriated many of those who were hunting them, sometimes just for fun, such as werewolves, felines, or witch hunters.

Erick, as representative, had got a position in the diplomatic service, therefore he was inviolable by law and any action against him was illegal, especially kidnapping and captivity. The Guild's officials told them that releasing Erick had given all members of Gary's group a reward and special treatment but that would be discussed separately and personally. Officially, Draco was announced as responsible for Erick's disappearance and was now prosecuted by Guild's forces for an attempt to murder a diplomat. Although Sean officially denied having anything to do with Erick's kidnapping, Gary didn't believe in his story. But Gary didn't want to mingle into this case too much, after all, Sean was his far-related uncle. There were too many mysteries hidden behind the event that lead to the circumstances of putting the casket in the British Museum in the first place, and therefore he felt inadequate to do anything about it.

According to Sean's explanations, the casket was lent to the museum from a private collection for exhibition reason only, in a hurry, without any knowledge about anyone trapped inside. And the fact of infecting Gary with Draco's blood was classified by the Guild, as a deliberate action for vampire's advantage, such as opening the casket. Probably, the factor to hurry to open it was included in the artefact itself. There was no written instruction on how to use the item, and lack of knowledge might lead to Draco's realisation that he would die very soon if Erick were to lie inside much longer. There were a lot of questions about what happened ten years ago, that led to closing Erick in the first place, but they could only speculate without any known facts. It was harder to guess without Draco and even slight specification for what precisely the coffin was used for.

Draco disappeared just after Gary lifted up the casket's lid, as far as some members of the theatrical team could recall. He was officially now on a list of fugitives, the most wanted by the Guild all over the world.

*

Gary wanted to talk about many things with Draco, but he knew it wouldn't happen, and maybe he would never have the opportunity to see him again in his short human life. Deep down, he regretted that he had taken for granted Draco's presence before the show. Back then, he thought that Draco would stay long after the opening of the casket. Gary's mind was wondering from one question to another, especially about those yellow marks on his skin that appeared in almost the same moment than Draco's. He was trying to find a way he might contact Draco, but Gary was guessing that such an old and experienced vampire like Draco was well-trained for centuries on how to efface his paths and stayed well-hidden.

'Tell me, please, how did you replace Erick with her?' said a tall and thin gentleman from the Guild and pointed at Jessica. The team looked at each other and laughed. Gary stared at Jessica with a big grin on his face.

'That was her brilliant idea, but Maya and her team did the job,' he said, nodding to Maya with encouragement to tell how it was done.

'There was a hatch in the stage's floor, in an exact place near the coffin, where they put Erick's body after taking him out …' Maya couldn't finish.

'So, that's why he was covered with a black cloth?' asked a woman from the Guild. There was a realisation on the Guild official's faces when they heard the way it was done.

'Yes, in the moment of exchanging, the actors were sitting in front of the coffin, humming in purpose to redirect crowd focus from the movement under the cover,' explained Sean with his normal, teacher-like tone.

'Maya and the others were waiting beneath the stage. They took Erick's body, lifted me up in a lying position and closed the hatch after, so the cloth's motion was limited to the minimum,' said Jessica.

'It took maybe thirty seconds to do it,' said Mark, smiling. He was holding the box with a pizza for himself and did a funny face to Gary's attempt to take the last piece of it. Gary mimicked him, went to the table, took an untapped box and made a gesture that all the food belonged to him. The boxes they brought were circling around, and everyone was eating pizza.

'We put a hat on Erick's head, covered him with a blanket, and sat him on a wheelchair. I swear, he looked like a little granddaddy on a family trip to the museum, who was taking a nap. That's why I couldn't play Juliet. My son was sitting on Erick's lap to make it more reliable,' continued Maya.

'But who called for you guys?' asked Gary, nodding to the nearest woman from the Guild.

'I did. I saw some vamps in a crowd that I know. They were standing behind, but I could spot them from the stage. I knew they would bring problems, so I called. Besides, we really didn't have any plans on what to do with Erick after the show,' said Sean, pouring whiskey into glasses and passing them to those who wanted. It was a very accurate explanation, but Gary somehow sensed that Sean had hidden motivation for his action.

'What will happen to him now?' asked Gary.

'We'll wake him up, but slowly. It'll take weeks or even months for him to recover. He was closed for too long in that artefact,' said a man from the Guild.

'What will happen to the coffin?' asked Robert, taking the offered glass with alcohol from Sean. He, like Gary, had a box with a pizza for himself.

'Well, technically it is lent to the British Museum from a private collection, but it still belongs to Draco. But, taking the circumstance into consideration, he might never physically come back for it. It'll stay in the museum for some time. But Draco still has rights to give disposition, and we'll have to send it to him. I don't think it'll be anytime soon,' replied Sean.

This evening ended with bottles of champagne, more fast foods, and the talks to early morning hours. About an hour after Gary's arrival, the werewolf's pack came in, bringing more alcohol, and a pile of cakes and sweets. Even James came to celebrate, but this time wearing jeans and a T-shirt. Although he tried to look casual, his manners were like he was always wearing the suit, regardless of situations. He was more interested in keeping company with the Guild officials, than socialising too much with the victorious team. Gary suspected that James was here for his own business than to celebrate the triumph. He congratulated Gary many times, but Gary wasn't entirely sure if James was referring to the show or the fact of killing Roseanne, one of the oldest and influential, almost untouchable, vampires in the whole of England, in bright light, with a lot of witnesses and working street cameras.

The party ceased after hours of recalling all major and little things that happened during the performance and during the preparation stage. Everyone said that Robert had stolen the show with his comments and public interactions, so often quoted during the party. The joke about the witch saying 'I'm in a wrong story' had been branded as the quintessence of this day, including the fight behind the museum. They all made a lot of jokes diminishing the lethal danger that was accompanying the performance, letting today's stress and tension vanish like the food and alcohol.

It was almost dawn when Gary went to bed, but he couldn't fall asleep so quickly. Too much sugar and the spontaneous party boosted his energy and replaced the hospital's tiredness. Thousands of questions were running wild in Gary's mind, and he felt he was eager to find the answers to all of them.

CHAPTER 26

18th July - Adam

Patric was lying on the floor inside his private prison, deep down under London's streets, crying. He was wearing his usual elegant shirt and suit trousers, but now they were ragged, torn in many places, almost fully covered by blood and some bits of flesh and dirt. The surroundings were severely damaged. The security office was destroyed entirely. Parts of computers were scattered around the whole space. They were broken into a thousand pieces like a glass thrown on the wall. Everything had long, scratching marks, even on the concrete walls.

About ten bodies were lying on the floor. Some of them still had a human silhouette, but some had missing limbs or heads. It wasn't possible to distinguish their gender mainly because the bodies were mutilated to an unrecognisable degree, that the scene brought to mind the most ferocious horror that could ever be made. There were pieces of flesh thrown around the chamber, with some that stuck on the high ceiling.

Patric had never had a rage to such uncontrollable level, when he didn't remember what he was doing. Now, after hours of devastating almost everything around, he had curled up on the floor and let himself cry. At that moment, the long-restrained tears overflowed with bitterness, had flown not only from his face, but inside his whole being.

The pictures of situations, when he had been humiliated, first as a small, poor human child, and then as thin teenager in ragged clothes, or as young man wearing stolen suits, desperately trying to fit in, climbing on the ladder of wealthy and influential people in society, were constantly flashing in his head. It was always in days like today, when everything that he cared about, collapsed like a fragile dying human. But today was the worst day that he had ever experienced in his whole life

He would never have had the social status he had now, if it wasn't for her. The first moment he saw Roseanne had turned his life upside-down, and twisted his destiny tightly with her, for more than a century. Patric knew that she was a vampire when he met her. But, back then, Patric was only a poor human, without any remarkable skills or talents, who would never be considered as a member of Erick's dynasty. He became a vampire for her, but not an ordinary one. Patric became an Upir, the predator for regular vampires, mainly because he didn't have any other option. He recalled the time in Rome when he accidentally met his vamp-Upir father and begged him for the change.

Upirs didn't form dynasties and weren't physically recognisable from any other vamps. But they didn't have the subconscious link that made them feel like a family, connected by the blood of their creator like all normal vampires had. Changing into an Upir was the only way that she finally could notice him.

*

His loud sob was the only sound in this chamber made in an unused, old part of London's underground. He couldn't remove from his memory the last moment, the last argument, the last view of her face, however badly he wanted. He couldn't stop her. She was always stronger than Patric. Centuries of being a vampire, practising how to influence someone's mind, made her pretty skilled in that field. She froze his mind and ran to the museum having hope to be the saviour of Erick, her vampire father.

When Patric finally woke up after an hour of being mentally blackout, she was already dead. He knew it when he saw Adam's skin start to peel off like a snake. Patric knew something went terribly wrong with Roseanne. Adam was one of her vampire sons. She created him for fun, only because he was a talented musician in opera in those times. And then, he had a phone call from his informant inside the Guild, about the incident behind the museum and about taking over Erick.

The rage, the killing, the smashing things around didn't help to numb the pain, he had felt inside not only his body but in the core of his existence.

He felt tired and hungry for more than the taste of vampires who he loved to bleed out to the last drop. It took a few hours for him to calm down to the level that he was able to think straight about what really were the consequences of her flurried actions.

Patric was lying flat on the ground, staring at the ceiling and thinking about his position in London's Viviters society, about all the political moves he had to make after this day that crushed his status quo so severely. Erick's dynasty was broken. The whole blood-line made by Roseanne died with her, slowly turning into atomic dust. There were thousands of her vampire children around the world that disappeared today without leaving bodies behind, like they had never existed. The worst thing was, her line had populated most of the dynasty, those with influence and power, and that could never be replaced. It would take at least the next two hundred years to climb back to that position. Erick was taken by the Guild to some safe-house. Nobody knew when he would be released, if he would ever be able to walk free. It was an apparent fact for everyone that Erick had a lot of enemies, but Patric was never one of them. Patric always admired him, and his skill of subtle political influence, that always had made unexpected twists in current course of events. All his life, Patric wanted to be like him very badly.

*

That was the reason he went back to the circus for Adam. Adam, this little, thin rat, had a piece of knowledge about old vampire rituals, skill, and powers even beyond Erick's abilities. And Adam knew how to use some of them, where to find a description of it and he could read in more than ten ancient languages. And now, he was gone like Roseanne.

Patric was thinking about all those benefits he lost today, and it wasn't his fault. Roseanne found out, by her spy from the Guild, about Erick, when and where they would collect him. But she was too late. The Guild had already intercepted Erick and drove away. Patric saw the last fight she had behind the museum and the moment when she died. He got the recordings from a camera installed on the museum wall sent to him by those who worked for him in the Guild.

Watching this on his mobile was the last thing he remembered before he fell into a rage.

*

His reasoning and logical thinking were slowly going back to normal, despite the immense emptiness he felt and physical pain of loss that still was piercing his body. He knew, that from now on nothing would ever be the same. The unpredictable, cold beast started showing his psychopathic face, laughing in his head in the voice of his Upir father. His words were echoing in Patric's head time and time again. The warning of a dark, merciless path that was unfolding in front of Patric right now and seemed like the best invitation to live without a heartbreak, caused him to struggle for the right decision. He knew he would always feel the pain, every time her face, voice, whisper, the picture from the past they had together would pop in his mind. The love for her, that he wanted to remove so hard, paralysed his mind, and still made him feel like a human.

*

Some barely audible noise caught his attention. It brought his senses back to reality. Patric thought he had killed all of those present in this place, regardless if they were prisoners or guards. He stood up with reluctance and walked to the last prison cell from where he heard the noise. It was open, as he left it. He looked around but didn't find anyone alive. He turned back and made one step when he heard something from under the bench that was standing at the end of the cell. Patric was sure that all he could find would only be rats lured from the sewers by intense blood smell.

But he was astonished at finding Adam lying on the floor, pressed to the most distant end, making him hardly seen. The bench that he was lying under, had a lot of deep scratches made by a furious Patric. His nails were much longer than a normal vampire, stronger and sharper like razors. With one pull, Patric threw away the bench exposing Adam, who squeaked like a small puppy and fully covered his head with his hands. Patric smiled faintly and came closer. He sat next to Adam, put a hand on his shoulder, and with the softest voice that he could have now, said; 'I'm not going to hurt you. Sit up. We need to talk.'

It took a while, but Adam finally sat opposite Patric with his knees tucked up to his chest. He peeped at Patric a few times, but his eyes were mainly staring on the floor.

'Roseanne is dead, but you're alive. How is that possible?' asked Patric, adjusting his sight to the dim light here. Now he started to notice the yellowish marks on Adam's skin that were appearing and disappearing randomly, healing him and replacing his dead skin with a new one. It looked like he was dropping old coating, like some animals were able to do. Adam seemed stable, but he looked like someone on his deathbed. But Patric knew if he survived such a traumatic event, he wouldn't die now.

'It's Draco's blood,' murmured Adam.

'How? He didn't change you, did he?' asked Patric.

'I'm the only one with double blood, his and Rose's. But Draco is not only a vampire. He is not even from this world,' answered Adam, but this time he was staring into Patric's eyes with a bit more courage.

CHAPTER 27

31st August - Unexpected Guest

Gary smiled to himself, watching again the movie about the first performance in the British Museum. It was more authentic and dramatic than the second one. He couldn't decide which one he should put on-line to his now working 'The Faded Photograph' website, comparing pros and cons of both shows. Although the second had more dialogue, better costumes, and theatrical pieces of equipment, and much better acting, his heart was with the first one.

The first movie he had made, the one with Airsoft competition, was only a week on different social media pages, but it already had hundreds of thousands of viewers, and a lot of positive comments. He looked at his work, and for the first time in life, he felt proud of himself. Gary made a lot of technically good movies from many different events, such as weddings or company parties, but they were for him like stamps on a stream of envelopes. They were like a job he wouldn't remember after a few days. But the first in forest movie had changed everything in his life. Gary had developed his own style. That was something he had never expected would happen so soon.

The late evening was hot and bright. Gary was alone at home. He started missing all those meetings they had had about the show. It all ended up pretty well for everyone. Gary wasn't sure if the Guild was so generous, or some vampire dynasties had something to do with all those presents that the group received.

Gary had got the newest and most expensive camera with a few additional gadgets. Moreover, he had got money for a new PC, that it would definitely make his work faster. Simon, Mark, Jessica, and Maya got some money as a reward as well, but not one of them said how much. But seeing their faces at the moment when they saw the cheque could tell a lot. But Sean was the one who won the life-changing jackpot. He had got a very fat cheque as a grant to organise his dream expedition to search for artefacts in the most distant parts of Asia. And now, Sean was so busy planning the journey, that sometimes he answered the phone talking in some long-forgotten language.

Gary was curious about what Robert had got from the Guild, but it seemed an inappropriate question to ask. Besides, Gary knew Robert would say something made-up with a sarcastic laugh.

*

There was one more thing that Gary received, but only he knew about it. It was an oblong, flat key-fob with a few, unmarked buttons, that looked like a key-chain. It was in an envelope, that someone put through the letter flap at night time, with only his name on it, without any signs that it was formally posted. Gary found it when he was passing the main door on his way to the kitchen for a night sandwich. Inside the envelope, there was a card attached to the fob, that looked similar to a business card, but there was only one nickname written on it from a less popular social media page. Gary checked it instantly, but it created more questions than he had before. On this page, there was only one picture. The picture was taken in a hurry. The night street was recognisable, but the image was blurred, like someone was walking fast. It was an image of the entrance to the Oxford Circus Underground Station in London, taken from the opposite side of the street. That puzzled Gary to the point when he had to give up of guessing. But he downloaded the picture and kept in a special folder on his PC.

*

It was late at night when Gary decided to go to bed. He went to the toilet first, leaving the window wide open. The room was lit only by two screens of his computer, exactly as Gary left when he went out. He came back to the room after a few minutes and headed straight to the window with the intention to close it. But when he did it, and he turned and shouted out of horror. A person was standing just behind him. Gary stepped back and covered his head with a protective gesture, but nothing happened. He wasn't attacked by the person who had invaded Gary's privacy.

It was Marie Tussaud, standing and looking like a normal alive human being. She was still wearing an old-fashioned black dress that she had on display in the wax figure museum. She put her finger on his lips, shushing the shout.

'Be quiet, Gary,' she said, smiling broadly.

Gary couldn't speak. His mind froze. He couldn't stop staring at this short, filigree figure, stunned by her presence. She gently put her finger on his chin and softly closed his mouth.

'I believe you know who I am?'

It was more a statement than a question. Gary nodded only. She gently sat on the spare chair standing next to his desk, indicating to him to join her by sitting on his chair. Gary sat, but he felt anxious. It wasn't only because of her unexpected visit at night time but because he realised about the mess he had in his room. Gary wanted to switch on the lamp on his desk, but she stopped him.

'I need your help,' she said, confidentially. She lowered her voice like she wanted to prevent any eavesdropping.

'What makes you think I can help you?' asked Gary.

'After the British Museum, there're some rumours about you among Viviters. But going to the point, one of my most valued items has been stolen. I need your help to get it back …' she didn't finish, interrupted by Gary's question.

'Me? Why?'

'If someone can do it, it'll be you,' she was smiling like a little granny passing cookies to children.

'Maybe the Guild …' Gary didn't finish, interrupted by her sharp voice.

'My primary suspect is from the Guild. I can't trust them,' she replied and pulled out from under her old-fashioned black cloak a paper folder and gave it to Gary.

'You have here all what you need, even how to find me.'